The Oasis of the Last Story

Tales from the Desert

By Michael Asher

About the Author

Michael Asher is an English writer, storyteller, and award-winning desert explorer.

Synopsis

Tormented with regrets for his military past, and hoping to find the part of himself he believes is missing, a young ex-special forces war veteran goes in search of the legendary Lost Oasis in the remote Sahara. Travelling by camel and on foot, he meets desert nomads with many strange and wonderful tales to tell. He works as a camel herder, is taken on as a hand with a salt-caravan, and becomes the apprentice of a nomad *kahin* or holy man, skilled in casting the sands – a method of divination. Over the long and arduous journey, experiencing heat, cold, hunger, thirst, danger, and deprivation, the *kahin's* arcane knowledge leads him into a rich world of spiritual beauty - a reality that transcends the mundane limits of civilization.

Searching for the Lost Oasis, in a landscape defined by outsiders as the ultimate in harshness and hostility, he finds instead a world where relations are governed by *muhanni* – kindness, generosity, mutual aid and well-being - where there is no fine boundary between humans and nature, and where survival depends not on conflict but on cooperation. Finally, obliged to complete his journey alone, he comes to understand that the Lost Oasis is a symbol not only of his lost self, but also of the enchantment that industrial man has driven from the Earth.

The Oasis of the Last Story is told through a web of tales from the desert, connected by a narrative of adventure and spiritual quest.

Flow

The morning after Rafig vanished, I was given a sign. It was early morning and I was in the desert making a fire by twirling sticks, with my camel, Ata, kneeling beside me. The sun was climbing up in the east in a brilliant aura of light, and the land was silent, waiting with bated breath for the unfolding of the day. I had set up three stones as a fire-place, with straw and wood between the stones. Suddenly the sticks started smoking, and the straw exploded with a flash and a whoosh, and the whoosh became something much louder, the sound of an immense entity approaching from behind.

It might almost have been rain creeping across the desert, the slow onset of a sandstorm, or even waves rolling on the shore. Yet I knew it could be none of those things. This was the *Hurra* – the deep Sahara - and it was dry and still, without a breath of wind or a touch of moisture. The ocean was unimaginably far.

I looked around and saw nothing, but the whooshing was coming closer, giving me the unnerving sensation of a phantom sneaking up on me unseen. I stood, and saw that Ata's ears were twitching – he had heard it too.

Then I looked up.

The sky above me was swarming with grey cranes. There were scores upon scores of them, flying in loose formation. Some were ranging low, and I could see their necks stretched out and their wings undulating. They were moving as a dense flock, each bird in its own space, flying together in perfect cohesion. The whooshing sound was the murmur of their wings, surging like the sea.

I stared at this crowd of flying people, transfixed by the force, grace, and majesty of the flow. Incredible power, I thought – power without restraint, running through the swarm like a current, power that spanned countless ages, shrinking the Distant Time to nothing. This tide of life had flowed over the desert long, long before it was green, before the lakes filled, before the rivers ran, and after, when the great waters dried up, and the rich colours were leached away and landscape reverted to rock and sand. It had flowed here since the wind blew, for it was the Great Spirit - the wind in another guise. As I watched, the flying folk suddenly changed direction, wheeling like a shoal of fish in an intricate swirling pattern, forming a spiral as a single body. It was as if the flock were a vast dark cloak that a giant hand had flapped in a perfect veronica - the most elegant maneuver I had ever seen.

The next thing I knew, there was a shift in my awareness. I was soaring with the flyers, looking down on a vast panorama that had opened up, while another part of me remained earthbound, taking in the landscape in all its sensory detail. For a moment I slipped into the flock, wings undulating on my shoulders, feeling my neck stretch, feeling my body move and flow, feeling the wind breathe me, feeling myself in flight, moving to a rhythm, drawn by a purpose. For a moment there was only one creature in all creation, and this river of flying people filling the sky, and the river itself a straw in this current, was something I had always known, had always been part of, and always would be. I never stopped being the human watching from the desert below, while there was no separation between myself, the cranes, and the rest of nature. There was just this wholeness, this power, this force – One Absolute Eternal Infinite - forever flowing on and on.

The winged ones passed, and the feeling passed, and my wings vanished, and the sense of flight disappeared, and I was standing by Ata, in the desert, watching a flurry of dots over a twin-peaked hill on skyline. I knew then that their coming had changed everything. I knew which path I should follow, which way I must go.

Caravan

I first encountered nomads one morning as I walked to school with the sun behind me and the breeze in my face. The school stood a little way out of town, and to get there one had to cross a stretch of desert. The buildings were enclosed by a broken wall of white stucco, and beyond it the Sahara rolled away west – a long succession of undulating pale beaches and sparse trees, with the ghosts of dark hills at the place where the earth touched the sky.

Since I had time before my first lesson of the day, I decided to walk past the school buildings and enjoy a few moments of peace. The landscape always enthralled me, but I saw it as a sleeping world, sacred, pristine in its emptiness – and unimaginably vast.

The sun was already brilliant, and the landscape rippled like a gently shaken carpet, in a wind that brought scents of ash and dust. Suddenly, I caught a movement in the middle distance. I focused on it and saw a mobile smudge a little bigger than my fist, moving rapidly towards me, growing larger as it approached. I fancied I could hear strange cries drifting across the landscape. I watched the coasting shape warily and had the impression that I was looking at a mythical creature – a giant centipede, or a spider with many legs. Then I knew what it was. *Camel caravan* was the only term I could think of, but it was not quite that. These were camels, certainly – scores of them, pressed shoulder to shoulder, flank to flank. They seemed to be floating effortlessly across the desert, and as they came nearer still, I saw that they were being driven by men in dust-colored robes and head-cloths. The herders were riding tall camels laden with saddlebags, sacks, water-skins and loops of rope. They were cracking whips, urging the herd on with strange chants. The camels pricked up their ears and listened, as if these were their native tongue.

I watched mesmerized as the herd drew abreast of me, close enough to make out individual animals – padded feet, angular heads, rounded humps, flicking tails. The riders were not looking my way, but I had the urge to speak to them. I waved and called out in Arabic. '*Peace be upon you.*'

The nearest rider lifted his eyes and stared as if seeing me for the first time.

'*And upon you be peace.*'

The man halted his camel and waited. I approached and found myself staring up into a face that was dust-caked and wind-scoured, etched with lines. The man wore a dagger in a leather sheath upside down on his arm, and wooden beads round his neck. He looked different from the townsfolk I knew.

We shook hands – his palm was rough and calloused.

'Where are you going?' I asked.

'We are taking these camels to Egypt,' he said, 'along the Pharoah's Road.' His words were gruff, and his voice was throaty and arid, as if the desert itself was speaking.

'What is the Pharaoh's Road?'

'A desert way. It has been used since the Distant Time.'

'Isn't Egypt far?'

'It is many sleeps from here.'

'Where have you come from?'

'From the southwest – also many sleeps.'

I was thrilled. When I had arrived here as a teacher, I had never dreamed that I would find anything like this. I had not believed it possible that there were still camel caravans – or herds – following ancient caravan tracks across the Sahara. It seemed like a dream. I had thought of the desert as empty – a sleeping land. Now it had woken up, and for a moment I was filled with elation. I had the impulse to say. *Take me with you. I want to go back to the Distant Time.*

The herd was already sliding away into the distance, though, and the rider was watching uneasily. The moment passed.

'Go in peace,' I told the man.

He peered at me. 'The blessing of the Great Spirit be upon you,' he said.

I stood watching as he caught up with the camels, until the herd itself grew smaller and dissolved into the haze.

Then I remembered school.

Comfort

I taught my classes with a mounting sense of excitement. On one hand, all I had seen was a camel-herd being driven across the desert. On the other, the caravan represented something entirely new. It was as if a door had swung open, as if a heavy curtain had been pulled away, revealing an unseen magical land beyond. Until that moment I had regarded the desert as a vacant place – now I knew that people lived and moved and had their being within it, it had come alive. If there was one caravan like this, if there were camel riders like that, there must be many, many more. There must be an entire desert world - a vast space where people lived as they had always done, where civilization had not prevailed.

At mid-morning, when classes halted for breakfast, I shared a pan of fava beans and *feta* cheese with my fellow teachers. We ate standing up, dipping fragments of fresh bread into the pan with our hands. I had been practicing the technique and was proud that I could now eat without dropping food – I no longer missed forks and spoons. Afterwards, when we had taken turns to pour water on each other's hands from a jug, and were drinking glasses of sweet tea, I spoke to Hamad, a teacher in the same faculty as myself, describing my encounter with the camel herd. 'The man called it the Pharaoh's Road,' I said.

'The Pharaoh's Road is the oldest caravan-route in the world,' Hamad told me. 'It was in use in the time of the ancient Egyptians before there were camels in Africa. And yes, they still take camel herds that way.'

'The camel-men – the herders – do they live in the desert?'

'They are nomads. There are many nomad tribes out there who still carry all their worldly goods on camel's back, following the rains, just as they have since time immemorial. They are scattered over a vast area. The desert is big, and there are places that few people have ever seen.'

'How is that possible?'

Hamad shrugged and grinned. 'That's what they say.'

'I'd like to go with the nomads,' I blurted out.

'Are you joking?' Hamad chuckled. 'The life of the desert is hard – heat and cold, wind and rain, hunger, thirst and fatigue. You sleep on the ground, you eat poor food, you never wash. Why would you want to live without comfort?'

'Some things are more important than comfort.'

'Like what?'

'I don't know ... like a *real* life?'

'Does comfort mean your life is not real?'

'Comfort is a drug that becomes addictive. When it is one's only object, it cuts one off from real life.'

'Your people are so restless,' Hamad laughed. 'It's as if you have lost something and must spend your time trying to find it again. What is it that you have lost?'

I grinned. 'I think we have lost ourselves.'

Lost

Certainly, I had felt lost in civilization. I had come to the end of a path that had turned out to be a cul-de-sac, and had run away. The small settlement in the palm groves of the Nile Valley, where I lived now - on the edge of the great desert - was as far away as I could get. It was the limits of the civilized world. Yet this desire to escape from the monotony and tedium - the sheer predictability of living in the town – had been with me as long as I can recall. It is not that my life was in any way materially deprived. My mother and father were caring enough - they were not rich, but they were prosperous, and we lived in prosperous times. I did not want for anything, and I went to what was called a good school. Yet I could never throw off the feeling that I was in an elaborate prison of some kind. For all the comfort, there was something missing, something I could not put my finger on. The world seemed artificial – a mad apparatus rattling on blindly - over-controlled, over-organized, bland, and unreal. Conformity was expected – to have one's own ideas was to rebel.

I came to the conclusion that the only way to escape from all this was to join the army - to seek the warrior's path. I enlisted as a soldier, took up the challenge of the toughest and most elite units – the special-forces. I put myself through some exacting tests of human endurance - I was conditioned to kill, and proud to wear the insignia of those crack bands. I reveled in the mystique that came from a sense of specialness, the ability to harness lethal force, from hardship shared. I fought in wars – it does not matter which war, because all wars are the same. I played my part in the killing, the atrocities - I saw comrades maimed and blown to pieces. Yet the warrior's path did not liberate mind or spirit – indeed, it was not a true warrior's path at all. I was not a warrior but a highly-trained servant. I had climbed to the very top of the ladder of violence only to find a desert there.

There was a close solidarity in the special-forces – one probably would have died for one's comrades – but, strangely, this was less about love than *esprit de corps* – a form of self-exaltation. There was also the feeling that one had achieved something that only a tiny minority of people were capable of – something that could not be bought. I was proud of that, and, despite it all that has happened since, a part of me remains so. Yet while I had reached a certain level of understanding– that I could extend physical limits by sheer determination – I also perceived the void in the fighter's life that echoed the emptiness of my world.

Then, one day, I shot my best friend. Of course, it was an accident. I had not meant to do it, at least I did not think I had. In any case, they held me responsible. I had fired the bullet that mortally wounded him, and at the very least I had been unprofessional. His name was Danny and the last I saw of him he was being carried off on a stretcher, still conscious, still talking. He died in the night.

There was an inquiry, and that was the end of it for me. I was guilty. It was an accident but I was guilty. I was guilty, but it was an accident. I had not meant to do it, but it was my fault that he was dead. I had been over-confident. I had been negligent. There was something missing in me, they said. When the guilt got too severe, I put a pistol to my own head, and came within an ace of squeezing the trigger. It was a message to myself that it was time to move on, to find the part of me they said was missing. I put the weapon away and resigned from the military. A week after that I answered a newspaper advertisement I had seen for volunteer teachers in a remote country in Africa. I applied for and was offered the job.

Animals

The morning after I had seen the camel herd, I woke from a dream I strained to remember. My mind raced to intercept images as they faded. I caught only a memory of sitting by a fire in the desert under a chorus of stars, with a dark-robed figure opposite me. The face was hooded, and I could not tell whether it was a man or a woman, because each time I glanced at the figure its form seemed to change. I felt a profound sense of awe, as if I were in the presence of a god or a goddess - as if I was involved in a deep and ancient mystery. There was the boom of a wind that seemed to well up from the bowels of the desert, the wings of giant birds beating, the bellowing of bulls, the bawl of thunder, dry lightning that seared vein patterns behind my eyes. The flames of the campfire flickered, I glimpsed white eyes in the fire, and suddenly a big cat emerged from the flames. Then the fire was gone and there was moonlight reflected on the luminous coat of what I took to be a white leopard. The animal stared at me and a voice that said *the animals will reveal the Lost Oasis. They will heal you, because you are animal, and one of us.*

Of the dream, it was only the crackling fire, the boom of the wind, the white leopard, and this voice that I recalled clearly. *The animals will reveal the Lost Oasis ...they will heal you ... you are animal, and one of us.*

It was the strangest, most vivid, dream I had ever had. The images, the sounds and the voice stayed in my head as I made tea on my charcoal brazier, and later, as I washed with a jug of water dipped from the large earthenware pot I kept in the corner. I had no idea what it meant but I had been talking with Hamad about lost selves – was it somehow connected with that? I was certain that the dream held a message for me, and that the message was somehow to do with animals, and a Lost Oasis. I had heard of a story-teller who lived on the *Other Side* – the east bank of the Nile. She was supposed to be good at interpreting dreams, and I wondered if she might be able to help.

Fates

At mid-day I took the ferry across the Nile and found the storyteller's mud-brick hut in the small village on the Other Side. I had been expecting an old woman, but Maya was young, with smooth, dark skin and intense eyes. She was carding thread on a wooden spindle when I arrived at the open door. She laid the spindle down, called me in, had me sit on a palmetto mat, and brought a bowl of water.

She sat opposite me, and I noticed that she was wearing a nose ring with tiny insets of amber and polished stone. I had heard that only married women wore them, though I saw no sign of a husband or children, so I guessed there must be exceptions. She stared at me with unwavering coolness - either she was slightly mad, I thought, or this was part of a technique designed to disarm her audience. I felt tempted to get up and leave, but controlled myself.

'All right,' she said at last. 'I see what you have come for. You came to this place from your country because you wanted to escape from the cage – the one you grew up in. Riches bring cages and the cage confines your being and imprisons your mind.'

I was astonished. Was I so transparent? I must be wearing my heart on my sleeve, I thought. I recalled my feelings after I had seen that caravan – a curtain pulled back, a door that opened into a different world – my sudden yearning to go off with the nomads.

'You feel it is time,' Maya went on. 'What was it your father said to you when you were a youth?'

I bristled again at this impertinence. How could she possibly know what my father had said years ago? She could *not* know, of course, except that all fathers were bound to have said something. And I remembered what my father had said distinctly. *You want to get yourself in the army, boy.* There it was – the truth that I had been hiding even from myself. Joining the army had not been just about escape, but also about conforming to my father's wishes – the values of a patriarchal society. Now I thought about it, I had wanted to be a writer, a poet perhaps, but my father had thought this an unworthy profession for a man.

He had been a soldier himself, but my mother was not greatly impressed with the idea of war or the military. As a young man, *her* father - my grandfather - had been permanently maimed in a terrific battle. His wound had not been treated properly. It had gone gangrenous, and though he had survived, his leg had not, and he had lived out his life in pain and poverty. My mother was a nurse – caring for others was her calling. She made no objection to my father's insistence, though – even if she had I would probably not have listened: I had been brought up in a milieu where warriors were heroes – a society exalting guns and glory. So I had got myself in the army, followed the military path, and realized finally that while there was adventure in the profession of violence, it was not genuinely heroic to excel in destroying things and people – especially people who were not equally well equipped. In any case, most casualties in war came from machines - from bombs and shells, not from gunfights.

I did not hold it against my father. I was glad to have had the opportunity, and on that path I had met many challenges, and learned a lot of valuable things I could not have learned elsewhere. The experience had affected me deeply – in some ways it had scarred me - but I was also grateful for the lessons I had learned. I had become a teacher to escape that old path. I had come here to distance myself from civilization, but Maya was right about this too – even here I was not outside the cage.

'I had a dream,' I said.

'What did you dream?'

I recounted all I could remember of my dream and afterwards she asked. 'Was it the white leopard who spoke?'

'Not exactly. The voice seemed to come from somewhere else.'

Her eyes sparkled. 'A man's voice or a woman's?'

'A woman's I think.'

'There was nothing in your dream to suggest the Lost Oasis except the voice?'

'That's it.'

'Very well.'

She considered it for a moment.

'I understand,' she said. 'Now let me tell you the story *I* know about the Lost Oasis, as my mother told it to me.'

She took a long breath and narrowed her eyes.

Oasis

'There was once a young man,' she said, 'who was herding camels on the fringe of the desert, when he realized a she-camel was missing. The animal's tracks led into the desert, and he followed them. All day he walked, across dunes and plains, and every time he reached a high place he thought, *now I shall see her*, but he never did. He kept on following the tracks. The sun beat down, and he grew more and more thirsty. At sunset he slept in the sand. Next day the young man followed the she-camel's tracks again but did not catch up with her. After a second night in the desert without water, he was so thirsty he could hardly move. On the morning of the third day, though, he found the tracks again. He forced himself after them, but soon he collapsed and could only crawl. He struggled to the top of a dune, thinking, *perhaps I shall see her now*, but he did not see her. What he did see was a green oasis – palms, vines, olives - trees of all kinds. They stretched as far as the horizon. With a last effort, the young man staggered towards the oasis. As soon as he was within the shade of the trees, he heard the tinkle of running water.

It was like music to his ears.

The oasis was bursting with life. There were gushing streams, pools, springs and waterfalls and date-palms heavy with dates. There were deep gorges and huge caves, and tangled forests of giant trees, where animals roamed. There were exotic flowers, mushrooms, olives, grapevines, and orchards with ripe fruit of every kind just waiting to be gathered. There were fish in the pools, ducks on the water, and flocks of birds that flitted from branch to branch. There were lovely young women, too, who danced and played music, and the boy danced with them until he was bewitched, until he forgot how long he had been there, why he had come, and even his own name.

Then one day he remembered the girl he was betrothed to, and it all came back. He felt a strong desire to return, to see his family, to see his beloved, and remember his self again.

The young maidens of the oasis were sad about this and tried to persuade him to stay, saying that there was a great secret hidden there that he had not yet learned, but would know if he remained longer, and it would change his life. The boy was afraid that, if he stayed, he would lose his self forever, so he asked for his she-camel, which had grown fat in the oasis. Taking the camel and a bag of dates, he set off the way he had come, eating the dates, and dropping the stones in the desert, so that he could retrace his steps should he wish to return.

When he arrived home, his family was astonished to see him. They said he had been away so long they had been sure he was dead, and the girl he had been betrothed to had married someone else. The boy was heartbroken and dismayed, as it did not seem to him that he had been away for any length of time. He settled back into the life of his village as best he could, but after a while he began to grow restless. He started to wonder what great secret it was the oasis maidens had talked about, and whether it would really have changed things. Overcome by a desire to return to the oasis, he wished his people farewell and set out to follow the date stones he had dropped in the desert. Try as he might, though, he never found any of the stones, and neither did he find the oasis again. He remained at home and grew old, never knowing what secret he might have learned had he stayed there, or how it might have changed his life.'

Maya paused and watched me closely. 'It's a story,' she said. 'I can't say it is true, but what is the truth, anyhow?'

I stared back at her. The story was a good one, but the meaning was not clear – it was open to interpretation. The boy had escaped the limitations of everyday life by chance - following a lost camel. He had found a kind of paradise, but had yearned to get back to normality. He had returned only to find that everything had changed. I could not work it out.

'Does the oasis have a name?' I asked.

She shook her head. 'It is simply called al-*Wahat al-Ghayba* – the Lost Oasis.'

'What about my dream? Do you think that it is connected in any way?'

'You dreamed of figure who was neither a man nor a woman. There was wind and thunder, and a white leopard. Oh, and a voice saying that animals would lead you to the Lost Oasis and heal you?'

'Yes,' I chuckled. 'Does that mean I'm sick?'

'The figure in the desert, neither man nor woman, both and neither, is a messenger. He - or she – brings a message that you need to be healed because you are not complete. You have lost part of the whole, and you will not be at peace until you have found that missing part.'

'You mean I will find what is missing at the Lost Oasis?'

'If you find the Lost Oasis, you will have found the missing part.'

'But does the Lost Oasis really exist?'

She laughed. 'What does *that* mean – exist?'

I gaped at her, puzzled. She laughed again.

I felt slightly irritated, but then, I thought, what had I really been expecting? There were no clear answers, only more questions. She had told me a good story that was all.

Back home that night, though, I lay on my bed so thrilled I could not sleep. If my experience in the military had given me anything, it was confidence in my ability to follow through. The Lost Oasis was only a story, but it had given me a purpose – a reason to venture beyond the limits, a reason to approach the wild.

So far I had not been in the desert, nor even sat on a camel. Yet I knew, without a shadow of a doubt, that Maya's tale had set me on a journey. I had seen a camel caravan in the desert. I was in the right place at the right time, and the quest for the Lost Oasis was going to be my life.

Market

The camel market was in the main square of the town and there were dozens of camels. As soon as I arrived, men in long white shirts and layered head-cloths crowded round me. A man called Jabir offered me a camel for ten guineas insisting that the animal was excellent. 'It is young and well-behaved,' he said. 'It won't bite you or give you any trouble.'

I glanced at the camel. It seemed very big, I thought. Its legs appeared ungainly and it had an extraordinarily long neck. There was something insect-like about the head, and I did not quite like the look in its enormous eyes, or the way it kept slavering and grinding its teeth. On the other hand, it looked like all the other camels, and I knew nothing about camels. I had never been this close to one before. Without even thinking, I started to bargain. A crowd gathered around us, laughing, and shouting. I offered the trader seven guineas, but he refused. I had already turned to walk away when Jabir ran up behind me and grabbed my arm. 'Have you got the money?' he demanded.

I hesitated, realizing that I had given in to an impulse - I had entered the transaction as if it were a game. I still had a chance to walk away, but the moment I agreed to buy the animal, there was no turning back. I licked dry lips.

'Yes,' I said.

'All right, it's a deal. I'll throw in a saddle and a water-skin for nothing.'

And there it was. In the blink of an eye, I had become the owner of a camel, a saddle, and a water-skin.

There were certain formalities to be gone through, such as obtaining a bill of sale from the market superintendent, and then, crowding around me, cat-calling and shouting encouragement, the locals showed me how to saddle the animal, how to couch it, how to mount and ride. It was the first time I had mounted a camel, and the sudden jerk forward took me by surprise. The onlookers encouraged me to take the head-rope, and I did a circuit around the square - it felt wonderful to be riding a camel at last – like a dream. It did not seem difficult while I was surrounded by people ready to help and give advice. I gave no thought as to what it might be like when I was alone in the desert.

Dusk

It was already dusk by the time I left the town. Jabir walked with me to the outskirts to point me in the right direction. 'The Pharoah's Road runs north,' he said. 'A camel-herd passed here two days ago, heading for Egypt. Just follow the tracks. If you travel quickly you will soon catch up with it.'

It sounded easy enough, I thought. I looked across the twilit desert, and noticed that the land was stony, a vast swath of pebbles that stretched as far as one could see in the dim light. It felt more like a rocky seashore than the desert.

When I mentioned this to Jabir, he told me. 'It is said that this was the mouth of a river that once met the Nile at this place. They call it the *Yellow Nile*. The stories run that the water flowed here from a mountain many sleeps to the west. Of course, that was long, long ago, in the Distant Time.'

He wished me farewell. 'That camel will look after you if you look after him,' he said. 'Now go in the safekeeping of God.'

I thanked him and urged my camel forward. Glancing to my right I could just make out the cluster of school buildings, where, one day, on my way to work, I had had a vision that changed my life. As the camel paced on over the stones, night fell quickly and soon the school was a memory, left behind in the dark.

Guardian

The moon came up, winking like a slow eye, watching me, and the sky was spangled with stars. The lights of the town were lost behind me. I felt serene and content to be there in the quiet and the great open spaces of the desert, alone with a camel pacing along placidly.

Soon, though, I started to feel uncomfortable. In the dark I could not see the tracks of the herd I was supposed to be following, so I could not be sure of my direction. I decided that while I had made a good start, it was enough for the first day.

That was when my problems began.

I tugged on the camel's head-rope to make it kneel, and the animal simply ignored me. I tugged harder and harder, but it seemed to take it as an excuse to mooch sideways and began grazing on the wide mat of grass that had appeared beneath us without my noticing.

After more futile tugging I leapt out of the saddle, only to find myself covered in viciously sharp burs that stuck in my arms, legs, and face. The faster I tried to pull them out, the more they stuck. They worked themselves inside my trousers, up the sleeves of my shirt and even into my lips and ears. This was totally unexpected - the desert was meant to be sand and rock with a few thorny trees. That it was the home of a grass that showered one with burs had never been mentioned in the stories.

I still had hold of the head-rope, but presently the animal began to wander further, into a stand of thorns. I yanked against it and the camel pulled harder, dragging me through the bushes – the cruel white spikes tore my shirt and scratched my face and hands. The tug-of-war seemed to last for hours. I was just wondering what I would do if the head-rope broke, when the camel sat down. As quickly as I could, I secured his front leg with a length of rope as Jabir had shown me.

I laid out my meagre possessions – a water-skin, tins of food, a blanket, and some clothes - and found to my dismay that everything was immediately covered in burs. I thought about lighting a fire but realized I had nothing to light it with, even if I could have found the firewood. I wrapped myself in my blanket, ignoring the burs as best I could, and tried to settle down. I could not sleep, though. My hands and face were sore and swollen. I was afraid the camel might run off – then I would truly be like the youth in the Lost Oasis story.

It hit me for the first time how ill-prepared I was. I had bought the camel on impulse, and though I had some water, I had little food, and no cooking utensils. I had no map, no compass, and no means of finding my way other than the promise of tracks I had not yet located.

I stared around into the night. I had been excited about stepping over the threshold of the wilderness, but now I saw that I had been too hasty. The desert was silent - empty, alien, and hostile. I began to wish I had not come, yet it was too late to turn back. I closed my eyes and tried to sleep. A moment later I felt a set of hairy legs scuttle over my face. I shivered and sat up, slapping my head and twitching, knowing that some very large crawling thing had just used me as a ramp. In the moonlight, I saw a spider as wide as my hand, with an enormous head and a strange double-pointed proboscis. It halted there, swiveling on a bloated abdomen, then faced me and raised its front legs in challenge. It seemed eyeless, and slowly its jaws opened – deep, serrated, chomping jaws, as vicious and menacing as anything I had ever seen. For a moment the spider seemed much larger than it was – a real monster, the guardian of the new world I had entered unbidden. I shuddered, and groped for something to crush it with. I found only my leather slipper, and by the time it was in my hand, the monster was gone.

This was nothing like I had imagined my first night in the desert. The camel-herd and the nomads I had seen were so perfectly fitted to the landscape they had seemed to wear it like a glove. Now, I could not understand how anyone could live in this place. The sense of serenity and peace I had felt at first had vanished. The moon went down abruptly, and there were no more stars.

Runaway

I tramped on for two days, not riding but pulling the camel behind me. With almost every step I cursed my foolish conceit in having set out alone into this wasteland. Quite early on the first morning, I came across a wide swath of tracks – hundreds of oval shapes superimposed on each other – that could only be those of the caravan I was looking for. If it had not been for those tracks, I would almost certainly have given up at that point.

The first problem was the camel. When I had seen the caravan on my way to school that day, the nomads had been so completely at ease on their mounts, and the camel-herd had drifted effortlessly across the desert. I had expected to ride my camel with the same facility as those men. Instead, after the first evening I dared not mount up in case I could not get off again, and I was obliged to lead the animal after me.

That might still have been all right, except that the camel showed no sign of wanting to go. It continually pulled back on the head-rope, doubling the effort, and causing me to swear endlessly. It felt as if I were dragging a grand piano uphill. If I turned to glance at the animal, hoping perhaps to intimidate it, I found myself staring into unwavering black eyes regarding me with what I took to be insane malevolence. While fixing me with its glare, the camel would lick its lips with a bloated pink tongue and gnash long, sharp-looking teeth, sending a shiver down my spine. Once, when I was standing in front of it, the camel made a belching sound and vomited gooey green cud all over me. The stink was nauseating and it stayed with me for days.

In a way I could not blame the animal for its behavior, because at night, when it should have been resting, I was unable to remove the saddle, as I had no idea how to put it back on. This meant that the animal had to sit upright for the entire night. I could not allow it to wander around grazing on any grasses we might come across, because I did not know how to hobble it. Anyway, I was pretty certain that once it got away from me it would never come back. The weather was scorching, and there was always grit on the wind. I had little water, and most of the time my mouth felt like sandpaper. Worse than that, though was the landscape itself – this endless sweep of featureless rock and sand, with its clumps of spiky grass and its thorny trees like bleached and distorted bones. It was a stark, strange, uncanny place – a place of mournful winds, eerie whispers, and surreal shadows. With every step I took it seemed to resent me more.

The nights were dark and lonely, and I found it hard to sleep, terrified that I would awake at sunrise to find the camel gone. Once I put my head down on my saddle bag and heard a high-pitched trilling sound, like a muted shriek, coming from beneath it. When the sound ceased, I thought I had imagined it. In the morning, though, I found a jade-colored scorpion there with crab-like claws and a scaly tail tipped with a sting ready to strike. I had been told that these small green scorpions were more deadly than the big black ones, and crushed it with my stick. The unnerving thing, though, was the knowledge that I had slept with the creature under my head all night. The memory of that trilling sound made me shudder.

As the hours turned into days, I grew exhausted, discouraged, and disillusioned. The desert was not my friend – it was out to kill me. Seeing that camel herd, hearing Maya's story of the Lost Oasis, had lulled me into a false confidence. I had thought it would be easy. Now I felt that I did not belong here and the whole idea seemed ludicrously childish –the stuff of fairy tales. How could there be an oasis in the desert that remained unknown? Often, I had the urge to give it up, and only the imagined sneers of Hamid and other fellow teachers prevented me from turning back. That and, perhaps, the mind-over-matter bravado that was the legacy from my army days.

Near noon on the third morning, I passed some low sand-dunes and was marching wearily towards a ridge of shattered rock on the skyline, when I came across a shallow wadi with stunted thorn-trees scattered along it. The wadi looked like a good place to rest. I headed for the first tree that offered a little shade and checked that there was no sandbur grass beneath it. The swelling the burs had caused on my hands and face had gone, and I had managed to remove the prickly seeds from my things, but I had no wish for another instalment. Finding the shade clear, I couched the camel.

Without letting go of the head-rope, I leaned across the saddle to get my water-skin – I had last drunk water at sunrise, and I was parched. The camel turned its head towards me, and I saw a warning in the insane black eyes. Suddenly, it jerked its head back, and whipped the head-rope out of my hand. It jumped to its feet, let out a blood-curdling bellow, and galloped off the way we had come.

I pelted after the animal, desperately trying to clutch the trailing head-rope. I managed to grab it, but it came away in my hand. I was left standing, staring at the useless rope. Even if I got near the camel now, I thought, there was no easy way to grab hold of it. I watched the camel's hindquarters swing away, its tail raised vertical in what looked suspiciously like a rude gesture. All I could do was wail, *'Come back! Come back!'*

To my surprise the camel stopped running. It began to shift about chewing at tufts of sword-grass. I saw my chance. I approached more cautiously this time. The animal waited till I was within an arm's length, then kicked up a spurt of sand and shot off again.

I pursued it, yelling. When it reached what it evidently felt was a safe distance, it halted and started to graze. I inched gingerly towards it. It chomped away happily till I was within an arm's length, then cantered off and began to climb the slope of a dune.

I laboured after it through hot, deep sand, falling even further behind. The next thing I knew, the camel had disappeared over the crest. Only then did I start to panic. Everything I had was on that camel – including food and water. I was several days from the Nile – it was summer and hot. I remembered how, in Maya's story, the boy had gone three days without water, and when he had stumbled across the Lost Oasis he had been in a terrible state.

I scrambled to the crest of the dune and saw the animal below, moving away steadily. It was already too far for me to catch, and my heart dropped. Then I noticed that, to the south, coming in my direction, were two camel-riders - dark scribbles on the blank sheet of the desert. Without even thinking, I began to jump up and down, waving my arms, shouting, 'The *camel*! The *camel*!'

Almost at once, the riders separated and began to work around the runaway camel with unhurried ease. One of them came close to it, leaned over, and grasped its nostrils. It seemed to freeze. The rider dropped out of the saddle and stood holding the camel's nose until the other arrived and slung a head-cloth around its neck.

I slid down the slip face of the dune towards them. They were youths, I saw, dressed in parchment-yellow shirts, wearing knives in sheaths upside down on their arms, and wooden beads around their necks.

'*Thank you*,' I wheezed.

Hungry

The youths stared at me with obvious indignation.

'The thanks is *to God*,' said one of them - a stocky young man with a slightly grave air. He spoke the last word with emphasis, as if they themselves had had nothing to do with it.

'When did you last feed this camel?' asked the other – a tall, spindly youth with a nervous grin.

'I let him eat grass when I stop,' I said.

'That is not enough,' said the grave-looking young man. 'On a journey like this, a camel needs to eat grain. There is little grazing on this part of the Pharaoh's Road.'

'He is hungry,' laughed the spindly youth. 'That is why he ran away.'

'The camel is the Gift of God,' the other added. 'He will not abandon you if you treat him well. Abuse him, though, and he will dump you in the desert.'

I felt ashamed. The last thing Jabir had said to me was that I must look after the camel. Deep down, I realized, I had thought of the animal as *it* - a clockwork mechanism that one

21

could stop and start at will, and that would go on working forever. I had not seen it as a conscious being of flesh and blood, with a spirit of its own.

The lanky youth took the head-rope from my hand, tied it loosely around the camel's head, and handed the free end back to me.

'Thank you,' I said.

He gave an exasperated gasp. 'The thanks is to *God*, don't you see?'

I thought I did - he was telling me that I did not have to thank them for saving my life, because to thank someone suggested that you were surprised they had acted like human beings, and therefore an insult. It seemed a little convoluted but that was only because I had been brought up to say empty *thank yous* for everything, and actually it made sense. It meant that, to them, kindness and altruism were normal.

'I am Khidir,' the youth said. 'This is Awad.'

We all shook hands.

'God is All-Knowing,' Awad said, 'but this is not good country for travelling alone. It is the edge of the *Hurra*. Few nomads wander here.'

'I was following those tracks,' I said, gesturing towards the strip of prints in the sand some way off. 'The tracks of a camel-herd. They told me it was two days ahead. I thought if I could catch up with it, the herders might take me with them.'

'We are travelling with that herd,' Awad told me, grinning. 'The guide, Brahim, sent us to fetch water.'

He nodded at their two camels, and for the first time I noticed they were laden with water-skins like bloated brown slugs. The camels looked heavier and more powerful than mine, and they were carrying two pairs of big water-skins apiece.

'You want to go down the Pharaoh's Road to Egypt?' Khidir enquired.

'I'm looking for the Lost Oasis,' I said. 'Have you ever heard of it?'

Khidir stopped and stared at me, then burst out laughing. 'The Lost Oasis? That is just a story they tell to children, my friend, don't you know that? There is no such place.'

'No, no,' Awad cut in. 'You are a stranger here – you know nothing. As my brother says, the Lost Oasis is a story, but perhaps - God alone is All-Knowing - it could be more than a story. If it exists, though, it must be deep in the *Hurra*. You cannot go there alone. Our guide, Brahim, has travelled in the desert more than most, and knows a great many things. Come with us. The herd is grazing in the Vale of Grasses. God willing, we will be there by last light.'

Donkey's Feet

Travelling with the nomad youths was a quite different experience from going it alone. First, they saddled my camel carefully, demonstrating how it should be done, then gave him a little grain from their own stock. While Awad squeezed his nostrils and held his mouth open, Khidir tipped several mouthfuls down his throat. The camel looked first startled then pleased: he began to perk up straight away.

Once we had all mounted and were following the tracks of the herd north, I noted that the camels kept pace with each other naturally, without interference from the riders. 'Let the head-rope go slack,' Awad instructed me. 'If you keep it tight the camel thinks you are trying to slow him down. Only pull it tight when you want him to stop. Camels like each other's company and as long as they are together you will have no trouble encouraging them.'

We rode silently for a while, then Awad asked me to tell him what I knew about the Lost Oasis. I described my dream and recounted the story as Maya had told it to me. When I had finished, Khidir laughed and said. 'It's a good story, but it's just a story. There is nowhere in the desert like that.'

Awad shook his head. 'Do you know the *Three Donkeys?*' he asked me.

'No,' I said. 'What's that?'

'It's a story, and it starts with a nomad following a lost camel like yours does. He also came to an oasis, but what he found there was something different.'

'What?'

'Let me tell you the story.'

'All right.'

'Anyway, there was once this nomad who was tracking a lost camel, when a strong wind blew up and swallowed the camel's tracks. The nomad's head was going round and round like a well-pulley, and he could no longer tell up from down or north from south. His water ran out and he had no food…'

He paused, flicked his head-rope gently, and made a clicking noise to encourage his camel. As he continued, I noticed that all three animals seemed to prick up their ears as if they, too, were listening to the story.

'A day passed,' he said, 'then another and another, and the nomad grew weaker and weaker, and felt that he would soon die. Then, one evening, as darkness fell, and he was thinking he would never see another dawn, he spotted the light of a fire in the distance, and heard singing – it sounded like the sweet voices of girls.

'He staggered towards the voices, but they seemed sometimes near, sometimes far away, and he began to think he would not reach them at all. Finally, just when he felt he could go no further, he found himself in an oasis with the shadows of palm trees, grass, and a pool of water. There was a blazing fire, and in its light he saw three young women dressed in robes, all three of them very beautiful.

'They greeted him in a friendly manner, and made him comfortable by the fire. They brought him water in a bowl and bade him drink only a little at a time. The water revived him. Then they brought him a bowl of sour camel's milk and a bowl of soft camel cheese, and bade him eat and drink a little at a time.

'When he had had enough, and felt satisfied, they filled two skins, one of water and one of sour milk, and laid them by him. They brought him saddle cushions and blankets and told him to sleep. As he drifted off into sleep the crackling fire comforted him, and the young women sang to him, with their sweet voices, and it was soothing, like the wind blowing in the grass, and the rain falling on dry ground.

'Then, as sleep overtook him, it seemed to the nomad that the girls' voices changed and grew deeper and harsher like the voices of wild animals. He opened his eyes and saw through the flames of the fire that, instead of beautiful maidens, he was looking at three donkeys in women's robes, with staring eyes, long snouts, flaring nostrils, and big teeth. Their song was the discordant braying of asses. The nomad was terrified but sleep held him in her tight grip, and he found he could not speak or even move.

'In the morning the nomad awoke to find himself lying on bare ground in the desert, with no cushions or blankets, and no trees, no grass, no water-pool, no trace of a fire. The maidens had vanished, and the skins they had filled for him were dry as bleached bones. His lips were cracked and his belly empty – he knew that he had neither eaten nor drunk, and he felt weaker than ever.

He wondered if he had seen the young women at all, and began to search for tracks. He found three sets of tracks, but not those of humans – they were donkey tracks, but looked as if the donkeys had been walking upright on two legs.'

Awad paused again. For a moment there was no sound but the slight creak of the saddles as the camels strode on.

'He had been tricked by the voices of jinns, you see,' he said. 'They can appear as humans, but they have donkey's feet.'

'So, what happened to him?' I asked.

'He stayed where he was, and later, by God's will, a nomad caravan came along and found him very near to death. He told them his story before God took him unto God.'

'I don't understand,' I said.

'Died,' said Khidir.

'Oh.'

I mulled over the story. It was similar in essence to Maya's, but different – the nomad's oasis had turned out to be a fatal illusion. Perhaps Awad's tale was closer to the truth than Maya's. Perhaps it was a warning, I thought.

I was just about top open my mouth to ask more questions, when Khidir said. 'We're here.'

Grandfather Fire

I looked up to see camels of all shapes, colours, and sizes, basking in long pools of shadow, dotted across a wide valley between sweeping dunes, thick with grass and sedges in vivid clumps. The sun was already tippling over the horizon when we arrived at Brahim's camp. The guide was sitting by a fire in the lee of piled equipment and saddles, and he rose to greet us - a broad-shouldered, wide-bodied man with ebony skin, a jaw like a slab and a tufty grey beard. After we had couched and unloaded our camels, he welcomed us with tea in small, thick glasses. As he and the youths talked, I gazed into the fire, watching the flames weave a graceful dance around the firewood. For the first time, I saw that the fire was a living creature - and for a moment I was awed.

'*Grandfather Fire*,' Brahim growled, and I looked up to find him watching me.

'What?'

'You were taken with the fire,' he said. 'Did you see anything in the flames?'

'Patterns,' I said. 'Dancing swirls.'

'If you look closely enough you may see the face of Grandfather Fire. The fire is truly alive, and once lit, it is the axis of the world. The space it illuminates becomes an island in the desert. When it goes out, and we move on, the place reverts to what it has always been. Only the firestones will tell of our passing.'

I nodded, fascinated. 'So if fire is our grandfather, what is our grandmother?' I asked.

'Water is our grandmother,' he said. 'The sun is our father - though some call him Father Sky - and our mother is the Earth.'

'I see. So they are all our relations?'

'Of course. All things that exist are our relations. Is it true you are looking for an oasis?'

'The Lost Oasis. Do you know of anywhere like that?'

'God is All-Knowing. I've heard the stories, that's all.'

'Stories for children,' Khidir cut in. 'If anyone knew where it was, it wouldn't be lost, would it?'

The guide laughed. 'That is true. Why are you searching for it?'

'It would be good to find somewhere that no-one else has been to.'

'Why?'

I could not think of an answer, and I realized I had not told him the truth. I was not on this journey so that I could claim boasting rights, nor was I here to conquer anything. I was genuinely searching for something that was lost.

'There are many oases in the *Hurra*,' he went on, 'and they have different names for different people. Perhaps your oasis is one of them, perhaps not, but in any case the *Hurra* is wide – in three moons one would not cross it all. One would need much water and food – and this is not a journey to make alone.'

Khidir snorted. 'It is not a journey for a townsman. You know nothing of desert ways – not even how to saddle a camel. You would never come back.'

His blunt comment irritated me. I was on a high horse, and had forgotten that, only a short time earlier, I had been standing on a dune shouting for help as my camel galloped off towards the horizon with everything I had on its back. And here I was declaring that I intended to find a place in the desert that no-one else had seen.

The guide made no comment - he did not seem to have heard. He was glancing over my shoulder. 'Praise be to God,' he said. 'They are here.'

I turned and saw the camel herd drifting out of the dusk. There were scores of camels, moving in a tight group, shoulder to shoulder, stepping so softly that they seemed to float. They reminded me at once of the herd I had seen on the way to school that day – the encounter that had set me on this journey.

Dark human figures were urging the camels forward with clicking, coaxing sounds. Brahim and the youths rose to their feet, and I did the same. I followed them as they went to meet the herd, and I was soon surrounded by stamping, sniffing, gurgling animals, whose heads wobbled over me like tall flowers in the wind. I mimed the others, holding up my hands, chanting 'Deh. Deh. Deh, which, in herder-talk, I understood, meant halt.

While we stayed on guard, the other herders moved around carrying masses of hobbling loops with wooden pegs - their clinking made a kind of music. The men would lift a camel's left front leg, fold it gently, then fit and peg the hobble while securing the leg-joint in the crook of their arm. After that they would ease the camel to its knees. One by one, the camels thumped down, and by the time the last sparklers of sunset had faded, the whole herd was settled. The men moved to their camp and under a soaring canopy of stars, and began to cook polenta, throwing handfuls of flour into a pot and stirring it with a sliver of wood, until it grew so thick the twig would no longer turn.

When it was deemed ready, Khidir poured sour camel's milk over it from a skin, and we ate with our hands, all of us crouching round the pot. I was glad I had already mastered this communal way of eating. I appreciated it now. I remembered how, in the army, men had eaten in groups strictly according to rank. That had always seemed wrong to me, as if they did not belong together. Eating out of the same pot, hunkering down close to the Earth, we were all one - there were no false barriers between us. When we had finished, Awad moved among us with water in a long-spouted jug, pouring a little into each man's upturned hands.

Afterwards we drank more tea around the fire, and the men talked endlessly of the wind, the sun, the rain, the grazing, the camels, and the way ahead. 'By the blessing of God, we have another man to help us,' Brahim said, nodding towards me. The herders peered at me, and I wondered if Awad and Khidir would tell them the story of how my camel had run away. I guessed they would – at least, Khidir would.

'It's true I have no experience,' I said, 'but I'm ready to learn.'

'One should always be ready to learn,' Brahim said, 'because the desert has much to teach. As for the Lost Oasis, the only people who can tell you about that are the nomads of the *Hurra*. They pitch their tents deep in the desert and know its secrets.'

'Where can I find them?'

'At Elai, perhaps. It is the last watering place on the Pharaoh's Road before Egypt, but nomads from the *Hurra* also water there. I cannot take you further, because soldiers guard the frontier, and they will not let you pass. In any case, Elai is better for you.'

'Thank you.' I said.

Khidir snorted again.

'I mean, thanks to God.'

'Yes, the thanks is to God,' Brahim repeated. 'If you want a story about a nomad following a lost camel, I have one for you, although perhaps it is not what you wish to hear.'

'Another one? Do all nomad stories start with stray camels?'

'Of course,' he laughed. 'Do you want to hear it?'

'Yes, of course,' I said.

Caravan of the Sun

All the herders stopped talking and gazed at the guide expectantly – they were evidently used to his stories, I thought.

'Well,' he began,' there was once a nomad who went in search of a lost she-camel. He followed her on foot, uphill and down dune, and across sandy plains for several sleeps. First he ran out of food, then he ran out of water, and soon he was so weak that he could no longer walk, and could only crawl. He crawled on until darkness fell, and he no longer knew where he was. At last he came to a vast hole in the desert. He climbed down to the bottom of the hole where he found another country – a country of trees and water-pools, and lush pastures. A beautiful woman was waiting for him – a woman neither young nor old, whose name was *al-Lat*. She said that this country was *Tihamat* – the country under the ground. She took him to her tent, gave him food, and told him, "Father will be here soon."

'She showed him a place behind her tent where she kept camels, goats and sheep in a stone pen. Some of the animals were thin, scratched and bruised, and others were sleek and fat. 'The wounded ones are those who have just come through the same hole as you,' she told him. 'The fat ones are those I have looked after for a while.'

He noticed that the she-camel he had been tracking was there, in a pen with the thin and wasted animals. When he asked for her, though, the woman shook her head. 'She arrived only recently' she said, 'and she needs my care.'

'They sat at the gap of the tent, and as they talked, a camel caravan passed silently across the desert, tended by camel-men with hunched shoulders and black cloaks, and he saw that the last camel was carrying on its back the star called *Day's Heart* – the Evening Star. As they passed the nomad called out "Take me with you." The camel-men did not stop, though, and the woman said again. "Father will be here soon."

'Before long another caravan drifted silently across the desert, led by camel-men in the same black cloaks. This time the last camel in the train was carrying *Zahara*, the Morning Star. Once again, the nomad wanted to join the caravan, and once again the woman shook her head and said. "Father will be here soon. He will take you with him."

'A little later a third caravan approached them across the desert, and when it came near, the woman nodded, and the nomad went to join it. The camel-men mounted him on a camel, and the nomad saw that the hunched men in cloaks were not men at all but black storks. The last camel in the train was carrying a litter covered with a black cloth, and riding in the litter was Father Sun. Though his light did not show, he gave out tremendous heat.

'The caravan travelled on and on across the desert, and for a while the nomad fell asleep, and when he awoke it seemed to him that stars were all around them and that the caravan was crossing the sky. Shortly, the black storks halted the caravan and told the nomad that it was the mid-day halt, and he must take off his clothes and throw them away. The nomad replied that he had no wish to get rid of his clothes. The black storks shook their heads and said. "We took you because we thought you were ready to throw away your clothes."

'So the caravan started again, and travelled on and on, till a tent appeared in the distance. The caravan stopped at the tent, and the nomad saw the woman al-Lat waiting for him, and realized that the caravan had returned him to the same place. After the caravan had departed, the nomad asked al-Lat for his camel once more, but she refused to hand the she-camel over. She took the nomad back to the hole in the desert, then guided him to his tents. 'Be one with your family,' she said, 'and do not go off without food and water in search of lost camels, for your time has not yet come.'

There was silence as the herdsmen pondered the story. It was a wonderful tale, I thought – the idea of the sun travelling with a caravan incognito was magnificent. Yet like the story Awad had told about the maidens who turned out to be jinns, it was slightly eery. Yet there were also motifs I could identify with. Just as the nomad had followed a runaway camel, and found another country, so I had followed my own runaway and met Awad and Khidir. The nomad had wanted to join the Caravan of the Sun, just as I had wanted to join Brahim's camel herd. The caravan had seemed to be taking him to the *Beyond*, but he had decided that he did not want to go, and had been given a second chance. I only hoped that if it came to it, the same opportunity would be given to me.

Before we rolled up in our blankets that night, Brahim called me over and presented me with a slender stick cut from a thorn tree. 'This is your *mahjin* - your camel-stick,' he said. 'Use it wisely. Never hit a camel hard, only tap him when you are riding. Remember that camels are people too.'

Brahim

Usually, we would be up in the cool before dawn, releasing the animals from their hobbles, allowing them to shift about grazing. After we had drunk tea and loaded our riding animals, Brahim would give the signal to mount, and we would canter around the scattered herd, gathering animals into groups, drawing the invisible net ever tighter. As the sun came up, spinning a gilded web across the pastel plains, we would move out into the wind, the camels pounding forward in an immense surge of power.

With the help of the herders, I learned to saddle camels, to hobble camels, to mount camels, to couch camels, to fit head-ropes, to canter, to wheel, to stay for long periods in the saddle. I learned the skills of holding the herd together, working around it, chasing strays back to the mass, keeping the animals almost constantly on the move. I became accustomed to halting for only a short break in the blazing sun of mid-day, and to driving the herd on until after dark.

Remembering what Brahim had told me that first night, I came to regard my own camel as a friend – he was by no means insane as I had imagined, but friendly and unassuming. He seemed to like my company, and had only run away that day thanks to my ignorance and neglect. I allowed him time to feed on grass and desert sages as I rode, and poured a little grain out on a cow-skin for him when we stopped for the night. I discovered that the nomads' animals had names, and I called him *Ata* - Gift - a name suggested by Awad, as a reminder that camels were a gift from God, and must be treated with respect.

Only Khidir remained critical. After his comment *you know nothing* I had been determined to watch, learn, and do everything as the nomads did – I could do it, I told myself. I was ex-special forces, and could do anything I set my mind to. Yet though I tried, I could not compete with men who had been handling camels since they could walk, and for whom travelling and living in the desert was a way of life. Whatever I did, no matter how happy with it I was – tying knots, saddling, loading, riding, herding - it was never good enough for Khidir. He would shake his head. *Not like that,* he would say. Sometimes he would snicker and again comment *you know nothing*, which I found infuriating. Often I had to stifle a rude rejoinder. I did not dislike Khidir, but I found myself avoiding him – as much as one could in a world with only half a dozen people in it.

Though the herd moved constantly, after a while I had the strange impression we were staying in the same place. The camels' feet made almost no sound as they walked, giving that odd sense of floating above the surface. The horizons seemed to remain always the same distance before us, always the same distance behind. The sun made its slow arc from sunrise to sunset and the shadows under the men, under the camels, under the rocks, changed in shape and size. Yet there was little sense of the days passing. Sometimes it seemed to me that this journey had no beginning and no end - we had been here for eternity and would remain here forever. At other times, though, I would drift off into long reveries about my youth, about the war, about Danny's death, about the hardships I had endured and the horrors I had been part of. The desert around me would fade out and I would engage in extended dialogues with myself that would continue until something – a sudden sound or movement - brought me abruptly out of the trance. Then I felt as if I had woken from sleep.

The sun grew fiercer as the season drew on, but the hardest days were those when a blistering wind hit us from the north. Although not a full-blown sandstorm, the wind carried dust that made our eyes smart. On these days, we would drop down from our saddles, cover our faces with our head-cloths, and walk behind the herd, using the great animal bodies as shelter. On foot, I realized for the first time how fast we were travelling. If I stopped even for a moment I would find when I looked up that the camels were already fading into the dust haze, and I had to run to catch up with them. The thought of being left alone in the desert without a camel and without water, was daunting.

The guide Brahim did not walk. He rode his camel into the eye of the wind, unperturbed by the dust, keeping the herd on perfect course. He steered our mobile world with iron precision, extending an arm and bawling *laymin-oooh* to order a move to the right, and *laysar-oooh* for a move to the left. Instantly we would range forward, making fine adjustments to the herd's direction.

I was interested to know how he was able to navigate so perfectly: I noticed that his attention alternated between the skyline and the desert surface, and that he made frequent small changes to the position of his camel. As I became more familiar with the nomads' talk, I realized, too, that they aligned themselves with the far-away, unseen, Nile - the nomad word for going north was *musaffal* – downriver: for going south, it was *musa'id* – upriver. How the desert people could orient themselves on a river they rarely or never saw fascinated me.

One morning, when the day was calm and I was riding beside him, Brahim told me of his own life.

'I was born in the desert,' he said, 'and when I was a boy – younger than Awad and Khidir - my uncle asked me to accompany him with a caravan to al-Gaa, the salt oasis. There were only the two of us. We had dug and loaded the salt and were on the way back, when God took my uncle unto God.'

'You mean, he died?'

'Yes, a sand-viper bit him, and he dropped dead, may God's mercy be upon him. I was quite without experience, and the camp of my family was still far. Yet I managed to bring the caravan back to our camp without losing a single camel or a load of salt. My family was proud because I was only a boy and I had brought the caravan in single-handedly, but I never believed that I had done it alone. God was with me - the Great Spirit that dwells within all of us, in the wind, in the desert grasses, in the birds, in the trees, in the sun and the clouds, in the wells and springs, and in the generosity and kindness of the nomads I met in the desert. Thereafter I acquired a name as a desert guide, and people started to trust me with herds like this one, being taken to Egypt. Yes, it needed courage and endurance to keep going after my uncle died, but such qualities are the gifts of God. The thanks is to God, always.'

News

One morning the guide led the herd across successive sheaves of sand that creaked under the camels' feet. As the sun rose higher dust-motes glinted among chains of fish-scale dunes, sand bars, and great crescents that towered over the desert floor in soft pink and gold. We drove the camels up a gentle slope and from the top we saw a party of nomads riding straight towards us. This sudden encounter was a surprise to me, as we had seen no-one since leaving the Vale of Grasses. When the strangers were near, Brahim halted the herd, and went to greet them. The rest of us followed. The travellers couched their camels and dismounted, then lined up to receive us – small men with weathered brown faces, wearing robes the colour of sand – they looked as if they had sprung from the desert itself.

Greeting was a ritual I learned by mimicry. One was expected to grip the other's hand firmly, look him straight in the eyes, and repeat:

By God's will you are well?

Upon you there is no evil, by God's will?

Thanks to God all is well,

By God's will your family is well?

Thanks to God, there is no evil. .

By God's will your herds and flocks are well?

Thanks to God, no evil is upon them …

… grasping, releasing, grasping, releasing, gazing intently into the other's face. It seemed almost like a contest to see who would give up first, but it gave one a good chance to weigh up a stranger and establish a rapport before any actual news was exchanged.

When the greeting was done, a lean old nomad with a wisp of beard and eyes the colour of stone, asked '*Sakanab*? What is the news?'

'The news is good,' Brahim said.

We all crouched down together, and the guide proceeded to give *sakanab* - a full account of everything he had seen and heard in the past few days – the spoor of gazelles, the prints of a hyena, the tracks of camels –where those camels were going, where they had come from – the direction and force of the wind, the texture of the clouds, traces of water, and most of all, the exact location and state of desert plants and grasses.

I was amazed not only by Brahim's prodigious memory, but also by the fact that he had absorbed all these details. It was as if, for him, every day had been a long and intimate communion with nature. Since I had met Brahim, I had covered every step of the same ground, yet my memory of what I had seen was almost a blank sheet - I might have been travelling in another dimension.

When the guide had finished, he asked '*Sakanab*? What is *your* news?

The nomads nodded and looked around at each other, as if unsure who should speak. By now I knew that there were no formal leaders among the desert people, and precedence was a very sensitive business. In the end, after a great deal of to-ing and fro-ing, the grey-haired man with the wispy beard agreed reluctantly to recount the *sakanab*. His account was as detailed as Brahim's had been, down to the track of a snake, or the presence of berries of a certain type. The thing that seemed to interest the herders most, though, was his mention of a place called Umm Sagar. 'The wells at Umm Sagar are almost dry,' he said. 'We watered our camels and filled our skins there, but we were scraping the bottom. Your herd would have gone thirsty.'

Brahim waited until the *sakanab* was finished, then asked a few pointed questions about the well. I thought he looked concerned.

We gave the travellers sugar and *tombac*, a dried leaf with a bitter taste - similar to but different from tobacco - that the herders smoked or tucked under their gums. There were no farewells, though. The nomads simply jumped on to their camels and rode off jauntily into the sands without a backward glance.

As we moved on later, I rode beside the guide. 'That was a remarkable feat,' I said. 'I mean to remember all those things. That must come from long practice.'

He seemed amused. 'There is no man here who could not have given the same account,' he said.

'*I* couldn't,' I told him.

Brahim chuckled. 'I have been watching you,' he said. 'Your heart is often working at something else. It is not set on what is around you.'

'What do you mean?'

'Your spirit is elsewhere.'

'You said there was much to learn, and I *have* learned,' I protested. 'I know more than I did when I came. I think I do things better now. '

'Yes, you have improved, but I am not talking about what you do with your hands, although that is also good. When I said that the desert has much to teach, I meant the desert herself.'

'I don't understand.'

'Are you *aware* of the desert? Do you feel her, smell her, hear and taste her?'

'Yes, sometimes.'

'Sometimes is not enough. She is never the same twice. If you do not allow the desert into your heart – if you shut yourself off from her - you will never be at ease here, and you will never be complete.'

'I don't think I shut myself off.'

'When your heart is working somewhere else, you are shut off. You are concerned only with yourself. You do not see or feel the world, so you are unable to recall what you have seen, or to pass it on to others.'

I felt irritated again. Perhaps I did spend a lot of time daydreaming - what right did this man have to tell me I should not?

'It's easy for you,' I said. 'You were brought up in the desert. I'm new to it.'

'All the more reason for you to learn. You shut yourself off from the desert because you are afraid - like a child wrapping his arms round himself or covering his head. You feel the desert is your enemy – the wind, the sun, the hunger, thirst, fatigue – danger. Like when my uncle died, bitten by a sand-viper. I was tempted to believe that the desert was my enemy then, but that would have killed me. Instead I remembered that she was no more my enemy than my hands or my eyes. The desert is Earth Mother - not a foe to be fought and defeated, but a force to which one must adjust one's tent.'

'*Tent*?'

'Desert people carry their tents on camel's back. They do not stay in one place like town folk, but follow the clouds and the rain. When we pitch our tents, we adjust the walls according to sun and wind. If the wind is blowing strongly from one direction, for example, we close the wall on that side, and open it on another.'

'I see – you adapt.'

'Yes, just as a thorn-tree bends in a strong wind. If the tree tried to stand straight against the wind it would be broken. One cannot control the wind, one must bend with it, so as not to break. If you regard the desert with hate or fear, that is what will come back to you. You must regard her with love - that is the only way you can know her talk.'

'You may call the desert *her*, but it is really only stones and sand isn't it? How can one love that?'

'Stone and sand, wind and rain, trees and grass, four-legged creatures, flying creatures, crawling creatures, and we two-legged creatures. The desert is all these and more – she is Earth Mother, and Earth Mother is one.'

'All right, but what about the desert's talk? Two-legged humans have language, but stones and sand, and all the other things, can't talk.'

Brahim laughed. 'They do not talk in words, but still they talk. You are not listening, that's all.'

He urged his camel forward and left me to consider what he had said. In the military I had learned about an effect called *ground-feel,* when a foot patrol began to sense the nature of the land they were moving in, and to use it to their advantage. In my experience, few soldiers were good at it, though. Mostly they considered the ground hostile. Still, it gave me a clue as to what Brahim meant. I thought about his ability to navigate in what I had seen as almost featureless terrain. Of course, I realized, it was not featureless to him – it was full of minute nuances that I had never noticed, including the wind and the sunlight, and the clouds – an endless kaleidoscope changing from moment to moment. I had started to think of our journey as timeless, and in one sense, I realized, it was – because the nomads focused mostly on the present. The past was finished, and the future had not yet happened. One was aware of the unfolding of a longer time-scale, of *sakanab,* of past learnings, of measures and provisions one must take, but one did not go into a dialogue with them - what mattered most was the now.

Lament

It was hotter than ever, and for the first time the camels started keening. It began as an occasional moan from within the herd, but as the sun rose higher and the shadows diminished, it spread to more and more animals - an eerie, mournful drone like an orchestra of badly tuned strings. It set my teeth on edge. Gone were the days when I had thought of a camel as a clockwork mechanism. The animals were burning up inside, and now I could feel it, just as if it were happening to me.

Awad rode up alongside. 'This is the herd's *lament of thirst,*' he said, with his customary air of gravitas. 'They have not watered for twelve sleeps. Camels do not get thirsty when they are grazing in green pastures, but in this heat, travelling continuously, twelve sleeps without drinking is hard for them.'

'Aren't we near the wells?' I inquired.

'You heard the *sakanab*. The news is that the wells are dry.'

In the late morning, Brahim called a halt in a wadi where there were some clumps of dried-out grass and skeletal thorn-trees. 'I asked God that we reach Umm Sagar by this afternoon,' he told us, 'but on this God has not struck for us. Our only choice now is to ride straight to the deep wells - the *sawani* - at Elai. If we travel fast, we can get there by tomorrow evening.'

'God is generous,' Awad said, 'but what if the *sawani* at Elai are also dry? By the time we arrive it will be too late.'

'You and Khidir ride to Elai and see the state of the deep wells,' the guide said. 'We will continue as far as the *Mushroom Stone*. Meet us there after sunset. Go in God's safe keeping.'

The youths mounted their camels and rode off without a word.

Brahim made his way among our camels, shaking our water-skins.

'God is generous,' he said, 'but our water is almost finished.'

It was already dusk when we brought the camel herd close to the *Mushroom Stone* – a dish-shaped slab of rock standing on a slim pedestal that wind and water had moulded over long ages. It did look uncannily like a giant mushroom, I thought. The stone lay in a grove of shattered boulders and standing rocks like surreal ornaments whittled with a giant knife. It had the feel of an ancient temple. In fact, Brahim told me the area was a *hattia* – a sacred place where no animal could be hunted and no tree felled. The gnarled rock faces were covered in runes and tribal brands that had been incised into them since the Distant Time. The slab seemed to be set so precariously on its pedestal that one shove would unbalance it. After we had settled the camels, the men hoisted themselves on each other's shoulders and took turns to try and push it down. They heaved and groaned, grunted and guffawed, but, of course, the stone did not budge. I was the last to try. I stood on Brahim's broad shoulders and while he gripped my ankles and gave encouraging growls – for the first time I realized how immensely strong he was. I strained against the rock with all my might, feeling the rough surface against my fingers. It felt faintly ridiculous to be pushing at a rock pedestal, and I quickly realised that the stone was not what it appeared to be. Rather than being separate, plate and pedestal were a single continuous formation moulded into that shape by the elements. It had probably been like this for ten thousand years.

'Every traveller who comes here tries his strength,' Brahim told me later, 'but no one has succeeded yet. The nomads know it cannot be done, of course, but trying one's strength against the stone gives a certain wisdom – the wisdom of stones.'

'Stones have wisdom?'

'One can learn from all beings – the trees, the stars, the sand, the hills … and the stones.'

'But are stones beings?'

'They are of the Great Spirit, but they are not aware as we are aware, or as animals and plants are aware. One cannot know what it is like to be a stone. They change, but slowly. This stone stood here in the Distant Time – one can tell that from the camel brands carved on it. Some of them belong to forgotten tribes.'

I tried to imagine how the desert would look like to this stone if it *were* aware – a crowded place, with humans and animals, storms and clouds, sunrises and sunsets, following one another at incredible speeds. For this stone, if it were conscious, the whole of human existence would have gone by in a moment.

'It is said that the *Mushroom Stone* was set here as the guardian of the land against the Anakim – the Lost Giants - sleeping under the sands,' Brahim went on. 'The day it falls is the day the giants awaken.'

Night Ride

We made camp near the *Mushroom Stone* with the camel-herd drawn around us, and sat around the fire. I was tired, though, and soon rolled myself up in my blanket. The next thing I knew, Brahim was shaking me awake, telling me to fetch my camel. 'They have returned from Elai,' he said. 'Thank God, the *sawani* – the deep wells - have water. Now we must get moving.'

It was pitch dark, and I would have liked to sleep longer. I forced myself to get up, though, took my head-rope, and went to find my camel. Within a short time, the other men had saddled their riding animals. We released the herd from their hobbles, mounted up, and soon the mass of camels was flowing into the darkness, while we worked around the periphery, chanting, tongue-clicking, keeping the animals pressed tight together.

For an eternity we rode on through the eerie otherworld of the desert night. I was aware only of the rocking motion of my camel, the herd's keening song, and the silvery coalescence of the animals moving before me. Though my legs and back were painful from the constant riding, I drifted often into the no-man's land between wakefulness and sleep, only to wrench myself up with a start from the sensation of falling. There was no water to drink, and my throat was rough as plaster – the sheer effort needed to hold on was exhausting. I could not see my companions in the darkness, and it took all my determination just to stay in the saddle, to keep my mount close to the herd in front of me.

Sometimes I saw waking visions – a flock of grey cranes flying overhead, a locust-swarm teeming past endlessly. I saw strange stalk-headed men pirouetting on air, and once a white leopard, and heard a voice saying *the animals will reveal the Lost Oasis. They will heal you, because you are animal, and one of us.* They were like visions I had had in the military while on night-watch in lonely places – vivid hallucinations with the eyes fully open. They reminded me of what I had come for, why I was there, riding a camel on an ancient desert road, under the eternal awning of the stars.

In fact, I had lost all sense of time. I might as well have been travelling forever, going nowhere, marching without moving. The night was the mouth of a vast cave opening ever wider, swallowing everything. I had been born and had lived all my life in the saddle - there was never a time that I had not been riding that camel, I felt.

Just when I was beginning to think that the night really was without end, though, a phantom whiteness appeared on the horizon. At first, I thought it must be another illusion of the night, but slowly it became a pale trace stretching across the world. I held my breath as the light thickened gradually into a rich redness that became streamers of flaming fire. Then I knew I had not imagined it – the dark soul of the night had passed, and the dawn was coming. Suddenly, Khidir, my most dedicated critic, broke away from the herd, rode over to me, and offered his hand, as if we were meeting for the first time. We shook with solemn ceremony. 'Peace be on you, brother,' he said.

'And on you be peace.'

'I salute you,' he went on. 'Perhaps you will find the Lost Oasis after all.'

To me Khidir's words marked a nodal point in my journey. From that moment I started to feel no longer an outsider. I really had taken a new path, and my quest proper had begun.

The coming of day gave me a fresh lease of life. I no longer felt drowsy or feared falling off my camel. I was in the saddle, sensing Ata's muscles strain and relax, feeling his soft pads touch the Earth, breathing the dust-scented air, taking in the carpet of sand, stands of esparto grass, evergreen tamarisk, tangled bushes of arak and caper. I began to notice things that must have been there before, but that I had somehow missed - horned grasshoppers in a thorn-tree, flocks of birds flitting like scattershot, strange droppings, the tracks of insects, tiny white flowers, tufts of grass, shiny black scarabs hustling past on quick legs, files of ants shuffling around nests like volcanic craters. I saw scorpions lurking at the mouth of their burrows, agora lizards skidding from rock to rock, skinks staring at me with eyes like polished gemstones. The desert was alive and bursting with activity: it came into focus in a way that I had never experienced before.

Souls

The deep wells at Elai were still distant, and we pushed the herd on quickly that morning. A low hot wind had started up from the north, and the camels were rumbling in distress, dragging their feet, stumbling. Occasionally animals would stagger away, sit down, and refuse to budge – the herders would cajole and wheedle them until they got going.

Awad drew my attention to a she-camel that had fallen behind. I saw that she was struggling, limping along with her head down, making sudden bursts forward, trying desperately to catch up with the others. I sensed that something was wrong – I knew by now that camels were social by nature and hated parting with their companions.

'It's the stones,' Awad commented. 'This she-camel grew up in the *goz*, on the desert's edge, where the earth is soft, and she is not used to the sharp stones of the Pharaoh's Road. If it is hot like this, those stones can burn through a camel's hoof.'

When we halted at mid-day, Brahim told us to tie the she-camel's legs with ropes and roll her over. 'Do it quickly,' he said. 'The water is still far, and the wind is blowing.'

The she-camel writhed and gnashed her teeth, and it took several of us to hold her down, dodging the flailing legs. The guide felt each of her pads carefully and showed us the sore on her right fore-hoof, where the thick skin had been sheared away.

He shook his head. 'A sore like this can kill a camel,' he said.

He called for a cow-skin. When it was brought, he cut a square from it with his knife. Then he took a long packing needle from his sheath, threaded a thin strip of leather through the eye, and stitched the patch to the hoof-pad. The she-camel didn't seem to mind this, and when it was finished, we untied the ropes and stood back as she jumped to her feet.

In the afternoon, though, it was the same. She struggled into the wind, lifting her foreleg high to compensate for the patch, but still she fell behind with a piteous groaning. By late afternoon, it was clear she could not go on. She sat down, and nothing we could do would make her get up again. She laid her head down in the sand and closed her eyes. We gathered around her and Brahim came over to us, looking grave.

He examined her closely, then said. 'She will not shift from this spot, but we cannot leave her for the vultures to peck her eyes out. That would not be right.'

It was clear what had to be done – even I knew - but it was equally clear that no one wanted to do it. I thought I understood why. I had learned that, for the nomads, camels were sacred animals – their entire lives revolved around them. They would slaughter a camel as a sacrifice, but always with regret and invocations. For them, the camel was the most beautiful of creatures. Their word for camel – *jamal* – was from the same root as their word for beauty - *jamaal*.

At last, Brahim drew his knife. He muttered a prayer – to me it sounded as if he were asking the she-camel's forgiveness. He looked grim as he plunged the blade into her neck. Blood surged in a torrent and soaked the sand, but in a moment wind-blown dust had covered it. 'Be one with the Great Spirit,' he said. 'I take your life, knowing that my own death walks with me every step of my journey, and I too will one day join the Great Spirit, while my body becomes food for the crawling things and the grasses. Death is always with us, as it is with all our relations – those that fly in the air, walk or crawl or grow on the Earth. It is said, *live long and you will see the camel slaughtered.*'

We mounted up at once, desperate to get the herd to water before more animals dropped. I remembered Brahim's story of how his uncle had died on his first journey and reflected on the suddenness of death in the desert. Here, it was present – it could not be hidden from view. In the civilized world I came from it was deliberately concealed, as if people wanted to deny it, to believe they were above nature, to feel they were immortal.

When I rode with Brahim later, I asked if he thought animals had souls. 'Of course,' he answered. 'Everything that is part of the Great Spirit has a soul, because the soul and the Great Spirit are the same. We are all born, and all must die – that is finite life. But death is not the end. We are all - grasses, flowers, trees, stones, humans, animals, sand, wind, stars, and the desert itself - part of the Great Spirit – the indestructible life that endures forever.'

He gestured suddenly and I looked up to see an unexpected sight - a rock wall that seemed to fill the entire skyline. The wall rose to blunt peaks in places and was faceted like a huge dark jewel - it appeared to be made of glistening ebony. Brahim pointed to a cleft - a natural arch - where the rock glowed gold in the melting afternoon sunlight. 'That is the *Gap*,' he said. 'The deep wells of Elai lie within that mountain.'

Wind

The *Gap* opened into a narrow gorge where the camels had to walk in file, following an ancient path beaten by hooves over countless generations. The path gave into a wide crater - a great arena of rock, with towering walls and thickets of ancient thorn trees. As I walked in, leading Ata, I saw that our coming had dislodged a pair of tawny eagles, who rode the wind over us with the faintest snap of wings.

The *sawani* or deep wells lay within the mountain in a fissure between the rocks above a wide wadi. They were narrow shafts lined with stones. We dropped cowhide buckets into them and hoisted them up, hand-over-hand, on ropes of plaited leather. The depth of the wells made it hard work, and I had just brought up a bucket half full of water, when Khidir told me. 'Not like that. You are too hasty – you should jiggle the bucket when it touches the water, or it will not fill properly. Perhaps you are trying to make it easier by pulling up a lighter weight?'

I had just started to feel that I was accepted – especially by Khidir – and the illusion was suddenly shattered. I felt a surge of anger.

'Can you do better?' I demanded.

'Of course I can.' He yanked the well-rope out of my hands, coiled the end of the rope around one hand and dropped the bucket into the shaft with the other. 'Another thing you do wrong is that you don't secure the rope to your hand,' he said. 'Like this you may drop the bucket into the well, and that would be a disgrace.'

He laughed, and I watched fuming as he braced his lean body over the shaft, jiggled the bucket around, then brought it up with swift, efficient pulls, hand over hand. He passed the full bucket to me. 'Now you take it down to the camels,' he said.

I did not argue, but I was still furious as I ran with the bucket down the rocky slope to where the camels massed around mud basins. The animals honked and trumpeted as they fought to get at the water. The old bulls among them roared, raised their heads, blew out pink mouth-bladders, and chanted menacingly - *blub-blub-blub-blub*.

We worked until after sunset. Finally, though, Brahim declared the wells dry. 'At least for now,' he said. 'The water will take time to return.'

When I finally rolled myself up in my blanket I fell asleep at once.

It seemed almost no time before Khidir was shaking me awake in the glow of dawn.

'What is it?' I demanded sleepily.

The youth dropped two empty water-skins on the ground next to me. 'Water,' he said. 'You must go to the well.'

'What? Brahim said the wells are dry.'

'There is another well down there in the wadi - a shallow one.' He pointed into the bushes. 'That way - not far. There is water, and it is sweet.'

If he knew that much, I thought, why didn't he go and get the water himself? I felt annoyed again, remembering how he had made fun of me the previous day, saying I was trying to shirk by raising a bucket that was only half full. What right did he have to wake me up and start giving orders? He was younger than I was and had nothing like my experience in life – he had no idea, even, what I had done - and he had been critical of me from the beginning.

'What about you and the others?' I demanded.

'You fill the skins. We fetch the camels.'

'And the bucket?'

'You will find it there.'

The first thing I noticed when I threw off my blanket was the cold. The past few days had been the hottest I remembered, yet now my breath was steamy, and I was shivering in my nomad *jibba*.

I picked up the skins and walked reluctantly through the bushes in the direction Khidir had shown me. I was still feeling irritated when I came to the wadi - a groove cut beneath shallow slopes covered in a tangle of thorn-bush. In the middle of the wadi-bed was a well with a stone-lined shaft. Beside it I found a soft cowhide bucket attached to a rope. I laid the water-skins down in the sand, picked up the rope, and tossed the bucket into the well, my hands already shaking with cold. There was a faint slap as it hit the water. I coiled the rope around my left hand, as Khidir had shown me, and wiggled the bucket around to fill it up. I tested the weight, as I had seen Khidir do, eased it off, then drew it up again slightly, until, satisfied it was full, I heaved it up to the well-head hand-over-hand.

The water was freezing, and the bitter wind numbed my hands. I was pleased with myself for drawing a full bucket, though, and it was only when I stood there holding it that the problem dawned on me. I picked up a water-skin awkwardly with one hand and tried to pour the water into it. Neither the mouth of the water-skin nor the bucket was rigid enough for the operation - the water spilled on the cold earth. It hit me with a familiar spurt of anger that this could not be done - not without a partner to hold the mouth open. Filling a water-skin was a two-man job. Y*ou fill the skins. We will fetch the camels* - had there been a smirk on Khidir's face when he said that? I was almost sure there had. *He set this up. He tricked me deliberately,* I thought.

For a moment I was lost. Then I had the idea of lodging the skin, mouth open, against a big stone, so that I could hold the bucket with both hands. *Aha, I'll show him.*

I drew a second bucket of water, tried to pour it into the water-skin. The skin simply toppled over as I was pouring. The water spread out like a stain on the desert surface.

I set the skin against the stone again, and threw the bucket back into the well. This time, though, my hands were trembling so much from the cold that I let the rope slip through my fingers, and dropped the bucket into the shaft, rope, and all. I heard it plop against the water below, and my heart thumped.

I should have secured the rope to my hand like Khidir told me. Now I've gone and dropped the bucket into the well.

I peered down the shaft. The well was sheer-sided, and there was no question of climbing down. I would have to go back to the smirking Khidir with empty water-skins, and admit that I had done the unthinkable. I could almost hear the youth's cutting comments. This would be the worst humiliation I had suffered since joining the herd weeks ago. After the night ride I had felt very pleased with myself. Khidir had even congratulated me, I thought - deceiving me so he could set me up again. I was such a clown that I couldn't even carry off this small task. I felt almost like crying.

There was a sudden movement and I looked up. A man had emerged like a spirit from behind some thorn-scrub not far away and began drifting silently towards me. As he came closer, I saw that he was a small man, old and wiry, with mahogany skin, bright grey eyes, and a few silver hairs on his chin. He wore his desert-stained rags with dignity. He stopped, we shook hands, and as we gripped and released, the old man regarded me keenly. I liked his face. His expression was concerned, and slightly amused, I thought. I had the feeling that he had been watching me for some time.

He peered into the well. Then, without a word, he walked back to the scrub on the other side of the wadi bed and vanished into it. I waited, shivering in the wind. A long time seemed to pass, and I began to wonder if the old man was coming back. When I thought about it, he had not *said* he would come back. I had almost given up on him, when he was there, moving towards me, carrying what turned out to be a long, slender, thorn-branch. I realized it must have taken some time and effort to find a branch of that length. Without any comment, he hunched over the well and used the branch as a fishing pole. Moments later he angled out the well-bucket and laid it down reverently on the sand.

'Thank you.' I told him.

'The thanks is to God,' he replied.

The thanks is always to God, I scolded myself. *I should know that by now.*

With hardly another word we worked together. While I hauled up the water, the old man held open the mouth of first one skin, then the other. It was surprisingly quick and easy, and I soon began to feel warmer from the activity.

When the skins were lying at our feet, bulging and well-tied, the old man squatted down with his back to the wind. I crouched opposite. He had not explained what he was doing here at the crack of dawn, nor inquired about me or my companions. I sensed that he knew more than he was saying.

He surveyed the two full skins for a while, then looked at me with warm eyes and disarming benevolence. 'You are angry,' he said,' because they sent you to fill the skins on your own.'

'Yes,' I said. 'It was a trick. I didn't expect that.'

The old man chuckled. 'Life is full of unexpected things. The question is, what did you learn from it?'

'I learned that filling a water-skin is a job for two.'

'So you learned that you need others – that you are not alone.'

I nodded. I had to admit that he was right, and now it occurred to me that sending me to fill the skins had been a test. Just two days ago, Brahim had warned me about shutting myself off from the world around me. After the night ride, I had felt changed, felt that I had passed some kind of initiation. Then, just when I might have started to feel self-important again, I had been set an impossible task.

I gazed at the man's face, and saw a deep strength I had not noticed before. Somehow his features were familiar, as if I had known him long ago.

'When you look at other people, you feel they are separate,' the man went on, 'but we are all connected.'

'How?' I asked.

'It is the wind that connects us. We are all the wind in another guise.'

It was such an unexpected observation from a stranger, here in a wadi, in a remote place, that I laughed.

The old man held up three gnarled fingers. 'When God breathes on us, that is wind,' he said. 'When we take the wind into our bodies, it is breath. When the wind is within us, that is spirit. Wind, breath and spirit. All three together are life, but they are all the same thing in a different guise.'

I tried to take in this sudden revelation. It was difficult to be certain what I had heard, because the Arabic words seemed entangled and related in complex ways. *Rih* meant *wind*, for example, but *ruh*, from the same root, meant *spirit*, also *divine breath*, or the *breath of life*. *Tanaffus*, meaning *to breathe in and out* - was from the same root as *nafas*, which could mean *soul*, *psyche*, *mind*, *human being*, or *self*. I sensed that the old man was telling me something profound, but what I got from this jumbled utterance was the idea that wind, breath, and spirit, were different aspects of the living essence. There was more, though, because the word he had used for life, *hayy*, actually meant *liv-ing* – a continuous process rather than a finite state. I remembered what Brahim had told me about finite life and indestructible life. There was also a level of our interaction that was beyond meaning, I realized, because what was passing between us was itself a rippling of the wind, and our utterances were modulations of breath, so much so that the word *hayy* – life or living - sounded like a sudden forceful expulsion of air, while *tanaffus* – to breathe - was the in-and-out sound of regular breathing itself. I was just starting to feel that this was a transcendant moment, when the old man was on his feet, smiling. 'The wind,' he said, 'is what connects us with all beings. Do not forget.'

Then, without a word of explanation, he was off, scurrying towards the thorn-scrub, and shortly after, he had vanished once more. It was so abrupt that for a moment I found myself doubting that he had been there. I considered the full water-skins, and the footprints in the sand. *No – he really was here. But what was that about breath and wind and spirit? Maybe I just didn't catch what he said.*

I turned my attention to the skins. I could not carry both, so I would have to take one and come back for the other. I crouched down and with some effort lifted one over my shoulder. I stood up with a grunt. I followed my own footprints back to camp, feeling the skin wet and heavy against my shoulder. The desert wind chilled my back. *When God breathes on us that is wind,* I thought. Wind was the movement of air, and the word for life – *hayy* – was itself a movement of air. *Fish don't talk about water,* as they said - one mostly forgot air was present, but one would be dead without it, just like a fish out of water. In that sense, the wind was shared by every being. The air inside one was contiguous with the wind, like a sort of Mobius strip endlessly twisting back on itself. The vegetation fashioned the air one breathed, and modified the air one breathed out, in an endless cycle. When that cycle ceased, all life ceased. The air – the wind – was life itself. And if the wind was the life-force – the divine breath - then all beings were just the wind in different guises. Was that what the old man had been telling me? Or had I just taken in the words and drifted off on a desert fugue? Perhaps, I thought, but I had also learned something more prosaic. One could not fill a water-skin alone, because water-skins were the creation of a culture where people were members of a community first, and individuals second –where people were not isolated units, separate from one another. And the idea that we were all an incarnation of the wind – that the wind was the animating spirit of the world – also meant that we were not separate, just extensions of *one* thing - the whole of existence was a singularity. And if it was all a singularity, there was no distinction between me and the sky, between me and Earth Mother, between me and the water, between me and Grandfather Fire – or between me and my companions. *We are not strangers, but of the same being.* This must be what is meant by the Great Spirit, I thought.

I was near the camp now, and, as I came out of the scrub I saw that the others had brought back the camels, who were shifting and grunting restlessly in their hobbles. Khidir was sitting cross-legged by the fire, with steam rising from a soot-covered kettle. He was facing in the opposite direction and it was only as I laid the heavy skin down nearby that he turned. He stared at the water-skin then eyed me with a look of utter astonishment.

'You filled them?' he gasped.

'Of course I filled them,' I said, keeping my face blank. 'Why? Were you expecting a problem?'

Before he could say anything I added. 'The other water-skin is down there by the well. Perhaps you could go and get it.'

I knew he would see the old man's tracks when he got there, and put the story together, but I didn't care.

Fish Eaters

Later that morning, Brahim called me over to meet a man who was sitting with him in his camp. As the stranger rose to greet me I realized with a shock that he was no stranger – it was the old man who had helped me at the well. He was clad in the same earth-stained rags, though he now wore an arm-dagger and carried an antique one-shot rifle slung from his shoulder.

'We have met,' I said shaking hands. 'In the wadi, at first light.'

The old man nodded but made no other answer. For a moment I thought he was going to deny that it was he who had helped me, but he didn't. Just in time, I stopped myself thanking him for his help in retrieving the well bucket and filling the water-skins. The thanks was to God, I recalled.

We sat down together, and Brahim introduced the old man as Rafig. He had arrived in the night, alone, with a small caravan of camels, the guide said, bound for al-Gaa salt-oasis. He had made camp on the other side of the crater and wandered over this side to inspect the wells.

'He tells me he bumped into you,' Brahim went on. 'You were drawing water to fill water-skins at dawn. Why were you doing that?'

'Khidir's request,' I said wryly.

Brahim chuckled. 'It takes two men to fill a skin,' he said.

'So I discovered.'

Brahim exchanged a glance with the old man and I wondered how much the guide knew – did he know that I had dropped the bucket into the well?

'Rafig is a wise man,' he went on. 'He understands a great deal about jinns, and no-one knows the *Hurra* better than he.'

'Brahim gives me too much praise,' Rafig told me. 'I know a little of jinns and a little of the *Hurra*. I am just a *kahin*.'

I wondered what a *kahin* was. I wasn't sure what was meant by jinn, either, and I recalled Awad's tale of the nomad and the beautiful young women who had turned into donkeys. I thought of my dream back in the Nile Valley – the figure who might have been either a man or a woman, or both. Was that a jinn?

'I was telling Rafig about you,' Brahim said, 'and your search for the Lost Oasis.'

Rafig regarded me with the same open, friendly manner I had seen in the wadi, and asked me to repeat my story. After some hesitation, I described the dream I had had, the white leopard and the voice saying *the animals will heal you, because you are animal, and one of us.*

Then I recounted Maya's tale of the Lost Oasis, of the youth who had gone in search of a she-camel and found a green paradise with trees, running water, and beautiful maidens. When my tale was finished, Rafig considered it in silence for a moment, then he said, 'That is a good story, but it is not a nomad's story. The young man kept camels, but he lived in a settled village on the desert edge.'

'That's true. But do you know anything about the Lost Oasis?'

'I don't know what is meant by *lost*,' he said. 'If a camel strays and one does not know where it is, one might say it is lost. When a place is lost, is it because one has forgotten where it is, or because it is no longer where it used to be?'

'I don't know,' I said. 'I suppose it *is* a strange sort of idea.'

'I do recall the story my father once told me,' Rafig went on. 'He was returning from Libya on a route called the Siren Road, with his kinsman, Barak. They were overtaken by the Poison Wind – a wind that blows from the south at the start of the *Ged* – the *Hot Hot* season. They were separated in the storm, and my father's water ran out. He was very thirsty, and ready for God to take him unto God, when he stumbled across an oasis with palm trees. There, he found water, and he sheltered among the palms till the storm blew out.

'Later, he tried to find Barak, but in the end he gave up as all tracks had been swallowed by the wind. Eventually he found his way back to the tents of our people – luckily for me, as I was not born yet. He called that place he had found, *the Oasis of Last Chance,* because it had saved his life. He could never tell exactly where it was, though, nor did he ever see it again.'

I was excited by Rafig's story. It sounded almost as if it had come out of the same bag as Brahim's tale of the nomad tricked by the voices of jinns, yet it seemed to refer to a real oasis.'

'So your father's relative was never found?' I asked.

'Ah, the story does not end there. A long time afterwards, just when the memory of him was beginning to fade, Barak returned.'

'What?'

'Yes, as God is my witness, he just walked into our camp one day. I was small then, but I remember it. Everyone had thought God had taken him unto God, and so it was as if he had sprung out of the Earth, reborn. When they asked where he had been, he said that he had been found by Fish-Eaters and had stayed with them. He had taken a wife among them and had children.'

'Fish Eaters?'

'Fish-Eaters is our name for the people who live deep in the *Hurra*,' Brahim explained. 'They are nomads like us but they speak a different tongue.'

'And they eat *fish*? In the desert?'

Brahim chuckled. 'Their camel-brand is called a fish,' he said, 'and it is said that in the Distant Time they made their camps near the Great Water, and lived on the fish they caught.'

'Fish Eater country lies to the west,' Rafig said, 'though there have always been Fish Eaters who have wandered into nomad lands, and many have lived among nomads.'

'So what happened to Barak?' I inquired.

'He returned to the Fish Eaters. I never saw him again.'

'What about the oasis your father found – could it have been the Lost Oasis?'

'God only is All-Knowing. My father did not find any maidens there, or if he did, he kept it quiet. As for a secret, if he learned one he must have forgotten it. 'So you don't believe the Lost Oasis is just a story?'

'Certainly there are oases in the *Hurra* where nobody lives. Tell me, though, what does this so-called Lost Oasis mean to you? Why do you want to find it?' He narrowed his eyes and watched me carefully.

I remembered suddenly that this was the man who had told me about wind, breath, and spirit. There was a deep lesson there, I thought, but though I believed I had understood on one level, on another I had yet to feel it.

'I don't know,' I said. 'If it exists I have to find it, and if it doesn't, I would like to know for certain.'

'So it is certainty you are looking for?'

He went silent again - there was a keen-ness in his face that I had not noticed previously.

'Do you think you could help me find this ... *Oasis of Last Chance*?' I said.

'By God, that is a hard one,' he said, laughing. 'I could not promise anything of the sort. I am a simple man, and Brahim has exaggerated my knowledge of the desert. In any case I have my own mission. I am taking a salt-caravan to al-Gaa, where I must dig out salt, load it on my camels, and deliver it to my clan in the Wadi al-Ma. Have you any idea how much work that involves?'

'Not really,' I said. I considered it for a moment, then added. 'Maybe I could come with you?'

'You?' He laughed again. 'Brahim tells me you are new to the desert. He says you are ready to learn, but I do not have the patience to train a novice – the work of a salt-caravan is hard.'

'I can learn can't I?'

He gave me a stern glance, and I glared back indignantly, sure he was remembering how I had dropped the bucket into the well. It was true that if he had not come along the bucket would probably still be there, and I would be the object of ridicule by Khidir and the others.

He watched me for a while, then said. 'If I take you, you must follow my lead without question. You must be ready to do the work with good heart, and not let your spirit wander.'

Brahim snorted, and I guessed the guide had told Rafig about my tendency to drift off. That must be why the old man was so reluctant to take me, I thought.

'I'll do everything you say,' I said.

He looked me up and down.

'Very well' he said. 'The Great Spirit will be our companion.'

'And after that you will help me find the Lost Oasis?'

He chuckled again. 'Let us say that working with the salt-caravan will be a chance for me to see if you are worthy.'

'Worthy? You mean like a kind of test?'

'Perhaps.'

'So if you are satisfied with me on the salt-caravan, you will take me to the Lost Oasis?'

This time he laughed so hard that the tears ran down his cheeks. 'I did not say I would take you anywhere other than the salt-place. I don't know if the Lost Oasis exists, and I am certainly not saying I can find it.'

'And you won't even tell me if you are ready to go with me to … er … *look* for any oasis until after I have helped you with the salt-caravan? That seems a pretty stiff bargain to me.'

'God knows, it is. It is your choice. If you come with me, we will share the work: we will eat the same food, and we will trust one another. Whatever I decide, you will not be abandoned. You have my word on that.'

I stared at him and then turned to look at Brahim, who nodded.

I swallowed. Rafig was a stranger I had met only that morning, and he seemed eccentric to say the least. Still, there was something about him I liked, and that made me trust him. It was a big leap of faith, but the whole idea of heading off alone into the desert had been crazy in the first place, and only made possible by the overweening self-confidence I had learned in the special-forces. There was nothing to be gained by holding back at this point, I thought.

'All right,' I said. 'I'm in.'

Parting

I was excited at the prospect of travelling with Rafig, but when it came time to saddle my camel, I felt reluctant to leave Brahim and the others. I had only been with them a few weeks, but it seemed that I had always known them. I already thought of them as kin. They had taught me so much, not just of desert skills, but how to see the desert, how to feel her presence, how to grasp her language by listening to her with all the senses. I embraced each of the herders in turn and was astonished to feel the affection that flowed from them, after I had come to them only a short time ago as an outsider. They seemed as averse to letting me go as I was to leave. I told myself that though I had learned important lessons from them, it was time to move on. I joked about runaway camels with Awad and Khidir, but it did not make the parting any easier. When I turned from them, feeling unexpected tears in my eyes, Brahim hugged me and put a bundle into my hands. It was a knife in a decorated leather sheath – the very same knife he had used to slaughter the lame she-camel, I thought. I drew it and examined the broad iron blade and carved wooden handle.

'I can't take this,' I said. 'It's yours.'

'I have another,' Brahim said. 'I noticed that you did not have a knife.'

It was true – and embarrassing for an ex-military man: I had forgotten to bring so much as a pocket-knife.

I returned the blade to its sheath. There was a loop of plaited leather attached, so that one could wear it on the arm – upside down for easier drawing. It was an incredibly generous gift, which I did not deserve, I thought. Yet I knew it would be an affront to refuse.

I choked back my thanks.

'You will be safe with Rafig,' Brahim told me. 'He is modest, as befits a man, but it is not given to all to be a *kahin* – a diviner. One must be of strong character, pure in spirit, sensitive, able to see the unknown and know the unseen. Once you have eaten bread and salt together, he will not let you down.'

'May the Great Spirit be with you,' I said. 'Go in His safekeeping.'

'The Great Spirit will always be with us,' Brahim said, 'and so will you, for in our hearts there is no true parting.'

Firestones

Rafig led me to his camp on the other side of the crater, where he had left his camels - I counted fourteen of them browsing in the thorn trees. He told me to dump my saddle and kit in the lee of a pile of pack-saddles in a sandy swath, where two water-skins hung from a wooden tripod. I unloaded Ata, then led him to join Rafig's animals – that made fifteen. All those camels seemed quite a handful for one man, I thought. Then I remembered Brahim's tale about the death of his uncle, and reflected that handling a caravan must be second nature to a nomad – something boys and girls started learning as soon as they could walk.

We retired to the camp, where I spread out my blanket and watched the sun as it dropped towards the walls of the crater through serried layers of cloud.

After dark Rafig fetched three stones to make a fireplace. He placed the stones in a triangular pattern in the sand and put a handful of bone-dry grass and twigs in front of him. Then he took a sharpened stick and a flat wedge of wood, and rolled the stick against the wood, twirling it fast between his palms, until the wood began to smolder. He placed smoking chips in the dry grass, blew steadily till it caught fire, then laid the smoldering grass under the twigs in the fireplace.

Red flames leapt up like curling fingers. Rafig opened one of the water-skins on the tripod, poured water into a bowl, and filled a battered kettle. He added a handful of tea-leaves and set the kettle on the firestones.

He delved in a saddle-bag, brought out some thick crusts of bread, broke them up into a wooden bowl, and poured liquid butter over them from a gourd. He added a sprinkle of salt.

Then he tipped some dried dates into another bowl and set both bowls between us.

'In the name of God,' he said. 'Eat'.

We both took bread and chewed it.

I put my hand out to take more but Rafig stopped me.

'Wait,' he said, giving me a grave glance. 'Once travelers have shared bread and salt, they are travelling-companions. The bond is sacred.'

'How do you mean, *sacred*?' I asked.

'I mean a man must not do harm to his companion or mistreat him in any way. He must not lie, nor try to cheat him, nor fail to share. He must contribute to the work equally and not fall short. If there is a problem with others - whoever they are – he must take his companion's part. A man never abandons his companion, nor betrays him, under any circumstances, even threat of death. That is *bowga'a* – treachery. Treachery to a companion is the most heinous of acts.'

The idea was not strange to me thanks to my military experience. Indeed, for a moment it evoked an intense pang of regret, a momentary image of my friend Danny – the young man I had mortally wounded. I had fallen short. I had not given him the care I should have done – was that *bowga'a*? I supposed it was.

'I get it,' I said, nodding, 'but what if your companion does something wrong against someone else? I mean, do you go along with that?'

'A man does not create problems for his companion. He tries to prevent him from doing wrong or making mistakes. If it does happen – and it sometimes does – one's duty is to stick with him whatever.'

'*Whoa*,' I said. 'How does one know what is wrong?'

He laughed. 'One just knows.'

'All right, but how would *others* know, if you were in the deep desert, the *Hurra*, say?'

'Nothing in the desert is hidden from God – not forever. God brings all things to light be they as small as a mustard-seed, be they hidden in a rock or in heaven or Earth. Acts of treachery will come out and are never forgotten.'

'Never?'

'Of course. No-one trusts a treacherous man. He loses all honor and is shunned by his clan. That is the worst thing that can happen.'

I swallowed, realizing that this was a serious matter - and we had already shared bread and salt.

'If it is not good for you, you may leave,' Rafig said.

'No,' I said, swallowing again. 'It's fine. Why would it not be?'

'Good, then let's eat.'

We finished the bread and dates and used sand to clean our fingers.

'Tell me,' I said. 'Is this …*bowga'a* … connected with what you told me in the wadi this morning? About the wind, the breath and the spirit?'

Rafig laughed again. 'I was trying to explain that all beings are the wind in different guises. That is a way of saying that we are all each other - we are not separate from God, nor from Earth Mother.'

'I see, but why did you tell me that this morning, out of the blue?'

'I could see that you were feeling self-important - you were out of harmony with others and with the world.'

'How do you know? I did what I was asked.'

'You resented it. I could tell from your manner. You did not think you should have been asked. I watched you for a while and you did not see me – you were not aware. Because of that, you dropped the bucket in the well, and you had no idea how to retrieve it. I could have left you to work it out for yourself, but it was clear that you were not accustomed to the desert, and would never think of using what Earth Mother offers.'

'You think Khidir sent me to get water knowing I wouldn't be able to do it?'

'I think he was trying to teach you, perhaps. There are ways of doing and being that were given to us by the Ancestors. One may think one knows better, but that is simply self-importance talking. It was not hard to get the bucket out of that well, but if it had been a *sanya* – a deep well – it would have been different, because no thorn-branch would have been long enough. Dropping the bucket into a well is a serious matter - in some circumstances it could mean death, not only for oneself, but also for others.'

'Why did Khidir not fill the water-skins, then?'

'No doubt he had other jobs. A man never shies away from work, because every task he takes on, no matter how humble, is a way of enhancing his reputation as one who helps the community.'

'I see, but isn't valuing one's reputation self-importance too?'

'Only if one tries to use it to make oneself better than others. If one has the good of the community in mind, reputation is not a bad thing. It is a reputation for being *as good as* others, not better than them.'

I considered it, and saw he was right. Acquiring a name for being *as* generous and hospitable as others was quite different from gaining a reputation for accumulating wealth at others' expense.

'All right.'

'Now you tell *me* something. How come you dropped the bucket in the well?'

'It was a mistake – my hands were shaking with cold.'

'Yes, but you made this mistake because you were not aware. What distracted you was your jinn.'

'*My* jinn? What *is* a jinn, then?'

'Jinns are of different kinds. Some appear as humans or animals, but most are invisible. Everyone is born with an evil jinn – a twin that stays with you until you die. This type of jinn is called a *qarin* - and your *qarin* can lure you into evil deeds.'

'I don't understand. You said I was distracted by a jinn. Was that jinn in me, or in the wadi? You said jinns are strong in lonely places. If they are in a place, how can they also be in a person?'

Rafig laughed gleefully. 'You have a lot of questions, and you think everything can be explained in words, but words cannot describe what is whole and indivisible. Words themselves divide the truth. Yes, jinns can be in you and in the wadi at the same time. That's why they are jinns. They disturb their victims by making them self-important, restless, greedy, selfish, or obsessed with power. They bring never-ending thoughts – *waswasa* – demon serpents, or devil's voices, speaking in one's head all day long. They can even make one ill. When a man is wrapped up in himself and his heart is intent on something far away - that is a jinn.'

I still didn't understand. 'So you are saying I am possessed by a jinn?'

The old man laughed again, and his teeth showed white in the starlight. '*Possessed* means a jinn controls you – a man in this state is mad - *majnuun*. You are not mad. Your jinn raises its head only from time to time. I saw it in your eyes for a moment, which is why I was wary of taking you with me on a journey.'

'Then why *did* you take me?'

'Because you need my help, I need yours. I cannot take the salt caravan back alone.'

'But how is it you travel alone anyway?' I asked. 'Awad and Khidir told me it was not good to travel alone here. And wasn't that also the lesson from the water-skins? Don't you have any family to help?'

Rafig's face turned stony, and at once I felt I had said something out of place.

'I had a son,' he said, 'but God has taken him unto God. He had an encounter with a bull camel. Bull camels in heat are the most dangerous animals alive'

'I'm sorry,' I said.

 I wanted to know more, but his manner was not conducive, and I could not blame him. After that, for a moment, I did not know what to say.

Fire

After we had drunk tea, Rafig added the remaining wood to the fire, building up the flames. The strong tea had made my head buzz. I gazed into the flames and again saw images dancing there - stories woven in front of my eyes. I knew suddenly that these flames and this fire must have woven the stories and peopled the myths of my ancestors over aeons, and those same ancestors who were in me, had gazed into this same fire, as their voices wove around the fire, and wove the fire into stories, and the voices and the stories and the fire were one.

'The fire is where all stories begin,' Rafig said. Once again it was as if he had seen into my thoughts. 'Even jinns come from fire.'

'And where does the fire come from?'

He smiled. 'The wide-eared fox stole it from the giants. Didn't you know that?'

'No, go on.'

'It was in the Distant Time, when men and animals spoke the same language and could become each other and remain as each other for a long time. There was no fire then, and people ate their food raw. On cold nights they shivered. The only beings who had fire were the Fire Giants. They lived in a far-off mountain called Fire Mountain, which had been stung by the Lightning Scorpions and so had fire. The Children of Adam could see the fire smoking from far away, but no-one could get near the mountain because it lay across a wide, waterless desert called the *Plain of Forgetting*. Many had tried to cross it, but by the time they reached the other side, they had forgotten why they had come. So they lay down and died.

One day the wide-eared fox came along. He saw that they were suffering, and told them he would cross the *Plain of Forgetting* to Fire Mountain, and steal fire.

'Why do you want to do this?' the people asked him.

'It's the sort of thing I do,' said the fox.

'How will you remember why you are there?' asked the people. 'All the humans who have tried so far have forgotten, and have died.'

'I will think about it,' said fox.

He asked his friend falcon how he could stop himself forgetting. Falcon, who was wise, told him that near Fire Mountain, he would find a tall *tarout* tree, and growing on the lowest branch of the tree there would be a tree-mushroom. If he ate some of the mushroom, his memory would be restored.

So the wide-eared fox trotted off across the *Plain of Forgetting* and as he trotted he could see the smoke rising from Fire Mountain. On and on he ran, as the sun rose three times, and on the morning of the third day he found himself near the mountain. By that time, though, he was so tired, hungry and thirsty, that he could no longer remember why he was there. He lay down thinking that it would be very restful to sleep in the desert.

He had just closed his eyes when he heard the chattering of ants beneath him, and soon they emerged from their tunnels saying, "Don't sleep, Brother Fox. You must go to the *tarout* tree and eat some of the tree-mushroom."

So the wide-eared fox got up and with the help of the ants, came to the *tarout* tree, where he found the mushroom growing on the lowest branch. He broke off some of the mushroom and ate it, and soon remembered that he was there to steal fire from the giants.

Just then he heard the voices of the giants bellowing above him and saw the smoke from their fire. He climbed up the mountain till he came to the place they had built their huts and saw the fire blazing between three stones. There were three giants – father, mother, and daughter. All three had massive heads, and claws instead of hands. As the fox watched, he heard Father shout, in his booming voice, *we must not allow humans to have fire, for then they will be as we are.*

The three giants danced round the fire in exaltation.

The wide-eared fox was afraid but he braced himself - he sauntered to the fire and calmly sat down, basking in its warmth. The giants stopped dancing and glared at him fiercely, but in the end they said *that is only a fox, we do not have to worry about a fox.* They went on dancing, and danced around the fire till it burned down to embers, and they became exhausted and fell down.

Then, quick as a flash, the wide-eared fox dipped his tail in the embers so that the tip caught alight. At that moment the giants smelled the burning fur, and awoke. They saw what the fox was doing, and let out great bellows of rage. The fox ran for it, and dashed down the mountain with his tail on fire. The giants leapt after him in great strides, roaring. Father came so close that he grabbed for the fox's tail with his claw. In that instant, though, Falcon swooped out of the sky and picked up the wide-eared fox in her talons. She had followed him and had watched the goings-on from a distance.

Leaving the raging giants far below, Falcon flew high in the sky, and across the desert to the camp of the humans. There was singing and dancing as the fox presented them with the stolen fire. From that day on, no human needed to suffer the cold, and they could cook their food instead of eating it raw. Not the wide-eared fox, though. He was punished for his impudence by never being able to use the fire – and always after that, he had a dark tip on his tail where the fur had been burned.'

Rafig chuckled. I smiled and nodded. 'What about the ants and the falcon,' I asked. 'Didn't they get any recognition?'

'They are in the story,' he said. 'To be in a story is great recognition.'

We watched the fire until it burned down to the three firestones, and I remembered all the firestones I had seen on the Pharaoh's Road. I realized now that they told a tale of nomad camps that spanned time beyond reckoning. It reminded me of my feeling that this journey had no end and no beginning - for time changed shape in the desert. If there were no past and future, I thought, if time were an eternal now, then all our predecessors and successors were journeying here beside us, and we were all on the same migration together.

Sandlines.

When I woke next morning, Rafig was already sitting by the fire making tea.

'Peace be on you,' he said as I moved to sit opposite.

'And on you.'

He poured out the tea. 'You sleep like a donkey,' he said chuckling. 'He who sleeps like the donkey may never wake up.'

'I *am* awake,' I said.

'Yes, you are now, but one day you may not be. You were sleeping so heavily, anyone could have come and taken the camels.'

'No, I would have woken,' I protested.

Rafig laughed and I drank the tea, remembering how, on military patrols we had slept on a hair-trigger, just as Rafig was saying – the slightest movement would wake us up. The old man was right - that was one skill I had forgotten.

'Now we must collect firewood,' he said. 'There is little wood between here and al-Gaa. Break no branches off unless they are dead – mostly, pick the wood that has fallen from the trees.'

We separated among the whitethorn acacias where the camels were browsing. There was plenty of deadfall lying in the sand – obviously this place was not frequented overmuch. I picked up what I could carry, brought it back, and threw it on a pile Rafig was making. The old man put down his firewood and picked up a piece of mine.

'Is this firewood?' he demanded, holding it up. He peeled off a length of bark and showed me the rotten marrow beneath. He squeezed the branch and it crumbled into pieces with hardly any effort.

'No good,' he said. 'White ants.'

He bent over the wood-pile, and extracted about half of the pieces I had brought, shredding them and throwing the termite-eaten remains aside, chanting, 'no good … no good … no good.'

Despite myself, I was irritated. Rafig picked up a smooth, yellowish piece of wood, which did not appear to have any traces of white ants on it. 'Sodom's Apple,' he commented. 'The smoke makes you sick, and it burns without heat. No good.'

He threw it aside, selected out several other pieces like it, and tossed them too.

He picked up another piece with prickly thorns still on it and held it almost under my nose. 'Whitethorn,' he smiled. 'This is good. The smoke is fragrant.'

59

'Are you telling me that's the only kind of wood that is good?' I demanded.

'There are others,' he said, 'but most of what you brought is useless. Do your people not use firewood?'

'Not a lot,' I said.

'Well,' he said. 'We need plenty, so go back and this time bring the good stuff.'

When the wood was picked to Rafig's satisfaction, he showed me how to cut the thorns off and break it into short lengths, so it could be packed and carried easily.

After that we went to fetch the camels. Even though I felt I knew this job and had done it a hundred times with the herd, Rafig insisted on demonstrating how to fit the head-rope, tying it across the camel's head and around the throat, then how to remove the leg-hobble, which was looped and tied loosely round the camel's neck. We led the animals back to camp, couched them and attached the knee-hobbles. We laid out the pack-saddles and saddle-bags, and fitted them one at a time. 'Saddling and loading needs all your attention,' Rafig commented. 'If one saddles a camel badly, it is like dropping the bucket in the well. Many, many serious problems develop from that small thing.'

All the camels were males, Rafig pointed out: she-camels were kept for milk and the nomads rarely trained them for riding or carrying. The animals were of various sizes and had different characters –one could tell their ages from the configuration of the teeth. The lead-camel was a bull called *Agha*, a giant animal with blubbery lips and hanging dewlaps of skin, who rumbled, snorted, and tossed his head imperiously as we saddled him.

When the caravan was ready, Rafig loaded his own camel, another big bull called *Hambarib* - Little Wind – and I loaded Ata. Then Rafig returned to the space where we had slept, and sat down. He called me over and I sat opposite. Without any explanation he started to smooth out the sand in front of him with his hands.

Suddenly he sat straight and closed his eyes: his lips moved as if he were reciting a silent prayer. Then I heard chanting, deep and insistent, that seemed at first to come from somewhere behind me. I was startled, and was about to look around when I realized that it had to be coming from Rafig himself - his lips were still moving and his body rocking slightly. For a moment the voices seemed to be coming from the right, then I was convinced they were coming from the left, then from behind Rafig. It was an eerie sensation that sent a shiver down my spine. As abruptly as they had started, the voices stopped. Rafig opened his eyes and began to make sets of impressions in the sand with a middle finger. I saw that the impressions were either single or double and that he built up the sets into horizontal stacks. His fingers leapt nimbly over the stacks as if he were making a calculation. When he seemed satisfied, he rubbed the stacks out and started again. I did not want to disturb his concentration, so I watched silently until he finally finished his design and sat back on his haunches.

'What is that?' I asked.

'*Sandlines*,' he said. 'Some call it *Casting the Sands*, *Striking Sand*, or *Earth Magic*. It is like … trying to write in sand what the wind says, or catching the voice of the Great Spirit.'

'So that is divination?' I asked. 'Do you believe we can see the future?'

Rafig laughed. 'What is the future?' he chuckled. '*Sandlines* gives a glimpse through *al-kashf* - the veil.'

'What veil?'

'The veil that prevents us normally from seeing the Great Spirit, seeing that we are of the Great Spirit and the Great Spirit's Dreaming.'

'You mean that the world is a dream?'

'Not your dream or my dream. The world is the Great Spirit's dream and in that dream there is no past or future – there is only now.'

He looked at me. 'Do *you* believe humans can see the future?'

'Not really, but I would still be interested to know what you saw.'

Dirty White

For years afterwards I wracked my memories of that day to be certain that events really did unfold as I remembered them. In the end I had to go back to the diary I kept at the time, though of course the diary entry was made on the evening of the same day, *after* the events had occurred, so is not entirely contemporary. However, it seems most unlikely that I would have changed the sequence in the written account to make a better story. For whom? The diary entry is actually very terse and there is no recorded reaction to events which looking back, seem extraordinary. On the other hand there is a degree of ambiguity that I would not have recalled had I been reliant on memory alone.

My record of Rafig's statement as to what he saw in the *Sandlines* that morning consists of only one sentence:-

> '*I saw either a white camel or a good man, and a woman, coming from behind – they saw us but we didn't see them.*'

My diary entry - now separated from the events by forty years – was made in English, not in the language we were speaking at the time – an unwritten dialect of Arabic. It is possible I might have misunderstood, misinterpreted, or mistranslated his utterance. For example, I am sure Rafig did not actually mention a *white camel*, since camels were never referred to as *white* in the nomad dialect. The colouring of camels involved a whole vocabulary of terms that were not used in any other context. While the word for white was *abyad*, what an outsider might have seen as a white male camel, the nomads called *aghbash* meaning something like *dirty white* (a she-camel would be *ghabsha*) This is, I am sure, what Rafig told me he had seen in the *Sandlines*, and I simply wrote *white camel* because there was no exact translation in English. Then there is the term *either* which seems to offer a choice between *a white camel* and *a good man*. According to the grammatical structure (*they saw us but we didn't see them*) the woman is present in both cases – there is the possibility of *a good man and a woman*, or *a white camel and a woman*. Again, since I wrote this after the event, having translated it into English, and since there are no commas in spoken language, it is difficult to be certain. What seems unequivocal however, is the positioning of these beings with relation to Rafig and myself: they would be coming from behind, and we would not see them, although they would see us.

Now I must compare this with what happened that day, also based on my diary entry. After the *Sandlines* reading, we returned to the camels, got them to their feet, checked the head-ropes, and made certain they were tied securely *head to tail* – meaning that the ropes were tied, not to the actual tail, but to the frame of the saddle carried by the preceding camel. Then we led them down the old trail to the Gap – the natural arch in the rock wall of Elai crater. It was only the day before that I had passed through it with Brahim and the herd, but that event already seemed to belong to a distant phase of my life.

Outside the Gap we halted the caravan, and Rafig pointed out the way to al-Gaa, the salt-oasis, which was our destination. I took a moment to orient myself. Brahim's herd had been travelling due north, parallel with the Nile – *downriver*, as they called it. The salt place lay to the west, in the *Hurra*. Beyond that, he told me, the desert stretched on and on as far as what he called the *Sunset Land* – or *Maghreb*.

Here is the conservation I recorded with Rafig at this point:

Self: 'How do you know the way?'

Rafig: 'I use the senses.' (He points to a distant rock pimple growing out of a shoulder of a jagged knoll, just visible on the skyline - probably a relict volcanic core.) 'That is *Hare's Ladder*– a Known Place. You must keep it against your right shoulder and turn your body slightly to the left. When we reach *Hare's Ladder* the pimple will be on our right.'

Self: 'So you navigate purely on landmarks?'

Rafig: 'No' (he holds up a hand.) 'Close your eyes.'

(I close them)

Rafig: 'Now, do you feel the wind?'

(I feel a slight breeze coming from behind me, tickling the back of my jaw on the right side. I open my eyes.)

Self: 'Northeast?'

Rafig: 'Yes. That wind comes from the Nile Valley. The moment you feel the wind on a different part of your head, it means you have changed direction.'

Self: What if *the wind* changes direction?

 Rafig: One knows that also, by other signs.

Self: Anything else?

Rafig: 'Yes. If you wish to find your way in the desert, you must not let your senses slip or allow your heart to work elsewhere. For now, fix your eyes on *Hare's Ladder*, and make sure you keep the wind on the place where you felt it. You must listen, watch the desert surface for signs, and observe its texture – is it soft sand or hard sand? Is it rocky with large stones or small stones, or gravel, or sand and gravel mixed? Watch how the shadows under the small stones change, and feel the earth under your feet.'

Self: 'All right.'

Rafig: 'Do you know the story of Blind Awda? He was a caravan guide on the Pharaoh's Road in my father's time.'

Self: 'A blind desert guide? Is that possible?'

Rafig: 'The story is well known. He was famous among the nomads, yet he could not see so much as his hand in front of his face. They said he knew the way simply from the direction of the wind, and from the texture and smell of the surface. That might have been part of it, but when they asked him how he did it, he said, "*I get a hot feeling in my head when I am taking the right path. I just know.*"

Self: 'That's amazing.

Rafig: 'Yes, now look at this.' (He points to something behind me and I turn to see two sets of human tracks – Rafig's and my own.)

Rafig: 'These are your tracks,' (bending over) 'Do you notice anything distinct about them? Examine them, then look at mine.'

(The tracks run parallel, so it is easy to compare them. Both of us are wearing nomad slippers or moccasins – hand-made cow-skin shoes with flat soles. Our feet are about the same size, but my footprints point straight ahead, while Rafig's turn slightly outwards. I tell him this.)

Rafig: (laughs) 'Your tracks are those of a determined man, but not a wary one. Any tracker can see you are not thinking about what is around you, only what is ahead. That is not good. You must know what is going on around you – even behind you – all the time.'

(I feel annoyed – as if I have been condemned by my own tracks)

Self: 'How do you know? Maybe that's just how my feet are.'

Rafig: (laughs) 'Tracks do not lie. A wary man turns from side to side as he walks, and it shows in his tracks. The desert is the Face of God, and the truth is written upon it. You must practice being present, and improve yourself.'

We set off, leading the caravan, and the desert rolls out before us, pinkish amber, undulating down to dark broken cliffs on the skyline. As we walk, leading the camels, the desert unfolds, rippled sand-sheets alternate with ranges of clinker- stones. There are tufts of sword-grass, ragged acacia trees, and the surface is dotted with the tracks of scores of gazelles. I see all this and I try to reach out to the landscape with my senses, taking in the smell on the air, feeling the wind on my neck, turning left and right to observe the desert from different angles. The sun is a fireball painting the land polished copper, crystalizing every stone in its unique form, casting long shadows. We guide the caravan across shoulders of shattered rock, wafer-thin flakes like broken glass, globs of lava, twisted nodules and black bubbles laid in beds of cream-coloured powder. Nothing stirs in the whole of this wilderness except the hot wind from the northeast. By the middle of the morning the heat is on us like a shroud, and we lead the caravan into a dry wash along whose banks grow a few thorn trees.

There, browsing among the trees, is an *aghbash* – white - camel.

I laugh. This morning Rafig predicted that we would see a white camel, and here it is. On its own, maybe, this is not so surprising. We are in the desert, and there are camels in the desert, and no doubt many of them are white. Still, Rafig said *a* camel, and this is one, not two or three. We halt to examine the camel. Rafig points out the neat hooves, graceful curve of neck, large head, and pricked-up ears. '*Hajin*,' he comments. 'A fast riding camel.'

We lead the caravan further along the wadi bed, and have been going perhaps another half hour, when we hear a high-pitched, urgent, angry voice coming from behind. We turn and see a man running towards us – a little man with a flying mop of hair and a wild beard. He is carrying a big rifle in one hand and a tiny water-skin in the other. He's excited, almost leaping towards us, and by the time he reaches us he's puffing and panting.

'What's wrong with you?' he gasps. 'I called you from right back there and you took no notice. I'm dying of thirst.'

'Our ears are heavy,' Rafig says. 'We didn't hear.'

It's true, but also a bit rich, I think, after Rafig gave me a lecture on remaining present in all circumstances – still, I didn't hear him either. When the little nomad gets his breath back he tells us that his family tents are pitched in the Wadi al-Ma to the south. 'God is Generous, but the rain has been poor,' he says. 'Many nomads have lost animals. I brought my sheep, goats, and camels into the *Hurra* to look for pasture, but I didn't find it. The sheep died, the goats are starving, and there's only one camel left.'

'We saw a beautiful white camel further down the wadi,' I say. 'Is that your camel?'

'*Don't attract the eye,*' he snaps. 'That camel is on its last legs. It belongs to God, but it happens to be in my safe-keeping.'

He glares at me so fiercely I almost take a step back.

'Let me give you water,' Rafig says, distracting him. He puts out his hand for the nomad's tiny water-skin, and together we fill it from one of our big ones. Rafig gives the bulging skin back to the nomad, then takes tea, sugar, dried dates, and flour from a saddlebag, and hands them over to him. The nomad wraps the supplies in cloth bundles, stows them in the pockets of his *jibba* and invokes God's blessing on us. Then he shoulders his rifle and trots back the way he came.

We watch him until he merges with the desert, then we exchange a glance.

'What was the problem about *the eye*?' I ask, perplexed. 'That camel didn't look to be on its last legs at all.'

Rafig chuckles. 'The *evil* eye,' he says. 'Never tell a nomad that he has beautiful animals or children. It may cause his *qarin* to appear.'

'So is a *qarin* the same as the evil eye?'

'No. The evil eye invites a person to feel self-important, and makes them vulnerable to their *qarin*. When self-importance possesses a person that is the *qarin* working.'

'How come you didn't hear him shout?'

'You distracted me. I was listening to you.'

'I see. It was my fault then.'

We get the camels moving, and carry on west. Of the next event I have no recollection. While I do remember the little nomad and can still picture his bushy beard, dirt-coloured *jibba* and tangled hair, I cannot remember meeting the young woman at all. The entry in my diary runs:

> '*Not long after, we spied a young woman under a tree – a lithe, slim girl, barefoot, with a long pole for her sheep.*'

I made no record of what we said to her, but I did note that she belonged to a different clan from that of the little nomad, so we must have exchanged some news at least.

We don't talk much for the rest of the day. One reason is the heat – the hot wind comes up and blasts us. I have already noticed how the heat can affect one's mood – how it makes one irritable and depressed – opening the way for the jinns Rafig told me about. The old man is silent and grumpy, disinclined to talk, except to his camel, and even that discourse does not sound very soothing. I wonder if he is annoyed with himself for not having heard the nomad's shout. The little man must have experienced a few moments of anguish when we failed to respond – failing to help another human in the desert is a disgrace.

When sun starts on the downward part of its journey, towards the end of the afternoon, though, it is a blessing. The aggravation engendered by the heat melts away slowly. When we finally halt for the night, we are exhausted. After careful consideration, Rafig chooses a place in a wadi where there are white-thorn bushes for the camels. Before we unload, though, he quarters the ground carefully.

'When you choose a place to sleep, make sure it feels right,' he says, 'and look out for the tracks of snakes and scorpions. A scorpion's tracks are like the marks of a person touching the sand with their fingertips. A snake moves sideways, so her tracks are a series of curves.'

After we have unloaded and unsaddled the animals, and set up our little camp, we lead them out into the shrub one by one, apply foreleg hobbles so that they will not wander too far, and remove the head-ropes. By the time they are all happily browsing it is full dark and the stars are out, peppering the velveteen sky. Rafig points out constellations – most are unfamiliar to me, and have animal names like *Wide-Eared Fox*, *Jumping Mouse*, and *Coney Night Caller*. One though, named *Shadad the Hunter*, I recognize as Orion. There are other tasks to perform now – hang our water-skins, which cannot be left on the ground, pile the pack-saddles into a wind-break, hunt for firewood in order to conserve what we have, make a fire, set up firestones, and finally, cook polenta, which we eat with sour camel's milk.

When dinner is over, it's time to go and collect the camels and drive them back to camp, where we couch them around our sleeping space. It's not until then that I can sit down on my blanket and get out my diary, which I write in the light of a torch. Now I have to sort out what happened today. If I remember Rafig's words this morning correctly, he predicted that we would see either *a white camel* and *a good man*, or a *white camel* and a *woman*. What we have actually seen is all three - a *white camel, a good man*, and a *woman*. Rafig predicted that they would come from behind, and that they would see us but we would not see them. In fact, only the *good man* came from behind, though he was angry because while he had seen us, we had not seen him. True, we saw both a *white camel* and a *woman*, but neither of them came from behind.

How can I explain this? Though Rafig's prediction was not precisely what happened, it had exactly the same elements: some of them – like *coming from behind* – seem too specific for coincidence. Looking back at it over forty years, though, all I can say is that I made the diary entry *after* the events of the day. Can I be absolutely certain that I did not change the contents of Rafig's prediction – even unconsciously - after the fact? And if I did change them, why would I not have made them more precise?

Only the previous morning, in the wadi, Rafig told me *the wind is what connects us with everything else that exists.* If everything is a singularity and exists as a continuum, is it possible that one's awareness of the present extends for longer than what is referred to as *now?* What is *now*, actually? Is it a static point or a moment of interaction when one's senses are focused on certain sensations*?* I remember the blind guide, Awda, and his claim that he *just knew* the way. Like every child who grew up in civilization, I've been taught that the universe is a collection of separate objects, and that as humans we are separate from nature, from each other, and from our bodies. But what if everything one has been taught to regard as separate is instead just part of one changeless, eternal being, whose barriers are a veil - an illusion? What if there is no *I*, but only an unfolding of the totality? What if every event is a crossroads where all paths come together, and all connections meet?

Pits

It was seven sleeps to al-Gaa, and it was a time of constant toil. I thought I had learned everything from Brahim and the others, but I soon came to realize that my time with the herd had been only overture and beginners. I had many lifetimes of desert lore to catch up on, but learning skills was not the hardest thing - it dawned on me slowly that when Rafig opened his eyes in the morning he saw a different world from the one I experienced. His was another reality conjured into being and molded over a hundred generations since the Distant Time - a dimension of which my own culture of machines and measurements was unaware. In my world, a dozen civilizations had risen and fallen since the time Rafig's people first came to this desert, and in all those ages the nomads had wanted no more than to live here, in the wilderness, as they had always lived.

Every day we saddled the camels, loaded them with such gear as there was, and got them moving, with Agha, the great bull camel, always in the lead. The desert rolled out before us, its vast yawning chasms like a siren voice calling us on, like an enticing drum-beat the camels seemed to hear and understand, as if it were speaking to them, and they pricked up their ears and lifted their feet, and moved to its rhythm, and when I looked at them they seemed to be smiling.

Rafig was an excellent guide, but unrelenting in his demand for perfection. As he had told me that first day, there was a way to do everything handed down from the Ancestors, and those ways had been tested by time. Rafig was quite right in his vigilance - one girth badly buckled, one hobble carelessly tied, one water-skin allowed to leak, could spell disaster for the whole enterprise.

The heat was tremendous. By late morning, the desert surface was too hot to walk on barefoot, and the sun was a razor flaying the sheen of colors from the sky. By that time we would be looking for a place to erect our *rakuba* – a shelter of blankets tied on acacia poles, with ropes secured to saddles or sacks of grain. Not even the most desert-hardened nomad, Rafig told me, would sit out in the sun when it was directly overhead in this season – and the *Ged* – the *Hot Hot* season - had not yet begun.

Around noon on the third day out of Elai we located a vein of sedges and stump-grass for the camels. There were no trees, so after unloading and unsaddling the caravan, we began to dig pits in the hot sand for the acacia poles. I was scooping out sand frantically with the knife Brahim had given me, when Rafig said. 'Not like that. The pit must be round, or the pole will not stand straight.'

I felt something inside go *snap*. 'This *is* round,' I retorted.

He shook his head. 'It is not round, it is oval. That is no good.'

I rocked back on my heels. 'It's hot,' I raged. 'I don't have time for this nonsense. What does it matter?'

'Very well,' Rafig said, and turned away.

He let me continue work on my pit, while he dug the other. When both were finished, he told me to bring the poles over and set them in the pits. I did so, and we filled the holes in with sand, packing it tight around the wood.

'Now,' Rafig said. 'Try the poles.'

Reluctantly, I shook the pole that I had inserted into my oval pit – it wobbled precariously. When I tried to shake the pole in Rafig's pit, though, it was as solid as a rock.

Rafig nodded. 'It needs to be round,' he said.

I had to dig my pit again, and we completed the shelter in silence. Rafig made a fire and cooked polenta. After we had eaten, we sat back in our tiny island of shade. Around us the desert stretched on endlessly – intricate wave-patterns on a pale peach-colored sand-sheet, with hardly a blemish, falling away to snake-scale dunes, with dark cliffs on one side, a crust of rough hills in the distance, and another parade of dunes beyond that. The whole landscape looked unreal: there was nothing moving out there except the shimmering heat.

'I have seen the shadow of the *qarin* in your eyes several times since we left,' Rafig told me, 'but this was the worst. Did I not say that jinns are strong in lonely places? When the right vessel comes along, they find a chance to attack.'

'I was in the army,' I said dryly, 'and I spent a long time being ordered about over trivial stuff. I didn't expect it here. I was in special-forces. I think I know how to dig a pit.'

'*Sahih*? Is that the truth?'

I bit my lip, wondering suddenly why I had made such a fuss. Rafig had told me before we started that I must follow his lead, and I had agreed. He had also told me there was only one way of doing things in the desert – the way tested by time, and I knew he was right.

'Maybe not.'

The old man gave me a stern glance. 'I don't know what special-forces is. It seems important to you, but whatever it is, it's in the past – you must put your self-importance behind you, because that is your *qarin* working.'

'Why should I put it behind me? I learned many things – and I'm proud of it.'

'If you learned useful things, do not forget them, but get rid of the pride that makes you feel self-important - that you are better than others. You wear it like a *jibba*. You think you do not need to be told how to dig a pit, nor fill a water-skin, nor to choose firewood, because you are too important for that.'

I stared at him, ready to give a cutting rejoinder. I could have mentioned the first day out when, after all his talk about staying in tune with the desert, he had not heard a thirsty man shouting – a man whose coming he had actually foreseen.

Instead I swallowed and looked down.

'Sorry,' I said. 'The jinn had me all right.'

'Stay vigilant. When it feels threatened, the jinn attacks the hardest.'

'What do you mean?'

'Your *qarin* will not accept that it has no power. It makes you think it is *you* speaking - the more you resist the harder it will scream and scrabble to convince you it is there.'

'I haven't heard the last of it then?'

'Stay alert, that's all.'

Lady Moon

When the shadows lengthened and the sun started to drop into its afternoon curve towards the western skyline, we packed up and moved the camels out. Sometimes Rafig and I walked together at the head of the caravan, but mostly I brought up the rear, walking behind Ata, the last camel on the string. Enthralled by the rhythm of the steadily undulating hind-quarters and the silently pacing feet, I had grown attached to camels now – I loved their movements, their shape, their smell - and as they had grown more familiar they had also come to seem even stranger and more magical. I had started by regarding Ata as a kind of mechanism, but now he was a person. He was an entity with his own distinct character, and - like all the other camels in the caravan – a shaman, with mystical powers of his own.

The knoll Rafig had called *Hare's Ladder* now lay far behind us and the plain of patterned sand dropped steadily into a vast *sangura* – endless flats of hard, powdery blue pumice. It was unexpected, alien, and unworldly, bounded on one side by a gallery of great rock piles like dumps from giants' quarries, and to the west by the outline of hills like ghosts in the shimmering sand-mist. The huge dimensions took one's breath away, searing the mind with the intimation of infinity, reducing the caravan to a tiny train of ants under the heavens. At the same time, the camels before me towered larger than life, with living shadows moving and stretching under their bellies. The sun slipped down its trajectory and lay tilted against the horizon, pulsing harmonics in rainbow colors that changed every time one looked at them, with interlocking arches of light radiating away from it as it sank into oblivion, leaving twists and sparklers of fire floating above. The night came down like a dark curtain, a breathing blackness, without even the stars to guide us. Soon we had to stop.

The desert surface absorbed heat in the daytime and one could feel the heat throbbing in the sand and stones for some while after sunset. When the throb finally played out, the moon came up, so huge, polished, and magnificent that I felt my spirit lift with it, and I almost imagined I heard the sound of a massed choir – spirit voices drifting out of the great and empty chasms of space - pitched in glorious complement. As the moon bathed the desert with green light and soft, luminous shadows, we went about settling the camels with grain in nosebags, arranging our camp, making a fire. Once again, as the flames licked up between the shards of wood we had brought from Elai, I felt as if another being was born between us. I thought of Rafig's story about how the wide-eared fox stole fire.

After we had eaten polenta, Rafig made tea and we sat drinking it, basking in moonlight. The moon was full, and staring up at the surface, so clear and white, it felt as if one might be able to stretch out and touch it.

'How far do you think the moon is?' I asked Rafig playfully.

'Oh, you could probably get hold of her if you found a tall enough tree.'

I looked at the old man's face to see if he was joking, but it didn't seem so. It hit me with a shock that, to him, the moon was the size and shape it appeared to be.

'Do you remember the Known Place we passed on the first day out of Elai – the *Hare's Ladder*?' he asked.

'The hill with the pimple that we left on our right?'

'Yes. That place is so-called because Brother Hare uses it as a way of climbing down from Lady Moon, and climbing back up again.' He paused and glanced upwards. 'Can you see Brother Hare up there?'

I shrugged. 'No, but people talk about the man in the moon, and I can't see him, either.'

'There is no man in the moon,' Rafig said, laughing. 'Look at the dark marks on the moon's face – you can clearly see hare's rounded nose and long ears, and he is doing something with his hands – some people say he is using a pestle and a mortar.'

I looked at the moon, and sure enough, I could see the shape of a hare, perhaps pounding something in a mortar.

'Brother Hare is Lady Moon's messenger,' Rafig said. 'He stalks among us, especially on nights like this, when the Lady is round and bright. After tonight she gets smaller and smaller until she dies. Then what? A slim silver blade appears – the *hilal*. She is very thin to start with, then she grows fatter and fatter until she can't grow any fatter without going pop – like tonight.'

'You mean she lives and dies like humans?'

'Of course –all beings do. Remember the wind, the breath and the spirit? We are all part of one flow, and the differences between us are only momentary appearances, like the ripples on the surface of running water. They appear to be distinct, but only for a time, then they dissolve into the flow, which is eternal. Once, long ago – in the Distant Time – Lady Moon called for Brother Hare, and told him to go to the Children of Adam and bring them an important message. 'Tell the humans this,' she said:

> *'As I die and dying live,*
>
> *So shall you die,*
>
> *And dying live.'*

'Very good,' said Hare. 'I will do as you ask,' and he climbed down the ladder.

He found Adam's Children and told them. 'I have an important message for you from Lady Moon.'

'From Lady Moon?' they said. 'Then it must be important. What is it?'

'She told me to say,

> *'As I die and in dying perish*
>
> *So shall you die*
>
> *And come to an end.'*

Adam's Children turned pale and started trembling. '*come to an end*,' they repeated, 'does that mean death is the end and there is nothing after?'

'That's about it,' said Brother Hare, and he ran away, dancing and laughing to himself, because he had cheated Bani Adam, and frightened them. He climbed

the ladder back up to the moon, still laughing. Lady Moon saw him and grew suspicious.

'What did you tell them?' she asked.'

Hare answered, 'I told them,

> *'As I die and in dying perish*
>
> *So shall you die*
>
> *And come to an end.'*

73

The moon was furious. 'That was not what I told you to say,' she shouted. She picked up a stick and whacked Brother Hare across the face with it, so hard that his lip was split in two. The hare remains with a split lip to this day.'

Rafig nodded at the moon again. 'If you look hard you can see it.'

I laughed, though when I thought about it, the meaning of the story wasn't quite clear.

'So that's why humans believe that death is the end of everything?' I asked.

Rafig nodded. 'Lady Moon's message was this – the way things appear is a momentary shape in the Great Spirit's Dreaming. When we convince ourselves that this shape is permanent – that we really *are* separate selves – we become weak and vulnerable. The evil jinn uses that opportunity to arise.'

'All right, but how is that related to death?'

'It is like the dance and the dancer. The dance is a movement of the dancer's body. We can distinguish between the dance and the dancer, yet there is never anything in the dance that is not the dancer. The dance is an activity of the dancer – they are not really two things, only one.'

'So we are the dance?'

'Not at all. We are both the dance *and* the dancer – they are not divided, don't you see? The dancer is the Great Spirit, and the dance is the Great Spirit's Dreaming – one is an activity of the other, but they are not separate, for there is nothing in the Great Spirit's Dreaming that is not the Great Spirit. When we die the dance of our life may be over, but the dance merges back into the dancer, with all the things the dancer has learned from that dance. The part of the Great Spirit's Dreaming that was us, blends back into the Great Spirit, though we were never really separate from it in the first place.'

'I understand your words,' I said, 'but it's just hard to imagine it other than a picture in my head.'

The old man nodded. 'Because the veil gets in the way. Your *qarin* tells you that the dance is all there is – that there is no dancer. It tells you that are a separate self, different from all others – special, like your … *special-forces*. This feeling of special-ness, of self-importance, becomes a burden of suffering. The jinn does not want to let go of its kingdom behind the veil – it wants to cry out this is *me, me. me,* and *me* is all there is. That is what we are struggling against.'

'Is the jinn real?'

'The jinn is real but not what it seems – it only has the power one gives to it. It is a being one helps to create, with no separate existence of its own. It tries to convince you that you are better or more important than others. The story of Lady Moon and Brother Hare reminds us that death is not the end of everything. Life is indestructible and we live for eternity in the One Absolute Infinite Eternal.'

Life

That night something woke me abruptly –- it was almost as if I had been shaken awake. Rafig was a dark bale in his blankets, and the camels were couched close together, drowsing. There was something else, though. I moved very slowly, felt under the saddle-bag I used as a pillow, slipped Brahim's knife into my hand. Then I saw the snake – a fat, thick, stumpy viper, pale scales and darker bands, sidewinding steadily towards me in the moonlight. I froze, with the knife in my hand. I stared at the slithering creature and it seemed that I could see her eyes fixed on me with a lidless, unfaltering stare, the horns pricking up, and the tongue flicking in and out as she coiled slowly and relentlessly towards me. I tried desperately to get up, but I could not move – as if the snake had hypnotized me into submission. In a moment she was face to face with me. Still I was paralyzed. She opened her jaws, showing the venomous sharp teeth and the thrashing forked tongue. I could not move. I could only wait for her to strike.   She reared over me and in that instant I opened my eyes, and sat up for real. At once I saw Rafig standing over what looked like a dark length of coiled cable, at least seven paces away.

The camels were staring at him inquisitively. He had his camel-stick in his hand, and for a moment I thought he would smash the snake, but instead he let the creature slither off into the rocks.

'I saw her,' I said. 'I must have been dreaming.'
'You shouted and thumped the ground in your sleep,' he told me. 'She circled round you but the thump must have startled her.'

As we sat by the fire next morning making tea, I asked him why he had not killed the snake. 'I thought about Brahim's uncle,' I said. 'He was bitten by a viper and dropped dead - just like that.'

'Yes, this snake can be deadly,' Rafig said. 'She reminds one of the closeness of death – of how death is always with us and can strike without warning. She tells us not to be distracted into forgetting that we are of the Great Spirit and the Great Spirit's Dreaming. On the other hand, though, the snake is also sacred - the embodiment of the Great Spirit, for she sheds her skin and her form changes, yet life continues through her.'

'Is that why you didn't kill her?'

He laughed. 'There was no need. She had done no harm. All living things are our relations and one does not kill a relation without good reason.'

'But what do you mean by *relations*?'

He thought for a moment, then said. 'All creatures exist in the Great Spirit, whether Adam's Children, animals, or plants, the skin is just a covering, you see, like clothes. Underneath the skin is the same essence that is shared by all things. If an animal were to shed its skin one would find a human underneath.'

I remembered the story Brahim had told that first night, about the nomad who had travelled with the *Caravan of the Sun*, but had refused to throw away his clothes.

'You mean one would find a man or a woman?' I asked.

Rafig laughed again. 'No, I mean that under the skin all creatures are people. They just look different. Sometimes one has to kill - if I thought the snake was about to strike I would have killed her. Never without a reason, though.'

He paused for a moment, then added. 'In our nomad tongue Sister Snake is *thu'ban*, but her true name is *hayya* – which means life.'

World Egg

It was six days since the camels had watered at Elai, and now they were starting to look thirsty, groaning and grinding their teeth. That morning there were no trees, but by noon we were in a field of giant boulders that stretched as far as the eye could see – they looked like stacks of great dark eggs, or single gigantic eggs tipped at angles in the sand, so that, in the high sun, they enclosed small pools of shade.

We halted the camels by one such stone, and after we had unloaded, we went to explore. The nests of rocks and boulders stretched as far as the eye could see, but there were no tracks and no sign of a well. We had been looking around for a little while, when Rafig stopped suddenly. I was momentarily aware of a dark streak of shadow on the sand, then there was a piercing screech and the snap of powerful wings in my ear. I yelled and ducked.

Rafig laughed. 'Sister Falcon,' he said, pointing.

I looked up to see a bird wheeling gracefully away from us, catching a glimpse of white breast, brown wings and a hooked bill. We both watched as the falcon – a peregrine, I thought –circled steadily in the cloudless sky.

'What is she doing here?' I asked Rafig.

'She is watching her nest,' he answered, indicating a pointed stone nearby. I noticed that the stone was striped with birdlime, and realized that the falcon must have been perched there all the time, so still that I had not noticed. I didn't see any nest, though. We walked towards the rock, and as we came near, Rafig stopped me again and nodded. Beneath the stone, in a patch of shade, lay a single egg, the size of a bantam egg, brick red and mottled.

I gasped. It seemed almost a miracle to find it here deep in the desert. 'Don't go any nearer,' Rafig said, glancing up at the still circling hawk. 'We don't want to scare her. The whole world could depend on that egg.'

I laughed. Shading our eyes, we both gazed up at the mother bird riding the air currents with her wingtips spread like fingers. I noticed that her circles were becoming tighter as little by little she dropped down towards us. 'She is a sun gazer,' Rafig commented. 'She sees behind the sun – sees more than we do. And she has already given us a message.'

'How?'

'Falcons drink often. She tells us water is near by her presence. Since the only water in this area is at al-Gaa, she tells us that it lies just beyond the horizon.'

Hyenas

We did not make the salt-place until after sunset. The sun went down in a brilliant aurora of light, and as my eyes grew accustomed to the dusk, I suddenly noticed what appeared to be a large dog running parallel with the caravan. I was startled, as had no idea where it had come from – one moment it had not been there, and the next it was. I could not see it clearly, but the first thing that alerted me was that it seemed to be keeping pace with the camels rather than running past them. The second thing was that Ata kept turning his head nervously towards the animal. Presently the *dog* was joined by another of equal size, then another and another and another, and now all of them were trotting in step with us. I heard no barking or growling, and there was something both ungainly and sinister – and un-doglike - in the way these animals moved.

These aren't dogs, an inner voice told me. *What would dogs be doing in the desert?*

I peered harder, catching a whiff of something acrid and animal, glimpsing thick bodies, humped shoulders with bristled manes running down backs, long snouts, eyes that glowed like red coals in the starlight. They lumbered along turning their ungainly heads sideways in a manner that seemed purposeful and malevolent.

I decided to tell Rafig, and ran up the side of the caravan away from the lolloping creatures. When I reached the head of the train, I saw that the old man had unslung his rifle and was cradling it his left elbow. He had obviously seen them.

'*Hyenas*,' he said, without stopping. 'I have never encountered them here before.'

Somehow the word *hyena* gave me a start. Instinct had warned me that the animals were not dogs, but to hear it said like this was still a surprise. I had never seen a hyena, and now there were four or five of them on the prowl only a stone's throw away.

I glanced dubiously at Rafig's home-made rifle. 'I could take a pot shot,' I suggested. 'If I hit one, it would scare the rest off, I reckon.'

'No,' Rafig shook his head. 'It would frighten our camels. In any case the hyenas have done nothing. Never kill a living creature simply because you are afraid.'

'Who said I was afraid? I'm thinking of the camels.'

Just then, Rafig tugged sharply on the head-rope of the lead camel, Agha, who had started to dart glances at the hyenas to his left. I was walking on the old man's right side, holding my camel stick, and I could no longer see the interlopers. I wondered if the camels would be spooked and break ranks – then we really would be in a pickle, I thought.

'They will not attack unless we stop,' Rafig said. 'They are tough animals, and can run from sunset to sunrise. Their usual game is to tire out their prey.'

He said I would be more use at the rear of the caravan, so I paused to let the camels pace by, and tagged on after Ata. Walking only a couple of paces behind him, I could make out the dark shapes of the hyenas further up to my left, padding silently, keeping perfect and deliberate time with the camels. The moon was not yet up, but splayed across the heavens, directly above us, lay the belt-stars and limb-stars of the constellation *Shadad the Hunter*. The night seemed to grow darker and the hyenas seemed to stay at precisely the same distance. I could sense the camels becoming increasingly nervous. I was a novice, perhaps, but I couldn't help thinking they would bolt, scatter, and leave us in the desert.

Then I saw a light blinking out like a beacon in the darkness. I knew Rafig had seen it too, because he shifted the direction of the caravan slightly and headed directly towards it. The surface beneath my feet changed suddenly from sandy to stony, and even the camels' pads, normally silent, began to crunch on the stones.   As we came nearer I realized that the light was an open fire, built up and blazing in the darkness like a beacon. Peering into the shadows I could no longer make out the shapes of the hyenas: it seemed that they had melted away as quickly and quietly as they had come.

Hermit

Rafig halted the caravan near the fire, and in its light, I saw what I assumed was a nomad camp – half tent, half brushwood shelter, in a corral of wooden stakes made from dried-out tree branches. A few camels and a donkey were hobbled nearby, and there was a small flock of goats inside the corral. A moment later a figure emerged from the shelter - a lean old man, with a beard, glowering features, red-flecked eyes, and a mop of matted grey hair. He wore no shoes and his feet were wide with splayed toes - he carried an old rifle like Rafig's in a hairy hand.

'*Faki*,' he said when he recognized Rafig. 'Where have you been? By God, you have become a stranger here.' His voice was curiously nasal, I thought.

The man, whom Rafig introduced as *the Hermit*, shook hands with us both. 'Welcome to al-Gaa,' he told me. 'I have seen no-one in a long time. Your coming is twice blest – once for me and once for the Great Spirit.'

He helped us unload the caravan. 'Do you want to sleep in the corral or out here with the camels, *Faki*?' he asked Rafig. 'I keep the fire going at night, so the *Night Cattle* don't bother my animals.'

'*Night Cattle*?' I inquired.

'Those beasts with humped shoulders, red eyes, and big teeth. Did you not see them?'

I realized he was trying to avoid using the word *hyenas* and I wondered why. *Night Cattle* seemed a strange way of putting it.

 'Yes, we saw them,' I said. 'So you don't hunt them?'

The Hermit shook his head. 'If they try to attack my camels or goats, I chase them away, but I do not go looking for them in their dens.   Some people say they are ugly, and there are many stories about them, but they are just another creature God made, after all.'

'Yes I suppose so.'

'They weren't here last time I came,' Rafig commented.

The Hermit made a sour face. 'They are nomads, *Faki*. God knows where they came from, but they have decided they like it here, at least for now. They won't come near the fire, though.'

'Better we sleep out with the camels then,' Rafig went on. 'In a corral there are too many blood suckers.'

'*Blood-suckers?*' I repeated.

'Goat-ticks,' Rafig laughed.

The Hermit showed us a place under some twisted *dom* palms where we could unroll our blankets. He helped us settle the camels, pile the saddles, and hang the water-skins. Later, he brought us water, and after a while, polenta in a huge wooden bowl, with a skin of sour camel's milk. After we had eaten, he fetched a pot of strong, sweet tea and served it in tiny glasses.

As we drank the tea, I asked him how long he had been here at al-Gaa. He said he could not remember how many years, but years did not matter, and days were only differentiated by the season. Salt-caravans came and went, he said, and he made a living by providing tools, and helping the camel-men dig salt in return for food and *tombac*. I recalled that it was here to al-Gaa that the guide Brahim had come as a boy, on his first journey in the desert, when his uncle had died on the way home. I asked the Hermit if he remembered Brahim.

'I knew him,' he replied. 'After his uncle died, may God's mercy be upon him, Brahim came here many times with the caravans.' He shook his mop of crinkly grey hair. 'Even then he had a name as a guide, but now he is one of the most renowned caravan leaders on the Pharaoh's Road – almost as famous as Awda.'

'The blind guide? You knew him, too?'

'Yes, he was a very old man then. He was strange, Awda.'

'How? Because he was blind?'

'Well, it was the way he behaved. He was an unusually strong man despite his age, and he had very acute senses of smell, taste, and hearing. He used to sniff things all the time and mumble to himself. He would sniff people, and even get down on all fours and sniff the earth – sometimes he would pick up things and lick them, and he could hear sounds and voices others did not hear - he would sometimes eavesdrop on distant conversations and astonish people by repeating what they had said when he was not present.'

'It must have been compensation for his eyesight.'

'Perhaps, but it was uncanny. His eyes were completely black, and his arms and legs were thick and hairy. He spoke in a sort of hoarse whisper. With that and his great strength, and his sniffing and licking and listening, it was like being near an animal.'

Rafig and I both laughed, and Rafig commented. 'It is said that he used to ride a huge old bull camel called *Anja*. The camel was always in heat, blowing a mouth-bladder, frothing and rumbling. He never bit Awda, but the guide used to order him to savage anyone he thought was threatening.'

'Yes, it is true, *Faki*' the Hermit chuckled. 'People were terrified of that camel.'

Rafig laughed again, and I recalled suddenly how he had told me that his son had been killed by a bull camel in heat. I was surprised that he was talking about such things so lightly after the way he had turned cold at Elai.

'How did Awda become blind?' I asked.

The Hermit shook his locks and shot a glance at Rafig. I noticed that his eyes glowed oddly red in the firelight.

'You know the story, *Faki*?'

'There are several stories,' Rafig said. 'Which do you mean?'

'Well, the tale goes that, as a young man, Awda lived in the *goz*, on the desert's southern fringes – an area well known for *Night Cattle*. One night he was walking alone in the bush, when he encountered a large, female beast. She did not run off, but stared at him, and beckoned him with her left foot. She turned and Awda caught the scent of her hind quarters. The smell overpowered him and put him in a trance, and when the animal turned and walked away, he followed like one enslaved. She led him to her den and disappeared inside.

'Awda tried desperately to follow her, but could not get in, so he stood outside waiting for her in the darkness, until, just before dawn, her clan returned. The *Night-Cattle* saw the boy standing there, and set upon him, going first for his eyes. Awda awoke from his trance, drew his knife, and fought them off. He managed to run away, and as the sun was up by now, the clan did not follow. 'He ran back to his camp, but the damage had already been done, and he had become blind. When the people asked him how he had found his camp, he answered, "*I had a hot feeling in my head that grew sharper as I came near.*"

'Afterwards, though his eyesight never recovered, he could find places without seeing landmarks, and in time he became the most noted guide among the nomads.'

I thought about the tale later, after the Hermit had retired to his shelter, leaving Rafig and me to build up the fire. It was a fantasy, of course, but it was also creepy when I knew there were real hyenas about, and I was glad to be in the fire's cheering orbit. For a while we sat together gazing into the flames, listening to the camels shifting and chewing the cud, then Rafig said.

'The Hermit's tale is common among the nomads – it is not only told about Awda. The story of a nomad being lured to a hyena's den by the smell of the animal's hind-parts is an old one. They say one young man was discovered with his head actually inside a hyena's burrow.'

'You mean it's a myth? Like the wide-eared fox stealing fire or the hare giving the wrong message to humans?'

'Yes, but all such tales have truth in them. Some of those who knew Awda tell a different story. They say he was not from the *goz*, and in fact no one knows where he came from, or who his people were. He had no family – no known parents, no brothers, no sisters. I have heard it said that he was a Fish-Eater from the deep *Hurra*, but I do not believe that. Others say that Awda himself was a hyena.'

'*What*?' I burst out laughing again.

'Yes, they say he belonged to the *Hyena People* – a clan of men and women who live far away in the desert – maybe in an oasis. They are of two kinds – hyenas who become humans, and humans who become hyenas. They have no children of their own but entice human children to join the clan in the way the Hermit described, except that they are taken far away and become hyenas themselves. Then there are hyenas who are born hyenas but can change their skins and become human – they also live among the *Hyena People*. The story goes that Awda was one of those – a hyena skin-walker who could appear human, and lived with humans.'

'The Hermit said he was like an animal.'

'Yes, some reckon Awda was not really blind – he only had poor eyesight. His other senses – taste, smell and hearing – were sharper than those of most humans – like a hyena's. He was very strong, hairy, and had red eyes and a nasal voice. No-one remembered him as a child or a youth – it seemed he just appeared fully grown one day. He was never married or had children of his own, and one day he just vanished.'

I laughed again. 'That's an even better story than the Hermit's.'

'Yes, and there's more. Some people say they have seen him.'

'Awda?'

'Yes, long after he was supposed to have vanished. Some nomads say they have glimpsed him, alone, deep in the *Hurra*, his eyes like burning embers, and big teeth, whooping and yipping, looking more like a hyena than ever, riding his giant bull-camel, Anja, blowing his mouth-bladder and rumbling like thunder.'

I rolled about laughing, the tale was so good. Then a thought struck me. 'What about the Hermit himself?' I asked. 'He has red eyes, a thick beard, and a nasal voice. Where does *he* come from?'

It was Rafig's turn to laugh. 'That is a good question. He has been here a long time – almost since anyone can remember, but he is not of the nomads and he is not a Fish Eater. I have a feeling that he came originally from the town, like you.'

'Like me? Well, I suppose all real hyenas come from the town, don't they?'

'Yes, perhaps, but you could ask him - I'm not certain. It is some time since I was here, and last time there were no hyenas.'

'Why does he call them *Night Cattle*?'

Rafig laughed again. 'God is All-Knowing, but for the same reason he does not wish to kill them, I think – I mean, what if they really *were* Hyena People? God forbid, one would be left with a dead body.'

We both roared with laughter, but then I remembered how reluctant Rafig himself had been, to let me shoot at the hyenas dogging our caravan – almost defensive, I thought.

I settled down in my blanket, gazing up at the star clusters that made up *Shadad*. The constellation had shifted slightly but was still visible. My head was awash with thoughts of the Distant Time, when men and animals spoke the same language and could become each other, of the shape-shifter in my dream in civilization, of blind guides, hermits and *Night-*

Cattle. The first time I had seen nomads I had wanted to go back with them to the Distant Time. It seemed to me that I had arrived.

As I drifted into sleep I heard, from not far away, the *whoop-whoop-whooping* of a hyena.

Rock Salt

The salt pan of al-Gaa had been invisible in the darkness, but I awoke after sunrise to see it stretching before us, a quicksilver sheen like the surface of a great lake, rimmed by the outlines of hills half-hidden in wavering haze.

'The Devil's Mirror' Rafig commented when he saw me looking.

He was making tea in the embers of the Hermit's fire – the smoking remnant of the blaze that had burned all night and given us comfort. The Hermit's shelter – a wool tent stretched over brushwood, enclosed by a fence - looked deserted. The corral was empty, and the few camels were gone - Rafig told me that our host had taken his stock off to grazing at first light, riding an old donkey.

As we drank our tea, he pointed out the deep thorn thickets and the swath of sedges and tuft-grass that lay on one side of the salt-pans. Nearer to our camp he indicated a large area of pits and rubble-piles, where, over the ages, nomads had dug out rock-salt. That was the prize of al-Gaa, Rafig explained – not the white salt one ate with one's food, but red salt or natron - the kind the nomads gave their livestock. After breakfast of dried dates and bread crusts, we collected the camels and led them off to a well on the northern side of the salt-pan, where we took turns to draw water. When that was done we brought them back to the *dom* palms, fitted the foreleg hobbles, and sent them to graze in the clumps of esparto grass that grew around the groves.

'Will they be all right here?' I asked Rafig.

'God is generous,' he said, getting my drift at once. 'Hyenas have no power in daylight. They are creatures of the night.'

By that time the Hermit's donkey was back, and we went to his shelter to barter some sugar and flour for the use of his rusty shovels and crowbars. In the harsh light of day, he looked older and more ordinary than he had seemed in the firelight – a disheveled figure with an unkempt beard and milky eyes, his body honed down to a husk of bone and ligament by toil, desert winds, and solitude. He gave us the tools, then escorted us to the salt-pan and showed us where to dig among the maze of pits. Soon we had stripped down to our *sirwal* – the baggy trousers we wore under our smocks or *jibbas* - and were attacking the salty earth with iron bars, quarrying chunks of the red salt with shovels and piling the chunks into heaps. The work was not backbreaking, but it was hard enough, and I was grateful that I had been schooled in the art of digging trenches in the army. Rafig worked solidly, totally focused on the task, cutting blocks and shoveling the salt with efficient movements and controlled energy.

The sun grew hotter and the wind dragged saline dust across the salt pan that stung our eyes and chafed our skin so that we had to don our *jibbas* again. By mid-morning, when the heat and dust had become intolerable, we were standing waist-high in hollows with pyramids of pink salt next to us. We laid down our tools and retired to the shade of the *dom* palms, where we checked on the camels, then drank tea and ate polenta.

We rested until the sun began to wane, and returned to the salt pits, carrying some large hemp sacks Rafig had brought with him. I resumed work with the tools, while Rafig filled sacks with lumps of salt, cramming them in until the sacks would take no more. Then he stitched them up with a packing needle and leather strips cut carefully from a length of cow-skin. By sunset, when we stopped work, six packs of salt stood ready for the loading. At sunset we brought in the camels, hobbled them in a semi-circle around our camp under the *dom* palms, and gave them grain in nose-bags. As darkness fell we heard a cacophony of eerie chuckles, so clear that even the camels turned their heads. Rafig and I peered into the darkness.

'That is the song hyenas sing when they leave their daytime places,' Rafig said.

'Laughing hyenas,' I said.

'It sounds like laughing, but it's a message – Sister Hyena has a whole language of her own just like the Children of Adam do.'

'It's very near, anyway.'

'Yes you are right.'

The scuffle of feet startled us, but it was only the Hermit, arriving with a pile of firewood. He built up the guard-fire, and we cooked and ate polenta together. After we had eaten, and were drinking tea in the light of the flames, I asked the Hermit if he knew anything about the Lost Oasis.

'I have heard the story,' he answered. 'A boy goes in search of a runaway camel and discovers a paradise in the desert, with green trees, water, and beautiful maidens. There is supposed to be a great secret there, but the boy leaves the oasis to visit his family before discovering what it is, and never finds the place again. That is a townsman's story – most nomads don't know it.'

'So I was told. How come *you* know it?'

He looked at me, his eyes once more glowing slightly red in the firelight.

'I lived in the town when I was young. I was tormented there and called a slave by people who believed they were free but were enslaved more hopelessly than I. Then I got into trouble, and I had to escape. I found a chance to go off with nomads into the desert, and eventually came here, where I own no more than I need to live, and am therefore free.'

I nodded. I wondered if he had meant the word *slave* literally. Then I remembered the storyteller Maya referring to civilization as *a cage* - those who were shut in the prison of society itself and obliged to sell their lives to a master were certainly slaves, I thought. I had been one of them, trained to kill on demand. Now, like the Hermit, I was outside that, but how long that situation would last I did not know.

'So the Lost Oasis is just a story?' I asked.

The Hermit laughed. 'God is All-Knowing. Perhaps it exists, or perhaps it existed once, and is now lost under the desert sands. The desert has not always been as it is today. Many old places are lost. Giants lived where nomads now wander with their camels.'

'You mean like the Giants in the story of how the wide-eared fox stole fire?'

'Perhaps. The nomads call the old people Anakim – the Lost Giants. Perhaps your Lost Oasis was a place of the Anakim. It is said that the Giants had a shrine in the desert that was sacred to their god…'

'Is that the same place as the Fire Mountain in the story?' I cut in.

'Perhaps. They called this god the *Twice Born*, or the *God of Many Names*, and it could appear as male or female, though it was neither and both at once, just it was young and old, both and neither. This god was heard in the talk of animals, the cries of birds, the wind in the trees, the breeze in the grass, the ripples in the water, the heat of the sun, the light of the stars, the patterns of the clouds. Its voice was everywhere in the desert, in the roar of the storm and the drumming of the sands that the nomads call *Azael's Drum*

Once again, the Hermit's words evoked a memory of my dream back in the Nile Valley – the one I had had the day I encountered the camel-caravan - the figure sitting by the flickering campfire that I had called a shape-shifter, who fluctuated between male and female, between youth and old age. I remembered lightning and thunder, the feeling that I was part of an ancient mystery.

'How do you know all this?' I asked.

'When I lived in the town, I was the servant of a scholar. He was studying the magic of the Pharaohs - the old Egyptian kings. I can both read and write, which was unusual for a servant, and |I used to read his books when I got the chance. Once he caught me reading them when I should have been doing my work, but instead of getting angry, he asked me what I had learned, and we used to discuss it. A *Town of the Twice Born* is mentioned in old manuscripts and said to be lost in the desert, like your Lost Oasis. The story is that the city can never be found twice. It is possible that this is front and back of the same story, for stories look different depending on where one stands.'

Wind Scorpion

The Hermit had finished his story and we were sitting in silence, staring into the flames, when a black shape scuttled suddenly across the swath of firelight. I saw at once that it was a gigantic camel-spider of the type that had run across my face on my first night in the desert – the one I had called *the Guardian*. It had the same hairy legs, a long, segmented abdomen, a head like a sightless bird's, and that sinister pointed snout, almost like a beak. I jumped to my feet and grabbed my camel-stick, shuddering. By that time, though, the spider had vanished into the shadows. I looked around for it. '*Horrible things,*' I said.

Both Rafig and the Hermit laughed. 'It is true, Brother Wind-Scorpion has a nasty bite,' the Hermit said, 'but he is not venomous like his cousin, the true scorpion.'

'You call it *Wind Scorpion*?'

'Yes, have you not seen how fast he runs? Like the wind. You will never catch him. Scorpion is slow, like a worn out camel. Brother Wind-Scorpion runs rings round scorpions, and eats them. He does not feel their sting.'

'Oh,' I said. Feeling slightly foolish, I sat down again.

'Wind-Scorpion is also called Camel Spider,' Rafig explained. 'He is not a spider like *Umm Kabut* though – not a spinner. He hates the sun, and loves the shadows. He comes out only at night.'

'You asked about the Lost Oasis,' the Hermit said. 'I know a tale about Brother Wind-Scorpion – Camel-Spider – and an oasis. It is called the *Oasis of the Last Story*.'

I laughed. 'All right,' I said. 'Go on.'

'In the Distant Time, the Wind-Scorpion was not a spider but a man. He was torn apart by Giants, and when it came to putting himself back together, he made a mess of it, and found that he had eight legs instead of two, and that his body was a hard shell on the outside, with no bones at all inside. He found he could still appear as a man when he wanted to, though, and could live among two-leggeds as one of them.

'At that time the Children of Adam had no stories to tell, and one could say they knew nothing. Wind-Scorpion, being inquisitive, found out that all the stories were kept by Sky Father in a big basket in the clouds. There was only one way to get to the sky then - by climbing a mountain called Sky Mountain. It was guarded by the Lightning Scorpions – the same scorpions who sting the Earth in a thunder-storm. At that time Wind-Scorpion did not fear the sunlight and came out by day. He climbed Sky Mountain, and when the Lightning Scorpions tried to stop him with their stings, he laughed at them- his skin was too hard for that. He went to ask Sky Father for the basket of stories.

'Sky Father showed him the basket, which was closed with a lid. He allowed Wind-Scorpion to peep inside, to see the stories that were in there, but refused to give it to him. He said that if human beings knew all the stories they would start to think that they were better than other beings, and as clever as Sky Father.

'Wind-Scorpion pretended to accept this, but instead he hid, and waited until Sky Father was asleep. Then he darted in and stole the basket of stories. Sky Father woke up and chased him, but with his eight long legs Wind-Scorpion could run as fast as the wind itself, and no-one could catch him, not even Sky Father. When he came to Sky Mountain, the Lightning Scorpions tried to stop him again, he was too fast for them. He climbed down Sky Mountain carrying the basket of stories and brought it safe to Earth Mother.

He dragged the basket across the desert intending to give it to the Children of Adam, but he could not resist lifting the lid and peeping into it from time to time. Each time he looked into it he learned a story, and became wiser. At last, he decided that he would not give the basket of stories to people, after all, but would keep it for himself and so become the wisest being on Earth.

He wondered where he could hide the basket, and remembered there was an oasis far away in the desert, where nobody lived. He decided to take the basket of stories there. On the first day all went well, and on the second day all went well. On the third day, though, a terrible storm blew up with a raging wind. When the storm had passed, the basket seemed lighter than it had been. Wind-Scorpion found the lid of the basket open, and when he looked inside he saw that almost all of the stories had fallen out and been blown away by the wind. He realized that the stories would be spread all over the world, and that the Children of Adam would pick them up and make them their own.

'He peered inside the basket again, and saw that only one story remained. He tipped it out, and found that it was the last story – the end of all the other stories combined. If all the stories were put together, this one would be the last, and though the other tales could be understood up to a point, without the last story their full meaning could not be known.

So Brother Wind Scorpion closed the lid and dragged the basket to the oasis, where he hid the last story in a place it would never be discovered. From that day to this no-one has found it, and while the world is full of stories, nobody knows where all the stories are leading, and what happens in the end.'

'What about Sky Father?' I asked. 'Did he take all this napping?'

'I was coming to that. Sky Father wanted to punish Wind Scorpion for stealing the basket of stories, and sent the sun to hunt for him high and low. That is why, to this day, Brother Wind Scorpion fears the sun and will always avoid it if he can.'

The Hermit laughed, and Rafig laughed, and I clapped my hands softly. 'That was a wonderful story,' I said, 'but tell me, does Brother Wind-Scorpion know what happens at the end of the story?'

'If so he has always kept the secret.'

'Perhaps that is the great secret to be found in the Lost Oasis,' Rafig chuckled. 'The one the youth in the tale could not wait long enough to find out.'

'That is true' the Hermit said, still laughing. 'Perhaps you yourself will find it and discover how all stories end.'

He stopped laughing suddenly and lifted his head. In the same instant I heard what sounded like a rhythmic panting coming from far off. It could only have been hyenas, but this was not the chuckling we had heard just after sunset - it was a deep, gasping, sigh that seemed almost human.

'*Night Cattle*,' the Hermit said. 'That is their hunting song.'

'What do they hunt here?' Rafig asked. 'Not camels, goats, or donkeys?'

'Gazelle,' the Hermit said. 'Also oryx, spiral-horn white antelope, wild goat, and hares.'

Rafig nodded. 'I have seen the tracks of Brother Hare and Sister Gazelle.'

'The others are rare.'

Later, when the Hermit had gone, we laid out our blankets near the fire. I noticed that Rafig kept his rifle close to him as he prepared to sleep.

Relations

The next morning the Hermit came to help us with the digging, and after that he joined us every day. We spent three more days quarrying rock salt, moving from one pit to another, as the packs slowly filled up. It was hard work in the blazing sun, and the salt-dust raised red spots on my arms and face. My companions were so cheerful and full of songs, stories, and poetry, though, that it was actually pleasant. In the evening we would retire wearily to our palm groves. The Hermit would join us for polenta and tea, after he had brought in his few camels and goats from their grazing in the thorn thickets to the north. Not a night went by without some sound from the hyenas -though as far as I know they never came near the camp.

The Hermit always seemed fascinated with the hyenas – he called their night-sounds *Night-Cattle music*, and when he spoke of them one could hear the admiration in his voice.

Rafig was always on the look-out for tracks, and on the second day he spotted the cloven-hoof prints of gazelle on the way back to our camp. 'A buck and three does,' he announced. 'They passed just after first light this morning.' Later, he showed me a pair of hoop-snares that he had made from acacia wood and leather. They were like small wheels with the spokes emanating inwards towards the hub – their sharp points not quite meeting there, but leaving a small space. The design of the hoop-snares, he said, came from the Ancestors in the Distant Time – the snare would be set over a shallow pit, covered in sand and dung, and tied to a heavy log. The animal's leg would be caught in the snare and though it might drag the hoop away, it would have to pull the log with it, and its sign would easily be followed. 'I will follow the gazelle tracks and set the snares in their path,' he said. 'Perhaps we will be lucky enough to catch the buck.'

'I thought you were against killing animals,' I said.

He looked surprised. 'It is wrong to kill any creature for pleasure, or because you are afraid,' he said. 'All beings – the standing people, the crawling people, the flying people, and the four-legged people - are our relations, and must be respected. Sometimes we need to defend ourselves, though, and sometimes we need to eat meat. That is perfectly good as long as we follow the law.'

'What law?'

'Spirit Mother's law. For instance, if my traps caught a doe or a *jadi*, I would let them go – I would only take a buck. These traps catch the animal fast, but do not inflict cruel wounds. In any case, all creatures eat other creatures. When God takes us unto God, and our bodies rot in the Earth, the plants, the crawlers and the fliers – even four-leggeds like the hyenas - flourish on them, too.'

He decided to go off and set the snares before it got dark. 'We have toiled in the sun,' he said as he left, 'and we will need meat for our journey. The hard work begins when we start loading the salt.'

He left his rifle with me in case I needed it, he said, and after he had gone I examined the weapon. I knew firearms well from my time in the military, but this was not like any weapon I had ever used. It looked and felt home-made, with a length of pipe for a barrel that broke open like a shotgun to expose a single cartridge in the breech. I drew the cartridge out with finger and thumb and saw that the brass case contained a flat-nosed lump of lead. I had to laugh. The barrel was smooth-bore, so I doubted that the flat-nose round could be fired with any accuracy – hitting the target would be at best a gamble, I thought. Although the firing mechanism could not have been made in a nomad camp, the stock had been beautifully carved from local wood. I replaced the cartridge in the breech and snapped it shut. No wonder Rafig preferred to use hoop-snares for catching gazelle. If there were any trouble from the hyenas, the best one could expect from a rifle like this was a loud bang that would scare them off.

By the afternoon of the third day we had filled twenty-eight packs with lumps of red salt – two for each camel in the caravan, excluding our riding-animals, Ata and Hambarib. Rafig had stitched each pack carefully and we lined them up in pairs on the salt-pan ready for loading. When that was done, the Hermit rode off on his donkey to bring in his animals. Rafig and I visited the well to wash off the caustic salt-dust, stripping down to our *sirwal*, splashing buckets of water over each other and gasping from the cold. We returned to the camp not long before sunset, and Rafig gave me some animal-fat called *wadek* that he used to salve camel-sores, saying it would be good for the salt-rash on my skin. He said he would go and check the hoop snares he had laid the previous day. Perhaps, if God willed, he added, we could celebrate the end of our toil by a feast of meat. Meanwhile I would bring in the camels, collect firewood, and rekindle the Hermit's fire, which had been out since that morning. Once again, Rafig handed me his old rifle.

'Watch out for the *Night Cattle*,' I joked as he left.

I anointed my arms and face liberally with *wadek*, which eased the irritation at once. Then I went to fetch our camels, methodically unfastening leg-hobbles and moving the animals back to our camp in threes and fours. When they were settled in the usual semi-circle around the camp, I went out to collect firewood, making a pile, and ferrying it back in several trips. By then it was twilight, with the sun turning to apricot and scintillating in its last display of glints and sparklers through the branches of the *dom* palms. I sat down by the ashes of the fire, and set about kindling a flame with fire-sticks as Rafig had taught me. It took a while, but eventually the spinning sticks generated enough heat to ignite the handful of dried grass I had brought. I fed the flame with tiny twigs, blew on it, and built it up with larger kindling until the fire was burning well.

I sat back, wondering why Rafig was taking so long. Perhaps a gazelle had been caught in the snare and had wandered off, dragging the log, obliging Rafig to track him. It was full dark, and the stars were out, with *Shadad the Hunter* lolling directly above me. It suddenly occurred to me that I had not given the camels their nose-bags of grain. I stood up and had started getting out the bags from Rafig's saddlebag, when there came a deep grunting cry from somewhere very near.

The cry startled me, sending an instant chill down my back. I dropped the nose-bags and picked up Rafig's rifle without even thinking. The sound came again, curiously human, and this time it seemed almost next to me. My insides suddenly felt hollow, and my scalp prickled. I peered into the darkness, noticed that the camels were fidgeting, turning their heads to scan the night, casting wary glances at something I couldn't see. I eased the rifle stock into my shoulder and held the weapon ready in both hands, tactical style. I had not touched a firearm since my army days, but the weapon I had carried then had been an extension of my body. It came back to me now in a familiar sense of comfort.

The camels were whimpering, straining against their hobbles - some rose on their knees, eyes bulging from the sockets. The panting-groaning cry came again, and I moved forward out of the span of the fire, keeping the stock in my shoulder. As I drew abreast of the camels, one of them – it was Ata, I realized - hauled himself fully upright and stood trembling, on three legs, looking as if he was about to snap the knee-hobble and leap off. I made calming noises to him, but at that moment I saw a pair of glowing red eyes leering at me out of the darkness, perhaps a dozen paces away.

The eyes fixed on me, and at once began to move in my direction, accompanied by that deep, primeval grunt I had no need to translate. I had the eerie sense I was in the presence of a malevolent intelligence that had planned this attack, singling me out, waiting till I was alone, luring me away from the fire. At the same time I sensed an immensely powerful body poised to attack. Nearer and nearer the burning eyes seemed to come, louder and louder the rhythmic grunt, till a silent scream rang in my ears. The beast seemed almost on me when I lifted the barrel and squeezed the trigger.

There was flat pop like a paper-bag bursting, a blinding flash, a puff of acrid smoke. Camels bellowed and hustled to their feet. I froze, knowing that I had let go my one shot and there was no chance of another. Beyond the camels, nothing moved in the darkness. The burning eyes had gone.

I lowered the rifle and heard a commotion behind me.

'*No God but God, what is it?*' Rafig's voice cried.

'A hyena,' I answered. 'She was coming at me.'

I don't know why I called the animal *she* – perhaps I was remembering what the Hermit had said about the female hyena being more aggressive.

A moment later the old man was at my shoulder, scanning the night.

'Are you sure it was a hyena?' he demanded.

Of course. What else could it have been?'

Before the question was even out of my mouth, though I actually found myself wondering. I had not seen the hyena, only the red eyes. The Hermit had reddish eyes, and where was he? This was the first time he had not come to our camp after sunset. It was a crazy idea, though - the camels had been terrified, and, in any case, why would he have been making that grunting-groaning sound? I recalled the talk about *Hyena People* a few nights previously, and dismissed the idea as ridiculous.

'Of course it was a hyena,' I said again. 'She was making that sort of groaning sound the Hermit called their *hunting song*. Look at the camels – they're terrified.'

'Did you hit her?'

'I think so, but I'm not sure. Anyway, she's gone.'

Rafig drew his knife from its arm-sheath and advanced into the darkness. I followed, covering him with the now-useless weapon. He strode ten or eleven paces before he knelt down and began feeling the ground. A moment later he stood up and showed me the dark smear of blood on his fingers.

'You hit her,' he said gravely, 'but she was some distance away when you fired?'

'No, she was almost on me,' I replied.

Cursed

After clearing the immediate area, making certain the wounded hyena was not skulking around, we returned to the fire, and made tea. Rafig took back his rifle, broke it open and removed the cartridge case using an iron ramrod. He inserted another round and snapped shut the breech. A few moments later, the Hermit joined us, anxious to know the reason for the shot. When I told him I had fired at a hyena, he took it as solemnly as Rafig had done, walked a circle round the camp with his rifle at the ready, as if to reassure himself. Then we put more wood on the fire and drank tea.

'Why did you shoot her?' the Hermit asked.

'She was coming straight at me,' I said. 'What else could I do?'

'You could have thrown a stone at her and shouted,' Rafig said. 'It would have been just as effective. In any case, she cannot have been nearer to you than ten paces.'

I tried to hold down my annoyance. On the one hand I had done my best to protect the camels – mostly Rafig's camels – and instead of congratulating me he seemed to be finding fault. On the other, I felt slightly shocked. The last time I had fired a weapon in combat I had mortally wounded my best friend, and the last time I had held one in my hands it had been pointing at my own head. I hadn't wanted anything to do with firearms after that, but now I had shot at a living being without even stopping to consider what I was doing. If Rafig was right, I could not be certain, even, that the animal had intended to attack. Of course it was dark and hard to judge distances, but the way I remembered it, the hyena had been a hair's breadth from jumping at me when I squeezed the trigger. I could have shouted and thrown a stone, and it probably would have scared her off, but the weapon was already in my hands and shooting had seemed the natural thing to do.

'*Night Cattle* don't usually attack Adam's Children,' the Hermit said. I could hear the resentment in his voice.

'What about Awda?' I protested. 'Didn't they tear out his eyes?'

'I told you that story was not true,' Rafig cut in. 'I have never heard of real hyenas tearing out a man's eyes unless it was a dead body. I know people who were bitten by hyenas, but in the night, when they were asleep.'

'You only winged her, anyway,' the Hermit said. 'Better you had shot her dead, because now she will be suffering and may die a painful death. Her pack will not forget it, and you will be cursed.'

I started to laugh but stopped myself. '*Cursed*?'

'The hyena is a magical animal,' the Hermit said. 'That much is true.'

'Yes,' Rafig nodded, 'and to kill other creatures out of fear is not good, as I told you. Spirit Mother will not like it. The Great Spirit created Sister Hyena as a hunter. When she hunts she is simply doing what the Great Spirit made her to do, so it cannot be evil.'

'If you didn't want me to shoot anything, why did you leave me your rifle?' I asked Rafig. 'I didn't ask for it.'

'I told you *just in case,*' he said. 'I left it to your judgment.'

It occurred to me suddenly that leaving me the rifle might have been a test, and that I had somehow failed it. Then I realized that Rafig could not possibly have predicted the hyena would come while he was away - not unless he had seen it in the *Sandlines*, of course.

'God knows, it is good to protect your companions, your family and your animals – even by killing, if there is no other choice,' Rafig said, 'but killing a living being is always regrettable.'

'What about when *you* hunt animals – the snares you set?'

'That is different, but it is also regrettable. We hunt in the name of the Great Spirit - Spirit Mother offers us these animals out of love. We hunt them without anger and without hate, not for pleasure nor for fame, but because our need is great. To kill for the sake of killing, though – when we are not hungry, or because we are afraid – risks angering Spirit Mother. We may be called to pay back with our lives or the lives of those close to us.'

'So I take it you did not snare the gazelles, after all.'

Rafig held up his hoops. 'The Great Spirit did not strike for us on this,' he said. After all, it has not been a very lucky evening.'

Later, before going to sleep, we heard a hullabaloo from the direction of the hyena dens. It sounded as if the *Night-Cattle* were riled up about something, I thought.

Gontar.

In the morning we returned to the site of the shooting and in the broad daylight were able to pick up hyena tracks and splotches of dried blood. Rafig measured out the first blood-spots from the place where I had fired, and, as he had said, it was about ten paces. We followed the spoor and it led us east across the salt-pans, abreast of the well, towards a rocky outcrop shrouded in acacia-bush, perhaps a thousand paces away. 'That's where their dens are,' Rafig said, pointing. 'They will be holed up there now.'

The spoor confirmed two things – first, that it really was a hyena I had shot, and second, that I had wounded her. Rafig didn't think her wound was grave, because the blood was not copious, but one couldn't be sure, as he said, and even a shallow wound might kill her in the long run.

We returned to our camp, saddled the camels, and led them out to the salt-workings, where we had lined up the packs the previous day. We maneuvered each camel between a pair of packs and couched them. The packs were too heavy for one man to lift – about a hundred and fifty kilos apiece, I guessed, making a total of about three hundred kilos per camel. This was the upper limit of a camel's carrying capacity – a rough measure the nomads referred to as a *gontar,* or *a camel- load.* Rafig called the Hermit to help us load. He had fixed poles of a wood called *inderab* between the horns of the pack saddles, so the weight of the salt would not rest directly on the camels' backs. This meant that the packs had to be lifted higher – to secure them over the pole with wooden pegs. Two men lifted a pack and pegged it, while a third man balanced the load on the other side. I understood now why Rafig had been so desperate to get someone to help him: it was hard and awkward work, even with three men, and I wondered how we would manage in the desert with only two.

Rafig was evidently worried about this also, as he asked the Hermit if he would like to accompany us as far as the Wadi al-Ma, which he estimated to be ten sleeps away. The Hermit considered the proposition. 'I can't go because I have to look after my livestock,' he said, 'but there is a nomad family whose tents are pitched not far from here – you will be there by sunset. You may ask them.'

As soon as a camel had been loaded with his two packs, we got him to his feet. Rafig explained to me that if the animal remained kneeling he would soon roll over and smash both pack and saddle. When the whole caravan was loaded, we had to get moving quickly. 'Once we start going, we don't stop,' Rafig said. 'If we stop for more than a moment the camels will sit down and roll on their packs. That would mean collecting the salt, repairing the packs, mending the saddles, and loading all over again.'

I whistled. Loading the salt packs was not something I would like to have done more than once a day, especially on an empty stomach – with our depleted food stocks and without the promised gazelle-meat, we were likely to arrive at the Wadi al-Ma half starved. Still, we gave the Hermit as much tea, dried dates and flour as we could spare, then Rafig invoked the blessing of God on him, and we led the small salt caravan off on a new stage of our journey.

Glint

We headed across a vast open plain almost the same pink hue as the rock-salt, leaving al-Gaa and its hyena-dens behind us to the north. We had changed direction, and were navigating on a whole new vocabulary of Known Places that Rafig pointed out to me as we walked. The ground alternated between sandy and stony, and the harder surface was cut by deep, meandering grooves, which Rafig told me had been made by the salt-caravans that had visited the oasis, as he put it 'not a few camels, but many, many camels, passing this way since the Distant Time.' The way was scattered with firestones, and one could clearly see places where camels had knelt down or been hobbled for the night. The tracks seemed so fresh that one could imagine the caravans that had made them a little way ahead of us, just beyond the horizon, when in fact we might have been divided from them by centuries, and the makers, humans and camels, had vanished long ago.

As the sun got up, the red surface came alive with heat haze that formed itself into strange ghost-shapes, silvery outlines, winking eyes, that, close-up, became thorn trees and low bushes like bony fingers groping out of the earth. The dust-colored surface was always tinged with a glint of mirage. There was a wind from the north that we kept on the back of our necks, and, now accustomed to the ever-changing desert surface, I followed its fine gradations with my feet. The camels seemed to gain momentum from their heavy loads, as if they were now in their real element - as if this was what they had been made for. They seemed like a flotilla of galleons that had unfurled their sheets and were bowling along in full sail ahead of the wind. They paced on as if each were mesmerized by the animal in front, their heads raised, ears pricked up, listening to the mystic rhythm of a unseen drum.

When I pointed out their new sense of determination to Rafig, he told me it was because they were going home. 'Camels know the way,' he said. 'I have seen animals lost during migrations appear at their family's tent far from where they were last seen, after many moons.'

Although I tried to stay focused on the present, the desert around me in all its living glory, my thoughts still wandered. I heard devil's voices - what Rafig called *waswasa* - in my head. In particular I could not help going over my memories of shooting the hyena, and how she had turned out to be much further away than I had judged. I remembered the Hermit's comment about being *cursed*, and although that seemed like nonsense, the thought of the wounded animal dying a painful death did trouble me. It was true, I'd had no real need to shoot her, I thought – I must have known this subconsciously as I remembered thinking that Rafig's old weapon was good enough only to make a bang. There was that feeling I had had that the hyena had waited till I was alone, and was out to get me. If I'd told Rafig about that, I was sure he would have said it was the work of a jinn, and going over it in my head, it did feel like paranoia. Then there was the Hermit, who had been friendly and hospitable, but whose attitude now struck me as odd. Why had he called hyenas *Night Cattle*? Why had he referred to their vocalizations as *music* when it was more like cat's miaowing? Why had he seemed so fascinated with them?

When I asked Rafig, he said. 'I did not tell you, but *Night-Cattle* is a name used mostly by magicians who believe that hyenas are their familiars. Cattle are livestock, like camels or goats, so *Night Cattle* suggests one controls them like livestock.'

I was stunned. 'But humans can't control hyenas, can they?'

'Only God is All-Knowing. Perhaps they can in some cases, perhaps not. The important thing is that they *believe* they can.'

'So is the Hermit a magician?'

'There are stories. He has lived alone for a very long time in the heat, the salt wind and the glare of the *Devil's Mirror*. If one stares into a mirror for a long time, one may eventually become what one sees. He has no children and never had a wife. He is not of the nomads, but not of your town people, either. He knows a great many stories, songs, poems, and much about desert lore – animal remedies and plant medicine. He says he comes from the town and was a slave once, but nothing of his original family.' He paused. 'Ah, but there are always stories about those who live alone. Perhaps the hyena is just his spirit animal. That would not be strange – we all have a special creature to guide us.'

'Really? What is yours?'

'Mine is the crow – I see him in dreams. And you? You have such a creature? '

'I don't know.' I recalled the white cat I had seen in my dream in the Nile valley – a leopard, I had thought. 'It could be a white leopard. Are there such animals?'

'Yes, but they are like your Lost Oasis – if you found it you would be very fortunate.'

Gone was the mid-day halt and the rest under our makeshift shelter of blankets and acacia poles – we could not afford to stop the caravan even for a short break. Rafig said that camels disliked travelling through the mid-day heat as much as humans did, but unloading and then loading them again would have been an overwhelming effort, even if there had been more than two of us.

Not long before sunset we came to an outcrop of rocky crags covered with caper trees – spiky green bushes twice a man's height, with foliage like tangled hair, and multiple white trunks no thicker than an arm. Some of the shoots held bunches of pink berries. Rafig told me that the nomads collected them – they were edible and sweet. Among the caper-groves were acacia thorns and a tree Rafig called *lalob* which bore a yellow-brown fruit larger than the caper berries. There were many camel and goat tracks here, as well as dried out droppings, and I wondered if this was the place where the Hermit had said we might meet some nomads. Sure enough, a figure soon appeared out of the trees – a smallish man in a desert-stained *jibba* and *sirwal*, and a multi-layered head-cloth, who lifted his hand and shouted '*Stop. Stop.*'

When we did not respond at once, he ran and plonked himself in front of us yelling '*Stop, or by God, I will divorce my wife.*'

I did not expect Rafig to stop the caravan after what he had said about the problems it would entail, but to my surprise, he did. A moment later we were shaking hands with the nomad, who had a thin, intense face, and penetrating eyes.

'Come to our tent,' he repeated over and over. 'My name is Saadig. Your coming is blest.'

Maidens

The moment the greetings were over, Rafig hauled on the lead-camel's rope again and I helped him get the caravan moving, encouraging the camels with clicking sounds. We followed Saadig across a rise into a sandy depression among the trees, where there stood a single tent of camel's hair with a brushwood shelter nearby - a coil of blue smoke issued from its grass roof. In the distance, I saw a herd of camels and a flock of sheep and goats browsing among the trees. We halted the caravan, and a youth appeared – a short, lithe, dark-skinned boy whom Saadig introduced as Zubayr.

We couched the camels and the two nomads helped us lower the heavy salt packs, remove the saddles, and lead the animals off into the bush, where we hobbled them and left them to browse among the herds. When we returned to the tent we met three women in brightly colored wraps that passed over one shoulder, leaving the other bare. They wore nose-rings, earrings and anklets, and their black hair was arranged in long braids, oiled and plaited. They were Saadig's wife, Dhuli, and two daughters. All three were of striking beauty, with bright, clever eyes, and as I shook hands with Dhuli, I remembered with a jolt that Saadig had threatened to divorce her if we did not stop at his tent. I supposed he must have been joking. Saadig showed us a place to sleep not far from the tent, where we laid out or blankets, dumped our saddle-bags, and built our usual wind-break from the pack-saddles.

When we were ready Saadig escorted us to the tent. 'Make yourselves comfortable,' he said. 'You are welcome here.'

I looked around for the youth, Zubayr, but he seemed to have vanished. The women, I noticed, were occupied in the brushwood shelter – probably cooking, I thought.

We took off our slippers at the door-gap and sat down cross-legged on the woven palmetto mats our host laid on the ground. I had not been inside a nomad tent before – the Hermit's place at al-Gaa was more a makeshift shelter than a tent – and I found it surprisingly spacious. There was a three-stone fireplace on one side and many interesting odds and ends hanging from the ceiling at the back– saddle-bags, sacks, water-skins, ornamental gourds, coffers, and beautifully worked tassels on plaited bands studded with cowrie shells. The tent itself consisted of rectangles of woven wool stitched together and stretched over a frame of poles secured with ropes to wooden pegs. As the guide Brahim had once told me, tent walls could be lifted or lowered in response to wind, rain, and sun, making the tent an extension of the landscape. It had quite a different feel from a house, which was a permanent dwelling and made to defy the land and to defend its inhabitants against nature, rather than blend into it.

Saadig and Rafig exchanged *sakanab*, and began to talk about people and clans as if scouring a mental map of nomad connections, to locate their respective places in it. 'Ah, I know you now,' Saadig said at last. 'You are the *Kahin* Rafig, and your clan waters in the Wadi al-Ma.'

Rafig smiled and nodded, and, satisfied, our host looked at me. Rafig told him that although he did not know my family, I had his countenance. '*We have eaten bread and salt,*' he said.

By way of introducing himself, Saadig mentioned the name of his own family, drew their camel-brand with a finger in the sand, and told us that his was one of the *Hurra* clans who spent their lives in the deep desert. 'We used to roam far on our migrations,' he said. 'As far west as the land of the Fish Eaters.'

'What lies beyond that land?' I asked, curious.

'Only God is All-Knowing. The desert goes on and on until one comes to *Al-Gaf*, the mountains at the end of the world, and after that there is only *al-Kharab*, the Great Abyss, and there all stories end.'

I laughed, remembering the Hermit's tale, the Wind Scorpion and the *Oasis of the Last Story*.

I was intrigued to find out if the nomads moved at random, or whether there was a pattern to their wanderings. When I mentioned this to Saadig he chortled. 'There are seasons to the rains and the grasses,' he said. 'We watch the clouds, feel the winds, and observe the stars at night – they tell us when the seasons change. Now, for example, we are waiting for the fall of the *Night Maidens*. That is the cluster of stars you see above the night horizon in these days. When the Night Maidens fall, the Hot-Hot season begins – the *Ged* - and we move south to be nearer the wells. When the *Night Maidens* rise, the time of rains begins, and we move to the desert pastures called *the Lush*.'

I noticed that Saadig never referred to years, only seasons, and it hit me again that the nomads had no numbers for the years and no dates – birthdays and specific ages meant nothing to them - humans became elders when their hair turned grey, and time was a great cycle that always came around.

'We do not go so far west as we once did,' he told us, 'because, though God is Generous, the rains have been meagre in recent times. There is less water flowing in the wadis after the rains than there used to be, and some kinds of grasses have disappeared. There were once so many spiral-horn white antelope and oryx - even ostrich – one would see them in herds. They are still around but they are fewer than in the past.'

'Yes,' Rafig nodded. 'My father told me a story of how once, dying of thirst in the *Hurra*, he came across a herd of spiral-horn white antelope – perhaps thirty of them. He said a prayer asking their forgiveness, and shot an old buck he thought must have fathered many children. He drank the water from its stomach and it saved his life. Brother White Antelope is like Sister Gazelle - while there are green plants, he can live his whole life without drinking.'

'And Sister Ostrich,' said Saadig, smiling. 'When we were children we would find ostrich eggs in great piles. We would take one egg and it was enough food for a dozen people. I remember once an ostrich chased me and my sister – the bird fixed her eye on us as if ready to kill us. We ran faster than the Wind-Scorpion and collapsed laughing when we reached our tents. Now all one finds is broken shells.'

'Ostriches are favorite birds of jinns,' Rafig commented, chuckling. 'That was probably a jinn in disguise.'

We all laughed for a moment, then it occurred to me that Saadig might know something about the white leopard in my dream.

'Have you ever seen a white leopard?' I inquired. 'Rafig tells me they are very rare.'

'Sister Leopard is a special animal,' Saadig answered, nodding. 'Very rare, very shy. Once when I was a youth, when we had made camp near Fish Eater country, I found some curious tracks, like those of Sister Hyena but narrower. I wondered what animal had made them. I followed them a long way, until they entered a cave, and I peered inside. The cave was deep and in the light through the opening I saw that the walls were covered in many pictures in red and white. I had never seen anything like them before.

'I saw that there were pictures of all manner of creatures – ostrich, spiral-horn white antelope, oryx, gazelle, and many others like giraffe and elephant whose names are known only in stories – one could easily recognize them. I would have gone in and examined them, but then I saw the leopard at the far end of the cave.

'She was a wonderful creature, not much bigger than a large dog and her skin was as white as moonlight. She raised her head and growled at me, but made no move towards me. I had my rifle with me, but she was so beautiful I could not have shot her even had she attacked. I would have rather run away, I think. Then I saw that she had a cub with her, of the same moonlight whiteness. I left them alone, but sometimes when the moon is bright, I think of that cave of many pictures, and especially I think of that leopard and her cub.'

Saadig's story was enchanting, and I felt reluctant to mention the white leopard I had seen in my dream. This talk of animals fascinated me more than anything, though. Just as I had realized at al-Gaa, the nomads lived in a world where the boundary between human and animal was not rigid – where animals were people too.

Since he was talking of distant lands and strange incidents, I asked Saadig

if he had ever heard of the Lost Oasis.

The nomad laughed and shook his head. 'The old, old stories,' he chuckled. 'Many nomads will tell you they have come across a place in the desert, where there were green trees and running water that saved their lives …'

'Yes,' Rafig cut in. 'My father had that experience too.'

'…yet that place can never be found again, no matter how hard one looks. There are many places where my clan pitched their tents, deep in the *Hurra*, for instance - places I remember as rich pastures, with trees, water-pools, flying creatures, and crawling creatures, that are now barren and devoid of green. One returns and they are simply gone. The face of the desert changes always. I wonder - is that what is meant by *lost*?'

'I don't know,' I said.

At that moment the youth Zubayr staggered in with a tin tray laden with polenta doused in camel's milk and the savory-smelling meat of a goat slaughtered in our honor. He laid it down in the sand before us and Saadig said, 'In the name of God, let's eat.'

Kin

We ate in silence, pulling the joints of meat apart with our hands and teeth, rolling polenta into balls with our fingers. Whenever any of us showed signs of stalling, our host would cry '*Eat. Eat.* Is there something wrong with this food? It comes with the blessing of the Great Spirit!'

When we were finally finished and could eat no more, Zubayr took the tray, while we went outside and Saadig poured water on our hands from a spouted jug. It was already getting dark, and the camels were no longer visible in the shadows of the trees. Rafig looked uneasy, but Saadig told him that the animals were safe here, and suggested that we bring them in later. Zubayr came back from the brushwood shelter with a kettle and glasses, and we went back into the tent to drink tea.

Saadig kindled a fire for light and warmth. As we sat sipping our tea, and the others talked, I thought about hospitality. Among the nomads, I saw, it was a right rather than a privilege – something that was expected. Not to demand it shamed the host because it made him seem unworthy. That was why Saadig had threatened to divorce his wife, I realized – he was demonstrating the degree to which our refusal threatened his honor. To offer something in return would have been equally a disgrace – it was not a negotiation, and nomad reciprocity operated on a much wider level. Today we ate at Saadig's tent, and tomorrow Saadig might eat at someone else's tent, and receive the same treatment. We, in turn, would welcome guests into our camp and offer them the best we had. Saadig might not see us again after this night, but his gift would be passed around to whoever needed it, even if those people were complete strangers – though, of course, to the nomads there were really no strangers - all Adam's Children were of God's Face.

I realized that I had drifted off again, and was trying to focus on the conversation, when I realized suddenly that Rafig and Zubayr were speaking in a language I did not recognize - not Arabic, but something else. I looked at Rafig, astonished.

'What is that?' I asked when there was a pause in their dialogue.

Rafig gave me an apologetic glance. 'That is Fish Eater language,' he said. 'Zubayr here is a Fish Eater.'

'We call ourselves *Tu*,' Zubayr cut in, laughing. 'That means *kin* in your tongue. I came here on a lame camel from *Tu* country looking for work as a herdsboy. By the will of God I found Saadig here, who was ready to take me on.'

'Really?' I said, intrigued. I had assumed that the so-called Fish Eaters were somehow the deadly enemies of the nomads – the *Others*. Now I realized that, if there were no clear-cut boundaries between humans and animals, there could be no rigid barriers between tribes either.

'How come *you* know the language?' I asked Rafig.

'It is no secret that I am half Fish Eater myself,' he said. 'My father was of the *Tu*. He came into nomad country long ago, looking for work as a herdsboy – just like Zubayr. My grandfather took him on and he worked in return for the gift of she-camels, until he had built up a herd of his own. That is the way it goes among us - after all, camels are a gift of the Great Spirit and, though they are in our safe-keeping, they do not belong to us – how can anyone really own a living being? It is our duty to share the gift. My grandfather had several daughters, my mother amongst them. My father married her, and was adopted into the clan. I was their first-born and have two younger brothers and a sister. My father was proud to be a nomad, but never forgot he was also of the *Tu*. He taught me their language, and initiated me in the *Sandlines*. I was tested, and they said I had the right temperament for it, thanks to the Great Spirit. So I became a *kahin*.'

'*Wow*,' I said. 'You never told me that.'

'It is not really important. Fish Eaters, nomads – and you of the town - all of us are the Children of Adam, just the same.'

Stars

Afterwards, we went out in the starlight to fetch the camels. We had removed their hobbles and were driving them back to our resting place when I noticed the stars. There were so many – more than I had ever dreamed of. The very fabric of the night seemed slashed in two by a wide scar like the bubbling contents of a cauldron, with threads of light emanating from it glowing ruby-red and blue, hurling out spangles and necklaces of stars. I realized it must be the Milky Way, though I had never seen it like this before. Rafig called it the *Ram's Trail* – and pointed out several constellations I did not know, including *Coney Night Caller* the *Fish of Stories*, the *Cow*, and the *Wise Tortoise*. None of these seemed to correspond to the constellations I had been familiar with before the desert, although I knew *Shadad the Hunter* was Orion and the *Jadi* – the *Gazelle Calf* – was the North Star.

I was still star-gazing when Rafig froze and touched me on the arm.

'*Look*,' he hissed. '*There.*'

I was aware of movement in the dark shadows among the bushes. We both stared into the darkness and I listened carefully, turning my ear towards the movement with my mouth open, the way I had learned in the army. There was a faint rustle and a hardly-discernable grumble of breath – the sense that some large animal was moving about there among the caper trees. At first, I thought it must be a camel or perhaps a stray goat or sheep from Saadig's flocks. I remembered that he and Zubayr had already brought them in. On impulse, I took my torch out of my pocket, switched it on, and scanned the shadows. In the instant before Rafig shook his head, and I switched it off, I caught the reflection of burning red eyes, gleaming at us out of the darkness.

'*Hyena*,' Rafig said in an urgent whisper, 'No God but God, it has followed us here.'

He was carrying his rifle over his shoulder, but he did not unsling it. Instead we continued to drive the camels on until we reached our camping place. We settled and hobbled them in a semi-circle front of the wall of saddles, so that our sleeping space lay enclosed between the two half-circles. As we sat down on our blankets a few moments later, a low but distinct panting sound reached my ears - *ughh, ughh, ughh*. A chill ran down my spine. I was thinking I might have imagined it, when I saw Rafig sitting very still, staring back at me.

'It is far,' he said in a low voice.

'How could hyenas follow us?' I whispered. 'What does that mean?'

Rafig looked as if he were about to say something, then bit his lip, and shook his head.

I did not sleep well that night. Every time the camels stirred or shifted I opened my eyes and sat up. I thought Rafig was deep asleep until, at one point, he said. 'You no longer sleep the sleep of the donkey. That is good.'

She-camel.

As we drank tea with Sadig and Zubayr next morning, Rafig asked casually if there were any hyenas in the area.

'Not here,' Saadig said, 'but there are hyenas at al-Gaa. Did you not encounter them?'

'Yes, we did,' Rafig replied. I realized suddenly that he had left this part of our experience out of the *sakanab*, and I wondered why.

'Strange man the Hermit,' Saadig said, chuckling. 'Living there alone with those hyenas. You would almost think that he was one of them.'

Rafig and I laughed with him.

'Do you believe in the *Hyena People*?' I asked.

'God is All-Knowing,' he said, 'but people can become like animals, I do know that.'

Rafig and I were waiting for Saadig or Zubayr to mention hearing hyena-voices in the night, but neither did.

After breakfast of bread and dates, Rafig asked if Zubayr would accompany us on the salt-caravan, as far as Wadi al-Ma. We would be there in ten sleeps, he said. Saadig replied that he could ill spare the herdsboy but was expecting his sons back from a scouting expedition shortly, and would let him go if the youth so wished. Rafig offered Zubayr three fat ewes or a camel-calf from his own herds in return for the work, and the Fish Eater boy agreed. He went off at once to fetch his camel and gear.

Meanwhile, Saadig asked Rafig if he would throw the *Sandlines* for him. 'We lost a she-camel early in the season,' he explained. 'She wandered away. We set out to follow her, and a storm blew up and covered her tracks. She's a *tanya* – a two-tooth – and flighty. Could you find out where she is? God knows, perhaps she is dead.'

Rafig agreed. He washed his hands from a bowl of water, dried them, smoothed out the sand in front of him, sat still with his eyes closed for a moment, then began chanting what sounded like a rhythmic refrain, in a voice too low for me to pick up the words. His voice oscillated strangely, as I remembered from Elai, rising and falling in volume. After a moment he opened his eyes and began making marks in the sand with his fingertips. When he had finished, he surveyed the marks, making more in two squares he had drawn in the sand. Saadig and I looked on in silence. After a while, Rafig sighed, sat back, and said. 'The she-camel is alive. She was found by travelers, who took her with them. They have made camp near the *Beetle*' He paused. 'That is a hill not far from our way to the Wadi al-Ma, about five sleeps south of here.'

Saadig nodded gravely. 'God reward you. As Zubayr is with you, he can identify her – he knows her tracks and how she is branded. He will collect her, and you can take her with your caravan.'

A momentary shadow crossed Rafig's face, as if he felt Saadig's proposition might bring trouble. Then it was gone. 'Of course, God willing,' he said.

'Did the *Sandlines* tell you who took the she-camel?' Saadig asked.

'Fish-Eaters,' said Rafig.

Eagle

Despite the fact that we now had a third pair of hands, the following days were the hardest I remember. We would be up in the crisp cold of dawn, and as the camels usually foraged by night, we would have to walk a long way to find them and bring them back. Loading the rock-salt was the day's great effort. Two of us would lift a pack, and while a third strained to keep it in place, the other two raced round to the opposite side and lifted the second pack, pegging the two packs across the saddle-bar. It had to be done fast, because keeping the first pack in place was perilous - often the camel would jib and jostle and try to get up, and if so it was almost impossible to hold the load steady. If the pack dropped it might mean a crushed foot, so one had to leap out of the way and let it smash open on the ground. That caused a delay, with the laden camels threatening to roll over, and the unladen ones leaping up with their eyes on more grazing, while we picked up the scattered lumps of salt, repaired the broken pack, stuffed the salt back in, and stitched it up.

Once we got the caravan moving, we could not stop for a moment, though in the first days there seemed to be endless interruptions when ropes came loose, or bits of equipment fell off, and one of us would have to jog back to find them. The days were hot, and marching through the inferno of noon without a break was hard on men and camels. Day after day the *Hurra* opened up before us like pages of a book, each day a different world, breathtakingly vast, achingly strange - glistering plains, and silvery sand-sheets, and rugged ridges, dunes like serried overlays that shimmered mauve, pink and purple, and stumps and knolls and chocolate hills, carved and battered, boulder graveyards and thorn-clad dry-washes, and hills that were stacks of stones and scatters of debris that might have fallen from the sky. The caravan gusted on under full sail, dwarfed by the vast dimensions, reduced to a broken necklace of pearls on the great deck of contours, breasting endless horizons, bowling along through long strands of hard-packed sand, patches of gravelly sand, places where it was more stony than sandy, places where it was very stony, places where the sand was soft, and the camels' pads sunk in.

I learned from Rafig and Zubayr that there were words for every nuance, every shape and texture of rock, hill, and mountain – a round-topped hill, a hill with a sharp peak, a volcanic plug, a double cone, When Rafig described Known Places, his language conveyed a rich stream of images that enabled me to see and feel the landscape as a sensory map.

The way was also a map of stories, of the animals and plant communities that lived here – there were camel-tracks and man tracks, and the droppings and spoor of crawling people, four-leggeds, flying people, were everywhere. Mostly I walked at the head of the caravan next to Rafig, while Zubayr brought up the rear. One of the most memorable occurrences of those first few days out of Saadig's camp, was when, passing through an area of undulating sand and tussock-grass, Rafig pointed out a tawny eagle circling high above us. At first she was no bigger than a black dot, increasing in size as she dropped lower and lower out of the cloudless sky, until I could see her golden brown form, wingtips spread like fingers, and the sunlight on her talons, gliding, dropping slowly, then suddenly swooping to Earth in an action of dreadful certainty, and rising again with a four-legged drooping in her claws.

'A wide-eared fox,' Rafig exclaimed.

'*Wow,*' I said, watching the bird climbing steadily, balancing her burden, the great wings stirring and angling as she strove to touch the air-currents, circling again and gliding into a downward curve far away.

Rafig thought for a moment, then without breaking pace, or letting go the lead-camel's head rope, he chanted:

> '*On the wing she spies Brother Fox far below,*
>
> *Between them the desert and the sky.*
>
> *She drops, then in a swoop, long and low*
>
> *She glides towards him from on high,*
>
> *As he, caught in the open sees her shadow*
>
> *And, spellbound by her fiery eye,*
>
> *Raises his tail, spreads his ears wide,*
>
> *Frozen, knowing not where to hide*
>
> *While she in one swift movement, has her talons in his side,*
>
> *And rising into the sun, her plumes all aglow,*
>
> *Bears him off to her eyrie with exultant cry.'*

I stared at Rafig incredulously, stunned by his vivid words and musical rhymes - I guessed he must have put them together almost instantly. 'Did you just make that up?' I asked, 'or is it a song you knew already?'

'I know many songs,' he said, 'but they would not do, because every event is different – I mean, similar, perhaps, but not the same.'

'Is this part of being a *kahin*?'

'We call this singing *dobbayt*. It comes from the same source as the *Sandlines*, of course. It is not a special gift – among the nomads both men and women compose *dobbayt*. When one sings that song the words mould the landscape and show us the way. Thereafter I will remember this happened here, and the land will remember, and when I see that crag over there…' He indicated a hogs-back ridge to the east. '…that will be called *Eagle Swoop*, and it will become a Known Place, at least to me, and now to you also. If ever you pass this way again, you will see this place, and remember the eagle and the fox, and my words, and it will come alive for you.'

It was only then that I began to glimpse, if dimly, how the nomads brought forth the landscape together through language, how the landscape was not separate from them, but alive as they were alive, and how there was no landscape without the knowing of it, and this knowing they had created with each other and with Earth Mother in all her aspects, since the Distant Time. The desert was cradled in their words and their words were their knowing, and so the desert they saw and felt was an ever changing work they shaped together in their songs and stories.

Midday Brightness

When we halted the caravan around sunset that day, I was so hungry, thirsty and exhausted I felt like flinging myself down into the sand and not getting up, but this was the time for the most intense burst of toil. The first job was to run along the line helping each camel to sit down, then knee-hobble the animals with hobbling loops. This meant excavating a small tunnel under the camel's left foreleg, threading the loop through, pegging it on top. All the time the creatures were shifting, groaning, and rumbling, anxious to get the weight off their backs.

The next thing was to unload the salt-packs. Though this was not as hard as loading them, it was still difficult and had its risks, as the camel might jump at the crucial moment, just as the pegs were being removed. Again we had to work fast, before the camels got fed up with waiting and decided to roll over.

Once the pairs of salt packs were laid out on the ground, we released the knee-hobbles, and the animals stood up, clicking teeth, stretching, snapping. We led them clear of the camp, applied foreleg hobbles, removed the head-ropes, and trudged back. By that time the camels were shuffling away. There was no point keeping them near us as there was no grazing by our camp – we had to trust that they would not wander too far.

It was already dark. Zubayr filled a wooden bowl with water and offered it to Rafig, who refused and offered it to me. I refused and offered it to Zubayr, who refused, and offered it to Rafig. I thought the old man might refuse a second time, and the bowl would continue going from hand to hand all night, while we stared at the water, parched with thirst, but unable to drink. In fact, we had to go through this ritual every time we drank, because, though Rafig was the eldest, it was not done among the nomads to claim precedence, even under extreme conditions. This time, however, he gave in and drank, which meant we could all drink our fill.

Of all nomad customs, this endless deference over water seemed the least appropriate to the conditions. When I tentatively asked Rafig about it, he said.

'There is a story about that – Swaylim and Zabib. Have you heard it?'

'No,' I said.

He and Zubayr regarded me gravely. 'Let me tell it,' Zubayr said, after a moment. He composed himself, then began.

'There were once two nomads - Swaylim and Zabib - who were travelling to a place in the *Hurra*, when their water ran out. After a while they decided to slaughter one of the camels and drink the water from its stomach. They did not want to do it, but it was the only way, so after many prayers and supplications, they slaughtered the camel and drank its stomach water. I have never drunk it myself, but I know people who have, and they say it tastes like vomit. It eased their thirst, but not for very long, and soon they had to slaughter the second camel and drink its gut-water also. That gave them momentary relief, but it did not last, and now there were no more camels to slaughter.

'They continued walking and after a while Swaylim collapsed and could not get up. 'Leave me here,' he told Zabib, 'and you go on and find water.'

'Very well,' Zabib said, 'but I swear by the Sun and his Midday Brightness and by the Lady Moon that follows, as we have eaten bread and salt together, if I find water I shall not drink till you drink'

So Zabib left him and staggered on alone until he reached a wadi, where he saw a camel grazing. He mounted the camel bareback, and it took him to a nomad camp. There was a woman there, and as soon as he saw her, he fell off the camel. The woman fetched a nomad called Durays, who came to Zabib and offered him water. Even though he was dying of thirst, Zabib refused to drink.

'I have sworn by the Sun and his Midday Brightness and by the Lady Moon that follows,' he said, 'not to drink till my friend Swaylim has drunk.'

'Where is your friend Swaylim?'

'He is lying in the desert south of here.'

'Then I will find him.'

Then Durays saddled a camel and followed Zabib's tracks until he found Swaylim, who was still alive. He offered him water, but Swaylim asked.

'Has my friend Zabib drunk? Because I swear by the Sun and his Midday Brightness and the Lady Moon that follows, that I will not drink till he has drunk. '

Durays knew that both nomads would die unless he took the burden of honour on himself.

'Yes,' he said. 'Your friend Zabib has drunk.'

'Ah,' Swaylim said. 'Since he has done so, I can drink. Give me the water.'

When he had drunk, the nomad put Swaylim on his camel and took him back to the camp, where Zabib was waiting.

When Zabib saw Swaylim he asked, 'have you drunk?'

'Yes,' said Daud, 'because Durays told me you had drunk.'

112

'Ah,' Zabib said. 'That was not true, for I kept my oath. Since you have drunk, though, I can also drink.'

So Zabib drank and both were saved, and their honour was also saved, by Durays who took the burden of honour on himself.'

The story made me laugh. It was honour taken to a ludicrous level. Yet it brought home just how seriously the nomads regarded the sanctity of companionship, and how important they considered their good names – they would rather die than give in to precedence, which is why, though one was dying of thirst, the drinking bowl might be passed round all night.

It was a good story, and it served its purpose, I thought.

Fox Woman

Zubayr brought firewood from the stock we carried, while Rafig found stones for the hearth, set them up, and twirled his fire-sticks. I filled a kettle from one of our water-skins, as there was no convenient tree, we had hung them from Rafig's tripod. We could not leave water-bags on the ground as, seeking the warmer earth, the water would seep out through the porous skin. Flames flared up suddenly in the hearth, the firelight reflected for a moment on the nomad's faces, and there it was – this place in the desert, not so different from any other place, had become *our* place, and our centre of the universe for this night. As Brahim had told me that first night with the herd, the fire was the hub of the world, and our world fanned out like ripples in concentric circles from this hearth, as far as the line where the smoke could no longer be detected – and that was the limit between our camp and the wild.

The kettle steamed, and when we drew in round the fire, the sky was full of stars so near and vivid I felt I could touch them. The whole weight of the heavens seemed to be dipping down on us, flotillas of brilliant sparkles and spangles, all of them people, all of them voices talking to us, and the dark velveteen veil of the cosmos, spanned once again by the folds of the *Ram's Trail,* and tonight inhabited by the recumbent gold form of Lady Moon.

Zubayr had seen the eagle earlier, but, at the back of the caravan, he had not heard Rafig's *dobbayt.* I asked the old man to repeat it for his benefit, and he did so, to Zubayr's pleasure. 'Ah,' the youth said at last, 'but the eagle was the friend of the wide-eared fox when he wanted to steal fire from the Giants, wasn't she? Did she not rescue him from their clutches?'

'That was in the Distant Time,' Rafig laughed. 'All animals were friends then, or could be if they chose, and humans and animals could become each other and spoke the same language. Anyway, it was a falcon.'

'Yes,' Zubayr nodded, but among my people – our people - it is well known that foxes can become humans. There was a man, for example, who once went in search of a stray camel in the desert…'

'Always a stray camel …' I cut in.

'… anyway, he took no food with him and soon became hungry. One evening he set a hoop-snare near his sleeping place, and in the morning he found a wide-eared fox with her leg caught in the snare. He was tempted to kill and eat the fox, but she was so small and beautiful that he could not do it, despite his hunger. Instead, he let her go.

'He did not find his lost camel, so he returned to his camp …'

'Do Fish-Eaters have tents like nomads?' I cut in again.

'No, they are made from palmetto strands and grass, not camel's hair … but do not interrupt …'

'Sorry.'

'So the man saw from afar that there was smoke coming from his camp, which was odd because he lived alone and had no wife. When he arrived, he found a lovely young woman there – a stranger who had black eyes with no pupils, and long bushy hair. As soon as he arrived, she brought him a plate of goat's meat, which he ate gratefully. When he had finished eating, he asked. 'Which is your clan and how come you are here?'

'Then the young woman asked him. 'Was the meat good?'

'Yes it was good, may God be blessed.'

'Then do not ask about my clan, or how I came here. If ever I am gone, do not follow my tracks, for I will surely return to you. Promise me, and I will be a good and loyal wife.'

So he promised, and they became man and wife, and they were happy together, and the goats flourished and the camels grew fat, and gave more milk than they could drink. Still, the man could not help being curious about his wife with the black eyes that had no pupils. She had a mark on her leg, he noticed, like the mark of a hoop-snare, and sharp, white teeth. Sometimes she could not sleep at night for, as she said, "I can hear the ants moving about in their tunnels beneath us – their voices are so loud." The man could not hear the ants at all, and realized that her hearing must be acute.

One night – it was the night of the full moon – the man awoke and found the woman gone. He looked for her tracks and saw that they led off into the desert. Forgetting his promise, he began to follow them in the bright moonlight, and after a time, he saw that they entered a small burrow. He watched the burrow for a long time, and, near morning, saw a wide-eared fox emerge, looking exactly like the one he had caught in the trap while following his lost camel.

He was so startled that he ran back to his camp, only to find his wife had arrived there before him. She was in tears. 'You have broken your promise,' she said. 'Had you trusted me, had you not followed my tracks, I would have remained with you always, and been a good and loyal wife to you.'

'She turned and walked into the desert. This time the man did not follow her - he knew he would never find her again.

'The next day a stray camel arrived in his camp. It was the animal he had been tracking long before, when he had come across the wide-eared fox. 'I am happy to see you, old friend,' he told the camel, 'but I would have been happier had I not, through my own fault, lost the beautiful creature I found when looking for you."

Rafig and I laughed and nodded. 'That is a good story,' Rafig said, 'but did you know this man?'

'No, only that he was one of our people.'

'Ah but is it not strange that he lived alone, apart from his clan?'

'Yes,' said Zubayr, 'he was probably a hermit or a *faki* – a holy man. There are many among the Fish-Eaters.'

'Such things are more likely to happen to hermits or *fakis* than others,' Rafig said, and I could see he was thinking about the Hermit at al-Gaa. It reminded me that I had hardly thought of the hyena since we had left Saadig's camp.

Later that night, though, I awoke suddenly to the sound of a chittering, chuckling call, and sat up sharply.   I sensed movement, and switching on my torch, I caught the faintest hint of red eyes lurking in the darkness. I felt a sudden prickling of the scalp, and a chill went down my spine. When I shone the torch-beam directly at the eyes, though, they vanished. I sat there for a long time in the darkness, watching and listening, but there was nothing more.

As we set off on foot to fetch the camels next morning, I told Rafig what had happened in the night. 'Perhaps it was a jinn,' I said.

A little farther on, the old man showed me some tracks cut clearly into the sand. 'Jinns leave donkey-tracks,' he said. 'These could be a dog, but there are no dogs without humans. They look more like hyena-tracks to me.'

Beetle

That morning we came across tracks of another kind - a wide swath of camel-tracks from a small herd that Rafig thought was moving south ahead of us. The old man handed me the head-rope, and went to inspect them. I kept the caravan moving, and when I looked back a moment later, both Rafig and Zubayr were crouching over the tracks, pointing and conversing animatedly. I knew Rafig was an expert tracker - like the best nomad trackers, he could remember the track of every camel he had ever seen. Although my observation had come on in leaps and bounds since I had first travelled with Brahim, I was not in the same league as Rafig, or even Zubayr.   I did know that when fresh, camel-tracks displayed a complex pattern of ridges as distinctive as a human fingerprint. The detail diminished with passing days and changing weather, and was eventually erased, leaving an oval frame and the imprints of two prominent toes. In sand, the wind wiped away these ovals quite quickly, but in gravel they could remain for ages.

I kept the caravan going, and in a short while the others ran to catch up with me. 'Those are Fish-Eater camels,' Rafig declared, breathlessly. 'They were grazing around here, and they have been taken back to *the Beetle.*

'How do you know that?'

'The *Beetle* is a Known Place – we will be there before sunset. I saw it in the *Sandlines* as the place where Saadig's she-camel was being herded by Fish Eaters ...'

'And the she-camel is there,' Zubayr cut in excitedly. 'I recognized her tracks among the others. It is just as Rafig said.'

'What will you do then?' I inquired.

'Ask the Fish-Eaters to give her back.'

Rafig took the head-rope and adjusted the course of the caravan until he had brought it in line with the Fish-Eater tracks. We followed the trail for a while until it veered off southwest. Rafig pointed out a round-topped knoll in that direction, which he said was the *Beetle,* and we shifted the caravan again and headed directly towards it.

We came to the Fish-Eater camp half way through the afternoon, when the sun was already drifting down through fans of slate-coloured dust. The stony surface tipped towards the serpent of a wadi that meandered across the desert, passing beneath the hump of a bare black hill, that, looked at in a certain way, I thought, might possibly have resembled a gigantic beetle. The wadi-banks were clad in fair-sized *heraz* acacias, and, some distance to the south, there were stands of grasses that Rafig identified even from this distance as *samn* and *hallif,* where a score of camels were grazing. The animals shuffled around, lowering their great heads amid the tufts, while two men watched them. Nearer to us, smoke rose in a pencil-line from a fire burning in a camp under the trees. Two more men were moving about there, building up a heap of firewood – tall, lean figures in dust-coloured *jibbas,* with smooth faces and tangled plumes of curly hair.

Although the men had clearly seen us, they did not come to greet us, but simply watched as we couched our camels and lowered the heavy salt-packs. This was not discourtesy, Rafig commented, but simply because the men were also travellers. They had no womenfolk and no tents – for them this was just a temporary camp.

When we had finished unloading, we turned the camels out to graze, and went to meet them. They seemed friendly enough, and welcomed us to the fire where we sat down to exchange news. The *Tu* speaker, a dark man with a head like a creased basalt block, heavy brow ridges, and eyes that were wide and alert, told us he was called Atman. His companion, a much smaller man – almost a miniature version of Atman – was called Hatim. I noticed that both carried rifles similar to Rafig's but of a different style, and, rather than arm-daggers, both wore curved knives on broad leather belts at their waists.

'I see at least one of you is of the *Tu*,' Atman commented, gesturing to our camels. 'Either that or you have acquired a *Tu* camel.'

I remembered that Zubayr's camel carried the so-called fish brand of his people – actually two curved lines joining at the top and overlapping at the bottom. The camel was some distance away, though, and I marvelled at the Fish Eaters' eyesight.

Rafig and Zubayr exchanged a glance, and I recalled that they had had a discussion, partly in *Tu*, as to if they should reveal themselves to the Fish Eaters, and whether this would be an advantage.

Zubayr laughed, nodded, and began to speak in *Tu*, and soon he and the Fish-Eaters were involved in a lively discussion. Rafig did not join in. He kept his face impassive, and as he did not much resemble our hosts physically, I doubted they would guess he was half-Fish Eater. The talk went on and on, and by the time they switched back to Arabic, they all looked pleased, as if they had discovered some mutual connection.

'These men are distant cousins on my mother's side,' Zubayr announced, smiling. 'Their family is from Oyo, a great mountain with many valleys and caves and forests of a tree called *tarout*.'

'Wasn't *tarout* the tree in the story of how the wide-eared fox stole fire?' I asked. 'The one that grew near the Fire Mountain?'

The others laughed, and Atman nodded. 'If the Great Spirit wills, we shall travel back there now. God has not struck for us in nomad country. We came here because the rains have been poor in *Tu*, and found that they have been even worse here.'

'God is Generous,' Rafig said. 'How many sleeps will it take you to get there, and in which direction does it lie?'

'If one heads northwest from here for seventeen sleeps, one comes across a place of palm-trees called *Bitter Pool* in our tongue. From there it is seven sleeps to Oyo, heading northwest, but the way is hard and waterless, across a plain called *at-Tiih*, the *Plain of Straying,* and a maze of dunes we call the *Labyrinth of Sand*. On the south side of Oyo lies another empty expanse called the *Plain of Forgetting*. If one does not know the way, Oyo is hard to approach.'

'The *Plain of Forgetting* is familiar,' Rafig said.

'Isn't that also from the story of the fox stealing fire?' I cut in. 'The plain where travellers lose their memory and lay down to die in the desert.'

'Well, perhaps it is the same one,' Rafig chuckled.

'Have you ever been there?' Atman asked.

'No, but I once knew someone who had.'

Atman and Hatim exchanged a glance, and I knew Rafig had said something they regarded as significant. Atman looked around, and I followed his gaze. Some way to our left, the other two Fish-Eaters had gathered the camels together, and were driving them slowly towards us. We all watched in silence as the animals glided through the last of the afternoon light, their elongated shadows floating beside them across a surface turned liquid amber. In a short while the men were halting them some way from the camp. I saw Zubayr squinting at them with narrowed eyes, no doubt trying to make out Saadig's lost she-camel among them, though the distance was too far, I thought. Once all the camels were hobbled, the two men came over to shake hands, then sat down with Atman and Hatim, facing us. I noticed that both of them carried one-shot rifles, which meant the Fish-Eaters had four weapons to our one – and Rafig hadn't even brought his rifle over.

'Now,' Atman said, dropping his friendly manner. 'You say you are taking your rock salt to nomads in the Wadi al-Ma. I know that is where your people water their animals, but it lies due south, not in this direction. Your caravan is heavily laden, so you must have had a good reason for leaving the way. Perhaps you will tell us what it is.'

I suddenly noticed that all four Fish-Eaters had their hands on their rifles. They were gazing at us intently. My scalp prickled and my heart started to thump. There was a constriction in my throat and a hollowness in my stomach that was familiar, but which I hadn't experienced for a long while. We were a hair's breadth away from a confrontation, I felt, and the way things were stacked, it was unlikely that we would come out of it well.

Two-Tooth

For a moment there was no sound but the camels rumbling and the fire crackling. Then Rafig laughed, so loud it made me jump. 'Of course,' he chuckled. 'I should have known. There are many *kahins* among the *Tu*, are there not? My father was one, after all.'

'Your father?' Atman said, and a look of understanding came into his eyes. 'Yes, my father was of the *Tu.*'

'Ah. It was he who told you of the *Plain of Forgetting*. That name is known only to us.'

'The *Sandlines* showed you?' Rafig asked.

'It showed me that there were three men coming, a red stranger…' He glanced at me. '… and two of our kin. We discovered a connection with Zubayr, but you did not commit yourself, even though I guessed that, when we were speaking *Tu*, you understood our talk.'

Rafig smiled. 'The *Tu* language and the *Sandlines* are gifts my father left me – may the mercy of God be upon him.'

'And no doubt the skill to cast the sand, also,' Atman said. 'The ability to see is not given to everyone– only those in whom the influence of the jinn is not strong.'

'Every man and woman may cast the sand,' Rafig said, 'but not all can read it well.'

'So,' Atman said, nodding. 'Tell us why you are here, and I will tell you whether *I* have read it well.'

'You have a she-camel,' Rafig said, '- a two-tooth - that you found in the desert, perhaps a moon ago. This young man …' he nodded at Zubayr … 'your distant relative, is a herder in the camp of the owner of this she-camel, and we have come to ask for her, on his behalf.'

Atman said something in *Tu*, and this time Rafig responded in the same language. They conversed for a while and I guessed they were trying to find some mutual connection as Atman and Zubayr had done previously. At one point I heard the name Barak mentioned, and remembered that this was Rafig's father's kinsman, who had been found in the desert by the Fish Eaters, and had stayed with them. When they finally changed back to Arabic, our hosts seemed more at ease.

'I will tell you what happened,' Atman said. 'About one moon past, when the Lady Moon was starting to wane, there came a sudden storm from the south, unexpected in this season. We were grazing our camels near al-Gaa at the time. The storm began in the morning and lasted all day. When it finished we picked up the tracks of a lone she-camel heading west, and joked that she must have escaped from humans, and was making her way to the *Night Camels*. We decided to follow her trail, and after a while we caught up with her. We saw that she was only a two-tooth, not yet mature, and that she bore a nomad brand. We did not know which clan, and as her tracks had been swallowed by the storm, we could not retrace them.'

'It is true,' Zubayr said. 'I lost her tracks in the storm.'

'We were not sure what to do with her,' Atman went on, 'but in the end we decided to take her with us. That way she would be in our safe-keeping until someone came to look for her, as we knew they would.'

Rafig guffawed and Atman seemed slightly offended. 'She was but a two-tooth,' he protested. 'She had no milk, and was not ready for breeding, so it was no great advantage to us to take her.'

'You had no obligation either to leave her or to take her,' said Rafig. 'So your decision was just.'

'God is generous,' Hatim cut in, 'but how can you be sure she is the animal you are looking for?'

'She was my charge,' Zubayr said, 'and I know her well. She has a lizard-brand on her left flank ...' He pointed to his right cheek. '... and a circle ... here. She also has a fresh scar on her withers, where she had an abscess, and we treated her with a hot iron.'

Atman exchanged a glance with Hatim. 'God is All-Knowing,' he said. 'She is the one.'

Later, we walked together to the Fish-Eater herd. Zubayr picked out a slim-legged, brownish-coloured she-camel without being told, and when he released her from her hobble, she warbled and nuzzled him affectionately – it was clear that she knew him. We stood round while Atman and Rafig checked that her brands and marks corresponded with what Zubayr had said. When that was agreed, Atman handed her over. Taking her with us, we went to collect our own animals, and brought them back to our camp. By then, the desert had turned plum-coloured as the sun touched the distant horizon and seemed to break like a gilded egg-yolk spreading light along the edge of the world. Then even that last remnant faded and Lady Moon rose and the night was soft blue and luminous with the slow sailing-boats of the stars.

Night Camels

When we returned to the Fish Eater camp, the fire was blazing, and Atman called us over to eat polenta with sour camel's milk. Afterwards, we sat together by the fire and the Fish Eaters served us tea.

'Tell me,' I said to Atman. 'You said you joked that the she-camel was heading for the camp of the *Night Camels*. What does that mean?'

'You know that when camels stray from their human keepers, they almost always return,' Atman said. 'They feel happy when they are with the Children of Adam, who water them and feed them when they are hungry. There are a few who do not, who long for the freedom of the desert. If they get a chance to escape they do not return, but find their way eventually to the camp of the *Night Camels,* in the desert.'

'That's a good story,' I said, 'but it's just a story, isn't it?'

Atman sighed. 'One must judge for oneself. Once, long ago, when I was a youth like Zubayr here, I had a strange experience. A male camel strayed from our herd and I set off on foot to track him down. I followed his tracks for three sleeps, and by the third sunset I was tired, thirsty, and hungry. For some time I had felt as if I was not alone - as if someone was watching me. Then - Lady Moon was as bright as she is tonight - I noticed a man standing in front of me. As I came near, I saw it was an old man dressed in animal-skins. His face was wizened and weathered, and he had large eyes, drooping lips, and a fat, red tongue that kept flopping from his mouth. He invited me to go to his camp, and though I understood his talk, his voice was like the blubbering of an old bull camel. I followed him and noticed that, although he was wearing skin slippers, the tracks he left in the sand were those of a camel.

'When we arrived at his camp, I was surprised to see lamps blazing trails between many tents, and camp-fires, with dozens of men, women and children gathered around them. The old man took me to his tent, where his wife sat by a fire. She was a beautiful woman, with braided hair, a long neck, and fine eyelashes. When the old man spoke to her, though, she answered in a warbling voice, like the voice of a she-camel. She showed me a place to sleep and brought me a bowl of food, which I realized was bitter *arak* leaves. It tasted all right, but afterwards I found I could no longer remember the names of my wife and children, and even why I had come there. Later, I went to sleep in the place they had shown me, but in the night I was woken up by a young man.

"Do you know me?" he asked – and his voice sounded like the rumbling of a young camel. "I am he whose tracks you were following – the one who strayed from your herd."

Then I remembered why I was there.

'Will you not come back with me?' I asked him.

He shook his head. "I will not return," he said, "for I am of the *Night Camels* now. As for you, though, you must leave, or you will forget everything and become as we are. You do not belong here."

'So I got up quickly and left the camp of the *Night Camels* and walked back to the shelters of my people, arriving hungry and exhausted after three sleeps. When I got there, they were amazed to see me. "You have been away for a whole moon," they said. "We were beginning to think God had taken you unto God." By my reckoning, though, I had only been away for six sleeps.'

Atman paused and looked round at us, his face half in shadow, half illuminated by the firelight. 'That was what happened, as the Great Spirit is my witness, though whether it was a dream or not I cannot tell.'

'It does not matter,' Rafig said. 'For encounters in dreams are also encounters in the world.'

I sat up suddenly. I had been enthralled by the story, but what Rafig had said set me thinking of my dream in the Nile Valley – the white leopard and the voice saying, *the animals will show you the Lost Oasis. They will heal you for you are animal and one of us.* It was after that dream that I had gone to see the storyteller Maya, and she had told me her tale about the Lost Oasis, which in a way was eerily similar to the tale Atman had just told us. It was as if I had just heard the original – nomad - version of the story, which though identical in structure, was not about a place, but about the boundaries between animals and humans – a theme of many of the stories I had heard among the nomads. It was also uncannily like the message in my dream, I thought. I suddenly understood what Rafig meant when he said *encounters in dreams are also encounters in the world.*

'Did you feel … well… as if you were becoming animal?' I asked Atman hesitantly.

'That wasn't quite it,' he answered, 'but I did feel that I was squeezing through a veil between two worlds. It was not going somewhere new so much as returning to where I had been before, but had forgotten.' He hesitated. 'Talking of animals, did you know you are being followed?'

Rafig, Zubayr and I went silent, staring at him. Once again, his wide eyes were pits of darkness in the firelight.

'The *Sandlines* showed me clearly - three men, and camels, and after you … something else – not human, whether one animal or more, I could not tell.'

We continued to stare at him, then Rafig said. 'I did not see that. What kind of animal was it?'

'The kind that hunts others,' Atman said. He paused for a moment, then continued. 'Only God is All-Knowing. When we were grazing the camels near al-Gaa, we heard the cries of hyenas, and though they never bothered us, we were on our guard.'

That night, for the third time since leaving al-Gaa, I heard the shrill shriek of a hyena in the darkness. When I woke in the morning, though, no one else mentioned it, and though I searched the area carefully, I found no tracks. When I looked in the direction of the Fish-Eaters' camp, they and their camels were gone.

Voices

On the second day after acquiring the she-camel, I started to feel hungry – not just the peckish feeling one has before meals, but something deeper and more insistent, like a deep ache or sickness. We had been moderately hungry from the outset – there had not been enough food for Rafig and me. I had brought nothing, and had relied on sharing the old man's provisions. Zubayr had added some flour, dried dates, and skins of sour camel's milk, but not sufficient to last till we reached journey's end – Rafig estimated another five sleeps. We were now down to only one meal a day – in the evening. We marched the whole day, non-stop, on empty stomachs.

On that day I experienced the gnawing of hunger as soon as I awoke, and remembered with a sinking feeling that an entire day must pass before I could eat. That morning we had a particularly long walk to find the camels and, by the time we got them back to our camp, I already felt shattered. After heaving the first few packs into place I was panting with exertion and after a couple more, I lurched away with my head spinning. I hoped my companions would not notice, though nothing can be hidden in the desert – at least they made no comment. I knelt down and took deep breaths, then returned to help, knowing that the loading was almost impossible with only two pairs of hands, and that Rafig and Zubayr were as hungry as I was.

Before we set off Rafig handed out dried leaves of *tombac*, and showed me how to keep it in my mouth between the gums and lower lip. 'Do not chew it or swallow it,' he said. 'Just let it rest in your mouth. It will help with the hunger and the fatigue.'

That morning, though, I had to push myself on in a way I had not experienced since I had been in the war - the heat, the fatigue, and worst of all, the craving for food, dominated my thoughts. No matter how much I tried to direct my mind to the present, it always reverted to images of eating – platters of fish, and tender chicken and roast meat, mountains of mashed potato with butter, salad and fruit. I remembered the polenta and goat meat we had dined on at Saadig's tent, and how we had scraped the grease off our hands afterwards. I craved that grease now - if I licked my finger, I could almost taste it. The bitter *tombac* kept the gnawing sensation away for a time, but soon it dissolved to almost nothing, and the hunger returned.

Every step became a penance, but there was no chance to rest and no escape from the withering sun. The heat was manic, dispiriting, sapping the will to go on, and the landscape reflected my inner void, a dead and desolate plain without trees or grass, without birds or crawling things, unrolling before us moment after monotonous moment, empty and aching and limp, like the corpse of a world long ago gutted by titanic vultures, leaving only the bare and sun-bleached bones – the blunted rocks, the lifeless sand, and the dumb and stupefied hills. The wind came lazily, rising in muffled cries like the screams of distant victims, falling away in strange whispers, tuneless whistles, aching sighs underfoot.

As the day grew hotter the camels became fractious. There were frequent stoppages as utensils dropped, saddles slipped, packs split and shed lumps of rock-salt. We would have to cut the camel concerned out of the caravan, so as not to halt our progress, working as fast as possible, while the animal kicked and rumbled and dribbled green cud over us, and we shouted at it and swore at each other. Each event strained us more, and its import was magnified by the heat and the longing for food, and the need to keep the caravan going. We tramped on hour after featureless hour into the inferno of the sun, into the endless hungry horizon. I knew it would pass, I told myself it would pass, but telling myself did not help, and my stomach felt like poison and my head was floating and my feet were on fire. *You are weak,* a voice whispered to me. *You are feeble, and pathetic, and stupid, not worthy of this journey, nor to travel with the desert folk, nor of this quest. You should not be here – thinking yourself so clever, so strong, so high and mighty, when you are nothing but a feeble person. Look at you, see the old woman that you are.* The worst, though, was when the voices in my head turned against Rafig. *He is nothing but an old fake and a phony, putting on an aura of sanctity to dupe others. He saw you coming that time at Elai, when he mystified you with nonsense about wind, breath and spirit. He tricked you into working with him on this caravan for nothing, and when you get wherever it is you are going he will ditch you – probably take your camel and leave you in the desert. He is the one who has the rifle, not you. He has no intention of helping you find any lost oasis – and all that is just nonsense anyway.*

Something kept telling me that the old man was leading the caravan in the wrong direction, veering off to the east rather than due south. I inspected the shadows underfoot, under the camels, under the stones, as Rafig had taught me, I tried to feel the wind on my face, but there was no wind, and there were no obvious landmarks on the horizon.

'Are you sure this is the right way?' I demanded at last. 'You're heading east.'

He inspected me closely without stopping the caravan. 'Hunger can spin one's head around,' he said.

'Yes,' I said.

I thought he was admitting his mistake, but we tramped on and the camels glided on behind us, and still he did not adjust position. I sought out the shadows again, my eyes searching the skyline frantically for something to fix on. An indignant voice screamed inside me, but I fought it back and fought it back, until, at last I could hold it in no longer.

'If we keep going this way, we will end up lost in the *Hurra*,' I blurted out.

He cast me a cool glance through narrowed eyes. 'Only God is all knowing,' he said.

He continued leading the caravan in the same direction, at the same pace, leaving me feeling snubbed. The heat and the hunger and the anger seemed to swell like a sour bubble inside me so that I could not distinguish one feeling from another. Rafig was always so certain he was right, I told myself, but no one was infallible. Again and again my *waswasa* grumbled, again and again my lips twitched as I suppressed the urge to tell him. We were going wrong and the old man would kill us all. My grip tightened on my camel-stick, my other fist clenched. I gritted my teeth.

'Rafig,' I yelled suddenly. 'You're going the wrong way. We should take the shortest route. We haven't got time for this.'

The old man eyed me calmly, and without halting the camels, turned and called Zubayr from the back of the caravan. The youth ran up and Rafig handed the head-rope to him and told him to continue. He led me off a little way from the camel-train.

'I see the jinn in your eyes,' he said.

'*Really*?' I answered. 'How do I know the same thing does not apply to you?'

'You must trust me,' he said. 'That's all.'

'Yes,' I nodded, 'But ….' Suddenly I knew this was not me talking – this voice was the jinn in my head, the jinn born with me – the *qarin*. Even Brahim had warned me against it, and Rafig had mentioned it often.

'The jinn claims to be you, but it is not you,' Rafig said. 'It is the false you, your enemy. How can it be you if it speaks to you? There cannot be two *yous* – one must be false. The jinn is treacherous and will kill you if you listen to it. This is not your true self speaking, for your true self is one with the Great Spirit – eternal, absolute, infinite. It cannot be destroyed. Your true self is in tune with all the things around you, which in truth are no-things – not truly *other*, but only you in another guise … remember

'The wind in another guise …'

'That's right – the breath and the spirit are but the wind. That was the first thing I told you when we met. The desert is not hostile, nor the sun our enemy, for the desert is us. The desert did not invite us here, and to live in the desert one must become of the desert, and become the desert. We do not control the desert, but she may give us sustenance if we come to her with humility. If not, if God does not strike for us on this, then we can only do our utmost, and the rest is written.'

It was then that I remembered how, on that first night at Elai, I had undertaken, to trust and protect Rafig, my travelling companion, even under threat of death. Zubayr, too, had eaten bread and salt with us, and I realized that whatever the jinn whispered to me was empty. Rafig, Zubayr and I came from different worlds, but that did not matter. They were myself in another guise and I must trust them completely. Between us there was a pact, and the pact was the word, and the word must not be broken.

Sandburs

By mid-afternoon we had entered the belt called the *Lush*, where rich pastures often sprang up in the season of the rains. It did not look very lush now, differing only from the desolation we had crossed that morning in its stands of sparse, dried-out grasses. There were stark hills in the distance, with low dunes around them, but the hills gave the sense that they were relics of great mountains that had once stood here, whose faces had cracked and shattered from the onslaught of wind and water, from the extremes of heat and cold, and the broken skin fallen away to lie in screes around them.

We led the caravan up and down undulating salients, letting our shadows flit and stretch behind us, until, with the sun a thumb and forefinger's measure from the skyline, we came to a swath of grass – waist-high plants growing, not in clumps like sword-grass, but in wide straw-colored ribbons among the low-lying sands. Rafig declared that we had found God's Bounty. The place looked quite desperate to me but I had been forcing one foot after the other all afternoon. My legs and feet were rebelling against me in twitches and muscle spasms, and I longed to rest. We couched the camels, settling them one by one, then, starting with lead-camel, Agha, released their loads and lowered them gently to the ground. Half way through the work I felt a bolus spin rhythmically in my head, with a bull-roarer, *waah, waah, WAAH,* sound. I staggered backwards, and had to steady myself against the saddle. I held on until the bull-roarer roar grew fainter, then continued with the work. I knew the other two had noticed, but neither of them said anything.

We hobbled the camels, sent them off towards the grasses, and piled up the saddles around the space Rafig had chosen as our camp. 'Take a deep breath,' he said. 'It needs some more work, but now we can eat.'

'Eat what?' I demanded. 'We have only a handful of flour left. That's not going to last us five sleeps.'

I thought of the hoop-snares the old man had put out for gazelle at al-Gaa, and had found empty the night I had shot the hyena. How I wished he had caught a gazelle - I could almost taste its succulent meat. Rafig pointed at the grasses, and I saw that the camels were already tucking into them with gusto.

'I told you we had found God's Bounty,' the old man said.

'But that is camel-food.'

'It is *haskanit*. It is good for Bani Adam, too.'

Rafig told us to empty two saddlebags, then led us over to the nearest stand of grass. Close up, I saw that the *haskanit* was a tall goat-grass with heavy ears, full of prickly seeds. With a shock, I realized that it was the same sandbur grass that had given me so much pain on my very first night in the desert - the grass that had made my hands sore for days. Rafig showed us how to take the sandbur stalks by thumb and forefinger and shake the sharp seeds into the saddlebags. We practiced a little under his watchful eye, then he left us, saying that he was going to look for old camel-dung – we would need it for fuel, as we had run out of firewood, and there was none to be found here.

Zubayr and I worked separately to fill our bags, and I was quickly reminded of my ordeal on that first night. The sandbur seeds stuck in my hands and covered the sleeves of my *jibba*. They leapt up and lodged themselves in my hair and beard. When I tried to remove them, they pierced my fingertips, leaving them red and sore.

By the time we had filled our saddle-bags, my fingers were swollen from the burs, and I noticed that Zubayr's were in the same condition. When we got back to camp, Rafig was already piling up the camel dung he had collected - not the little black balls I was used to, but hard flat pats left by massed camel herds grazing in the *Lush* during the season of the rains. The grass was so abundant then, he said, that a camel's droppings were moist and a different shape – the pats had long since been dried hard by the sun.

Rafig also showed us two stones he had found - a flat slab and a cylindrical stone with smooth sides, like a rolling-pin. Both stones looked as though they had been worn down by use. As I examined them, Rafig said, 'this is the work of the Old People – the Anakim – the Lost Giants.'

'The *Lost Giants*?' I said. 'These things don't seem so giant.'

The old man shrugged. 'God alone is All Knowing. One finds their tools almost everywhere in the *Hurra*.'

He shook his head when he saw our sore and bloated hands but told us he would find some medicine for us later. We tipped the seeds on to a cow-skin he had spread out, then he showed us how to smash them on the stone slab, remove the chaff, and grind them to flour with the roller. It was painstaking work, hunkering over a hand-mill on empty stomachs and working the roller with hands that itched painfully from the sandburs. Zubayr and I took it in turns to grind the seeds under the supervision of Rafig.

When we had a heap of greenish flour, Rafig scooped it into a pan. He added a little water from a skin and some salt, and began to knead it into a dough. While he was doing that, Zubayr made fire, twirling a stick between his palms against a base, until it was hot enough to ignite a handful of dried grass. He transferred the flame to the dried camel-dung, and when the first pat began to smoke, the youth crouched on all-fours and blew into it. A glowing spot appeared in the dung, and grew bigger as Zubayr blew, spreading around the fuel. Even when it burst into low flame, though, there was little heat. Rafig removed his slipper and used it as a fan, and after that Zubayr and I shared the task of fanning the smouldering dung. We fanned ferociously until our arms ached, but the fire never quite took off - if we slackened the fanning for even a moment it threatened to go out.

When the dough was ready, Rafig placed the pan on the three stones he had arranged around the fire. Again, we shared the job of fanning the flame, working so intently in our craving for food that we hardly noticed the sun going down and the darkness engulfing us. We fanned and fanned, taking turns, as the dough hardened and browned, and the unmistakable smell of baked bread touched our nostrils, almost mesmerizing us. By the time Rafig declared the bread well and truly done, Lady Moon was up, and the desert sky was brilliant with stars. There was a neat brown loaf in the pan. We stared at it in wonder. Rafig drew his sharp knife, cut it into three portions, and we eyed each other. Even though we were starving, even though the process of preparation had been so long and painful, we observed the nomad custom of restraint. The pause allowed me to reflect for a moment on the food, on where it had come from, how the Earth had provided it, astonishingly, in the so-called desert wastes, and how everything we had was the gift of Earth Mother. It seemed another age before Rafig exclaimed, 'Come on. Eat.'

We dipped our hands into the pot and found that each of us had a piece of bread not much larger than our own hands. We ate it slowly, piece by piece, savouring it. I have never forgotten the taste of that bread.

Lush

Though we were still hungry after eating the bread, the edge of the craving had gone. Rafig went off into the night and came back with a stone – in the light of my torch I saw it was covered in grey and red lichen. He scraped the lichen off with his knife, mashed it in a pan with a little water, and applied it to our fingers as we held them out for him. The relief was almost immediate. *The Gift of the Stones*, Rafig said.

Afterwards, the three of us sat huddled in our blankets under the stars – tonight there was no fire to cheer us, but at least we had eaten well enough.

'That sandbur grass has saved our lives,' I commented. 'I can only imagine what this area must be like after the rains.'

'There are camels as many as ants from a disturbed ant-hill,' Rafig said. 'The *Lush* does not flourish every season, but when it does, it is truly the Bounty of God. For the nomads there is no better time than when *elbil* – the camel herds – are eating green grass. Here they are deep in the *Hurra*, and they are free. They do not need anything, because they have more camel's milk than they can drink, and that is both food and water. Yes, when the rains are abundant this is a different country – alive with grasses, flowers, birds and butterflies, green as far as the horizon in every direction. There are gazelles in herds, even oryx and spiral-horn white antelope. The camels eat and eat and eat. Sometimes they grow so fat that their humps split.'

We all laughed. It hardly seemed possible that the desert could be so bountiful, yet I knew what he was saying must be true.

'*The Lush* was found long ago,' Rafig said, 'by our ancestor – at least my ancestor on my mother's side - called Kabaysh, a name that comes from our nomad word *kabsh*, a *ram*. It is said that Kabaysh came here from the Great Water, leading his sheep ...'

'Great Water?' I asked. 'What is that?'

'God only is All Knowing. Perhaps it was the Nile, or perhaps a great lake that existed in the desert then – the same one that gave the Fish-Eaters their name. Anyway, they had travelled for many days and were hungry, for there was no grazing to be found. One morning, Kabaysh awoke to find the tracks of a wild ram near his camp. His ewes seemed contented, so he guessed the ram had visited them in the night. He decided to follow the ram's tracks, thinking that he might hunt him down and eat his meat. He tracked the animal to a *gelti* - a rainwater pool in the rocks, far from here - where he found a magnificent wild ram with spiral horns of four hand-spans, floundering in the water.

He was about to shoot the ram when the animal spoke. In those days, of course, men and animals could still speak together. "My leg is trapped by a big stone under the water," the ram said. "If you will not shoot me with your arrow, and will help me to get out, perhaps I shall be able to help you."

Kabaysh did not really believe the ram would be able to help him, but he took pity on the animal anyway. He put down his bow, jumped into the water and freed the ram's leg. Then they both waded to the bank.

'Once out of the pool, the shepherd saw that, unlike nomad sheep, the wild ram had long legs and a long tail. Instead of running away as Kabaysh had expected, the ram told him. "You are looking for pasture and your sheep are hungry: because of your kindness, I shall help you. When you leave here lead your flock in the direction of the sunrise, till you come to a dune overlooking a great desert plain that stretches as far as some bare, broken hills. Spend the night on that dune, and in the morning, you will find something wonderful."

Then the wild ram ran off into the desert.

'Kabaysh followed the animal's instructions, leading his flock east until they came to a dune. From the top they could see an arid desert plain stretching as far as sparse hills on the horizon. There was nothing for the sheep to eat, but they were tired, and they slept on the dune.

'In the night there was a great storm, with rain and thunder, and lightning scorpions that stung the earth all the way across the great plain below them. When the sun rose, they saw a wondrous sight. The plain had become a lush garden of green, with grasses as high as a man's thigh, and yellow flowers as far as the eye could see. There were wide-eared foxes and gazelles there and creeping people and flying people – a whole world flourishing in the desert.

'The shepherd thanked the Great Spirit for their deliverance, knowing that the wild ram was the Great Spirit in another guise. He and his sheep spent many sleeps in the green pastures, which he called *the Lush*. The ewes grew fat and in due course gave birth to lambs, and behold, the lambs were long-legged and long-tailed like the wild ram, rather than short-legged and short-tailed like their mothers. So, God gave nomads *the Lush*, and also the long-legged, long-tailed desert sheep.'

'There are no sheep in *the Lush* in these days,' Zubayr commented. 'That must have been in the Distant Time.'

'Certainly, they say the *Lush* blooms less often than it used to. Ah, where are the rains of yesteryear?'

'*Truth*,' Zubayr said.

That night I slept soundly, undisturbed by the cries of hyenas. This area and the plain we had crossed that morning were too arid even for them. At last we had thrown off our followers, I thought.

Thirst

Voices woke me at first light and I opened my eyes to see Rafig and Zubayr crouching by the large water-skin we had hung from a pack-saddle. The skin had lost its bulge and lay limp between the saddle-horns, almost empty, while the sand around it was obviously damp. For a moment I tried to remember whether I had failed to tie the skin securely – a grave sin in the desert – but I had not been the last to draw water, I recalled. They looked concerned. I got up and crouched next to them, and Zubayr showed me a ragged tear in the water-skin just below the mouth.

'Not cut by a knife,' Rafig said. 'Too rough. Somebody tore it open with their teeth.'

I stared at him. 'You mean, an *animal*?'

'Look at this,' Zubayr said grimly. He showed me several sets of tracks that formed circles around the torn water-skin. Some of the tracks were indistinct, but others clearly etched into the surface. The tracks were those of a carnivore – large and wide-footed, with a pad and four toes showing, each with a pointed claw-tip. I knew by now that dogs left such a print – or almost any hunting animal that did not retract its claws – but this was unlikely to be dogs.

'*Hyenas*,' Zubayr declared. 'Atman said they were following us.'

A shiver ran down my spine and my scalp prickled. If hyenas had entered our camp in the night, they must have done so in absolute silence, without alerting the camels, and without us being aware of it. Rafig had said that hyenas sometimes bit sleeping humans, and we had been completely vulnerable. Instead of attacking us, though, it seemed that they had deliberately torn open a water-skin and wasted our vital water supply. The chilling thing was that this appeared to be an act of calculated cruelty dreamed up by an almost-human mind. I wondered for an instant if it could have been humans disguised as hyenas, but I saw where that thought was going and dismissed it.

'Why would hyenas follow us?' Zubayr asked.

We had not told him about the incident at al-Gaa, when I had shot the hyena. I recounted the story to him briefly now, even though I knew that to do so was to admit to myself that a hyena was capable of understanding who was responsible, and of planning revenge.

Rafig stood up. 'Never mind that now,' he said. 'We have two small water-skins, and there is a little water left in that one.'

'The small skins also have only a little water in them,' Zubayr said. 'We must find more soon.'

'If God wills we shall be at *Broken Hobble* by sunset,' Rafig said. 'There is a deep well there.'

Zubayr and I exchanged a glance. We both knew this would mean a whole day marching in the heat with no food, and only a few mouthfuls of water. In these temperatures moisture-loss was far more dangerous than hunger. It was as if the hyenas had deliberately conspired to condemn us to the drawn-out torture of thirst.

'Come on,' Rafig said. 'Let us load the salt.'

Loading fourteen camels each with a *gontar* – about three hundred kilos, I reckoned – was a desperate trial in our frail and thirsty condition. We managed it by sheer willpower. When the caravan was ready, we tightened our belts and got the camels moving, leaving the grind-stone and roller we had used to make bread out of goat-grass, leaving the tracks and marks where we had rested for the night, leaving that little piece of the *Lush* to become itself again.

We tramped on, hauling the camels, and at least they had perked up after a night grazing on the nutritious *haskanit.* They looked smug and superior this morning, many of them had green rings round their drooping lips from eating the sandburs, and they walked with their heads up, lifting their feet, undulating along with that curiously harmonious flowing motion, as if they were not separate animals, but one huge many-legged, coiling snake.

As the sun rose higher, though, the thirst set in. It began with a dryness of the lips and an itching in the eyes. With no saliva to moisten my lips they quickly began to crack, and my tongue, drying out, grew fatter and was soon covered in thick white paste. My tongue stuck on my bloated lips, making my words slur like the talk of a drunk. These symptoms were followed closely by a pain in the kidneys which grew steadily more acute, until I was forced to bend at the waist. The others were in the same condition as me. Now, I could not get the idea of water out of my head, no matter how I tried. In comparison, the desire for food the previous day had been trivial. Thirst was a stream of images, of cascading falls, clear springs, surging torrents, torrential rain, diving into a forest pool, feeling the coolness in the throat and on the skin. In my mind I dropped a stone into a stream and saw the water splash up in slow motion, saw the shock-wave spread out in a perfect circle, saw the ripples run away, slowly, slowly, wave and counter-wave, ripples within ripples within ripples, and the ripples were the *qarin*, the separate self I had believed I was, when, in fact, the only real *I* was the river - the flow - and when the ripples had played out against themselves, the true *I* would still be there, flowing on and on and on. Yet the sheer craving for moisture was a strident voice over-riding all these images, and it did not come from any jinn, but from some part of me that had been there since the beginning of time. I felt as if my throat had been scrubbed with sandpaper and that my eyes were sinking into their sockets. I had never been here before, not even in the war – *this is what* real *thirst is like*, I thought.

We strode on and the camels rocked on imperturbably, and the thirst was a fermenting fungus in my stomach, and the heat was a deadly pulse, and the hot wind was in our faces, and the sun was a devil's eye. Soon, I had that familiar feeling that we were going nowhere. The horizon before us was blank infinity, and the desert behind a featureless stage. Only the sun and shadows shifted. The caravan had become our world, and our world was marching on the spot, marking time. *Let the day pass*, an inner voice told me. *Let Father Sun pass over. Let the coolness come. Let us reach water.* My mind began to wander. I found myself thinking about the Lost Oasis, realizing that I had almost forgotten why I was looking for it. *Because it contains a secret that could change my life, and change the world?* Did I still believe that? I was roused from my internal wandering by a cry from Rafig and I suddenly became aware that my attention had strayed - for a long time, hours perhaps, I had become locked in myself and had not taken in anything of my surroundings. The old man was pointing and gesturing. On the horizon lay a sharp hill almost the same misty grey as the sky.

'*Broken Hobble,*' he croaked.

We found the well in a wadi at the foot of the rocky hill not long before sunset. Leaving the camels with Zubayr, Rafig and I stumbled over to the well head, clasping our waists with both hands, trying to stay upright, our swollen tongues protruding from broken lips. The shaft was wide and very deep – much deeper than the one at Elai, where Rafig had fished out the bucket. In fact, it was so deep that I could not see the water. Rafig picked up a pebble and dropped it over the rim. We both heard the dull *thunk* as the stone hit dry rock.

Hobble

We camped in trees nearby and sent the camels out to find what grazing they could. After dark we made tea with the last of the water, and huddled round the fire in blankets, sipping slowly from our glasses. I felt the hot liquid working, clearing my throat, stripping fur off my tongue. For a moment I experienced an uplift.

Rafig took out the torn water-skin, and began to stitch up the rip with a packing needle and leather strips cut from the piece of cowhide he carried. 'We need tar to waterproof it,' he explained, 'but it will be all right for now – I mean, if we had any water, it would.'

'I still can't believe that hyenas did it,' I said.

There was silence for a moment, then Zubayr said, 'I once knew a man among the *Tu* who shot a hyena - he said the animal had been taking his sheep. When he examined the carcass, though, it was a woman – a pregnant woman from another clan. The woman's family demanded blood-compensation for both the woman and the unborn infant. The man said that when he shot the hyena, he did not know it was a woman. Other witnesses said he knew, because the hyena had visited his camp before, and he had seen her standing on her hind feet like a human, and had told others she was really a woman.'

'All right,' I said. 'Am I supposed to believe that?'

'God is All-Knowing,' Zubayr grinned. 'It's just a story.'

'Are you saying I behaved badly, shooting the hyena, and that's why the well is dry?'

'No, the well is dry because there is drought on the land. You did not bring that. If we had not lost that water in the night, it would not have been a problem.'

I thought about it for a moment, as the fire crackled. I thought about the dry well and wondered why they called this place *Broken Hobble*. When I asked Rafig, the old man coughed and cleared his throat. 'The story goes that a nomad was herding camels near here in the Distant Time,' he said, 'and his camels were thirsty and giving out the *lament of thirst*. The nomad kept all his animals hobbled as he feared they would wander off and leave him. One she-camel said, '*Let me free from my hobble and I will find water.*' The nomad was afraid she would not come back, though, so he refused to let her go.

'The next night the camels were very thirsty, and the she-camel asked him again to let her go. Again, he refused, thinking that it was an excuse to escape – perhaps she planned to find the *Night Camels* and live with them, he thought.

'The following day the camels were so weak from thirst that again the she-camel begged the herder to let her go. He refused for the third time. In the night, though, he awoke to discover that the she-camel had broken her hobble and was gone. He followed her tracks to this well and found her waiting patiently for him. She had smelled water and located it, but could not reach it without his help. The nomad went to fetch the rest of the camels, then fashioned a rope and bucket and drew water for them all.

'Later he passed the story on to his clan, and after that, the nomads no longer kept grazing camels hobbled in the *Hurra*. They only had to remain at a well and let the camels wander in search of grazing, and when they became thirsty, they would return, knowing that the Children of Adam would draw water for them.'

'That is a good story,' I said. 'Except that there is no longer any water at *Broken Hobble.*'

'God is All Knowing,' Rafig said, 'but there is another well not far away, *Salt-Bush Grasping,*'

'There is drought on the land, *Faki*,' Zubayr said. 'That well may also be dry.'

'*Salt-Bush Grasping* is not like this well. It is an '*ayn* – an eye or spring. The water there does not depend on rain. Many nomads pitch their tents in that area, and they keep the water flowing, drawing it every day...' He paused, then nodded thoughtfully. 'Still, only the Great Spirit is All Knowing.'

I wondered how long we could go on if there were no water at *Salt-Bush Grasping.* There were the camels and their stomach juices – they had grazed well on the sandbur grass. I did not want to think about slaughtering Ata, though, or any of the other camels either.

An idea suddenly occurred to me. 'Why not throw the *Sandlines*?' I asked Rafig. 'Find out if there is indeed water at *Salt-Bush Grasping.*'

The old man shook his head. 'I threw the *Sandlines* last night, but they gave me no clear answer.'

He turned away, and I found myself wondering if the *Sandlines* had given an answer Rafig did not wish to share. Perhaps, in telling us that there were wells ahead, the old man was just trying to keep up our spirits. I dismissed the idea almost at once. The nomads had faith that the Great Spirit would provide what they needed. If it did not, whatever happened was written.

That night the hunger and thirst would not let me sleep except in snatches. I tossed and turned under my blanket, and at one point awoke to see the glowing embers of the fire, and beyond it a dark shadow that looked like a huge animal. I glanced at the camels, who were still rumbling and belching- they did not seem to have noticed anything. I sat up and, staring at the shadow, saw that it was not an animal but a woman with flowing black hair and glowing red eyes. She was wearing a black wrap, but her smoothly rounded belly was clearly visible beneath it. She stared at me, and although her lips did not move, a voice said, *there are things that appear to be hyenas, but are not.*

Then I woke up a second time, to find the woman gone, the camels asleep with their heads resting on the ground, and Rafig and Zubayr still covered with their blankets.

Breath

How we managed to load the camels next morning, I do not know. It was as if we had been blessed with a second wind. Afterwards, though, we felt shattered again and all three of us had to rest, sitting in the sand for a few moments to recover our strength, while the laden camels fidgeted. We did not try to talk - our tongues were furred once more and our lips cracked and swollen. We helped each other to our feet, got the camels moving, and led them out of the canyon and into a blue plain like a vast wrinkled animal skin pinned out to dry and tan in the sun, where the sand-dust rose in a seething miasma, and the wind set whirling devils spinning along the rim of the world. The camels plodded on, huffing and rumbling, snorting dust, snapping teeth, flapping eyelids, and their pack saddles creaked and murmured. In the midday brightness, when our shadows had become dark nail-parings underfoot, we spotted dark cliffs on the horizon and I squinted at them with a gaze gone misty from the heat and thirst and hunger. Today I would not let myself withdraw from the world, would not give rein to the jinn inside me. I clenched my teeth and worked every agonized step deliberately, willing my body forward, feeling Earth Mother beneath my feet, drawing me down into her, feeling in the wind a merciless tongue lapping moisture from my body. *No*, I told myself. *The sun is not my enemy and the desert is not my foe. I am the wind in another guise. I am the wind, and I am the eye of the wind, and I am that which the wind blows, that blows the wind.*

I looked up and saw pointed peaks looming above us, and underfoot the surface had become a stony scree. Shortly we came on a narrow camel-path winding down through the stones into a canyon, and Rafig adjusted the head-rope, leading the caravan along the path and through a gap leading to a long corridor between rock walls, etched and chiseled into shelves and alcoves. In places ancient runes had been scratched into the rock, with tribal camel brands in the shapes of crude matchstick men, lizards, fishes, circles, crescent moons, crosses and stars. The walls gave some shelter from the sun and wind, and I was beginning to breathe more freely again, when I saw in front of me the stone parapet of a well under an overhanging rock.

'*Salt-Bush Grasping,*' Rafig announced.

He halted the caravan, passed the rope to me, and he and Zubayr went to inspect the well. I watched the two of them as they leaned over the parapet, and peered inside, licking my lacerated lips with a tongue like a windsock. When they turned away their expressions were crest-fallen. They shuffled over to where I stood. 'There is water,' Rafig panted, 'but too deep … twenty men deep, maybe even thirty. God is generous …we do not have a rope that long.'

I searched the old man's face desperately. 'Maybe we can climb down … get to the water.'

Rafig shook his head. 'The well is steep. One cannot climb down. Imagine thirty men each with one arm held above his head, standing on each other's shoulders. That is the depth of the water.'

In my thirst-fuddled state it took me a moment to work out that this was about sixty metres – more than a hundred and eighty feet.

'What if we join head-ropes?' Zubayr suggested.

Rafig shook his head again. 'Still too short.'

I saw Zubayr's boyish face fall slightly, and my heart sank. No water. Only God knew what we would do now. *The hyenas did this*, I thought. *They deliberately wasted our water to make sure we would die an agonizing death in the desert.* I remembered the pregnant woman in my dream. *There are things that appear to be hyenas, but are not.*

'What do we do?' I asked Rafig.

He took the head-rope from me, stood up straight.

'We go in God's safekeeping,' he said.

Wind

We left the chasm behind us and pressed on across a vast plain with a new desperation, weak from hunger, weak from thirst. Every step was torture, and my breath came in gasps. My head began to swing like a weight and only determination drove me on. I kept close to Rafig, but sometimes the caravan seemed to recede, to become smaller and more distant, as if the scale of the world were in a state of flux. The pendulum in my head, the rhythmic rotation of that bull-roarer, *waaazz, waaazz, WAAAZZ,* fading in and out like Rafig's chanting for the *Sandlines,* now from the front, now from the rear, now from one side, now from the other. A dense mist gathered at the edge of my vision, and though I fought to keep it away, I realized that I was becoming detached from myself. My legs were walking, but I was not walking across the desert, because there was no *I* to be walking there. The desert was being walked, but not by me - there was no me, only the Great Spirit, the great flow enfolding and unfolding, like the ebb and flow of a tide, like the long shadow of sunrise that enfolded itself into a tiny ball at noon and unfolded slowly again towards sunset. *Once upon a time a boy went in search of the Lost Oasis. He searched for the oasis in the desert for days under the hot sun until he was so thirsty, he could hardly walk.* I was the boy in the tale, and I was the tale being told. My legs were the legs of the boy in the tale, who could hardly walk, and I was the hot eye of the sun looking down on the boy from afar, looking down on myself looking down, observing black specks on the landscape of indestructible life, men, and camels, moving in a direction, intent on a purpose. *I am the wind, and I am the eye of the wind, and I am that which the wind blows, that blows the wind.* I was walking in the desert, then there was just walking through the desert, and no person walking. I was looking at the action of a moment, and there was the action of the moment with no-one looking, and there was the entire flux of existence unfolding, the whole oceanic wave of being that washed everything in its stream, in the spirit, the breath shared with the trees and the grasses, the nomads, the camels, the gazelle, the wide-eared fox, the hare, the hyena, the eagle and the ants, the water and the winds, the earth and the fire, the Great River, the Great Unfolding of All Things. The flowing, the flowering, the Great Spirit, was one, and in every breath, the universe, the flow of wind, and waves and clouds and stars, of galaxies, moons, and planets, rushed through me like a flood and left me ajar.

Battikh

'*Wake up.*' Rafig was shaking me, and I opened my eyes to found myself lying in hot sand. I could not remember how I had got there. The last thing I recalled, I had been tramping along beside the caravan with my head in the clouds.

'*Drink,*' the old man said. I felt liquid rushing into my mouth – it was sweet and delicious. I swallowed, spluttered, and sat up.

'The spirit left you,' Rafig said. 'I was afraid for a moment, but now it is back. You saw something, no?'

He held out an object that looked like a green cup – the same vessel from which he had been squeezing liquid into my mouth. I took it and realized it was a dwarf *battikh* – a watermelon - cut in half. The liquid that had rushed into my blood like a flood was watermelon juice.

I squeezed more juice greedily into my mouth, bit into the sticky wet pulp. It was the most exquisite thing I had ever tasted. I felt the liquid trickle down my throat, unclog my mouth and ease the pain in my stomach. I could actually feel the moisture spread through my body, and feel the warmth and well-being as it reached into the remotest extremities like an angel's hand. I looked round, saw the heavily laden camels shifting in deep ripples of sand, saw Zubayr sucking juice from a *battikha*. To my astonishment, the sands around the caravan were an interlocking web of rich green vine-shoots, a complex network of vines, with little oases of green leaves and yellow flowers, and at intervals dozens upon dozens of *battikh* growing on them in long spreads. It was a miniature universe and each melon was a tiny planet with a vivid pattern of fields and forests, oceans and deserts on its skin.

'*What*?' I gasped, standing up. '*Battikh*? Is this a dream?'

Rafig chuckled. 'Everything is the Great Spirit's Dreaming, but no, you are not asleep now. God is generous – we were in his safekeeping and he has struck for us on this. Here is the Lost Oasis you were searching for – a paradise in the sands.'

Gazelles

We could not afford to halt the camels here for long, so we detached Ata and Hambarib from the caravan and filled their saddle-bags with *battikh*. I cut one in half and fed it to Ata - he bit into it happily, slurping at the succulent pulp, then swallowing it whole and staring at me in anticipation, waiting for another. The effect of the *battikh*-juice was magical – in a moment all the brooding thoughts had gone and I was a new person. Rafig, too, had recovered some of his energy, and was walking around with a spring-laden gait, stuffing *battikh* in his pockets and balancing piles of them in his hands. When there was no space on our camels for more *battikh*, we ate a couple each, fed the skins to the camels, and led the animals hurriedly towards the caravan – it had already become a blot on the horizon.

As we walked I tried to recall what had happened before Rafig had roused me. At first I had been walking in the desert, and at the same time I had been somewhere above, looking down on myself walking in the desert, and also looking down on myself looking down, in endless recursion, as if I were gazing into reflecting mirrors stretching to infinity. At the same time I recalled feeling a deep sense of connection with all around me. There had been the realization that what I had always imagined was *I*, was not my true self at all. My true self was something much bigger – inconceivably large. My body did not end at my extremities but extended out into the desert and beyond – it spanned the entire universe. No, it was more than that, I thought - my body *was* the universe - what I thought of as *I* was an excitation of awareness, a ripple in the flowing of mind, and there was no universe, really, but only this flowing, this consciousness, this mind-at-large, this great mind where all minds had their being, and I was both the finite, evanescent ripples, and the flowing itself, and there was no me at all, but only this walking in the desert, with no-one walking, and this walking was the flowing that went on forever.

'What happened to me?' I asked Rafig.

'You collapsed at almost the same moment Zubayr shouted out that he had found the *battikh* patch. No God but God, I have seen some strange things, but this was very odd indeed. The oddest thing of all is that they are sweet melons, not bitter ones.'

'Why is that odd?'

'Sweet melons are rare. Bitter ones are more abundant, but they are poisonous.'

'How did you know these were not the poisonous type?'

'The pattern on the skin is different. We use the seeds of the bitter melon for medicine and we extract tar from them to waterproof skins, so the pattern is familiar.'

'Why did you say that was the Lost Oasis?'

'Because it was a tiny oasis that we found by chance, like the boy in your story –or perhaps because we were guided here by the Great Spirit. *Battikh* are a miracle – a gift from God. They flourish only for a brief moment and will not be found again – as in your story of the Lost Oasis. But though they may vanish, they are not gone forever. The fruits dry out in the sun, and detach themselves from the vines, and the wind bowls the husks along, scattering seeds through the desert. The seeds lie in the sand, perhaps for ages, until the rains come again, and then the small paradise in the sands flourishes once more, though not in quite the same way or quite the same place. This scattering of seeds depends on the sun and the power of the wind, so these *battikh* are themselves the wind in another guise.'

I remembered the words Rafig had spoken in the wadi at Elai – it seemed so long ago now. The thought struck me powerfully, and by the time we caught up with Zubayr and the caravan, the world had readjusted itself, and I felt my position in it subtly different. I had no doubt that this oasis of *battikh* had saved our lives, and, like the sandbur grass, the plants had come at precisely the right moment.

All three of us were dragging along at the head of the caravan, sucking watermelons, carrying more in our pockets, when Zubayr said, '*There,*' and pointed to three dark shapes that drifted across the amber plain before us - gazelles, running fast, kicking up spurts of dust. They wheeled round in a long arc and dashed away south showing white tails like bobbing beacons.

'That is the second sign from the Great Spirit today,' Rafig said.

'How?' I asked.

'The gazelles came to guide us. They tell us that the Wadi Safra is in that direction – south – and it is near.'

The animals will reveal the Lost Oasis said a voice in my head. *You are animal and one of us.* I had now begun to glimpse the meaning of that message, I thought. The animals were emissaries of the Great Spirit. These gazelles showing us the way were an unfolding of the Great Mystery, just as the *battikh* were. The Great Spirit was my spirit also, as it was the spirit of the gazelles dashing across the desert. Plants, animals, humans and everything that existed were excitations of the Great Spirit, and in that spirit the only number was one.

'When I was a boy,' Rafig told me, 'I kept a young gazelle in a pen of stones. I fed her well, but she became ill, and I thought she might die. Then my father told me to let her go, because, he said, she was born to run free among the grasses and the thorn trees, among the eagles and the crows, the ants and the beetles, the hares and the foxes, the spiders, and the snakes. He said God did not make her to live in a pen of stones, but to feel Earth Mother under her hooves, the wind and rain on her skin, and to live among the voices of other creatures.'

'You let her go?'

'Of course. I learned that the Children of Adam are like the gazelles. We are born free to live in the wild, to live without walls or barriers. We are born to love each other in a world where wind, waters, clouds and rain, animals, and plants, are our family. When we are cut off from that family, like people where you come from - the town - we forget who we are. Even our love for our own kin becomes weak.'

I thought of my upbringing in civilization – how I had always felt that there was something missing, and, after Danny's death, how desperately I had wanted to get away. 'Have you ever been in the town?' I asked Rafig.

'Yes,' the old man said. 'It is the place where all tracks run out, and you cannot find your way nor hear the voices of the desert. There is much noise, but the noise is empty - there is a great silence beneath it. Townspeople have little love, for love does not flourish where one feels oneself separate from the Great Spirit.'

'They don't know they are separate, though.'

'They know, but they will not let themselves admit it. They amass wealth and accumulate things, or puff themselves up with pride over achievements, to ease this separation, but it avails them nothing.'

I remembered the storyteller Maya telling me that I was not whole, that there was a lost part of me that I might find if I found the Lost Oasis. I had thought my true goal was to find a place – an *actual* oasis. Since I had left the town I had heard stories about many kinds of lost oases, the most recent being the evanescent oasis of the *battikh* that had appeared like magic and saved us, just at the moment when I was starting to understand that it was not so much a place as a way of being I was searching for.

143

A Tree

The talk petered out as our bodies started to remind us that we were hungry. The fruit had restored the balance of moisture, but it had not given us the energy we needed for intense physical effort. Soon we were trudging along in silence once more, plodding, panting, following the gazelle tracks, bearing on our backs the burden of the midday brightness. At one point, I looked up to see a man riding a camel in the desert far to the south. '*Look,*' I called to the others, 'A nomad.'

'That is not a nomad,' Zubayr said. 'It is a tree.'

'We haven't seen a tree for days,' I said. 'It is a nomad I tell you.'

'There are no nomads here,' said Zubayr. 'The nomads have moved south - did you not notice there were none at *Salt-Bush Grasping*?'

'Perhaps it is a traveler.'

'What traveler? It is a tree.'

It seemed forever before we came near to the nomad on the camel, and I had already started to feel it was odd that the man had not moved. When we came up to him, though, I saw that Zubayr had been right. It was a tree.

As we passed the tree, though, Rafig stopped to gaze at its branches. '*Arak,*' he said.

It was the tree with the bitter leaves that camels seemed to like, but which made their breath smell - the leaves Atman the Fish-Eater claimed to have been fed during his stay with the *Night Camels*.

'It is true that we have not seen a tree for many sleeps,' Rafig said wearily, 'and *arak* do grow aplenty in the Wadi Safra.'

He paused and glanced again at the tree – it had a crooked trunk that looked like a mass of coiled ropes, and its bark was cracked and scaly. I noticed that its branches were bare – only bunches of dried leaves remained.

Rafig shook his head. 'This tree has not known rain this season,' he said.

He was about to turn when Zubayr let out a cry. '*There,*' he shouted, pointing south. '*The wadi.*'

I looked up and shading my eyes, saw a greenish grey band stretching the entire length of the skyline. Almost directly in front of us a single spiral of smoke rose above the horizon.

'Is that a tree?' I asked Zubayr.

'No,' the youth cracked a smile. 'That is nomads.'

Stone

Leading the caravan towards the nomad camp, we were startled by a pair of crows who hopped and skipped away from us, cawing. They flapped their wings and took to the air, rising easily on currents.

Rafig watched them circling, and I remembered him saying that the crow was his spirit-animal.

A little further on we came across the skeleton of a camel with the skin stretched tight over it like a drum, and gouges in the belly where the carrion creatures had feasted - I wondered if it was the crows or something larger. After that we came to a place where the bones of animals were scattered widely, and the skulls of goats and sheep lay cracked and gaping in the sunlight.

The nomad camp was a single tent, small and unkempt, and a brushwood shelter, set in a thick grove of shriveled *arak* and whitethorn trees on the edge of the wadi. We had almost reached the camp when a thin, ragged nomad with a wild black beard and matted hair emerged with a bowl of water. The man held the bowl out to us. '*Drink. Drink,*' he said.

 The watermelon juice had eased our thirst earlier, but the morning had been hot, and we were still thirsty – we had not drunk our fill for days. None of us wanted to accept the bowl first, and I remembered the story of Swaylim and Zabib, and how, even on the verge of death, it was not done among nomads to drink water before another. Finally, I let myself be persuaded, even though I knew I should not have. I took the bowl and squatted down to drink. I sensed the water cool and clean against my broken lips and was about to take a long drink when Rafig shouted. '*Don't.*'

'*What?*'

'Do not glug it down. It will hit you like a stone dropping from the sky. Take only sips.'

With an effort I forced myself to take only a little. After so long without moisture other than *battikh* juice, it tasted like nectar. At once I could feel it freeing up my whole body, releasing my muscles and lifting my mood. When I had drunk a few mouthfuls, the thin nomad took back the bowl from me, nodding approval. He handed it to Zubayr, who passed it to Rafig, who passed it back to Zubayr, who finally drank.

The nomad shook hands with us and introduced himself as Rai. 'Your coming is blest,' he said. It sounded as though he meant it.

As we unloaded the camels, stacked the saddles and made camp, I saw that the wadi was a blasted heath – a wasteland of tortured trees and sun-bleached bushes like crooked fingers, all unpeeling bark, thorns and prickles. The little grass I saw was parched and dried-out, burned brown or siena. I did not need Rafig to tell me that there was nothing for our camels to eat here. Worse, the smell of putrefaction hung heavily on the air, and here and there were animal carcasses in various states of decomposition. Out of the corner of my eyes I noticed shadows flitting across the sand, and looked up to see two crows gyrating above us – the same ones, I guessed, that we had startled earlier.

'*I saw the crows and walked in their trail*,' Rafig said, and I realized suddenly that he was quoting.

'*Every night they led me to a place,*

Every sleep in a different place.

I followed the crows till I found you.'

'This is a dead land,' Zubayr commented with a shiver. 'One smells death here. I wonder why Rai stays, when all the nomads have moved south.'

'God is All-Knowing ...' Rafig said.

' ... and man will discover,' said Zubayr.

' ... that life rises from death,' Rafig cut in, 'and as I die and dying live, so shall we all die and dying live – as Lady Moon told Brother Hare.'

We walked over to the tent to greet Rai's wife, Halima, and two young sons, Nasib and Sakhir – both boys nearing manhood. As we were shaking hands, an older girl emerged from the brushwood shelter, and Rai introduced her as his daughter, Shamsa. I gazed at her and saw large, dark eyes and braided black hair cascading over bare brown shoulders. We shook hands, our eyes met, and I felt something flare up between us, like the scintillation of a falling star. *It will hit you like a stone dropping from the sky.* A tidal wave crashed on the shore of primeval waters, and the wings of a tawny eagle cracked as it swooped on a wide-eared fox, like a quiver running through creation. It was the sacred breath of Earth Mother gushing across stones, speaking a language older than the desert. For a moment I stood frozen like the fox transfixed by the shadow of the eagle. She was young, yet she was more ancient than the desert, as mysterious as the desert wind, yet so familiar that we were indivisible, as we were indivisible from the wind and the desert. *We are the wind, and we are the eye of the wind, and we are that which the wind blows, that blows the wind.*

At that moment, I felt a tale begin in the telling, a new weft woven into the Great Mystery that told the story of all that had ever been or ever would be. *Long, long ago, a young man and a beautiful young woman met in a desert place where there had once flowed a great river ...*

'Welcome,' said Shamsa

'Thank you.'

'The thanks is to God,'

'Oh, yes.'

'I will go and fetch firewood.'

As she glided away, somebody guffawed. I turned to see Zubayr, his face creased with amusement. '*Thank you. Thank you,*' he mimicked. 'Don't you know yet that the thanks is to God? You look as if a lightning scorpion stung you.'

'That's what I feel like.'

'Careful, brother. You are not in a fit state for wooing.'

'*Wooing?*' I spluttered.

Zubayr laughed.

Shamsa and her mother spread mats for us under a leafless acacia tree. The girl brought us water, averting her eyes when she noticed that I was watching her. I hadn't realized it myself until she did that, and I cast my eyes down too late, hearing another a snicker from Zubayr. I started to wonder if he was jealous.

Rai sat down with us and asked for our news.

'The news is good,' Rafig said. He recounted almost everything significant we had experienced, from our meeting with the little nomad, al-Gaa, the Hermit, Saadig's camp, the Fish Eaters, our struggle with hunger and thirst, the sandbur bread, the wells, and the *battikh*. Rai listened in silence.

Soon, the women brought us polenta, dried dates, and sweet tea, and though we were starving we followed Rai's advice, eating slowly, savoring every mouthful. I noticed there was no goat slaughtered in our honor, and though I was grateful for everything we had been given, I was also curious. Now I thought of it, I had not noticed any camels, goats, or sheep around the camp, only carcasses, and I could not help thinking of the crows we had seen, the dead camel, and the animal boneyard.

'It has been a hard season,' Rai admitted 'God is generous, but he has not struck for us with the *'ushub* - the grazing. All our clan have departed for the south, because it is so poor. You will not find another nomad tent here in the Wadi Safra.'

'We have seen it so,' Rafig said. 'There were no nomads at *Salt-Bush Grasping* either. That is why we could not water.'

'Yes, the *'ayn* there is thirty men deep. One cannot water without a long rope and a pulley, and a camel to draw up the buckets. I suppose you do not have such a rope.'

'No. I have visited that *'ayn* many times, but this is the first time I have found her dead.'

'The nomads around the *'ayn* started talking of jinns,' Rai said. 'The rope kept on breaking, and once the pulley-frame came apart and fell into the shaft. They lowered a boy into the shaft on a rope and he got stung by a scorpion. One of the camels they used to draw water went lame, and another - a bull-camel in heat - bit off another herdsboy's fingers. There was no grazing for their animals and they began to die. To cap it all they were plagued by hyenas.'

'*Hyenas*?' My ears pricked up. 'You mean the ones we saw at al-Gaa?'

'Hyenas are hyenas,' Rai chuckled, 'but – God is All-Knowing - they may be the same ones. They have been wandering around like nomads this season, far and wide, because so many animals have died in the drought. It has been a good season for them - they are the only people who have grown fat - hyenas are hunters, but eat carrion if they can find it.'

Rafig and I exchanged a glance. Perhaps the hyenas we had heard calling, and whose tracks we had found, were not following us after all, or at least not for purposes of revenge, as I had begun to imagine. Perhaps the fact that they were ranging much more widely than they normally did was simply due to the drought conditions. I thought of my dream the previous night, and of Zubayr's story of the Fish-Eater who had shot a hyena that turned out to be a pregnant woman. It struck me that things usually had a rational explanation.

'Do you believe hyenas can become people?' I asked Rai.

The nomad's lean face was grave. 'Perhaps. I know the stories – the *Hyena People*, Blind Awda bewitched by a she-hyena and so on – but one must remember that Sister Hyena is the incarnation of a jinn, and if you kill her, her malevolent spirit will never rest until it has taken revenge on you.'

For a moment there was silence. I stared at Rai, then at Rafig, who looked down. I wondered why the old man had not mentioned this. Rai had spoken as if it was something everyone knew, and Rafig, who was a *kahin*, must certainly have known. On one hand it sounded like nonsense, on the other it might explain why, when I had shot the hyena at al-Gaa, both Rafig and the Hermit had seemed disturbed.

I cleared my throat, ready to make a comment, when Rafig cut in, changing the subject.

'Why do you stay here, Rai?' he asked.

The nomad gave him a sheepish glance, but there was a touch of gratitude in it, as if he was pleased someone had at last asked the question.

'God is generous, *Faki*,' he said, 'but we cannot move because we have no camels. All our camels died in the drought - sheep and goats too.'

I stared at him, wondering if I had heard right. He had spoken casually as if the matter was of little importance, without a trace of self-pity.

Rafig did not seem surprised, though – I guessed he had worked it out already. 'The crows and the bones and the smell of rotting meat,' he said. 'I thought you might have some animals left. I did not know things were this bad– I have been away from my clan's tents for three moons – on the way to al-Gaa I travelled up the Pharaoh's Road and spent time in the markets – I did not come this way. Do you have a place to go?'

'We will go to the camp of my wife's brother, Hassan. It is in the Wadi al-Ma, three sleeps away. If we remain here much longer we will be out of provisions.'

I gulped, thinking of the food he had given us so generously.

'We are going to the Wadi al-Ma,' Rafig said. 'Travel with us, Rai, and use our animals. We have three riding camels who are not laden, and then there is that she-camel I got back from the Fish Eaters. She might carry something.'

I cast a glance at Zubyar, aware that Rafig had just promised the use of our camels without asking. The youth smiled back at me and nodded.

Queen

I did not begrudge them Ata, of course, and to object to Rafig's generous offer would have been churlish after Rai's hospitality - how his family must feel I could only imagine. I had not been in nomad country long, but long enough to understand that everything they had was the gift of the desert, through their animals. It was not physically possible for humans to travel the distances between grazing, carrying enough water and food to survive there, without their camels, and the goats and sheep provided milk, meat, and almost all else they needed. It seemed to me that a nomad family who had lost their livestock had lost the world.

We got little sleep that night, and when the Morning Star the nomads called *Zahara* came up, heralding the dawn, we saddled *Ata*, *Hambarib*, and Zubayr's camel, *Warakh*, and led them over and to the nomads' tent, where we couched and hobbled them for loading. Rai helped the women and boys strike the tent, roll it up, tie up poles and pack away tent-pegs. They dismantled the brushwood shelter, stacking up the posts for firewood. It was all done in a precise order, and everything had a place. They quickly stowed all their possessions in pots and gourds, sacks, wooden chests and saddlebags. I halted to watch Shamsa at work in the starlight, until Zubayr nudged me.

'What are you staring at?' he demanded.

'Nothing.'

'Oh, is that what you call it? Nothing? Not a gazelle, a spiral-horn white antelope, or a wide-eared fox like the one in the story? Come on, there's rock-salt to be loaded.'

As Zubayr, Rafig and I heaved our packs of salt on the backs of our kneeling camels, Zubayr said, 'I think our brother here has found his Lost Oasis.'

'Rubbish,' I said. 'A cat can look at a queen, can't he?'

Rafig finished pegging a pair of salt packs. 'There are no queens among the nomads,' he laughed. 'In any case, nomad girls are often promised to their first cousins, so she might not be free.'

By the time everything was in place, the sun was a gold edge on the horizon and the sky was alive with streaks of flaming fire. Rafig took the head-rope, while Zubayr and I helped Rai's wife Halima, and the boys, Nasib and Sakhir, mount the camels. Shamsa waited till last, and when her turn came, she shook her head so that her braided locks swayed like a curtain, and laughed shyly. 'I'm not riding,' she told me. 'I am strong and can walk as well as any man.'

She untied a red head-cloth sewn with cowrie shells from her waist and looped it neatly around her hair, then helped us raise the camels to their feet.

'We go in God's safe-keeping,' Rafig announced.

Catfish

The *Well of the Catfish* was a short distance from the camp, and was marked by a round white stone with a hole in the centre, and the skull of a donkey placed on a cairn. I examined the donkey-skull and found inside it a piece of hide into which had been sewn the mummified head of a snake – a viper, I thought.

Rafig and Zubayr took the salt-caravan on, while Rai and I couched the riding camels, and, with Nasib and Sakhir, took turns to draw water. There was a mud basin, where we poured water for the camels, and while Shamsa and Halima supervised the animals, the four of us filled the water-skins.

'Why is there a donkey's skull?' I asked Rai, nodding at the cairn, 'and a white stone with a hole in it, and a viper's head sewn into a piece of leather?'

'To ward off the evil eye,' Rai told me at once, hauling up a bucket hand over hand. 'This well is precious to us, for as long as there is water, there is life.'

'What *is* the evil eye exactly?' I asked, remembering the thirsty nomad near Elai, and his reaction when I had praised his camel.

'It is the *Eye of Envy*. Whenever one looks at anything with an admiring glance, a jinn attaches itself to that glance as it leaves one's eye. The jinn may bring evil to the object of admiration.'

I balked, remembering how I had felt when I had looked at Shamsa the previous day. The last thing I intended was to bring harm to her.

'All wells have a benevolent spirit,' Rai went on. 'We put up these amulets to help keep evil jinns away.'

'All right, I understand the skull and the viper's head – but the stone with the hole?'

'No ordinary stone – some say stones like these were made by the Anakim – the Lost Giants – in the Distant Time.'

I held the mouth of a water-skin open, and he tipped the bucket, pouring the water in without spilling a drop.

'Jinns are easily scared, then,' I said.

'There are certain things they do not like - tar, salt, or the smoke of bitter plants. They do not like skulls, nor white stones with holes in, nor the heads of snakes – especially vipers.'

The water-skin was full, I realized. Grasping the mouth tightly, I laid it down on its side, while Rai tied it.   When that was done, the boys picked it up by the saddle-loops and carried it over to where the camels were drinking. I took the bucket and dropped it into the well. After I had hoisted enough water to fill another bag, one of the boys took the bucket, while Rai and I looked on.

'Are jinns also afraid of catfish?' I asked him. 'Is that how the well got its name?'

The nomad laughed. 'No. The story is that, once, in the Distant Time, a Fish Eater came walking along the Wadi Safra in the hot season. He had come from his own country far to the west, and he had foundered his camel. He was dying of thirst, but of course the well was dead – there were no nomads here. The well is seven men deep, and the Fish Eater did not have a rope, so do you know what he did?'

'No.'

'He jumped into the well. It must have taken a lot of courage, but he did it, leaving only his sandals at the well-head in case anyone should come by. He was not hurt and the water was only up to his chest, so he drank his fill and just waited, putting his trust in the Great Spirit.'

'What happened to him?'

'A party of nomads came along, saw his sandals at the well-head, and realized there was a Fish Eater in the well.'

'How did they know it was a Fish Eater?'

'Because of the sandals. Fish Eaters wear sandals, nomads wear slippers. Anyway, shouting down the shaft, they realized that the man was alive. They had a rope with them, and pulled him out. He told them he had been in the well for several days, and that, every time he had felt himself slipping under the water, a great catfish with long whiskers had appeared and buoyed him up. She was the spirit of the well, she said. Her name was *Labuna* and she had told him stories to keep him awake. She said she had been here since the time before the desert was the desert, when great rivers ran and there were great waters that one could follow for many moons and not find an end of them, and the waters were full of fish.'

This was fascinating, and I wanted to ask more, but the water-skins were full, and we had to catch up with Rafig and Zubayr. We loaded the skins on the camels, helped Halima and the boys into the saddle, and got them to their feet.

Muhanni

It took half the morning to cross the Wadi Safra, and, with the camels, we followed the contours of the land, dipping gently from the high banks through acres of sun-dried grasses and skeleton trees. There were low dunes with grass-clumps and endless hillocks of sand with stunted caper bushes, and twisted *arak*, as far as the eye could see. There was almost nothing for the camels to eat, though. Quite often we came across the carcasses of animals picked clean by vultures, hyenas, jackals, and crows, whose tracks Rafig or Rai pointed out. The core of the wadi was a channel of sand rippled, not by wind, but by water. Though dry as a bone now, I guessed that water must run freely here when the rains were abundant.

We had strung the riding camels together, and Rai led them from the front, following Rafig and Zubayr with the main caravan. Shamsa and I walked behind the riding camels. At first we were shy with each other – I could not think what to say and felt self-conscious. I was not one of her people, not a nomad - I had not grown up here, and did not know their ways, especially with women. She was the only nomad woman I had been close to - perhaps she would not even understand me, I thought. I recalled the startling images that had come into my head when we had met the previous day. I had felt drawn to her with a powerful, magnetic pull, and at the time I had been somehow certain that she felt the same as I did – as if we were not strangers, but had always known each other. I remembered how that sentence had appeared in my head - *Long, long ago, a young man and a beautiful young woman met in a desert place where there had once flowed a great river* ... as if the whole story had happened already. That gave me a cue, I realized.

'Tell me,' I said. 'Is it true that long ago the Wadi Safra used to be a great river?'

She smiled, showing clean white teeth. 'Oh yes,' she said. 'So the old stories say – the ones my father tells us. In the Distant Time it was called the Yellow Nile, and water flowed down from Fish Eater country to the west, as far east as the bend in the Nile. That was before anyone alive now was born, before our grandfathers and our grandfathers' grandfathers' grandfathers ...'

' ... oh, grandfathers' grandfathers' grandfathers,' I said, laughing. 'It was long, long ago. I get the picture.'

She laughed too, and I realized at once that I had been right: we knew each other.

'Your father told me the story about the *Well of the Catfish*,' I said. 'How the Fish Eater was saved by a great catfish called *Labuna*, the spirit of the well, who had remained there since the time the desert was covered in water.'

She squinted sideways at me as we walked. 'Do you know the story of the flood?' she asked.

'Not really.'

'Well, long ago …' she chuckled, 'of course, it's always long ago - *al-Lat* - Earth Mother - became angry with the Children of Adam, and caused the rain to fall so hard that all the rain of a season fell in a single day, and it rained for many days – day after day after day – until the whole world was covered in water, flowing in raging torrents as far as *al-Qaf* – the mountains at the end of the world.'

She stopped talking and glanced at me to see if I had understood. I nodded.

'Well, the rain fell with crashes of thunder and lightning scorpions, on the palaces of kings and the hoarders of treasure, who had broken their covenant with Earth Mother through selfishness and greed, and they and all their works were washed away - nothing remained, not even a memory.

'Of all Adam's Children, there was only one who escaped with his family. That was a man called Wadd, who alone had kept his covenant with Earth Mother. Forewarned by her, Wadd, with his brothers and their wives and children, and all their animals, and all the creatures they could save, had climbed to the top of *al-Qaf* – the mountains at the end of the world. They remained there for forty sleeps, and on the last morning two ravens appeared out of the clouds. The ravens told Wadd that Earth Mother's rage was spent, and that the flood waters were going down.

'So Wadd and his family and all the creatures they had taken with them, came down from the mountain, and found a world that was green and lush, with forests and prairies of grass, running with water from many streams and rivers and great lakes, teeming with fish – including catfish like *Labuna* - and their people multiplied, and their animals multiplied, and the creatures they had saved from the floods multiplied, and they lived in a fat land where they had milk and honey, meat and bread, and they stood in need of nothing. Wadd and all his clan were grateful for their deliverance, and swore in the name of Earth Mother that they would never break their covenant, and would ever after love the Great Spirit, the Earth and all her creatures, and love themselves and love all Adam's children, and they would practice *muhanni* forever.'

'What a tale,' I said. 'What is *muhanni* then?'

'Giving us the use of your camels to move to my uncle's camp is *muhanni*. It is the nomad way.'

'How does it work?'

She giggled. Then she noticed that we had fallen behind a little and hurried to catch up with the caravan. I followed her and for a while we walked in step, watching the camels as they slouched and swayed ahead of us. After a moment, Shamsa said.

'You asked about *muhanni*. Do you know Shadad?'

'Shadad the Hunter? You mean the constellation - the stars?'

'Yes, he is up there. There are many stories about him. He lived in the Distant Time, and wore a cloak of lion-skin – there were lions in those days. He carried a great bow that only he could bend, a throwing stick, and a spear.   Once, he had been travelling across the desert for many days on his camel and was exhausted, hungry and thirsty, when a buck gazelle crossed his path. Knowing the Great Spirit had sent the gazelle to save his life, and that the animal was old, and was offering himself, he brought it down with his bow and arrow.

He made camp, then giving thanks to the Great Spirit, he skinned the old gazelle and cooked the meat on the fire - so hungry was he that the smell of roasting meat made him feel faint. The meat was roasted, and he laid the succulent pieces on a stone, and was just about to eat, when he saw a nomad family coming – a man and his wife and children. They had no animals with them, for the animals had died in the drought.

Shadad rose to meet them with a smile on his face, and bade them sit by his fire, and he gave them water, and offered them the meat of the gazelle. Even though they begged him to eat with them he refused saying.

'The Great Spirit has brought you as my guests, and your coming is blest. Eat until you can eat no more.'

The next morning, Shadad mounted all the nomads on his camel, andnled them over dunes, and plains and mountains, to the camp of his clan. There, he made them welcome, gave them a place to build their shelter, gave them a camel from his herd to fetch water and firewood, and made sure they had food and milk for as long as they wished.

'Since the nomad had no animals, Shadad invited him to help herd his camels, goats and sheep, and in return gave him a she-camel in calf every season, or two if the rains were abundant. The she-camels gave birth to their calves and the calves grew and multiplied, and soon the nomad had a herd of his own. He exchanged some camels for goats and sheep, and they also multiplied, and the nomad and his family wanted for nothing. One season, when the rains came, they decided to take their animals to the Lush.

'They went to Shadad to thank him, and he told them, 'give thanks only to the Great Spirit, for we are one in the wind, the breath and the spirit, and we are all part of the Face of God.'

'So the nomad and his family left Shadad's camp, and from that day, whenever they encountered others, they would share with them, and help them, and extend to them kindness and generosity, mutual aid and well-being, and those others would do the same for others, and the others for yet other others, and so *muhanni* grew like an ever-branching tree among the nomads, and everyone had a duty to assist everyone else, even strangers, and, while there was food, no one ever went hungry or remained without a helping hand.'

Shamsa spoke in a musical tone, almost as if she were reciting poetry, and her dark eyes flashed, and her voice was girlish and lilting – almost entrancing. I guessed she was accustomed to telling stories, like most of the nomads I had encountered. The concept of *muhanni*, too, was a revelation – everything Rafig and Brahim and others had told me about the nomad way, became suddenly clear. The nomads lived in sharing communities, where everyone was equal, no-one accumulated wealth, and where greed and selfishness were treated with contempt. By sharing, the nomads nurtured the whole community, and no-one was left out - all that was expected of them was the good will to treat others in the same way.

'Now I understand why you and your family don't seem sad despite having lost your animals,' I told Shamsa. 'I thought that to lose your livestock must be to lose the world, but I see it is not like that.'

She laughed and nodded. 'We will not go hungry because all our people have is shared. Though it is sad that our animals have died, it is as it is. God is generous. No, we have no need to be afraid, because we are not alone.'

Hunted

The caravan paced on, and we walked together, and the day was silent except for the creaking of saddles and salt-packs, the slap of water in the skins, the rumbling and snorting of camels and occasional snatches of conversation from the others. For me there was just the voice of this woman mingling with my voice, and our words crossing and weaving around each other like musical counterpoints, in windings and configurations, intertwining like serpents on a caduceus, as we told tales that formed and broke, that reshaped the desert and remodeled the sky – stories of lost oases, shape-shifters, and swooping eagles, trickster foxes and poison winds, from beyond and from the deeps within us, strange and familiar, affirming what we had known from the instant we had met, that we were not strangers, that we had always known each other, and we *were* each other, and had simply been waiting for this moment to manifest.

We left the sandy plain and entered a wilderness of black stones where the land rose up to a wall of hills like monstrous shoulder bones, and the caravan was confined to ancient paths threading through the stones, so narrow that Shamsa and I had to walk one behind the other. The hills were bare, blue and sand-sculpted - ancient protrusions from the desert, thrusting in fluted buttresses out of delves and depressions where seams of sand showed through, and where bony trees with pale trunks plied tentatively between the rocks.

The sun was dipping as we reached the saddle between the hills, and the shadows of the camels were spidery shapes on the rough surface, and from the top we looked over a vast blue-black plain of sand and scrub that rolled on and on, until it dissolved into greyness far to the south. Letting the caravan descend into the valley, we turned to view the way we had come, Shamsa pointed out something in the distance. The land was half in darkness with bright spots picked out by the last lucid rays of the sun, and at first I could not see anything. Then, with her insistence, I made out a dark curlicue moving through one of the brighter peaks. From here it looked no bigger than a fly, but I thought it might be a man on a camel. Shamsa's eyesight was more acute than mine, though. 'It is an animal,' she said, peering intently. 'A four-legged, but not a dog or a goat or a sheep.' She paused, then said. 'I think it is a hyena. It seems to be following our trail.'

Her words chilled me. I had not thought about hyenas all day, transported elsewhere by my conversation with her. Now I remembered what her father, Rai had said about hyenas being jinns and about their malevolent spirits taking revenge.

'It isn't sunset yet,' I said. 'Don't hyenas come out only at night?'

She laughed. 'My father told me they prefer the dark, but they will come out in daytime if they are disturbed. Anyway, this is the last of the light.'

I nodded. Then, casting a last glance in that direction I said.

'Come on. The caravan will leave us behind.'

We hurried to catch up before full darkness fell, and followed the camels as they shuffled down paths that fanned out like veins through the dark stony wasteland, down to the pebbled skirts of the hills, where Rafig and Zubayr, still at the head of the caravan, found a sandy salient just outside the boulder field large enough for all the camels to rest. There were many firestones here, and fragments of ropes and broken harness and hobbles, and nubs of blackened firewood, and piles of dry camel-droppings, showing that this was a place favored by caravans, though there was nothing here for the camels to eat.

Rai and his family helped us to unload the salt packs, and after dark we built two fires in the lee of the piled saddles and the women cooked polenta on one of them. Since we had almost no provisions left, we had to rely on the flour and dates Rai and his family had brought with them – there was enough for all of us, though it would not last us to our destination, and from the next day, we knew, we would have to trust in the Great Spirit.

Afterwards we sat round a single fire, the women and boys on one side, the men on the other, talking, telling stories. I stared into the fire, glimpsing the face of Shamsa, soft and insubstantial through the flames. Later, we left the women and boys to sleep near the fire, took our blankets a few paces away and settled down to sleep.

Voice

I fell asleep quickly, and I dreamed of Shamsa, and of wings beating, soaring across great open spaces, and I awoke suddenly to hear her voice calling my name out of the darkness. I sat up and looked around. I could not see much - just the dark patches that I assumed were the other men sleeping nearby, the faintest glow of the fire, and a lighter area where the camels slumbered with their heads lowered. The voice came again – that lilting, musical voice, enticingly girlish. I threw my blanket aside, put on my slippers, and picked up my torch. I worked the switch, but there was no light – I guessed the battery was dead. I put it down, picked up my stick, and started walking towards the place I thought the voice had come from, away from the camp and out into the darkling desert. Shamsa called a third time, and this time the tone was urgent, as if she were in trouble. I was tempted to call back to her, but when I opened my mouth no sound emerged.

The voice came once more, almost shrill, close at hand, and I walked faster, fancying I saw the girl's outline in the wan starlight. When I was within a short distance, though, the shadow seemed to fade into deeper folds of the darkness. I halted. Almost at once the girl's voice came again, now from far away – the same mournful call, more urgent than ever. For some reason, I was still unable to call back, but I made my way towards her, moving faster, stumbling over stones. As I came nearer I made out another shadow, and this time the merest hint of red eyes in the darkness. The shadow called my name, but the voice was deep and throaty - it no longer sounded like Shamsa. Still, I was stumbling my way to the spot, when once again the outline vanished. I stopped and listened. There was absolute silence.

I was in pitch darkness. There were pale stars above me, but I had not been watching them and was unable to judge direction. Our camp was invisible, and I had absolutely no idea where it lay, or how to get back there. I turned round and walked the way I thought I had come, but after some paces I began to doubt, turned to my right, and hurried in that direction.

I walked for what seemed like a long time, trying to make out the shapes of the hills. The darkness remained utterly impenetrable, though, and I was sure this could not be the right direction. I wheeled round again, but now I had not the faintest idea which way I had come - I was more hopelessly adrift than ever. I started to walk fast, then to run, without even caring where I was going – just to get away, to get somewhere, to escape from the imprisoning night. I was totally lost in a way that I had never experienced before, and it was frightening.

I stopped again, desperately casting this way and that. I was just thinking that either I would have to stay here till morning, or shout for help, when suddenly a voice called my name again. This time it was clearly not Shamsa, but a man's voice, coming from behind. I turned and saw a dark figure almost on top of me.

'What are you doing?' the voice said. 'Why did you wander off in the middle of the night?'

It was Rafig. I could not see him properly in the darkness but I was certain it was he.

'Shamsa,' I stammered. 'She called to me.'

'That girl is sound asleep back in camp,' Rafig said.

Mimesis

It took us only two more sleeps to bring the caravan to the camp of Shamsa's uncle, Hassan, and both nights we were lucky enough to find nomads, who welcomed us and brought us meat, polenta and camel's milk. Shamsa and I walked together for much of the journey, though I never told her what had happened that night when I thought I had heard her calling. We saw no more of the hyena we had glimpsed from the pass in the hills, and I never mentioned it again. Neither did it trouble us in those two days.

On the second morning, though, I walked at the head of the caravan with Rafig, while Zubayr and Shamsa brought up the rear. Rafig kept laughing at me for looking back to see what the two of them were up to, though I swear I did not realize I was doing it.

'*Oh, she is like the Lady Moon on a dark night,*' the old man recited, chuckling.

Her slender figure, the glamour of her eyes,

Entrance you.

Her black hair falls down her back,

But beware the snakes hidden in her braids,

For though her body is as soft as a gazelle's,

Her heart is harder than a rock.'

'That is not true,' I told him, laughing, 'not unless snakes mean life, as you told me. I can't help thinking of how I heard her voice calling to me from the desert, though. Was I dreaming do you think?'

'Perhaps,' Rafig said. 'Some people walk in their sleep. It makes no difference, though – dreaming and waking are all in the Great Spirit.'

We walked without speaking for a while, and the only sound was our slippers crunching on the surface of the desert. We were crossing a barren plain of browns and burnt sienna, towards coils of dust-smoke rising on the skyline as if from hidden fires.

'I remember you told Atman that an encounter in a dream is an encounter in the world,' I said to Rafig, 'but now you say it's an encounter in the Great Spirit. Isn't that different?'

'*How?*' the old man laughed. 'The Great Spirit is not in the world – the world is in the Great Spirit. Dreaming and waking are in both the world *and* the Great Spirit, for everything we experience is the Great Spirit's Dreaming.'

I laughed, not because it didn't make sense, but because it somehow seemed self-evident, yet at the same time went against all I had been brought up to believe. 'All right,' I said, 'but if that is so – I mean if there is only *one* thing - the *Great Spirit*, the *Great Spirit's Dreaming*, whatever you wish to call it – why do you not have *my* dream? Why do I not have yours? Why can I not tell what you are thinking – or read the thoughts of the camels here?'

'Because of *al-Kashfa* - the veil,' Rafig said. 'Do you not remember I spoke of this before? Although we are all one in the Great Spirit, there is a veil between our thoughts and dreams and those of others that prevents us from seeing beyond. *Al-Khashfa* is thin and flimsy, though, and sometimes we may glimpse the Face of God through it. That is what happens with the *Sandlines* and other ways of seeing – in dreams and in trance. Sometimes it can come suddenly for no reason. The day we found the *battikh*, for instance, just before your spirit left you, you looked as if you were seeing another world.'

'I remember,' I said. 'Yes. I had this feeling ... I was walking in the desert, then there was just walking in the desert, but nobody walking.'

Rafig nodded and chuckled.

I thought it over and the camels padded softly behind us, and the water in the skins made a squishing sound from the swaying motion of their walk. I could hear voices from the rear of the caravan and guessed Shamsa and Zubayr were talking. I felt a pang of jealousy, wondering if they were getting on well together, wondering whether Shamsa preferred his company to mine. I suppressed the urge to look behind. I thought instead of the powerful feeling of connection I had had when I had first met her – how I had been certain she felt the same. I wondered if, at that moment, we had glimpsed the real through the veil that seemed to separate us, just as Rafig had described.

My thoughts returned to the curious events of the other night, and right on cue, Rafig said. 'God is All-Knowing, but it is said that hyenas can imitate human voices. Sometimes they will lure people into the desert by mimicking the voice of someone they love, enticing them further and further into the wilderness until they are far from help, then attacking and eating them.'

This was uncannily similar to how I remembered the events of that night: hearing Shamsa's voice, following the sound of it as it retreated, until I was hopelessly lost – except that nothing had attacked and eaten me, of course.

'Why didn't you tell me about the hyena's revenge?' I asked. 'You know – what Rai said – that hyenas are jinns embodied, and if you kill one, her malevolent spirit will not rest until she has wrought revenge on you.'

'We cannot be certain you killed one,' Rafig said, but he looked uneasy, I thought. 'You shot at one and there was blood, that's all. In any case, not everyone believes hyenas are jinns.'

'If I remember rightly, the Hermit said I was *cursed*,' I replied. 'I didn't understand it then, but I do now. Whatever one says, *something* ripped open our water-skin, which resulted in the torture of thirst for all of us – and I collapsed. We were saved only by the *battikh*. *Something* lured me into the desert on a pitch-dark night, too. I'm wondering if it could be the same pregnant woman with red eyes I saw sitting by the fire at *Broken Hobble*, and the voice saying *some things appear to be hyenas, but are not.*'

Rafig blinked. 'You saw a woman? Why did you not mention it?'

'Why didn't *you* tell me that hyenas are jinns back at al-Gaa?'

'Because jinns are all around us as well as inside us, and they have *very* keen ears.'

Peace

It was afternoon when we reached the Wadi al-Ma, a vast belt of trees standing on both sides of a dry river bed that coiled through the desert like an enormous serpent. I guessed it had been part of the great river system that had once criss-crossed the desert – a system that had included the Wadi Safra, the so-called *Yellow Nile.*

The tents of Hassan's clan were pitched on the banks of the sandy bed, in a dense thicket of acacia trees, some of them massive and ancient. We followed the water-course as it cut through the forest tunnel, passing through dappled light, through herds of browsing camels, flocks of sheep and goats moving in clouds of acrid-smelling dust. A little further on, men, women and children were gathered round a *sanya* – a deep well – and we saw camels hoisting heavy buckets of water by long ropes on a wooden pulley. It spun and rattled as the buckets came up.

Rai led us to a cluster of camel's hair tents neatly pitched on the wadi side, and we climbed the bank and couched the caravan in the shade of the tall trees. We started unloading rock-salt for what Rafig said would be the last time. He belonged to another, but related, clan, he explained, and though his folk watered further up the same wadi, the rock salt would remain here. The interested parties would have to bring fresh camels to pick up their share.

As we were easing the salt-packs down, Hassan came to welcome us. In contrast to his brother-in-law, the lean, wild-looking Rai, Hassan was robustly cheerful –rather too plump and well fed for a nomad, with a trim beard and a head like a gourd. He shook hands heartily with us all, declared our arrival blest, and showed Rai where he and his family might pitch their tent.

Rai, Halima, Shamsa, and the boys, had already couched the riding camels, and were unloading them in the same systematic way –- items in exact reverse order to that in which they had been packed. After we had unsaddled the salt-camels and sent them out to browse in the trees, we helped the family unpack their baggage and put up the tent. Hassan came over to supervise with his two sons – bright, lively boys named Sayf and Dahil. They were obviously delighted to see Shamsa and her brothers and were soon laughing together. It gave me a pang when I remembered that these boys were Shamsa's first cousins and that she might be engaged to one of them. Then I considered the age difference – they were little more than children, and she was a grown woman. It seemed unlikely, I thought.

'Let your camels rest and eat,' Hassan told us. 'God's witness, we have had no rain here this season, but there are still leaves on the trees, and grass left from past rains. As for your animals, it is easy to see that the journey to al-Gaa has drained their strength.'

Later, Hassan called Rai, Rafig, Zubayr and me over, spreading a rug under a tree nearby. He introduced us to his wife, Nayla, a moon-faced woman with almond-shaped eyes and high cheek-bones, wearing a gold nose-ring, who brought us fresh camel's milk in a huge bowl of carved black wood. She handed the bowl to Rafig, who took it with both hands, and offered it to me. I refused, ready to go through the usual ritual of deferment, but Rafig shook his head. 'You must drink first because here you are the least known, and the least known is the most honored.'

'What do you mean, *least known?*'

'Apart from Rai, none of us is truly known here, but Zubayr and I have connections with the family. In that sense you are the least known, and therefore the most welcome.' He held out the bowl again. 'Camel's milk is sacred to the nomads, and drinking is a sacrament. You must drink crouching, not standing or sitting, and you must grasp the bowl with both hands.'

I crouched, took the bowl with both hands, and drank in gulps. The milk was frothy and warm and had a slight salty taste. I imagined I could discern in it the mellow flavour of desert flowers. It was, I thought, the perfect reward for our hard journey.

I passed the bowl back to Rafig, who passed it to Zubayr, who drank and passed it to Rai, and as the bowl went round it struck me that the drinking had a ceremonial quality - the milk was nature's gift, coming to us through the camels, directly from the desert plants. In drinking it we were drinking the desert.

The nomads began to exchange the news, and I sat back and watched the sunset throw a pattern of colours among the branches, seeing campfires winking out of the shadows along the wadi banks, watching camels and flocks of goats and sheep moving placidly along the sandy bed in a sheen of dust. Birds trilled in the trees, and from somewhere came the clicking rasp of an unseen animal Rafig told me was a *coney*. I remembered the constellation named *Coney Night Caller,* and though I had no idea what the animal looked like, I understood now why she was famous for her night calls. I was a stranger here yet I felt at peace. I had left the town in search of the Lost Oasis, and though I had not found it, and was not sure that it even existed, I had already found so much more than I could have dreamed of. There was a palpable atmosphere of trust and contentment in this place – and despite having been here only a short time, deep down I knew it. It was this life, close to the Earth, shorn of all pretensions and trifles that I had come to see, to feel, to be part of.

Shaken

Hasan had slaughtered a sheep in our honor and after dark, when we had brought in our camels and laid out our own camp, we returned to his tent for the feast. Our host and his two sons brought in great trays of meat and polenta and we all tucked in. '*Eat. Eat.*' Hassan roared whenever one of us hesitated. 'Is there something wrong with this food? Your coming is blest. You are welcome here.'

Afterwards as we sat drinking tea, Hassan told his brother-in-law, Rai, that, in the morning, he would bring him a camel, and would make sure the family did not go short of food and milk. 'Then, when you are ready,' he said, 'I would be honored if you would herd camels with my sons, Sayf and Dahil here. They need a man of your experience to guide them.'

Rai did not thank his brother-in-law, neither did Hassan treat him as anything other than a respected guest. There was no sense that Hassan was granting a favor - it seemed rather that by being there, Rai was doing a favor to Hassan. 'The Children of Adam do not control the rain nor the sun,' Hassan said, as if in explanation. 'Humans are not in charge of the blowing of the wind, nor the growing of the grass, nor the blooming of the trees, nor the flight of the grey cranes over the desert. It is as God wills. Today drought has taken your animals, Rai, and tomorrow it may be mine. The wealth of the nomads does not lie in camels, goats, or sheep. It lies in the love that we have for our people. To love and trust the Great Spirit, all Adam's children, and each other – that is the way to live.'

Hassan and Rafig had not met before, but when Rafig introduced himself, our host looked slightly puzzled. 'Of course I know of your family, *Faki*,' he said, 'and your reputation, but I had heard that some misfortune had befallen you, and that you had gone away.'

Rafig smiled thinly. 'God took my son unto God, may God's mercy be upon him,' he said. 'He ran foul of a bull-camel in heat.'

'God's mercy be upon him,' Hassan echoed, 'and His peace be upon you, *Faki*. It seems our news is not always sound.' He still looked doubtful, though. He had obviously heard something different, and since nomad news was notorious for its accuracy, was loathe to let it go.

They continued talking, exploring connections between families, and in due course the conversation drifted in my direction. Although I knew by now that nomads considered it rude to ask directly what a stranger's business was, I felt that I was obliged to give an account of myself. I muttered something about searching for the Lost Oasis, glancing at Rafig. I was aware that the *kahin* had taken me with him on the salt-caravan partly as a test of my worthiness, and I was not at all sure that I had passed it. There had been the business of shooting the hyena, wandering out into the desert at night in response to what might have been a hallucination, the numerous times my lurking jinn had turned up.

Rafig made no comment, but Hassan said. 'I have heard such tales – everyone has - but to me they are but the story of the desert. Like a rug shaken by the wind, the landscape flaps, ripples, and rolls, while remaining the same rug. Rain falls in the *Lush*, and green grass and yellow flowers bloom as far as one can see - a paradise. Nomads arrive there with their camels from every direction. Then the rain stops, the grass fades and the *Lush* is lush no longer. The nomads leave, and the wind wails over a red land. You may search for your paradise, but you will not find it because the grasses and the flowers have gone.'

'You mean there is no such place as the Lost Oasis?' I asked.

Hassan laughed. 'When you look at a cloud, you may think you see something in it – a man riding a camel, say, or a dog chasing a hare. If you continue to watch, though, you see that the cloud is constantly changing at the edges, and soon it does not look like what you thought you saw at all.'

'Like a mirage in the desert? The *Devil's Mirror*?'

'Yes. In due course the cloud vanishes, leaving the sky. The sky is always the same – at least while the sun is up - it only seems to change because of the clouds, but it is the clouds that change, not the sky. The Lost Oasis is a story like the clouds. The moment you think you know what it is, it has already become something else.'

'I understand,' I said. 'You are saying it's just a story, but isn't it so that there is no story without an element of truth?'

'Truth is not always what it seems,' Hassan said, smiling. 'Something tells me that you have not really come to find the Lost Oasis. Perhaps it is a lost part of yourself you are looking for.'

I nodded, wondering if this was hint about Shamsa. Rai must have told his brother-in-law that his daughter – Hassan's niece – and I, had enjoyed each other's company on the journey here from Wadi Safra. That much must have been obvious – in the desert, nothing could be hidden. Was the *lost part of me* Hassan had referred to an oblique reference to any thoughts I might have about his niece as my *soul mate*?

'Perhaps,' I said, 'but I still have to find out if the Lost Oasis exists. That is the task I have set myself.'

Hassan nodded. 'Very well. A man knows what he must do, but such a journey involves great hardship and difficulty. If the Lost Oasis does exist, it can only be deep in the *Hurra*, and this is not the best season for a journey into that region. The *Night Maidens* will soon fall, and after that the desert knows no coolness. Many have died of thirst there. Why not be patient till the *Night Maidens* rise?

I told him that I would consider his words, but I knew I could make no decision until I had talked with Rafig.

Chance

Afterwards, Rafig, and I walked back in the darkness to our camp under the trees, leaving Zubayr talking with Rai and Hassan. We checked our camels to make sure they were comfortable. I found Ata in the moonlight and chucked him under the chin – he snapped at my fingers playfully and ground his teeth, reminding me that it was a while since I had ridden him. His last job had been carrying Shamsa's mother, Halima, and her family's household goods.

The two of us sat down on our blankets and I asked Rafig politely why he had made no comment about our proposed journey to look for the Lost Oasis. I told him that I understood the salt-caravan had been a test of my merit, and that he had never committed to the Lost Oasis quest. I said that I thought I had done my best, although I knew I might have let him down on some occasions and had perhaps fallen short. If so, then I would understand, but I believed this was the moment of truth, and I knew by now that he was an honest man and would tell me the truth.

170

Rafig considered it carefully for a moment, then said. 'God is All Knowing and nothing is hidden from Him. Lies are no good to you. You worked hard on the journey – you dug the salt, and you loaded the camels, and you marched all day, and you accepted heat, thirst, hunger and fatigue mostly without complaint. You did not fall short in effort. On the other hand, you sometimes let the jinn take over, such as when you shot the hyena – that was a mistake. It rendered you – and us - vulnerable to attack by the unseen.'

'So you *do* believe that hyenas are jinns then?'

'Jinns are everywhere, in some hyenas, and certainly in ourselves. As I told you, we all have the *qarin* we are born with – the twin that may lure us into evil. Lies are of no use to you - you still have that self-importance, the jinn's voice speaking in you. That is not good, but at least you are aware of it, and that is the first and most crucial step in overcoming it.'

'So you will help me find the Lost Oasis?'

Rafig shook his head. 'I know nothing of any Lost Oasis,' he said.

Something cold passed down my spine as I stared at him. It seemed that the inner voice that had been nagging at me since we had left al-Gaa had been right. It had been a mistake to trust this man, and now, after all the hardship and the struggle I had endured, he was going to ditch me. I remembered how, earlier that evening, Hassan had seemed to regard Rafig with suspicion and had looked at him as if he were not telling the truth. So much, I thought, for bread and salt.

'Very well,' I said. 'I will go alone.'

Rafig raised an eyebrow. Then he laughed.

'Why?' he said. 'I did not say I would not go with you. I have said from the start that I know of no Lost Oasis. I can promise only to try and help you find the oasis my father told me about – the one he called the *Oasis of Last Chance*. Be clear I said *try*. I promise no more and no less – and may the Great Spirit go with us.'

I felt flushed with relief. How could I ever have doubted him? I was so relieved I wanted to hug him and thank him effusively, but I restrained myself, knowing it was not appropriate. 'God bless you,' was all I could say.

'The way will not be easy,' he added, 'but we will take only two camels and travel fast. First, though, you must remain here for a few sleeps. Tomorrow I will go to greet my family and tell them the rock-salt is here. I will take another camel for now, and *Hambarib* will have a chance to eat and rest before the journey. I will be back shortly.'

'What about the hyena?' I asked. 'Do you think she will give us a break now we are here?'

Rafig looked troubled. 'Perhaps, but if she is truly a jinn she will return to plague us until she has taken her revenge. We must consider what to do about that.'

I nodded. 'Very well.'

'You and Zubayr look after the camels while I am gone. You are welcome here, but you are Hassan's guest, so be careful about your conduct with Shamsa. I know … *she is as lovely as a rising moon and as graceful as a spiral-horn white antelope, and one glance from her gazelle-like eyes takes your breath away,* and all that … but if you have serious intentions, you must find out if she is spoken for, even among nomads, nothing causes more conflict than jealousy over a woman.'

Litters

Rafig left early the next morning, and during the following days Zubayr and I kept each other company, herding the camels and watering them at the *sanya* further down the wadi. Sometimes we would ask Shamsa's brothers, Nasim and Shakhr, to keep an eye on our animals, and wander around visiting tents. Always the nomads would make us feel welcome, as if we had done them great honor by our visit. They would invite us to sit in the shade and bring us bowls of fresh camel's milk, tea, polenta, or meat. They were so welcoming and warm that just being with them was a pleasure. They loved nothing more than to talk and tell stories, yet they were always busy with their hands.

The women used wooden spindles to make yarn from the wool of camels, goats, and sheep. Once, we stopped to watch some women weaving the yarn into squares on a flat loom pieced together from sticks, using a gazelle-horn as a shuttle. Zubayr said they would later stitch the squares into a rectangle called a *shugga*, which would form part of a tent. 'Our *Tu* women do not have this art,' he said. 'We make our tents from the fibre of dwarf palms – that is more like basketwork. We build our lodges from brushwood and grass.'

We watched nomad men making water-skins, pinning out a hide in the sun, and smearing it with a paste made from sheep or goat brains, mixed with the crushed bark of white-thorn trees. They would shape the dried skin into a bag, stitching it at the edges, fashioning the legs into saddle-loops, then filling the whole thing with sand and leaving it to dry. When the water-skin was ready, they would waterproof it with tar made from the crushed seeds of bitter melons - the ones Rafig had talked about. We also watched men making camel saddles and litters from the light, tough wood of caper or white-thorn trees that grew in the wadi, carving the parts with their razor-sharp knives, binding them together with strips of goat-hide. The litter was a framework of light wood superimposed on a saddle, over which drapes and covers could be laid to provide shade, almost like a tiny house on camel's back. When I asked one nomad why he was making a litter, he sighed.

'We make these for the great migration to the north,' he said, 'so that women and infants may travel out of the sun. The rains have been so poor these last seasons, though – we only moved a short way, then returned. Ah, but to see the whole clan moving at once with all they have on camel's back, and the litters in bright colors, and the camels wearing ostrich feather plumes, and the saddlery shimmering with cowrie shells, and the camel herds moving and the goat and sheep flocks moving in a golden sheen of dust – now that is a sight that fills one's heart with joy.'

'I hope to see that,' I said.

The man shook his head. 'Only if God strikes for us on the rains this season,' he said. 'The Great Spirit is Generous – we shall see.'

We talked to women potters who molded pots from red clay, firing them with charcoal in a kiln of stones. We watched a gunsmith make a one-shot rifle like Rafig's, working on a portable anvil on a spike stuck in the earth, while another man made flat-nosed lead bullets in on a bellows-fed fire. Women and girls spent much time shaking water-skins on frames to make buttermilk, or on their hands and knees grinding grain on flat stones, like the one we had used to grind sandbur seeds in *the Lush*.

After a few days in the camp, I began to feel as If I had been there forever. The way the nomads lived called strongly to me. They owned little, yet their lives were rich and meaningful. I envied them. Just being with them gave me a glimpse of how joyous life could have been for everyone, I thought.

Hearts

The main question on my mind during those days was whether Shamsa was promised to someone else. Zubayr told me that nomad girls and boys might be betrothed when they were quite small, so it could have been arranged long ago, he said, before either party even understood what it meant. Perhaps the cousin simply had not yet acquired enough livestock to pay the bride price.

Sometimes, though, I felt that Zubayr was doing his best to discourage my interest in Shamsa, and I wondered how he felt about her. He had talked to her often on the journey from Wadi Safra – though not as much as I had - and obviously he liked her and enjoyed her company. As a Fish-Eater he was an outsider here, but still more of a known quantity than I, a stranger who was not from this desert world at all. I had felt a sense of competition with him, starting with the remarks he had made on the day we had both met Shamsa, and although I did not believe there had been the same attraction between the two of them, this might have been just my jinn talking, because such things were not always clear.

The best time to take the camels to the well, we discovered, was around sunset, when the cool set in. This was when the young, unmarried girls chose to meet together to fill water-skins, to water sheep and goats, to chat, exchange anecdotes, and tell stories. There were often young, men there at that time, too, watering camels, ogling the girls, hovering around their groups and listening to their tales.

Watering the animals was quite easy as the water was camel-drawn and when our turn came, all we had to do was hitch a camel to the well-rope. While one of us made sure the rope was properly set in the groove on the pulley, and that the buckets came up without snagging, the other drove the camel forward. The pulley-wheel squeaked and groaned and the heavy buckets sailed up to the well-head, where the young men would help each other carry the water to the mud basins. They worked together with joy, I noticed – laughing, cracking jokes, singing, even reciting poetry – especially if the girls were listening:

'The pull of my heart

Is the pull of a well-rope

Taut on the camel's back

Drawing up water.

The sigh of my love

Is the moan of a pulley

Turning, turning

As the bucket rises up.'

The thirsty camels pressed in around the basins, lowering their heads, sucking up great draughts of water, their neck-muscles rippling under the skin, lifting their heads, blowing hard through their nostrils, grinding their teeth, smacking and wobbling their lips, showering everyone with cool drops. The young men encouraged them with watering chants as old as the desert:

Aw. Aw. Aw.

Aw-cha. Aw-cha. Aw-cha.

Aw. Aw. Aw.

It seemed to me that there was a harmonic resonance that ran through the whole company, as if this work, with water, with animals, with the Earth, and with each other, was a privilege rather than a penance, as if they were taking part in some deep religious ritual. Just being with them and among them made me feel happy. This, I realized, was the principle of *muhanni* in action – this was how work should be.

Every time we watered our animals now we would bring lumps of pink rock-salt and place them in the basin – Zubayr told me that the salt improved the animals' condition and appetite. It was a great satisfaction, I felt, being there in the desert twilight, as the cool began to settle on the wadi, under the moon and stars, in the bitter scent of the dust and the savory musk of the animals, the sunset songs of birds, the thrilling cadences of girls' voices, the watering-chants of the young men, the well-rope creaking and the pulley rumbling as it turned and turned, the snorts of the camels, the slurp and gulp of their drinking, as they drank down the water mixed with the salt we had dug out of the salt-pan with our own hands, and brought here on such a hard and hazardous journey. One could feel proud of that.

That evening we had harnessed Zubayr's big camel *Warakh* to the well-rope and while Zubayr drove him forward, I leaned over the parapet to make sure the buckets came up cleanly. When we were finished I handed the rope over to a nomad who looked rather older than the rest and a tad surly – a broad-shouldered man, short and thickset, with a slightly pugnacious face, who introduced himself as Arjan. He was wearing new slippers, a furled white head-cloth, and an unusually clean, white *jibba*, I noticed.

After we had moved our camels into the trees nearby, Zubayr called me back to the well-head, where a girl was about to tell a story. The audience was made up mostly of other girls - graceful young ladies in brightly colored, calf-length wraps that left their shoulders bare. All of them had long black hair, oiled and braided, falling down beyond the pit of the back, and most wore hoop earrings, bracelets, and anklets, adding an extra elegance to their figures.   Arjan - the nomad in the clean *jibba* - was standing behind the crowd, listening, and staring intently at the young woman telling the story. I saw with surprise that the storyteller was Shamsa.

Dove-Woman

'This is the story of Abu Nadhif and the Dove-Woman, she announced, in the sweet, musical tones I had grown accustomed to on the journey.   She swung her curtain of braided hair over her bare shoulder, and began.   'Long ago in the time when animals and humans spoke the same language, a nomad named Abu Nadhif happened on a large *gelti* – a rainwater pool - in the desert, tucked into a hidden niche in the cliffs, surrounded by trees and grass and bushes.   As he stood there, a white dove flew down to the water's edge.

'The bird did not see Abu Nadhif, who was hiding in the trees, and it peeled off its feather robe, and behold, there stood a young woman as beautiful as the rising moon and as graceful as a spiral-horn white antelope in pasture. The young woman entered the pool and swam in the water, singing to herself. Abu Nadhif watched her, and was filled with a longing so intense that he thought he would go out of his mind.

When the young woman moved towards the middle of the pool, Abu Nadhif saw his chance and, quick as lightning, snatched her feather robe. The young woman noticed this and felt alarmed, hiding her body in the water.'

'Why have you stolen my feathers?' she demanded.

'Oh most beautiful one, because I am in love with you, and want you to be my wife' he answered.

'Give me back my feathers,' she said, 'so I can cover myself.'

'That I cannot do, adored one,' said Abu Nadhif, 'for then you will fly away and I will die of love.'

The young woman tried to persuade him, but seeing he was determined not to return her feathers, she came out of the water, and said:

I must marry you, but I will never be yours,

For I am she who throws the hearts of lovers into the fire.

So desperate was Abu Nadhif's passion that he laughed at this. He took the young woman back to his family's tents, where they lived together as man and wife, and he hid his wife's feather robe in a cave on a mountain where he thought she would not find it.

In due course the woman discovered that she was with child, but she continued to herd the sheep and goats as before. One day her goats wandered into the cave on the mountain where Abu Nadhif had hidden her feather robe. As soon as she entered the cave she recognized the scent of the feathers, and quickly found where they were hidden

She left the feather robe where it was and returned to the camp of Abu Nadhif, where she eventually gave birth to a boy. Abu Nadhif doted on the infant, who was his pride and joy. Shortly afterwards though, as they were sitting by the fire, the woman suddenly seized the infant and threw him into the flames, whereupon he vanished.

'Abu Nadhif was so shocked and distraught that he drew his dagger and tried to kill the woman, but she fled, outrunning all who pursued her, till she reached the cave where her feather robe was hidden. She put it on and flew to the top of the mountain.

When Abu Nadhif and his people arrived, they found her sitting in a high place on the mountain-top, waiting for them.

'Why have you done this?' Abu Nadhif demanded.

The Dove-Woman answered, 'Did I not tell you when you stole my feather robe,

I must marry you, but I will never be yours,

For I am she who throws the hearts of lovers into the fire?

Our son was your heart, and so I threw him into the fire. Not one hair of his head was harmed, though. He lives on in the land of the jinns, for I am the daughter of the shaykh of jinns, and we are creatures of fire. If you wish to see us again, you must seek for us there.'

And so saying, she spread her wings and flew back to her own country as fast as the wind, and there she found the boy alive and well.'

It was a wonderful story, I thought, with a powerful message, and the onlookers cheered and clapped. Except for Arjan - the thickset man in the clean *jibba*, I noticed, who pursed his lips and frowned.

'Who is that?' I asked Zubayr as we went to collect our camels in the moonlight.

The Fish-Eater youth chuckled. 'Arjan is Shamsa's first cousin,' he said, 'the eldest son of Hassan, our host. She is promised to him – I discovered that today. He has been away for a while, and has just returned.'

My heart sank. I should have known that Hassan would have a son older than Sayf and Duhil. Then I thought again about the story.

'He didn't seem very happy with Shamsa's tale, did he?' I said.

Zubayr laughed. 'It's hardly surprising - the story was for him, of course. Did you not see the clean clothes he was wearing? Abu Nadhif means *Mister Clean.*'

I thought about it all the way back to our camp, wondering if Shamsa's story might have been for me, also.

Reflected

'The message is clear, isn't it?' Zubayr said. 'Abu Nadhif forces Dove-Woman to marry him by stealing her feathers – she can't fly away.'

We were sitting by the fire in our own camp, in the moonlight, waiting for the kettle to boil. The camels were drawn up around us in a semi-circle as usual. There was a slight breeze, and the flames flickered, and the boughs of the great acacias above us creaked and rattled, as if they were talking in croaky voices. The camels burped and chewed, and from somewhere the clicking wheeze of a coney started up.

The kettle began to steam, and Zubayr dragged it off the firestones with bare hands and placed it in the sand in front of him. He unwrapped two small glasses from a piece of cloth, dusted and wiped them, and set them down between us.

'Yes,' I said. 'She tells him frankly that, while she has no choice but to marry him, she does not love him. She flies away as soon as she gets the chance.'

Zubayr flipped off the lid of the kettle, letting out more steam. He stirred the tea with a stick, then put the lid back on.

'Why did Shamsa choose tonight to tell that story?' he asked. 'I mean, the day her cousin returned with his new clothes? She used the name *Mister Clean* on purpose - she was clearly trying to put him off. The thing is, she said it in front of everyone, and he obviously was not happy.'

'Where does that leave me?' I asked.

'Only God is All-Knowing,' Zubayr said. 'Perhaps it leaves you with a chance, at least in her heart, perhaps not. Tell me, though – have you really thought about this? All right, I know … *she is like the moon and the stars, and all the flowers of* the Lush, *and her eyes are like sun and its mid-day brightness, and the eyes of all the gazelles of the* Hurra *rolled into one*, and so on and so forth … but marrying her means taking on her family and a lot of duties.'

I knew he was right - I was captivated by Shamsa – I had fallen in love with her the moment our eyes first met - but I had hardly thought it through. Once I was married to a nomad girl, I would have to stay here in the desert and become a nomad. There would be no returning to the town. Taking her away from the free life to live in the cage of civilization would be pure sadism, I thought.

Zubayr lifted the kettle and poured tea carefully into each glass, not spilling a drop. He set the vessel down again and handed me a glass. I blew into it then took a sip. It was hot, sweet, and very strong.

'Even supposing she wants you,' Zubayr went on, picking up his own glass, tasting the tea, 'how will you pay the bride price? Her family – Rai and Halima and the others - will never agree to a marriage without that. They have just lost all their animals, remember? On the other hand, Hassan is their benefactor - they don't have much to gain by supporting you.'

'I have only one camel.'

'Ah, exactly. Then there is your quest for this … Lost Oasis. You said you would be leaving as soon as Rafig gets back. Apart from the fact that they probably think you are mad to go on such a pointless journey, especially in the hot season … and the chance that you may not return …'

'May not return? What do you mean?'

'Only God is All-Knowing, but the *Hurra* can be a dangerous place … I am just saying …'

'All right, I've got it.'

For a moment there was silence but for the crackle of the fire and the slurp of tea.

'Everyone heard Shamsa's story tonight,' Zubayr said after a while. 'There will be a lot of questions – about you as well as other things. If you are not here to speak for yourself, it might go the other way.'

'You mean she might marry Arjan after all?'

'They were promised to each other when they were small …'

'Arjan looks a lot older …'

'All right, when *she* was small … that's still a powerful bond, and it is supported by nomad custom. Don't forget, Dove-Woman in the story was obliged to marry Abu Nadhif, *even though* it was against her will.'

I suddenly felt miserable. Although I suspected that Zubayr himself had an interest in Shamsa, and might be trying to put me off for that reason, what he had said was still sound. I wondered if I should postpone … no, abandon … my quest for the Lost Oasis. Zubayr had called it pointless, and in a sense it was – at least for anyone but me. Yet it was the dream that had brought me here, and I owed it to myself to see it through - I could not settle down to another life until I had completed that. Was that my jinn talking? I did not think so – just the opposite. It was my jinn that was trying to distract me from my purpose. I suddenly saw the true nature of the Evil Eye –and why the nomads did not express love and admiration openly. The Eye was my feeling of love for Shamsa in a dark mirror, distorted by possessiveness and jealousy - an imperfect shadow image, reflected back in the fear of others.

I realized that I had taken our mutual feelings for granted, though. I had never told Shamsa how I felt, nor asked how she felt about me. Somehow I had imagined that we both *just knew*.

I drained my glass and put it down in the sand. 'The only thing I can do is talk to her,' I said.

Ogre

When Zubayr and I returned from taking the camels to browse the following morning I saw Shamsa leaving her family's tent with the camel Hassan had given them. The animal was carrying empty water-skins, neatly rolled and tied to the saddle, so clearly she was heading for the well. I was about to rush to catch up with her when Zubayr stopped me and showed me four figures marching directly towards us. Three of them were young men from neighboring tents, dressed in the usual sand-hued garments. The fourth, standing out from the others in a clean white *jibba* and a layered white head-cloth, was Hassan's son Arjan – *Mister Clean* himself. They looked determined, and all of them were carrying camel-sticks, I noticed.

I cast a last glance at the figure of Shamsa, as she disappeared around a bend in the wadi, and we went forward to welcome our visitors. When I shook hands with Arjan he squeezed my fingers – an action the nomads considered rude. The three of them sat down on our mat with their camel-sticks across their knees, and refused the tea Zubayr offered.

We sat down opposite them.

'You are the Fish-Eater who is working as a herdsboy with our relative Saadig,' he said, looking at Zubayr, 'and who helped the *Kahin* Rafig bring rock-salt.' He nodded at the neat piles of salt we had made around our camp.

'I am of the *Tu*, yes,' Zubayr answered. I knew he did not mind being called a Fish-Eater, and that there was no stigma attached to being a herdsboy - many nomads worked for other households, just as Rafig's own father had done. The way Arjan had said it, though, was borderline offensive. And after all, I thought, he knew our names, and that we were his father's guests.

'…and you,' he said, looking at me, 'are the … *other one* …who came with the *Kahin's* salt-caravan.'

He made it sound as if I was something the dog had dug up.

'Quite true,' I said as brightly as possible. 'We saw you at the well last night.' I was tempted to add, *when Shamsa told the story of the Dove-Woman*, but I sensed the jinn working, and refrained.

'Yes,' Arjan said, glancing sideways at his companions, whose faces I remembered from the well. The men stared back at him blankly, and I wondered how much they sympathized with him. I remembered Rafig's parting words *nothing causes so much conflict as jealousy over a woman.*

'How did you like the story my cousin Shamsa told?'

Zubayr and I both nodded. 'I like stories,' I said.

'Good,' Arjan said, 'because I have another story to tell you. Would you like to hear it?'

'I can't wait,' I said.

'Long ago – it was probably in the Distant Time – there was a race of giant ogres who liked to kill and eat the Children of Adam. They were ugly, but could change themselves into handsome young men when they wanted to, and use their charms to entice young women. They would lure them into a trap then kill and eat them.

'One of these ogres took a fancy to a certain nomad woman and decided that he would live among the prey. She was already promised to a young man of her own clan, but the ogre made himself into a fine-looking, big-talking fellow. He came to the clan's camp as a stranger, and captured her heart. *That is the husband I must have*, she told herself. Her family argued against it, saying that though the man was handsome and seemed respectable, he had come from nowhere, and nobody knew who he was. The young woman's heart was set on marrying him, though, and so it came to pass.

'The couple lived together with the woman's clan and were happy for a while, but the ogre could not forget he was an ogre. One night the wife awoke in bed to find her husband clutching her bare breast, with a red gleam in his eyes. '*I remember that my father used to feed us food like this*,' he said.

The woman was so horrified that she jumped out of bed and ran to tell the clan, *my husband is an ogre who was raised eating the flesh of young women*. Enraged, the people came out with bows and arrows, spears and daggers and surrounded the woman's tent, so that the ogre could not escape. Then they set fire to it and burned the ogre alive. That was the end of him.'

Arjan stared at us triumphantly, and for a moment we both eyed him in silence. I felt the urge to laugh. *That's me*, I thought, *the ogre*. Instead, I said. 'That's a good story.'

'Yes, it is a good story,' Zubayr agreed, 'but I have heard it before, and you have not told it all, Arjan. You missed the part where Sky Father, who had seen all this, grew angry with the clan for their intolerance. After all, the ogre could not help his

184

childhood, and by marrying the woman he had obviously been trying to change his life. In the end, he did nothing but told her the truth. The clan killed him in a horrible way without giving him a chance to show that he was reformed. So Sky Father brought a terrible curse on the clan, and turned all of them – including the woman - to stone. They remain so to this day.'

Arjan chuckled coldly, glancing at his companions, who looked equally uneasy.

'Now let me tell you another story,' Zubayr went on before they could say anything. 'Let's call it the story of the woman and the herdsboy – yes, a herdsboy like me – perhaps he, too, was a Fish-Eater, or perhaps he came from another tribe.'

Crow's Trail

'The woman was young and beautiful,' Zubayr went on, 'and her family forced her to marry her cousin, to whom she had been promised when she was small. In fact – though nobody knew it - she was in love with the young herdsboy who tended her cousin's livestock, and who, as I have said, was from another tribe.

'Her family would not listen to her objections, so she married the cousin, and they lived together without trouble for a while. Then the husband had to travel far away for some reason – perhaps to journey down the Pharaoh's Road with a herd - and he left the wife, with the herdsboy to look after the camels, goats and sheep.

'As soon as the husband had gone, the wife announced that she was moving her tent to a far off place, as, of course, was her right. In fact she packed up the house camels and litter, and moved to a region that was barren, where there was nothing for the animals to eat or drink. She did not care, though, as she was with the herdsboy, beyond prying eyes, and while they spent days of bliss together, the carcasses of dead animals piled up around the tent.

One day, while the herdsboy was tending the camels not far away, the young woman saw two crows circle the camp and alight on a carcass. The woman did not know what the crows meant, but when she told the herder, he knew at once. *'The crows are a bad omen,'* he said, *'because they will bring the one who is searching for you.'*

Indeed, the husband, who had returned from his journey, and was searching for his wife and herds, followed the crows' trail to the camp, where he was horrified to see the piled up carcasses of his animals. When the wife saw him, though, she came running with a smile, and he suspected nothing. He asked what had happened to the animals, and she said. "The rains have not been abundant, O husband. God has not struck for us on this."'

Zubayr stopped talking and looked at Sharig and his companions, who were staring at him with distaste.

'That is the end of the story,' he said, smiling.

'That woman was a disgrace,' Arjan declared in an angry voice. 'That must be a Fish-Eater story, for no nomad woman would do as she did.'

'Of course not,' Zubayr said, thoughtfully. 'It is only a story, but it shows what misfortunes may follow when a young woman's feelings are denied.'

I smiled to myself, though I could not help wondering if the story were at least partly about Zubayr's own feeling for Shamsa - he had chosen a tale about a herdsboy, after all. Whatever the case, he had made the point with all the eloquence I had come to regard as normal among desert people. The message must have struck home, because a moment later our four guests got up and left.

Love's Lament

That afternoon, we drove our camels to the well, where we found Shamsa with the usual crowd of girls, filling water-skins, watering goats and sheep at the basins. I wondered why she had remained here so long – perhaps waiting for me, I thought. Her story about the Dove-Woman the previous night had been a public declaration of her feelings – at least about Arjan - and, since nothing remained a secret among the nomads for long, everyone must also have heard about his visit to our camp with his cronies.

We left the camels near the watering-basins, and approached the well-head where the girls made way for us. Shamsa averted her eyes and watched us from behind half-closed lids. As if it had been planned, the girls clustered around Zubayr and began questioning him about our journey with the salt-caravan. He looked pleased. While they were distracted, I took the opportunity to draw Shamsa away from the crowd, a little further down the wadi where we would not be overheard. I knew we would not have long. Everyone would be aware of what was going on – that we had to talk - but on the other hand, among the nomads, two people in conversation was never considered a bar to others joining in.

At first Shamsa looked discomfited to be separated from her friends, but she let herself be led, and we climbed the wadi bank to stand under an old acacia. The sun was about to go down, setting fire to the wadi-bed, and drawing streamers of flame from the thorny branches above us. Shamsa's face was full of life, and I saw in her eyes two bright points like candle-flames – twin reflections of the sun's last gleaming. Birds began a chorus of trills and long musical cadenzas, and from somewhere a coney began to call – a whistle followed by a guttural scrape, giving way to a high-pitched squeal of sadness.

'Sister Coney's lament,' Shamsa said. 'Calling for her lost lover across the emptiness. Will he ever return?'

She looked at me then – a look like the thrust of a knife deep inside me. It made the skin at the back of my neck prickle. I knew it was not Arjan and it was not Zubayr -it was *us*. I had been right all along - the moment we met we had seen through the veil between separate souls that Rafig had talked about, to glimpse the one soul beyond.

'If God wills, he will return,' I said. 'Of course.'

'Yet there are many dangers in the *Hurra* during the *Ged* – the *Hot-Hot* season – and the way is long. Many things may change before he returns. There are other suitors, and custom is on their side – they may call a clan meeting to press their claim. Her family may believe that a suitor at home is better than another far away in the desert, whatever her feelings.'

Her face, turned to mine, was so full of spirit that I wanted to kiss her, though I knew kissing in public was taboo among the nomads.

'Why did her lover leave?' she asked wistfully. 'Why did he go away in the first place?'

'He had to go – he was drawn by a feeling inside him that he could not resist. He was looking for a part of him he felt was missing.'

'Perhaps that missing part was always here.'

'Perhaps, and perhaps that is what he had to discover.'

I said it, but it sounded lame even to me. I knew her and she knew me. Deep down both of us knew we were each the missing part of the other. Yet still I had to go on my quest, unwise, dubiously planned as it was – I had to make my golden journey if only to prove myself worthy – worthy to myself, that was, because Shamsa needed no such bravado.

'Sister Coney is faithful,' she said. 'She is here every night with her lament. One day, though, she may not come. Faithful as she is, something beyond her control might happen. Or she may decide that her lament is futile - that her lover is not coming.'

'He will come,' I said. 'He swears by Earth Mother, by the light of Father Sky and his splendor, by the rain, the thunder and the lightning flash, by the wind, and the breath and the spirit.'

I hardly knew where my rhetoric had come from. Shamsa laughed but with a touch of bitterness, and I saw that the flecks in her eyes had turned silver, and might have been tears.

'She will wait for her lover as long as she is able, but she does not swear because she cannot tell what the new dawn may bring, and here in the desert everything changes – there is drought, there is hunger, the winds come, the rain falls, and the Children of Adam migrate to other pastures. She may not even be here when her lover returns.'

Tears were filling my own eyes now, and I fought them back. 'Wherever you go,' I said, 'I will find you.'

The sun went down, the wadi darkened, and a greyness descended from a night sky not yet lit by stars or moonlight. Shamsa leaned forward and kissed me – a kiss so warm and powerful and unexpected, it took my breath away. Her braided hair wafted over my face for a moment, sending quivers through my body.

'Go in the safekeeping of God,' she said.

Then she hurried off towards the well, her bare feet kissing the soft sand silently. I watched her go with a sense of hollowness creeping up inside me, knowing that now it was too late to change my mind, and that I might have lost her forever.

I stared at the night sky for a long time, seeing stars pop up, ignited suddenly in the velvet darkness. A tight cluster of stars hung just above the horizon.

'*The Night Maidens fall*,' a voice said.

I glanced sideways and recognized Zubayr, his face shadowed so that only the whiteness of his teeth stood out.

'And now the *Ged* begins.'

'So be it,' I sighed.

High in the tree, Sister Coney began to call again, the plaintive lament for her lost lover.

Flurry

In my dreams Sister Coney's lament became the whoop of hyenas. I sat bolt upright in the moonlight and listened - the whoop came again, spine-chilling and very near. I woke up Zubayr, and the two of us put on our slippers and went to investigate. The camels did not seem to be agitated, and we heard and saw nothing more.

In the morning Rafig returned, couching and unloading his camel nearby. He told us that his family were well, and that he was ready to start the journey. As well as bags of provisions, he had brought four large water-skins from his own camp, though they had some leaks and needed repair. The three of us sat down and Rafig showed me how to mend a hole in the skin by inserting a ball of hard camel-dung behind it, tying it from the outside with a thin strip of bark dampened in water – the bark tightened as it dried. I tried to focus carefully on the task, aware that it was crucial, aware that the materials I was using came directly from nature – the animal skin, the bark, the camel-dung. One required no tools, not even a needle.

When all the skins were watertight Rafig brought out a gourd full of tar, made from the crushed seeds of the bitter melons he had talked about, and we used twigs to paste it over the skins. 'When new, the tar makes the water taste foul,' he commented, 'but it stops the skins leaking. Better drink foul than go thirsty.'

As we worked, we told him about Shamsa's story of the Dove-Woman, and about our visit from Arjan and his friends, and the tales Zubayr had told them. The old man looked each of us, shook his head and said nothing. When I mentioned having heard the hyena in the night, he seemed concerned, though. 'God is All Knowing,' he said. 'I dreamed of a hyena last night.' He paused, remembering. 'I was staying at the camp of my relative further down the wadi, sleeping outside the tent. I dreamed of a hyena with a wounded leg, all bloody - and a white dove. The hyena seized the dove in her jaws, and was about to crush her, when a crow landed on the hyena's head and whispered in her ear. I do not know what the crow said, but the hyena let the dove go, and it flew away in a flurry of wings. Then I woke up.'

'*Really*?' I said, astonished.

'Did you see Lady Moon when you awoke?' Zubayr demanded.

Rafig nodded and pointed at the sky with his pasting twig. 'She was there.'

Zubayr glanced at me. 'That is where she was when you woke *me* up,' he said.

'You mean it was the same time?

Rafig laughed and paused in his pasting. 'I did not know what the dream meant, but now you have told me about Shamsa's story of the Dove Woman, perhaps I do.' He fell silent for a moment. 'Or perhaps I don't.'

We did not say anything more about Rafig's dream at that time, but talked about our arrangements for the journey. We planned to take only our two riding camels with us, and each would carry two water-skins. Unless we ran into the Poison Wind, the water would last us ten sleeps, but Rafig was confident we would find more. He said we should put our trust in the Great Spirit. I agreed, but then I remembered how our water-skin had been ripped open while we slept, and our vital water spilt. If that happened in the deep *Hurra* during the *Hot Hot,* God help us, I thought.

Rafig asked Zubayr if he would stay with the camels here until we returned. He could keep an eye on the rock salt and assist any member of Rafig's clan who came to claim their share. Zubayr agreed at once. He seemed quite happy to stay here, and it crossed my mind again that he might have designs on Shamsa's affections, and hoped to take advantage of my absence to put forward his suit. It gave me a twinge, but then I dismissed it - he was aware of our feelings for each other, and could not behave in that underhand way – not after we had eaten bread and salt.

It remained only to fill the water-skins. We went to fetch Ata and Hambarib, and led them to the well, where nomads were already at work, with an old camel plying the rope and the pulley spinning and groaning. Shamsa was not there, but I noticed Arjan working among the group of young men at the basins. He glowered at Zubayr and me, but he was friendly enough with Rafig, who had not met him previously, and who made a point of greeting him. While they were talking, the young men and women allowed us access to the basins and helped us fill our water-skins. They all wished us luck on our journey and invoked the safe-keeping of the Great Spirit.

Raven

When the water-skins were full, we couched our camels and slung them from the saddle-horns, then roused the animals and walked them back to camp. On the way we came to a place where a lone she-camel wandered, circling a crude wooden frame with an animal skin pinned to it. The skin smelt pungent, and the she-camel tottered round and round it, occasionally extending her head towards it and sniffing, then continuing her aimless patrol, giving out deep, rumbling sighs that reminded me of the herd's *lament of thirst*. The animal was obviously distressed. Suddenly a large black bird with a shiny beak and penetrating eyes landed on her head, flapping its wings and cawing, but holding on firmly with its feet as she continued her round.

'*You*,' Rafig cried out suddenly. '*You.*'

He glared at the bird, but made no attempt to scare it away, and it seemed to be doing no harm to the she-camel, merely enjoying a free ride, jockeying on her head as she paced aimlessly around the frame. After a while it seemed to grow tired of the sport and flew away.

'What's this about?' I asked Rafig.

'Her calf died,' he said. 'We call a she-camel like this a *khaluj*. She cannot get over the loss of her offspring, and the nomads set up the calf's skin to help her deal with her grief and to make sure her milk continues. Of course, she knows the smell of her calf. You see, the feelings of a camel are no different to those of Bani Adam. There is nothing worse for any creature than the loss of its children, whether for the mother or the father.'

'And the bird?'

He paused before answering and seemed to drift off for a moment. 'I thought it was a crow,' he said, 'but it was a raven.'

He seemed quite affected by the sight of the she-camel, and I remembered suddenly that he had lost his own son – he had said to a rampaging bull-camel. I had thought it curious at the time, but now it came back to me more strongly, and I wondered if Rafig was holding something back about his son's death.

We walked in silence for a while, driving the camels in front of us, through the dappled light of the trees that arched over the wadi-bank. The camels kicked up dust – its pungent smell had become familiar to me now and part of the ambience of the place. To my surprise, Rafig broke the silence to talk about his dream last night. 'My

192

first thought,' he told me, 'was that it referred to you. The blooded hyena was the spirit of the hyena you shot at al-Gaa, and the white dove was yourself – she was about to devour you in revenge.'

'What about the crow, then?'

'I assumed that was myself, warning the hyena off – because the crow is my spirit-guide. When I saw that raven on the *khaluj's* head though, it was a sign. I knew it was not a crow but a raven.'

'Is there a difference?'

'Crows and ravens are brothers but not the same. Raven is the trickster who stole a bagful of stars, the moon and daylight, from the greedy giants who were keeping it for themselves. You saw back there how he rode on the *khaluj's* head - as if he were making fun of her, and reminding her that her grief was futile.'

'So if the raven in your dream wasn't you, who was it?' I asked.

Rafig's eyes lit up. 'My son,' he said, 'is the only person I know has a raven as a spirit-guide.'

Averse

We were back at camp by late afternoon, where we hung the water-skins from the horns of our saddles and laid out our mats in the shade of the trees. Hassan's wife, Nayla, with her younger sons, Sayf and Duhil, arrived carrying leather bags of flour and dried dates, several skins of sour camel's milk, and liquid butter in decorated gourds with plaited straps. Rafig told her he had met her son Arjan at the well, and called God's blessing on her. After she had gone, he showed us the flour, sugar, tea and sour milk he had brought from his own camp, together with two sacks of sorghum grain for the camels.

'If God wills, neither we nor the camels will go hungry,' he said.

Under his supervision we wrapped up the dry foodstuff and stowed it away in cow-skin saddle-bags, hanging the skins of sour milk and the gourds from saddle-horns.

As the sun began to dip, and the heat lost its sharp edge, we sat by a fire Zubayr kindled, and drank glasses of tea, watching the sunlight turn from white to gold through the spiky branches of the trees.

'It was generous of Nayla to give us that food,' I commented. 'Especially since … well, you know … in view of the fact that Arjan is her eldest son, and he and I are … sort of … rivals.'

'You are a guest,' Rafig said, 'and guests are sacred. Rivals means nothing in comparison – even if you had a blood feud with the family they would be obliged to offer you hospitality, and to defend you against all comers, including their own family. Arjan cannot harm a hair of your head while you are a guest here – it would be a disgrace as great as *bowga'a* – the betrayal of a travelling companion. No-one would ever speak to him again.'

'When one leaves, one remains in the host's safekeeping,' Zubayr added. 'Until the last food one ate as a guest has left one's body – that is reckoned at one sleep. If Arjan planned to do anything to you, he would have to follow you into the *Hurra*.'

I asked if he thought Arjan might pull something like that. Zubayr laughed. 'When it comes to a woman, anything is possible.'

I felt a sudden pang of sympathy for Arjan. Shamsa was a beautiful, captivating girl, and he had pinned his hopes on marrying her since he was old enough to understand what marriage meant. To find the mat pulled from under him at the last moment, must have been devastating, I thought. I was a stranger who had appeared from nowhere like the ogre in his story, and - however inadvertently - I had stolen the affections of his childhood sweetheart. To him I *must* be an ogre, I thought.

Zubayr must have guessed what I was thinking, because he said. 'When Shamsa told the Dove-Woman story the other night, it wasn't just about you. I don't think she wanted to marry Arjan – the story never mentioned a rival.'

I nodded. 'It makes me feel bad, though, as if I've thrown a stone into a quiet pool and set ripples in motion. Tell me ….' I looked at Rafig. 'Is this my evil jinn working – my *qarin.*'

Rafig's look was serious. 'I understand that you feel sympathy for Arjan,' he said, 'as do I. It is a terrible thing to have one's expectations in love ruined. Love is not jinn's work, though.

194

Love is something altogether more powerful than a mere jinn. I have seen you with Shamsa – it is God's love, true love – a feeling beyond your ability to control. It is the love that falls like a stone out of the sky and knocks you down. You feel she returns your love – it is shared, not one sided, and it is equal. There is no element of force in it, and your aim is not to boast that you are a better man than Arjan. No, this is not your jinn working. On the contrary, trying to force a woman to marry one when she is *averse* - when it is against her will - is the jinn.'

'That makes me feel better,' I said.

'Now,' said Rafig. 'I must ask the Great Spirit how to find that oasis.'

Mystery

Zubayr brought water in a wooden bowl, and Rafig washed his hands and dried them on a piece of cloth. He sat down in the sand and composed himself, closing his eyes, reciting a silent prayer. Then he opened his eyes and said.

'I am of the Great Spirit, who may speak through me, as may the spirits of all the ancestors who have struck our sand before me. We go in search of the oasis my father found on his way back from Libya – the one he called *the Oasis of Last Chance*. I pray for an indication as to how to reach it, and as to whether our journey will be fruitful.'

He closed his eyes again and began to rock backwards and forwards, chanting in a rhythmic voice that reminded me at once of the bull-roarer reverberation I had heard just before collapsing from thirst in the desert, oscillating, faint then loud again, *whazz-whazz-WHAZZ,* and I jumped as his voice seemed to come from behind me, so clear and vivid that I was tempted to look around, although I could see Rafig in front of me, as I could see the flames of the fire.

Suddenly Rafig stopped chanting, opened his eyes wide, and began to smooth out the sand in front of him. At once he started making impressions in the surface with the tip of his right middle finger as I had seen him do at Elai. Again, he made the marks in stacks, one above the other, some double imprints, others single. Once a stack was completed, he moved to its

195

right and started another, working so fast that I could tell that single and double marks came at random. Zubayr and I watched entranced as he finished stack after stack. When he finally sat back and surveyed his handiwork, I counted sixteen stacks in all – the same number I had counted at Elai.

Rafig stared into space for a moment, blinking. Then he leaned forward and, as before, drew two boxes in the sand with quick strokes of a finger. When he had filled both boxes with marks, he sat back again, closed his eyes for a few moments, then opened them, and scanned each box closely.

'*First Pouch* shows the way,' he said, leaning over, pointing at the marks. 'Here is the *Sky Tree* and here is the *Windmother*. Then we have *Saddle Unravels*, and *the Outer*. *Sky Tree* is the tree at the top of the pass into the *Oversight* - the pass is two sleeps from here. *Windmother* is a prominent rock at the end of the *Horn Dance*, and *Saddle Unravels* is a well under a rocky knoll lying to the north. Both are known places. *The Outer* I do not know, but it may be revealed.'

'What about the other square?' Zubayr inquired.

'That is *Second Pouch*. It tells us about the possibility of success. The lines give me *Camels Quench their Thirst, Dragon's Tail, Leg Trip-Up*, and *Joy*.'

'So dragons come into it?' I asked.

'The dragon is a creature of *Tihamat* – the shadow world,' Rafig said, 'but his is the knowledge of *al-falak* - the stars, the winds, and the waters. *Dragon's Head* means success, but *Dragon's Tail* means calamity.'

'Oh, that doesn't sound encouraging,' I said, 'but at least the camels get to quench their thirst, and joy is involved.'

'*Leg Trip-Up* means a misfortune,' Rafig said. 'So we have misfortune and calamity, and things do not always happen in the same order they come up in the *Sandlines*.'

'You mean there could be joy *before* a calamity?'

'We are all in the hands of the Great Mystery,' he said.

A Ghost

Later that evening we were called to Hassan's tent for a last feast of goat's meat, together with Rai and his boys. Hassan's younger sons were also present, but not Arjan. Rafig must have noticed his absence because he asked Hassan about him, only to receive a non-committal answer – it would have been impolite to press it further. I noticed it, though, and I recalled what Zubayr had said about Arjan following us into the desert. It seemed unlikely, because my going away was to his advantage, but I intended to return, and one never knew. That gave me a pang of distress over Shamsa. In view of what she had said, I wondered if I was doing the right thing in leaving. I had made my mind up, though, and, assuming I was alive, nothing would prevent me from coming back.

In the morning, Rai, Hassan, and their families turned out to help us load our camels and wish us well – only Arjan and Shamsa were missing. Rafig refused any offers of assistance, though. 'I am old and know how to saddle and load my own camel,' he said chortling. 'If anything goes wrong, only I am to blame.'

When the camels were ready, Hassan presented his hands, palms uppermost, fingers spread, in supplication. '*Blessings'* he said. There was a moment of silence while the crowd held up their hands and repeated the word.

'The blessings of God be upon you,' Hassan went on. 'Our spirits go with you in the Great Spirit. There is no true parting, and you go in the safe-keeping of God.'

'*Amen.*'

I cocked my leg around the front pommel of my saddle, and Ata rose at once, blowing and grunting. Rafig mounted Hambarib, and we set off at once, descending the bank and riding across the soft sand of the wadi bed at a trot.

As we approached the trees on the far bank, I saw a figure standing in the shade – a girl in a dark wrap, with long black hair falling over bare shoulders. It was Shamsa and she was waving at us. A bolt of raw sorrow shot through me, as I remembered her voice and the power of that kiss - the pull of her body and the waft of her long hair. It was all I could do to stop myself racing over to her at once, and declaring that I would stay. I had to force myself on, hoping Rafig would not notice the tears in my eyes, and I kept turning to look at her until she was behind us and I could look no more. I was glad when we were out of the trees and into the sunlight, with *the Oversight* the faintest shadow on the skyline, like a lost world.

Rafig tapped Hambarib with his stick, and rapped his feet on the camel's withers. The animal lifted its head, pricked up its ears, and stepped out. Ata, raised his head and strove to keep pace with his companion. I felt a surge of warmth towards him – all the way from al-Gaa I had not ridden Ata, but now we were one again. It seemed a very long time indeed since the day he had run off into the desert, to be stopped by the nomad boys.

We rode across furrowed pleats of sand that the wind had swept off patches of grey lava, where thorn bushes pressed out of cracks and fissures like the legs of spiders. As we moved towards the mountain, we saw many camel hair tents pitched in groves of acacia along dry watercourses and Rafig pointed out dust clouds made by flocks and herds moving towards the wells. He said that more nomads than ever were concentrated around the wadi because of the drought in the *Hurra*. 'Not like the old days,' he told me. 'There were open pools then, and one did not have to rely on deep wells. The grass grew tall because the rain was plentiful.'

At noon we halted at a well in the middle of the plain, where shock-haired nomad youths were using two camels to hoist up the water, each heaving a rope in a different direction. We couched the camels at some stone basins among flocks of sheep and goats who pawed at the ground in their effort to get at the water. The well-ropes creaked, and the pulleys shrieked and spun as the buckets sailed up to the well head, to be dragged off to the basins by the youths. It was hard work, I thought, but the nomads worked with the same kind of joyful glee I had seen at the well in the Wadi al-Ma, as if the water itself were a special gift that they had been granted. There were so many animals drinking that by the time the youths dropped the bucket in the well again, the basins were empty.

Our camels were not thirsty, and after they had drunk a little, we moved out of the well-field. We rested at the tent of a grey-haired nomad named Sliman whom Rafig said was his relative. After they had exchanged news, Sliman astonished me by asking Rafig if there were any news of his son.

'Sheep and goats have gone missing on *the Oversight*,' he added. 'There has been talk of *a Ghost*.'

Rafig looked worried and made a half-hearted answer. I wondered if I had heard right. The only spontaneous reference the *faki* had ever made to his son in my hearing was in connection with the raven that had perched on the she-camel's head the previous day. I had always understood that his son was dead, and I noted that Sliman had mentioned a *Ghost*. How this was connected with missing goats and sheep, I could not fathom.

After we had eaten polenta and dates, and drunk tea, our talk turned to our journey, and the Lost Oasis. When I asked Sliman if he knew of it, he shook his head. 'There is no such place as the Lost Oasis,' he said. 'I was born in the *Hurra*, and I have never heard of it. Some of our clan used to graze their camels in Libya, far along the Siren Road. It was easier in those days because one could find grass growing in the sands. Now you will never get beyond *the Outer*. There is nothing there. The *Night Maidens* have fallen, the weather is getting hot, and your camels will die.'

Rafig and I exchanged glances. It was unusual for a nomad host to speak in such a forthright manner, and there had also been the slightest trace of anger in Sliman's voice. We had both noticed his mention of *the Outer*, though – one of the places Rafig had seen in the *Sandlines*, and the only one he had not recognized.

Outer

We set off again in the afternoon, and rode across an open plain with seams of sunburned grass and sedges like miniature trees, with *the Oversight* now a translucent line on the horizon. Just before sunset we found a sandy gully, where there were whitethorns and caper trees. We made camp there as the shadows drew long across it. Setting up the camp was easier now, with only two saddles and two lots of equipment. The most important items, as always, were the water-skins, which we hung from the saddle-horns.

After we had eaten, we sat cross-legged by the fire under the stars, keeping an eye on the shadows of the camels as they browsed among the trees at the edge of the gully. We had not spoken much that afternoon, and although I had tried to focus on my surroundings, I had not been able to stop myself ruminating over what Sliman had told us. Now, I asked Rafig why our host had seemed so angry when I had asked about the Lost Oasis.'

'It is part of the world his family has had to abandon,' Rafig said. 'They were one of those clans who lived always in the *Hurra*, and they have been moving south, a little further every season, because the rains have been so poor. For him, the Lost Oasis represents the lost green of the deep desert he knew in his childhood, and the thought was bitter to him.'

I nodded. 'He said *you will never get beyond* the Outer.'

'The Outer could be an oasis on the Siren Road, maybe even the place my father stumbled across – the *Oasis of Last Chance.*'

'Sliman said there was nothing there.'

'No, he did not say that. He said there was nothing *beyond* the Outer. He helped us more than he knew, because if the Outer is on the Siren Road, then all we need to do is follow that way. *Windmother* and *Saddle Unravels* are Known Places on that route.'

The fire crackled. I thought it over for a moment, and suddenly another question occurred to me.

'Why did he ask you for news of your son? What was that about ghosts and missing goats and sheep?'

Rafig sighed and stared into the fire. 'I suppose the time has come tell you,' he said.

Morning Star

'You were talking of jinns last night,' Rafig went on. 'God is All Knowing, but if you wish to understand the harm they can do, listen to the story of my son. I had not intended to tell you, but now I must. Seeing that raven yesterday reminded me.'

I stared at him, puzzled. 'Forgive me,' I said gently. 'I thought God had taken your son unto God.'

Rafig glanced at me and the firelight sparked for an instant in his eyes.

'I know, and it is true in a way…'

'In a way? You said he had an encounter with a bull camel. You told me that the bull camel on heat was the most dangerous of all animals. Surely he must be either dead or alive.'

'One might say he is both dead and alive. I will tell you the story and you must judge for yourself.'

'Very well.'

Rafig was a *kahin*, so, if he had not told the truth about his son, he must have good reason, I thought.

'His name was … is … Adnan,' he began, 'and from being small he had all the signs of a *kahin* or a *faki*. He grew up a sensitive young man, thoughtful and kind. He was skilled at *dobbayt* from childhood – he would astound older people with the quickness and beauty of his song. While he was herding goats and sheep in the desert, though, he met a little girl called Zahara …'

'Ah, the *Morning Star*…' I said.

'Well, this little morning star belonged to another clan - I do not know when it happened, but I suppose they must have often seen each other, and talked when they were with the flocks.

'As they grew older they would meet, sit together and recite poetry – only for short periods, and there was nothing more to it than that. They were in love, though – I mean, as I said before, real, God-given love …'

'…the kind that falls like a stone out of the sky and knocks you down …?'

'… *ay – kayf hada.* The problem was that Zahara had been promised to her first cousin, Mughir, and when she came of age, he insisted on marrying her. Zahara did not love him and did not wish to marry him – she was *averse*. Now, as you have probably understood, *bil 'urf ar-ruhhal* - according to nomad custom - a male first cousin on the father's side has the right to marry his female cousin, but it is not obligatory. Often if one of the parties is *averse* then the matter is dropped, and they can marry the one they choose.'

Shamsa's words came into my head at once. '… *'custom is on their side – they may call a clan hearing to press their claim.'*

'In this case, though, the girl's family insisted on her marrying the cousin, rather than my son, Adnan, who was of another clan. When Adnan told me about it, I went to meet with the girl's family hoping to persuade them to change their minds. I threw the *Sandlines*, and it came up with bad omens for the marriage of Zahara and Mughir. I told the family this, but of course they said I had rigged it, and that Adnan was the one the omens were bad for, not their daughter.

'Adnan and Zahara continued to meet in the desert, ignoring the row going on around them - just sitting close, enjoying each other's company, and reciting *dobbayt* they had composed for each other. One day, though, when they were sitting together in that way, Mughir arrived with three companions – they had obviously decided to keep watch on her.

'The girl was afraid, and Adnan did not know whether they intended to kill him, or kill her, or kill them both. Of course, they were doing nothing wrong, I am sure of that. Adnan asked Zahara if she would feel safer at her father's tent. She said she would, and he escorted her to the family's camp, while Mughir and his cousins followed. The young men did not try to harm them, though, and they reached the tent safely.

Although Zahara's father respected Adnan for behaving with courage and dignity in this case, the family still insisted on her marrying Mughir, and of course there were no more trysts in the desert after that. It was announced that Zahara and Mughir would be married.

Adnan and I visited Zahara's family again and tried to talk them out of it, but their minds were made up – jinn, you see. The wedding took place, and Adnan became distraught. I thought he might do harm to himself or another, but instead he mounted his camel and vanished into the desert.'

Wild Man

In the light of the fire, Rafig's eyes had taken on a far-away look, and there was a sadness in his face – the same expression I recalled from when he had first mentioned his son at Elai. He added some fragments of wood to the flames, then continued. 'Seasons passed, and I heard no news of Adnan, but I did not believe that God had taken him unto God. Meanwhile, the Great Spirit had not struck for Zahara and Mughir on their marriage, just as the *Sandlines* had shown me. God took Zahara unto God.'

'She *died?*'

'Yes, nobody knows what the cause was, but some said it was out of sadness, pining for Adnan. Others tried to claim that Adnan had bewitched the marriage from jealousy – even that *I* had bewitched it. Of course, there were also those who said that Mughir had killed Zahara, because she had never lost her aversion to him. People say many things but only the Great Spirit is All-Knowing.

'I still heard nothing from Adnan, though I felt in my heart that he was alive. The *Sandlines* did not give any hint that he was dead, but neither did it show me where he might be.

'Then, after some while, a nomad told me that he had met a wild man on *the Oversight*, who, he said, looked like my son, though he was much changed. He said that the man was living in the desert with the animals, and seemed deranged. At once I set off on my camel to *the Oversight*.

'There were some tents on the plateau and from the nomads I heard rumors of a wild man who lived up there in the remote gullies and thickets. Some said he was half-human, half-animal, some that he was one of the *Hyena People*, and some claimed that he stole and ate sheep and goats, sneaking up on them in the night so quietly no-one heard him – they called him a *Ghost*.

'I scoured the mountain, travelling from valley to valley, crag to crag, looking in caves and overhangs and thickets, but did not find a trace of the *Ghost*. One night, though, I was sleeping in a wadi, when I was woken up by a cawing and frenzied fluttering of wings. Lady Moon was almost full that night and I opened my eyes to see a coal-black raven perched above me in a thorn tree, staring at me with eyes like awls. The raven flew a little further up the wadi and settled. I got up and walked towards it, and it flew off again. I realized that it was calling me to follow, and, remembering my son's spirit animal was a raven, I hastily loaded my camel, and went after it.

'For the rest of the night I followed the raven as it flew off and landed, always a little further on. Even if I could not see it, I heard its voice calling me. I scrambled down stony screes, forced my way through thorn-thickets, climbed steep escarpments, until, by the time the sunrise was a red slash across the horizon, I was tired out. I was in a water-course on the edge of a great forest of thorn-trees. I sat down to rest, and when I looked around the raven was gone – I had no idea whether or not I had dreamed it.

'I fell asleep, and when I awoke it was full daylight, and there was a dark figure standing over me. For a moment I was scared – I thought it was a *ghul*. "Father,' a rasping voice said, "I would talk to you while the threads of light are there, while I am able to feel, for I suspect I could easily forget you and no longer think of you."

'A chill went through me then, as I realized it was my son. Yet it was not Adnan – not the boy who had grown up in our tents. He was emaciated and sallow – the ribs showed through his chest, and his body was scarred and lacerated, stained from the desert. His hair was a wild jumble, and his eyes were red and restless – they seemed sunken into his head.

'I spoke to him, but he seemed unable to answer directly, or rather, his speech resembled the snarl of an animal – and in fact, his features had narrowed, his jaw looked wider and more prominent, and his face had a strange gaunt look that reminded me of a dog or a hyena. That may have been just my impression, but there was certainly something of the predator about him – a shadow in the eyes. He was intense, and seemed aware of every smell and every sound. His teeth were sharp and yellow, and he was barefoot and naked except for animal skins, though I noticed that he still wore a dagger on his arm.

'My first impression that he could not speak properly was only partly correct. He could talk, though he seemed to have lost almost all memory except for Zahara and their love. Once, when I mentioned the word *clan*, he came out with a snatch of *dobbayt* he must have composed himself:

'I know no clan but the jackal

No kin but the hyena, no cousin but the wide-eared fox.

The raven is my brother, and the jumping-mouse my sister.

They do not reveal secrets,

They do not tell lies.'

Apart from this he would only repeat the name *Zahara* over and over again, sometimes crying out, howling, and bursting into tears. We spent that day together and he kept repeating. "I feel I could forget you and no longer think of you."

'When it began to get dark, he suddenly drew his dagger. His red eyes were wild and I thought he was going to kill me, but instead he stuck the knife into the trunk of a thorn tree. "I feel I could forget his place," he said, 'and I no longer feel that I know. You must not come here again, for I feel I no longer know."

'Then I glanced at him and saw that he looked even more like a hyena than I had thought, and in a moment he was on his hands and knees sniffing the ground snuffling, and when he raised his arms it seemed that they were covered in fur. I was scared, and could not believe what I was seeing, but in that moment he let out a spine-chilling chuckle and loped off into the thorn forest with that limping way of running hyenas have. I could not believe it, but it seemed that I had just watched my son turn into a wild animal.

'Despite his warning I realized he must have left the knife in the tree as a marker– a Known Place where he might return. In fact, and despite his warning, I lingered there for many sleeps hoping he would come back. I found his den under a rock overhang, where there were firestones, animal skins, and the bones of many creatures, including goats and sheep – I knew then that the stories of his stealing livestock were true. It was somehow comforting to know that he used fire, because it meant he had not actually *become* an animal – and that what I had seen was partly an illusion. Numerous times I set off to track him through the acacia forest, but always his tracks eluded me. It was as if he had just disappeared. In the end I departed, leaving his knife stuck in the tree in case he ever needed it as a signpost to return home.

'However one looked at it, though, I realized that the son I knew simply was no longer there. He had not become an animal, perhaps, but he had crossed the threshold between human and animal and was trapped there, and could not get back.'

I stared at the old *faki* spellbound. If it had not been Rafig telling the story – if I had been in a different milieu and without the experiences I had had since leaving civilization – I would not have believed it at all. On the other hand, a lot of things now made sense – why Rafig had taken seriously the tales about Blind Awda and the Hyena-People, why he had been so upset that I had shot the hyena at al-Gaa, and why he was concerned that a hyena might be following us.

'I have told that story to few people,' Rafig said. 'Mostly I say that my son is dead, and, God have mercy on him, in one sense it is true.'

'Do you think he was …*is* … possessed by a jinn?' I asked.

'Perhaps the loss of Zahara to another was such a shock that his jinn emerged. Losing his loved one was hard, but another person might have endured it.'

'But doesn't it show the depth of his love? One might say that had he been less affected, it would have shown his love was not so deep?'

'God only is All-Knowing. Adnan is not the only nomad ever to become a *Ghost*, and live among the wild animals, though *Ghosts* are mostly outcasts who have violated custom, which my son has not.'

'Did you see him again after that?' I asked.

He shook his head. 'That was in the cold season, before I began the journey to the salt-place. I spread the word among nomads on *the Oversight* to look out for him, and not to kill or hurt him, and I would compensate them for their animals if he took any more, though I never said that he was my son. I hope I may hear some news of him as we cross *the Oversight* on our way to the *Hurra.*'

The fire had burned low, and shortly we went to collect the camels, and brought them into our small camp. Rafig rolled up in his blanket and seemed to go to sleep almost at once. I sat there for a few moments, pondering Rafig's story, and taking in the immensity of the night sky, and the stars like galaxies of glittering diamond eyes. From somewhere across the moonlit plain came a cry, so distant that I could not tell whether it was animal or human, only that it seemed achingly sad.

Sky Tree

All next day we rode towards *the Oversight* until, in the later afternoon, the mountain loomed over us like a great squatting giant, a massive bald, shiny skull bowed against its knees, brooding and ready to rise and spring at any moment. Nearer still, one could make out dark flutings like the scales of a monstrous reptile, here and there shattered into screes and stone piles that gathered around its skirts, denuding a skin of raw stone hacked and gashed with cracks and fissures.

A narrow gully wound up into the heart of the plateau, and, slipping down from our camels, we led them up the winding path until we reached the sandy bed of a wadi that, in the rains, brought water down from the summit. Now it was dry, and the rock face towered above us, a grey wall weathered into chunks and chimneys.

We reached the top of the water-course, and there, standing above the bed on a rocky promontory was a tree so vast that it seemed to be holding up the sky, and when I squinted up at it trying to gauge its dimensions, it seemed that its upper branches were on fire, bursting into brilliant plumes of flame, and I thought I could smell smoke and hear the roar of the burning. Yet the branches were not being consumed, and as we got nearer I realized that it was the trick of the downing sun, and the blown dust, and the wind in the branches. The tree was truly massive - its gnarled and knotted trunk was buttressed by coiled roots thicker than a man's body, and thirty people could have stood shoulder to shoulder around it. This living column towered so high above us we had to bend backwards to see the top, and the branches there were like titanic fingers, twisting around each other, supporting spreads of leaves in wide umbrellas. On the topmost branch I spotted a huge martial eagle, framed against the fiery sky, with its fierce hook of a beak shiny in the light, its feathered chest like broad ripples, its vast wings half unfolded. It took off as I watched, flapped once, fell down towards us with its gleaming black eye fixed on me, then flapped once more, and sailed off towards the flaming horizon.

We couched the camels under the tree, and Rafig opened a water-skin, poured water into a wooden bowl and passed it to me. I refused, and passed it back to him. He took the bowl and drank, then pushed it back into my hands.

'This is the Sky Tree,' he announced, 'and there is no other tree like her in the whole of the nomad lands. It is said that she is older than the desert, as old as the hills – she stood here when this land was forest. There were many more of her kind here then, but they have gone. She is the last of an ancient race.'

'Was that before or after the flood?' I asked chuckling, remembering Shamsa's story.

'God only is All-Knowing,' he said,

We sat in silence for a while, feeling the breeze on our faces, gazing across the vast plain we had crossed that day, a patchwork of mottled green, brown, and shadow, bathed in the fluid fire-flame shades that heralded the sunset. The Wadi al-Ma with its great acacias was a grey blur in the far distance. I thought of Shamsa and the last time I had seen her, waving in the shadow of those trees. I thought about Arjan and his cousins. Suddenly, voices drew me out of my daydream, and I saw a party of nomads coming up the wadi.

Amuck

There were two keen-eyed men with beards and matted hair and two small boys, driving a few sheep and goats. One of the men was leading a pair of bony camels that carried water-skins, while the other strode along holding a firearm with a wide muzzle like a trumpet. A thin white dog with wide paws ran at his feet.

Rafig and I stood up to greet them. The men couched the camels and sat down with us to drink water and exchange *sakanab* – the news. The boys chased the dog, and the dog chased the goats and sheep.

'I know you,' the man with the blunderbuss said to Rafig. 'You are the *Kahin* Rafig. I am Musa son of Khalid. This is my brother Kabir, and my sons.'

It was dusk when we moved with our new companions to a place further up the wadi, where we made camp a short distance from them in a grove of tamarisk and ironwood. After full dark, the brothers slaughtered a goat, roasted the meat on hot stones, and called us to share it. Musa said that in times past they had grazed their animals deep in the *Hurra* - like many other families they had moved south because of poor rains.

He warned us about Fish Eaters. 'The rains have been even worse than ours in Fish-Eater land this season,' he said. 'They are moving east into nomad country, looking for camels.'

'I have known some very decent Fish-Eaters,' Rafig said.

'Yes, yes, the Fish-Eaters are Adam's Children, *kayfana*,' Kabir said. 'Still, when hard days come, many, even nomads, will turn to *the Amuck*.'

'Not in the *Ged*, surely,' Rafig said.

Musa shrugged. 'God is All-Knowing, but only yesterday we spotted a party of four nomads on camels, all armed with rifles, heading this way, into the plateau. Their camels were carrying two big water-skins apiece. Kabir here said to me "those men are going into the *Hurra*, otherwise they would not be carrying so much water. Why would they be going there in this season if not for *the Amuck*?"'

Rafig was suddenly interested. 'Did you recognize them?' he asked. 'You did not see their camel-brands?'

'Too far away,' Kabir answered, 'and that was another thing. They saw us but did not come for *sakanab*.'

Rafig nodded. By now, I understood that most nomads would go far out of their way to get *sakanab,* knowing that their lives might depend on it. Deliberately avoiding a chance to hear it was out of character.

'They were coming from the Wadi al-Ma – where you came from,' Musa said.

He had seen our water-skins, and had clearly deduced that we were also heading into the *Hurra.* I knew the nomads considered it rude to ask questions about others' intentions, but the brothers were obviously curious.

I told them about the Lost Oasis, and they listened carefully.

'I know the stories,' Musa said at last. 'The Lost Oasis is a place of sweet water, green grass, and dates as big as your thumb falling from the trees. The wind there is always cool.'

'Do you know where it is?'

'It's just a story,' he laughed. 'I can't imagine a place of cool wind in the *Hurra* – especially after the *Night Maidens* go down, but perhaps this Lost Oasis is not in the desert at all.'

'What do you mean? I asked. 'If it is not in the desert, where is it?'

'In another place,' Musa said, nodding towards the Sky Tree – she was hardly visible in the darkness. 'It is said that Sky Tree is an entrance to *Tihamat,* the land that lies beneath this one, and can be entered only by certain secret paths. It is to this place that the souls of dead animals go when they die, looking for an opportunity to be reborn.'

I laughed. 'So you think the Lost Oasis could be down there?'

'Perhaps. Let me tell you a story.'

Snake Woman

'Back in the Distant Time,' Musa went on, 'when Sky Tree was not as old as she is now, but was already old, and had roots that went down deep into Earth Mother's womb, three brothers arrived from the *Hurra,* looking for water. They sat down under the tree, and the youngest went to sleep. The two older brothers decided to move on without him. "He is very slow," they said, "and in any case, if we find water, why should we share it with him? Instead of a third share, we shall have half." So they left him and went off.

'When the youngest brother awoke it was dark, and he was terrified. He did not know where the others had gone. All around on the mountain he heard the sounds of wild animals – the cry of jackals and the howl of hyenas, the rustle of wide-eared foxes and the hoot of owls. Suddenly a white snake appeared from among the roots of the tree and reared up in front of him. It had green eyes with pupils like slits, and a flicking tongue. The young man was afraid, but the snake told him. 'Do not be afraid as I mean you no harm. Look behind me and you will see a hole among the roots of the tree. Enter that hole and you will find a tunnel winding down into Earth Mother's womb. At the bottom of the tunnel is a door. Open the door and you will be in another country. The young man entered the hole and found himself in a tunnel just as the snake had said. He followed the winding tunnel down into Earth Mother's womb, and came to the door. When he opened the door, he found himself in another country that appeared to be the opposite of the desert above. Here, in the warm sunlight there were vast plains of rich green grass, and whole forests of trees like Sky Tree and orchards where the trees were heavy with ripe fruit. There were fields of flowers that were alive with bees, and sparkling rivers, pools, great lakes and waterfalls. The sky was full of rainclouds and flocks of birds and the land was teeming with animals such as gazelles, spiral-horn white antelopes, oryx, giraffes and elephants. There were herds of fat cattle and sheep and goats in flocks stretching as far as the horizon.

'The young man saw a figure in the distance, and when he approached he realized that it was a tall, slender young woman with long hair. She had green eyes with pupils like slits, he noticed. 'I am *al-Lat*,' she said, 'and this is our country, *Tihamat*.' She bade him follow her and he did so, noticing that, despite having shapely feet, she left curving tracks in the earth.

She took him to the tents of her family, whom he found kind, generous and hospitable, though their eyes, like hers, were green with slits for pupils, and when they spoke it sounded like the lisping of snakes. They treated him as an honored guest, and he feasted and drank milk. Afterwards they begged him to stay with them there and gave him cattle and goats and sheep so that he would have a herd and flocks of his own.

'The young man decided to stay in that country, and asked for al-Lat as his wife. The family agreed and the woman agreed, and they were married. On their wedding night, she said to him. "I will be a loyal wife to you, but if ever you awake in the night and do not find me, and you see a snake slithering away, promise that you will not kill it, nor ask any questions."

'The young man promised, and kept his promise, and they lived together happily and his livestock grew fat and he had everything he needed. Every day there was fresh milk, and honey, and bread and meat and fat, and ripe fruit to eat, and he was content with his beautiful wife.

'One day, after he had been there a long time, two men appeared in the camp, ragged and thirsty and thin from hunger. They were the young man's two older brothers. The youth recognized them, but felt no rancor. He welcomed them to his tent, told his wife to bring firewood, and gave them the best of all he had – milk, bread, ripe fruit, fresh meat and fat. He told them that they could stay with him, and that he would give them cattle and goats and sheep, and his wife would find them wives from among her family.

As they were talking and feasting, the young man asked how the brothers had found their way here. They told him that they had been dying of thirst and hunger, when they had seen a white snake slither out of a crack in the rocks. The snake had spoken to them saying that if they entered the crack and followed a winding tunnel down into the bowels of Earth Mother, they would be in another country.

'They had done as the snake said, they told him, but first they had killed it and cut off its head – after all it was a snake. They opened a bag they had with them and showed the young brother and his wife the head of the snake they had killed. At once the wife screamed. "*That is my sister, Uzza,*" She hissed at them and a forked tongue flicked from her mouth. She changed into a white snake and slithered off, as did all her relatives from the nearby tents. In an instant the meat they were eating became full of maggots, the fruit became rotten, the milk went off and the bread turned mouldy, so that the brothers dropped the food in horror.

'In the same moment the whole camp vanished and the tents turned to dust. The sky grew dark and a great wind blew up. Gone were the trees and the green grasslands, the rivers and the pools and the waters. Gone were the fat cattle and the goats and sheep and all the animals. The land became a desert, and the brothers were enveloped in a cloud of dust so dense they could see nothing. When the dust cleared, they found themselves sitting under Sky Tree where they had started. They searched and searched for the hole in the tree that would take them back to the green land in Earth Mother's womb, but they never found it, neither did they ever again meet al-Lat, the Snake-Woman.'

Musa stopped talking and smiled at me. 'Which of those people was most subject to jinns?' he asked.

I thought about it for a moment. 'Obviously the elder brothers,' I said.

Musa nodded. 'They abandoned their brother, and they killed the snake who had helped them.'

'It is a good lesson,' Kabir added. 'One should not kill a snake without reason any more than one would kill a Child of Adam without reason. The snake's spirit does not die, but returns to wreak vengeance on its killer.'

I thought of the hyena I had shot at al-Gaa, and the way hyena-spirits seemed to have been plaguing me ever since. I wondered if the same applied.

Flayed

When we had finished eating, Musa and his brother gave us tea, and we sat cross-legged, enjoying the warmth of the fire.

'That was a good story,' I told them, 'and I have heard others like it, but I don't think the oasis we are looking for is under the Earth. Have you heard of a place in the desert called the *Outer*?'

The brothers exchanged a glance, then Kabir said. 'The *Outer* is what some people call the furthest oasis on the Siren Road. There is another oasis called the *Inner*, but that is deep in Egypt, far, far away on the other side of the *Hurra*.'

I caught Rafig's eye. It seemed his guess had been right. We might find the Outer by following the Siren Road. But what *was* this Siren Road, I wondered?

'Siren is a place in the north, in Libya, only reached after travelling several moons,' Kabir said when I inquired. 'The story goes that it stands on a mountain in a forest near a water they call *Great Green*. According to the tales, Siren was built by the Anakim – the Lost Giants - when they left the desert in the Distant Time, long ago. The Siren Road was the route they used to get there. One can still find what they left behind – graves and cairns and old tools and stone rings and pictures on the rocks.'

'Have you ever been to the Outer?' Rafig asked.

Both brothers shook their heads. 'Never, but we know its reputation,' Musa said. 'It is haunted by jinns who put a curse on all who enter.' He laughed. 'But maybe it's just Fish-Eaters.'

Later, after we had brought our camels into camp and knee-hobbled them, Rafig and I lay wrapped in our blankets, watching the moon as it sagged towards the dark wedge of the plateau, and was finally gone. I could hear Musa and his family moving about, and animals snuffling and shifting, some distance away.

I thought over what we had learned from the *sakanab,* especially about nomads with firearms moving into the *Hurra* in the *Hot Hot* season. I could not forget what Zubayr had said about Arjan following us into the desert – or maybe even *preceding* us? I recalled that Arjan had not been at his father's tent the night before we left, and that Hassan would not say where he had gone.

'What is *the Amuck*?' I asked Rafig.

'*The Amuck* means camel raiding. It happens especially in times of drought when desert people think their neighbors have more camels than they deserve.'

'You mean stealing?'

'No. Stealing is dishonest.'

'What's the difference?'

'Camels are the gift of God. One cannot steal what never belonged to anyone in the first place. One must defend those things life depends on, of course, but raiding camels is not immoral in the eyes of the Great Spirit, as long as it does not deprive others of life.'

'But how can it not?'

'By custom, raiders are supposed to leave their victims enough animals to survive – to take everything is not honorable. They will not molest women or children, and will only harm those men who stand in their way.'

'Which is all men?'

'Of course, yes. Men are harmed, even killed sometimes, but such deaths are never taken for granted, and in the long run blood-compensation is always paid.

I thought it over. 'Do you believe we are in danger from raiders – or Fish-Eaters?'

It was a moment before Rafig answered. 'I saw nothing like that in the *Sandlines*,' he said, 'but I did see *Leg Trip-Up* and *Dragon's Tail*.'

'No news about your son, then?'

'Maybe I will ask tomorrow.'

For a while I lay watching the stars, inhaling the darkness, listening to the camels chewing the cud, recalling that all of us shared the same breath - the same spirit that gave rise to trees, men, and clouds. With every breath a tide was surging through our being – the waves and ripples of an eternal ocean where men, trees, camels, rivers, sun, rain, moon, and stars, were born, lived, died, and yet lived on. As I watched, a star shot out of the darkness and streaked across the heavens on a burning tail, igniting into a ring of bright fragments, and a radiance so sharp it flayed the night.

We were up at first light, and went to take our leave of Musa and the others.

'By the way,' Rafig said, 'how long have you been herding on the plateau this season?'

'We came out of the *Hurra* two moons before the *Night Maidens* fell,' Musa said. 'Our tents are pitched on the north side of the plateau.'

'Have you had any trouble from hyenas?'

Musa eyed him curiously. 'There is a hyena clan about,' he said.

'What about … a *Ghost*?'

'I have heard stories, but not for a while. You may pass my tents on your way to the *Slant*. If so, you can ask my wife if she has any recent news.'

Rafig nodded. We walked back to our camels, took the head-ropes and led the animals out of the water-course, taking a last look at the great living tower of Sky Tree with her boughs like the fingers of giants clutching at the leaden sky. We mounted up and followed narrow camel-paths twisting through dense brakes of scrub and thorns, opening out here and there into expanses of pasture, then closing in again, dipping down into valleys, where sandy beds followed steep rocky bluffs and scattered screes. Near noon, when the shadows had shrunk to almost nothing, we came across a herd of camels grazing on esparto grass and acacia trees along a wadi-bank. There were no men around, but we saw a slim woman wrapped in a one-piece garment of bright red and yellow, wearing necklaces of beads, bracelets, and a nose ring. Her braided black hair fell down her back, reminding me painfully of Shamsa. Small children played around the camels, yelling, and chasing each other. Two tents were pitched on a salient above the bed of the water-course not far away.

The woman turned out to be Musa's wife, Khadija, and we halted in the shade with her long enough to give her news of her husband, and to drink the fresh camel's milk she offered. When Rafig enquired about the *Ghost*, she said.

'Did the Father-of-my-Children not tell you? When we first arrived here from the *Hurra*, there were many stories about a *Ghost* stealing goats and sheep. We were warned not to hunt it down or try to kill it, as we might end up with a blood-feud on our hands. Someone – they said he was a *faki* – had been here looking for it, saying – God forgive us, for He is All-Knowing – that it might be his son.'

Rafig nodded and I wondered if he were going to tell her that he was the *faki*, but he didn't. 'That was some time ago?' he inquired.

'Yes, we have not had any such news for a while. If it is a *Ghost*, it is either dead, or it has moved on.'

Rafig looked grave, but he called God's blessing on her, and we mounted up again and rode off, following the wadi-bed, then climbing up a path through steep screes of rocks until we came to the head of the pass called the *Slant*. It was marked by a wide cairn of stones, where we dismounted and saw below us the vast panorama of the desert, a great plain of grey dust under an untarnished sky of dazzling brilliance, a scintillating weave of gravel beaches and ripples of fish-scale dunes, sparkling with threads of light and phantom mirrors, simmering gently at the edges with dust-devils and columns of sand-smoke, and in the distance, layers of hills and ridges overlapping, rim upon rim, as far as the eye could see.

'The *Hurra*,' Rafig said solemnly, and I stood there and breathed in the desert wind with its scents of ash and bitter dust, and felt my spirit surge.

'Freedom,' Rafig went on, 'that a man confined in the town will never know nor dream of. From here one could ride a camel as far as my father's land of *Tu*, and beyond, west to the Sunset Land and north to Siren Land and the *Great Green* water, and in all that land one would find no walls or fences to keep one out. The desert is pure and clean and it is the place of liberty, and a life shared with all people – humans, plants and animals.'

He picked up a stone and added it to the cairn, and I did the same. 'Do you think your son is down there?' I asked him.

'God only is All-Knowing.' He scanned the horizons keenly as if he might get a glimpse of his son.

'O Oversight mountain,' he recited,

'Have you not seen Adnan?

Is he not down there in the desert,

With the spiral-horn white antelope and the gazelle?

I pray the Great Spirit

To show me my son.

He waited for a moment with his head cocked, as if listening for an answer, then turned to me.

'If God wills, we will find him.'

I paused and looked at him closely. 'Do you know the way? Can you trust the *Sandlines*?'

Rafig laughed. 'Trust? The *Sandlines* cannot be wrong – only my reading may be wrong. The *Sandlines* is a way of seeing the great web of strands that spans the world – the threads of light joining everything that exists. Of course it is not really strands, or threads of light –

those are just words. We call it the Great Spirit, and the Great Spirit's Dreaming, but these are also just names, for what it is cannot be grasped or explained by any Child of Adam - we too, are of it, and so are our words. Some people say it is a giant roc.'

'What's that?'

'A bird – like an eagle, but so huge it can pick up a bull-camel with each foot. Yet it is not really an eagle, or like an eagle. It is not like anything.'

'You do know the way – at least some of the way?'

'In the *Hurra* the threads of light join sacred places of water and plants that were created in the Distant Time the by Shadad the Hunter. In his dream, Shadad danced through the land, carrying a water-skin and playing on shepherd-pipes. He dreamed that he danced through the desert in long curves, like a snake, and wherever his dance crossed the path of the jinns, he made a Known Place, or poured water from his water-skin and made a well, a pool, or a *gelti*. Then he woke up and found himself in the land he had dreamed into being, and that it had *become*.'

Rafig pointed out a peak to the north, only just visible on the skyline.

'That is the *Windmother,*' he said. 'It stands at the far end of a long ridge, the *Horn Dance*, that we must keep on our right. I know the way as far as *Saddle Unravels*, after that it is as God wills. Let us go in peace, and may the Great Spirit be with us.'

We took our head-ropes and led our camels down into the *Hurra*.

Horn Dance

It took three sleeps to reach the *Horn Dance*, and once we were close, we wheeled our camels north along the gnarled and weathered rock wall, chocolate brown, rust red, pitted with caves and overhangs, that reared up in the near distance like a frozen tidal wave. Not long afterwards, Rafig spotted some interesting tracks and swung down from the saddle to examine them.

'This is curious,' he commented. 'One would have said they are the tracks of a hyena, though they are too narrow, and while there were once hyenas here, nomads have not seen them here for many seasons. This track was made only this morning.'

I couched Ata and joined him, squinting at the prints. As Rafig had said they were fresh. The outlines were intact, and the claw-marks clearly incised.

'Not a dog?' I asked, remembering the lean white dog Musa and Kabir had had with them.

Rafig shook his head.

'Then what?'

He opened his eyes wide, as if a thought had suddenly occurred to him. 'Remember what Saadig said about the white leopard? He said its tracks were like a hyena's, only narrower.'

It was my turn to feel surprised. 'You think this could be a leopard?'

'Only God is All-Knowing.'

We mounted up again and began to follow the trail. 'She is moving north ahead of us,' Rafig said. 'I believe she has come to be our guide.'

'How do you know it's a *she*?'

'Only because the animal Saadig saw was a she-leopard.'

I remembered the white leopard in my dream. The voice I had heard was a woman's voice.

'Why should she guide us?' I asked.

Rafig gave me a curious look. 'Perhaps you know better than I do,' he said.

We followed the tracks in silence for a while. I was watching the ground, when something drew my interest. It was a white stone with a hole in it, almost identical to the one I had seen with the donkey-skull at the *Well of the Catfish* in the Wadi Safra – the amulet set up to scare away jinns.

'*Hold on,*' I told Rafig. I couched Ata again, slid out of the saddle and picked up the stone. It was flat and not quite as wide as my palm, and the hole was clearly too small for the fingers to pass through - it could not be a bracelet, I thought – not even a child's fingers would pass through. It was clearly man-made though. I beckoned to Rafig, who couched Hambarib and joined me. He looked at the stone. 'Ah, a giant's digging-stick,' he chuckled.

'What?'

'It is the work of the Anakim. You can fit a stick in the hole in the stone, and use it for digging. Our people still use such sticks but not often, and we do not make stones like this.'

I pushed my thumb through the hole and shook my head. It would never have occurred to me that it was a weight for a digging-stick, but now he had said it, it seemed obvious.

'See,' Rafig said. 'There are more.'

I looked around and gasped. The surface here was flat, hard sand, and it was covered in stones like this – some intact, some broken in fragments. There were stones of all shapes and sizes – some were clearly hand tools, knapped and facetted, but there were also arrow-heads, bone slivers, pottery shards, bits of shell, and grinding querns with roller-stones, like those we had used for grinding sandbur seeds in the *Lush*.

'What *is* this?' I asked Rafig.

'Anakim place,' he said. 'The giants lived here in the Distant Time.'

I picked up a fragment of pottery - reddish-yellow terra-cotta, decorated with an intricate pattern of notched bands. It was quite different from the sort of pottery I had seen nomad women making in the Wadi al-Ma. Their pottery was thicker and lacked the notched pattern – altogether cruder than this.

I crouched and ran my hand over the smooth surface of a grinding stone, like an enormous bar of grey soap worn down in the middle. I wondered how much grinding it had taken to reach that state. A very long time, I guessed – more than one person's lifetime, anyway. I picked up a triangular arrowhead – a slim flake with many facets, so finely wrought that the edge might still have drawn blood. I put the arrowhead in my pocket, and picked up a larger stone – like a big oyster with rounded sides and an edge. I weighed it in my right hand - it felt pleasantly heavy, but there was something else - it fitted my hand as perfectly as a glove. Like the arrowhead, this tool had been deftly carved, and it must have been polished, too, because the finish was smooth as marble. I switched it from hand to hand, marveling at its excellence. It was a cutting tool of some kind – not a knife, more like an axe without the shaft. There was a kind of power in it, I thought – it had been created with loving attention, yet it suited my hand so well, it was as if the maker had known I would one day arrive here and pick it up.

I gripped it and it was suddenly as if the ground underfoot trembled, and there was a crash of thunder and the sky went dark. Lightning scorpions flashed, black storm-heads cruised across the horizon, and rain came crashing down on gravel plains, splashing on mountain massifs, rushing down in streams and rivers, dissolving great dunes, washing down volumes of sand, forming vast inland waters that heaved and frothed and rippled.

The vision was vivid, but it lasted only an instant and then the clouds were gone and I was back under the radiant blueness of the desert sky. I held the stone tight, as if it were precious, as if I had just found the key to something - the key to everything, perhaps. I thought of the luxurious, green, watered land of *Tihamat* in Musa's Snake-Woman story, and of Shamsa's words, '*the rain fell … on the palaces of kings and the hoarders of treasure … and they and all their works were washed away - nothing remained, not even a memory.*'

I looked around, hoping to see some feature – a hill or a wadi – that might suggest a logic of habitation. The desert here was no different from the surrounding area, though – the great ridge on one side, with sand, stone, gravel, rock outcrops, an occasional thorn tree, a few stumps of faded grass. Once people had lived here, whether Anakim giants or others, I did not know, but not the nomads who wandered here today, I was sure of that.

I looked up to see that Rafig had moved over to a rock outcrop and was beckoning me. 'Here there are pictures,' he announced.

I saw that the rocks were covered in images – dancing, spidery shapes of men and cattle deeply engraved in the stone. The man-shapes were bizarre and alien, their limbs too long and their actions exaggerated - the bodies were headless, with only necks like featureless stalks. The cattle, though obviously cattle, were represented with impossibly long horns.

Rafig pointed at them. 'The *Horn Dance*,' he said. 'Shadad the Hunter came dancing here in his dream, and marked the way, where the giants' path crossed the path of the jinns. Some say the Siren Road starts from here.'

I pointed to the stalk-heads engraved on the rock. 'Are these Anakim?' I asked.

He shook his head. 'The stories say so, but God is All-Knowing.'

I took out the stone axe I had picked up and showed it to him - how it fitted into my hand. 'The Anakim are supposed to have been giants,' I said. 'I am not a giant and yet this stone might have been made for me.' I pointed at the rock pictures again. 'See, the men don't tower over the cattle like giants. They seem of ordinary size - unless the cattle were also giants.'

Rafig nodded but said nothing – perhaps *giants* did not mean the same thing to him as it did to me, I thought. After all, giant is relative.

'Do nomads make pictures like this? I asked.

He shook his head.

He was already moving again, indicating another, larger, rock outcrop with a stone face indented under a slight overhang. I joined him and saw there were more pictures of animal and human figures, with geometrical patterns such as whorls, zig-zags and parallel waves.

'See,' Rafig said again, pointing at the human outlines. The first thing I noticed was that, unlike the figures on the other outcrop, these ones had heads. To my astonishment, though, they were not human heads, but those of animals. Although it was hard to be sure, the heads looked cat-like – perhaps leopards or hyenas, or a mixture of both. Yet the bodies were clearly human – they were standing upright, wearing clothes of some kind, with five-fingered hands spread, and feet equally detailed. There were six or seven separate figures, but they were grouped close together in a pose that suggested dancing.

'*Masks*,' I said. 'The people who made these wore animal masks.'

'Perhaps,' Rafig nodded, 'though is said that the Anakim were able to see through the veil better than us, and were closer to the animals.'

'*Closer* to?'

These pictures suggested that the artists were more than just pet-lovers, I thought. I glanced at him and knew he was thinking about his son, Adnan, and what he had witnessed last time they had met. If truth be told, that was the idea that had first struck me when I had seen the pictures. I had rejected it, but now I looked at the images again, it was true that the heads did not look like masks. The human figures on the other outcrop had no heads – these had the heads of carnivores. It gave me an eerie feeling, something like what I had felt when Atman had told the story of the *Night Camels,* or when Rafig had told me about Adnan. Who knew what the artists had intended? These pictures were made very, very long ago, I realized.

Rafig's guided tour was not quite finished. He led me over to a place some paces away, where there was a stone circle. I was not as surprised as I might have been, as I remembered, when talking about the Anakim, Musa had mentioned such circles.

It was a ring of black basalt blocks spaced at wide intervals. The blocks stood higher than our knees, and stood out darkly against the pastel sand. I crouched down to look, ran my hands across the smooth surface of the stones. To me it felt polished, like the stone axe I had put in my pocket. 'These stones are too heavy for an ordinary man to lift,' Rafig said. 'They say it is an Anakim house.'

I counted sixteen blocks around the circumference, which, as far as I could judge, was absolutely round. It struck me as an odd coincidence that this was the number of strikes Rafig made when throwing the *Sandlines.* The stones might the foundation of a brushwood lodge, I thought, except that there were other, pointed stones within the circle, whose purpose was not immediately obvious.

I remembered what the Hermit had said... *A Town of the Twice Born is mentioned in old books, and said to be lost in the desert?*

Could this be the remains of that town, I wondered? '

When I asked Rafig what he thought, he looked around at the landscape - there was not a tree nor a tuft of grass. 'How could anyone build a town here in the desert?' he demanded.

It was true, I thought - the remains of what might have been a house, some stone engravings, and a mass of stone artifacts, did not make a town. The Hermit had suggested that this legend – *the Town of the Twice-Born* – might be the same place as the Lost Oasis. The oasis was supposed to have been lush and verdant, though, not arid desert like this. Perhaps the legend was never about a real town, but a metaphorical town - a place frequented by numbers of people over an extended period. Perhaps it meant a kind of superior nomad camp, like Hassan's place in the Wadi al-Ma, where we had come from – what would remain of *that* ten thousand years in the future? On the other hand, it was difficult to imagine that barren site ever resembled the Wadi al-Ma, a strip of ancient forest along a water-course in the desert that had clearly once been a river. On impulse, I took the stone hand-axe out of my pocket again and ran my fingers over it. My intuition had told me it was the key to some truth. When I found that truth, I thought, the Lost Oasis would be in sight.

Truth

We mounted our camels and rode north, keeping the Horn Dance ridge to our right. Soon after starting we picked up the strange tracks again – the ones Rafig thought might belong to a leopard. I still found it hard to believe, because leopards were so rare, but, as Rafig said, it was difficult to imagine what else it might be, discounting a dog or a dwarf hyena. The other thing that puzzled me was the presence of the claw-marks. Although I was not an expert, I remembered being told that leopards retracted their claws when walking, while dogs and hyenas were unable to. When I asked Rafig about this, though, he shook his head, reminding me that Saadig had said nothing about retracted claws in his story of the white leopard.

By early afternoon we had lost the tracks. 'Just vanished into sand,' as Rafig put it. Shortly after that, we came upon an area where the sand had been blown away, leaving only the desert's hard skin of wrinkled pumice. Here, the surface was scored by a wide band of grooves running parallel, meandering from side to side, crafted over the ages by the feet of camels. The grooves were almost identical to the ones we had followed south of al-Gaa, made by generations of salt-caravans.

'Is this the Siren Road?' I asked Rafig.

The old man shrugged. 'It's a road,' he said. 'It looks as if no-one has been here lately.'

We began to follow the caravan tracks. As our camels kicked up the dust that had lain between the stones, I felt as if something had been awoken by our arrival. It was as if this way, unused for so long, had been given life and was uncoiling its tentacles before us. A dialogue was in flow between us and the desert, and every step of the way we were tuning in to ancient memories, released from the unconscious by the movement of the camels – as if only camels need apply, for they alone could attain the correct frequency.

Day's Heart

We made camp at sunset under the *Windmother* - a weathered outcrop standing at the end of the *Horn Dance*. Its upper tier had been so etched out by sand, wind, and rain over the aeons that it looked like an enormous chess-piece. In the last of the daylight I saw how the eroded stone might be taken for an old woman with a granite face and voluminous robes, pondering over the fate of the world.

'The *Windmother* lives in a cave in al-Qaf, the mountains at the end of the earth,' Rafig said. 'It is in these mountains that all the wild spirits dwell. *Windmother* keeps the wind in her cave, tethered on a leash, so it bellows and fumes and roars to be let out. Sometimes she unleashes it, and often it rushes out and runs amuck, and she has to scream and rage and at it, and fasten the leash on it, and heave it back.

'Sometimes *Windmother* appears as a crone with no teeth, and one eye, and at other times she is a bird with the head of a woman, or a girl whose lovely voice one hears across the desert, and whose look turns one to stone.'

There was no grazing, so we filled nosebags with handfuls of grain for the camels. Rafig used his fire-sticks to kindle a blaze from the wood we had brought with us, and tonight, instead of polenta, we made *Umm Duffan – bread buried*. We kneaded dough into raw loaves, then buried the loaves in the sand under the embers of the fire. Darkness fell suddenly, leaving our fire a tiny spark, a pale imitation of the great clusters of stars above us. Rafig pointed out a star he called the *Day's Heart* – the *Evening Star* that, like Zahara, the *Morning Star*, did not sail round the heavens. 'Its rising awakens the strong feelings of the heart,' he said. 'It tells us that it is time for our *second eyes and ears* to open.'

'How many sleeps do you think it is to the Outer?' I asked him.

'God only is All-Knowing. Musa and Kabir had never been there, so could not say. After this, we cross the *Urg ash-Shayb* – Old Man Sands. It is jinn country - there is no water, no Known Place, and no tracks or grooves to be followed.'

'Is that why you said we must open our second eyes and ears?'

'Yes, and all our other senses. The *Day's Heart* gives warning. After Old Man Sands, we may perhaps pick up the Siren Road again, and follow it to *Saddle Unravels*.'

An idea occurred to me. 'Wasn't it the Anakim who made the Siren Road?' I asked.

'So the stories say.'

'The grooves we followed today were obviously made by camels, but in the rock pictures we saw no camels, only cattle. If the pictures are truly the work of the Anakim, it seems they had no camels, so how could they have made a camel-path?'

Rafig nodded. 'It is so,' he said. 'Cattle need green grass and water - in this desert they would die.'

I brought out the hand-axe I had found and laid it in front of me.

I had sensed it was a key, and now I almost heard the key go *snick* in the lock. A door opened in my mind like the hole that had opened for the Youngest Brother in the Mother Tree, and taken him down to the Earth Mother's womb.

'If the pictures don't lie,' I said, 'and the Anakim really did have long-horn cattle – the *Horn Dance*, you know - the desert cannot have been as it is now. In fact, Shamsa's stories about Wadd and the Flood, and even perhaps Musa's story of Tihamat, tell us that there were rivers and lakes here in the Distant Time. What one calls the *Hurra* now – *the Desert of Deserts* - must have been like the *Lush* in the rains, like your story of Kabaysh and the wild sheep - but much more, and season round, not just part of the time. Here it was not sand, gravel and stone, but green prairies, thickets and forests, lakes, streams and running rivers.'

Rafig laughed, nodding, as if I were a bright pupil who, posed with a problem, had finally worked out a solution.

I picked up the stone axe, noting again its perfect fit in my hand. I felt once more a jolt of power through my arm, saw, heard, and felt – even smelt - the cascade of sensations - the angry clouds and the throb of rain falling in the desert, the storms and the wadis bursting their banks, the smell of rain on hot sands, the roaring surge of waters, the waterfalls, lakes, and rivers, teeming with fish, trawled by crocodiles and hippopotami. Now I saw animals in majestic procession – elephant, giraffe, buffalo, bushbuck and waterbuck, wildebeest and hartebeest and eland, wild cow, spiral-horn white antelope, and white-eared cob, as many as ants on the landscape, following the rains into the forests and rich green savannahs. There were the hunter-people that slunk after them by day and night – lion and leopard, hyena, cheetah, wild dog. The skies were spanned by eagle and falcon and osprey, and ostrich stalked the savannah, herding droves of chicks. I saw cattle people, too, wandering with herds of longhorn cows, along riverbanks, gathering around the Great Waters, around massifs like the Horn Dance where today cattle could not live. These people used grindstones to make flour from the seeds of wild grasses like the sandbur, they dug for roots with weighted digging sticks, shaped clay into vessels for cooking, and hollowed out gourds to carry milk and water. They hunted spiral-horn white antelope, gazelle, oryx, eland, elephant, giraffe, and buffalo, and other creatures, on foot and face-to-face, with bows and arrows and spears. They used stone axes like the one I held in my hand, to cut wood for their fires, for their shelters, and to skin animals to make water-bags and pouches. The stone ring Rafig had shown me was not a house at all, but a sacred stone circle built to focus spiritual forces. Those people in the Distant Time did not feel they were separate from each other, from other humans, or from the Great Spirit. They glimpsed threads of light through the veil, and knew they were part of the universal spirit. The nomads – Rafig's people – had forgotten how to make rock pictures, perhaps, but this harmony of humans in the world was something they had not lost. I showed the stone axe to Rafig. 'This is the key, as sure as the *Sandlines*,' I said.

'The key to what?' he laughed.

'To the Lost Oasis. This key opens the door. It shows us that the Lost Oasis is not one place - the *whole desert* is the Lost Oasis. In the Distant Time, the desert was green and flowing with water. There were great rivers here – Wadi al-Ma was a river, and Wadi Safra was a river, just as Shamsa told me. All these rivers flowed into the Nile from the desert to the west.'

'Fish Eater country.'

'Yes, Fish Eater country. That is why your father's folk are called Fish Eaters, because in the Distant Time they lived near great rivers and lakes, and they ate fish.'

'It is as you say,' Rafig chuckled. 'As I told you, the Sky Tree is the last of her kind.'

I thought of the ostriches that were no longer to be found, the spiral-horn white antelopes and white leopards that were becoming extinct, the many types of grasses that were no more. I thought of nomads like Musa and Kabir and Sliman, moving south out of the *Hurra* because of the drought, and the Fish Eaters migrating into nomad country from the west.

'Something changed again,' I said. 'After the floods had subsided, the land turned arid. The clouds moved south. The rains did not come. The rivers and the lakes dried out, and the wind piled up their sandy beds into dunes. Only the oases were left, like green islands in an ocean.'

Rafig laughed even louder. 'I have never seen the ocean - or an island.'

'It's happening once more,' I said 'as it did in the Distant Time. The desert is drying out, and the dryness is spreading. Animals and plants are disappearing, pastures like the *Lush* no longer flourish as they once did, and the oases are changing. That is why no one knows the names now, nor where they are. Soon they will all vanish.'

'God is All-Knowing,' Rafig said. 'What you say may be true for you now. The world we see around us - both the desert and the land beyond it- is no more than ripples in the sand. The ripples change as the wind changes, but the sand itself remains. It is as God wills. All things are the excitations of the Great Spirit, and all must pass, but, just as the dragon eats its own tail, it comes round again.'

He paused and smiled at me as if everything I had said was obvious – and probably, to him, it was. For the first time since we had left the Wadi al-Ma, I felt as if he was testing me – as if this were all some elaborate seminar of self-revelation, with Rafig my self-appointed tutor. I found myself wondering why he had *really* agreed to accompany me on a harrowing journey by camel in the wrong season, without any benefit to himself. Then I wondered if this was my jinn coming out, and dismissed the notion that he might have an ulterior motive.

'None of this helps us find the Lost Oasis,' he said. 'Not the one in your story, anyway.'

'No, it doesn't,' I said, 'but it must be connected.'

The old man's eyes glinted in the firelight, and he smiled again, as if the pupil had at last said something very significant.

When he thought the bread was baked, Rafig cleared away the ash and embers from the fire with his camel-stick, and dug out the loaves. They were brown and crusty, but too hot to touch, and we had to handle them with our head-cloths. We held them up in the darkness and tapped off the sand and grit with our sticks – miraculously not a single grain remained attached to the crust. We left them to cool on our head-cloths, and after a while, picked them up and cut them into hunks with our knives. We arranged the hunks on a tray and poured liquid butter from a gourd over the pieces.

'In the name of the Great Spirit,' Rafig recited.

We ate the hot bread and liquid butter in silence under the stars. It was delicious after days of polenta.

Later, I was woken up by a chirruping cry that echoed across the desert. It sounded curiously bird-like – not a hyena's call. I lay listening as the cry became a rhythmic panting that moved steadily closer. Presently I heard the scamper of feet around the camp – a muffled, dogged padding. The camels lifted their heads and looked round, shifting in their hobbles. I sat up and caught a fleeting glimpse of pale white eyes reflected in the starlight.

'Sister Leopard,' Rafig said dreamily, and I realized that the old man must have been awake all the time. 'She brought us here, showed us the pictures and relics, and set us on the Siren Road. Now, her task is over.'

'Will we meet her again do you think?'

'God is All-Knowing.'

In the morning, though, there were no animal tracks in the sand around the camp or anywhere else nearby. When I told Rafig that he had spoken to me in the night, he shook his head.

'I heard nothing, and I did not speak to you. I slept the sleep of the donkey.'

I stared at Ata and for a moment our eyes locked. Then the camel looked away and snorted.

Old Man Sands

That morning we entered *Old Man Sands*, a sea of sand-waves stretching in every direction. As we slipped down from our camels and prepared to lead them by hand, I searched frantically for a landmark or something to rest my gaze on. There was nothing – not a tree, not a stone, not a blade of grass. The starkness was absolute and frightening. The grooves of the Siren Road had simply vanished under the sands, and here no mark could remain for long on the surface. It was as if we were standing on the edge of infinity - I had been in the desert for a while now, but I had never seen anything quite like it. I remembered the nomad adage that the desert was not hostile, and in truth there was a sweeping, soft, curvaceous beauty to the sand-eddies, whose surface was a floating carpet of ripples. Yet there was an anonymity to it also –a land where travellers had left no sign and no memories, and where one glanced round in desperation for an anchorage, finding everywhere the same. It was easy to understand how jinns might come to inhabit this sand-sea. To be here was to be nowhere, to relate to nothing, and nothing - apart from the Great Spirit - could be said to exist, unless it related to something.

'*The Face of God,*' Rafig chuckled. 'Do not get separated. Keep the wind in your left nostril. Your eyes are no good here.' That made me think of Awda, the nomad guide, rumoured to be of the legendary Hyena People, who was blind, but had excelled in his profession of piloting desert caravans. As we led the camels on, I began to appreciate how that was possible. *Old Man Sands* seemed beyond space and time, and one's normal sense of scale was useless.

From a distance, ripples on the surface gave the impression of being much bigger than they were, and I would find myself moving towards a mass of dunes, only to find them dissolving into sand-waves no higher than my little finger. Any dark mark on the surface - a pellet of dry camel dung, for instance - was as large as a black tent, and often we saw far-off campfires, and camels, and nomads, that turned out to be the sun's reflection on the surface. Huge eyes seemed to wink at us out of the sands, only to close like shutters as we approached them. There were sudden and unexplained gusts of sand like smoke-trickles, and dust-devils that waltzed eerily across our vision.

Once, forgetting Rafig's strict instructions to stay close, I turned and led Ata at right-angles to the old man's path, just to see what would happen. I walked no more than ten paces, and when I turned back to look at my tracks I saw that they meandered wildly. I hurried to catch up with the guide, realizing the full seriousness of what he had told me – without landmarks, travelling in a straight line here was impossible. Only the wind kept us on course and if the wind dropped we would be stranded.

When we made camp that night, we hobbled the camels near enough to touch. If they wandered off in the darkness they would be eaten up by the erg, and there would be no finding them. We made a fire with wood we had brought with us and for the second night made *Umm Duffan*.

After we had eaten the bread and liquid butter, we sat by the dwindling fire, watching the stars, as usual. 'What *is* this place?' I asked Rafig. 'Why is it so different?'

'Ah,' he said, 'that is a good story.'

Azael

'Once,' Rafig said, 'Old Man Sands was a Great Water, of the kind you talked about yesterday – full of fish and all sorts of water creatures. There was a giant called Azael who lived in the clouds with Sky Father, and he looked down and saw Earth Mother, and saw she was rich and fertile with many cattle and grasses, and animals, and he wanted to live here. He climbed down from Sky Father's tent in the clouds and asked for one of Earth Mother's daughters in marriage – and was so given. Azael and his wife had many children and those children became the Anakim – the lost giants whose work we saw yesterday.'

'If they *were* giants…'

'One can say they were between Azael's tribe and Adam's tribe. This was long ago, in the Distant Time …'

'You mean they got smaller ...'

'As to that, God only is All-Knowing, but Azael taught his sons to herd cattle, sheep and goats, and there was so much milk and meat that they multiplied. He became so strong that he started to think he was stronger than Sky Father, and that he himself should be Sky Father. He intended to climb up where he had come from, and throw down Sky Father. Unfortunately for him, Earth Mother learned of his plan and sent a raven up to the clouds with a message to Sky Father.

'Sky Father was angry, but he waited until Azael had climbed up to the sky, then turned him into a serpent, and threw him down into the Great Water.

'You shall never leave that place,' Sky Father told him. 'You shall swim there forever.'

'Azael had no choice but to stay, but he decided that if he could never leave, no-one else should have the water. He swam down to the bed of the water, and burrowed deep, deep, deep into it, till he found a great cave. He made that cave his home, and began to suck down the water. Day after day he sucked and he sucked and he sucked down the water, until none was left in the Great Water. Only the sand was left, to be dried out by the sun and blown by the wind, and so it remains till this day, as you see.

'Azael still lives down there – deep, deep down, in the cave, guarding the water. From time to time, though, he rises to the surface, and, in the form of a great serpent, swims through the sand to the edge of the erg as if the sand were water. He is old now – very old – he is *Old Man Sands* himself, and when he swims through the sand, the surface trembles, and the sand rumbles with his voice – some say it is his singing, and others that he beats a great drum as he swims, but whatever the case, it is as loud as thunder.'

'Azael's Drum?' I asked, 'didn't the Hermit mention that?'

'Perhaps,' Rafig said. 'Only God is All-Knowing, but it is said that *Old Man Sands* lurks under the sand in the erg, as a great *hashara* fish under water ...'

'What is a *hashara*?

'A creature that bites – a catfish, for example, or a scorpion.'

'A hyena?'

'No, a hyena is a four-legged, not a *hashara*. Anyway, Old Man Sands may appear as an old man in a black cloak, or a Crocodile-Man, or a Catfish-Man, or a Great Snake-Man, or sometimes as Sister Siren - a young woman in a black robe with black hair down to her knees. His drumming and singing leads travellers astray, spinning their heads around so that they do not know north from south, and luring them to their deaths. Many nomads have lost the way and died of thirst here in the *Urg ash-Shayb*. That is why one should never take anything for granted.'

After the fire died, we wrapped ourselves in our blankets and lay down. I dozed rather than slept, and when I awoke to what I thought was a stark cry in the night, I could not decide whether it was Old Man Sands, Sister Hyena, Sister Leopard or a *hashara*. I gave up trying to sleep after that, and lay awake, straining my ears, and though I did not hear any more strangled cries, I was certain I could hear a distant drum-beat, and maidens' voices singing.

Drum

Even after we got the camels moving next morning, I felt a presence – the sands seemed heavy as if they held something that I had not felt the previous day – as if the grains themselves were a spiral galaxy of crystal eyes, watching. The sand-waves and ripples were on the move, and one could imagine some great *hashara* creature swimming just under the desert's skin raising welts and undulations. I could not help thinking of *Old Man Sands* – Azael – as a sand-dwelling serpent. In places the camels' feet creaked and crepitated, sinking through the top-sand, revealing raw pink layers beneath, like wounds, and Rafig warned me about *sand deeps* – invisible pools of loose grains where a camel might be swallowed up completely.

By mid-morning we were moving towards a range of dunes that projected suddenly from the surface of the erg – high crescents in an endless interlocking maze, with puddled faces and knife-blade edges that seethed and simmered with fine dust. The dunes lay on our left side, and as we approached the skirts of the dune-field, Rafig, in front of me, extended his arm and pointed with his stick, yelling '*laymin-ooo'*, meaning we should shift to the right. At that moment *Old Man Sands* started booming.

It began abruptly with the surface under our feet shaking and trembling, so violently I felt it might knock me over. At once we were enveloped in a curtain of dust that hung in the air, and I could only just glimpse my companion. I was about to shout to him, when the air itself started jumping with a rhythmic kettle-drum tattoo, and from the direction of the dunes came a deep-throated chorus, perfectly in time with the drum-beat. The singing was unbelievably loud, and it sounded like human voices – men and women – humming and clapping and chanting in counterpoint. Moreover, the voices seemed to be calling to me – I could hear them singing my name, and I knew they had a message for me and me alone, and that I had to find out what that message was, and where it was coming from.

I turned towards the dunes, and in a moment I was climbing up a slope up into the dune-field, leading Ata after me. I did not turn to look at Rafig or shout to him – this was about *me*, I reasoned, and none of his business. He was always the big boss, I told myself – always prescribing what I should and should not do, whether it was lecturing me on jinns, digging holes, or collecting firewood. Like he was someone special. I wanted to find out where that song was coming from, and this was *my* time. Rafig could go swivel – I would catch up with him later.

A pall of sand-mist lay at the razor-edged crest of the dune and a moment later I plunged over it, bringing Ata with me. Now I was in the belly of the dunes, I saw that it was a labyrinth of shapes liked a honeycomb, arranged in cells, each one with its cell-walls, rising out of the pit at acute angles. The deep-throat thrum of the voices and the throb of the drum were even louder and more intoxicating, yet I still could not make out where they were coming from. Together, Ata and I slithered into one hollow and climbed breathlessly up the slope on the other side, then another and another. It was hard work, and in the next basin, I had to stop to rest. The drumming and the hum of the voices was almost deafening, so maddening in its insistence that I felt I was being drawn into it and absorbed by it, and that I was at risk of losing myself – of losing a sense of who I was and why I was here. Suddenly I held my hands over my ears to try and block it out. *'Shut up!'* I shouted. *'For God's sake stop.'*

As if in response the chanting shifted to a low resonance, a deep growling that no longer sounded human. I tried to turn away from its lure but by now I felt I could not.

The rumbling grew lower and lower as, heaving on the head-rope, I staggered up to the rim of another hollow. Then the noise stopped abruptly. There was silence but for the whispering of the wind. Almost at the same moment, a dark figure appeared on a low dune some distance away. I jumped – it must be Rafig, I thought. He must have left his camel down below, followed me, and somehow got in front. Then I realized with a shock that it was a woman – slim, and dressed in a black robe whose hem touched the sand. She had long black hair that swirled and twisted around her like a cloak, obscuring her features, and I could make out nothing but a hint of red eyes glowing like coals. The woman said nothing, but seemed to be sobbing. Suddenly she turned away and I saw from the new angle that her stomach beneath the robe was heavy and curved – she was clearly carrying an unborn child. I opened my mouth to call her, but no words emerged. She made off in the opposite direction, bent forward with a slightly limping gait. With a start, I noticed that she left no tracks in the sand. A moment later she vanished, and at the same time I remembered the pregnant woman I had seen in my dream at *Broken Hobble*, and the phrase, *there are people who appear to be hyenas, but are not.* Then another phrase came into my mind, *there are people who appear to be people, but are hyenas.*

I shivered and turned to Ata, who blinked at me and blew a raspberry – he seemed to be rolling his eyes. I realized that I was completely disoriented – I had no idea where to go. I turned one way, then the other, but I was trapped in a maze with no clear exit. I could not think why I had decided to go off on my own like this – it was irrational, and now I was beginning to panic.

It occurred to me that the only way out of this mess was to follow my own tracks, but when I wheeled Ata round I realized it was not going to be that easy. Some of the slopes I had descended were at acute angles – harder going up than coming down. By the time I had heaved the camel to the top of the first two, I was shattered, and just as we reached the crest Ata pulled back hard on the head-rope. It came away in my hand, and I froze, rooted to the spot. This had happened before – the day he had run off, only to be caught by Awad and Khidir. I thought he and I were friends now - that we trusted each other - but if he chose to run off again, carrying my water, I would be in dire trouble.

I dared not make a sudden move, just in case. Slowly, talking to him calmly, I eased myself forward. He did not shift, and he allowed me to loop the rope gently round his head.   By the time we were moving again, though, I had almost lost hope of finding Rafig.

I shuffled disconsolately up another couple of dune-faces, collapsing on to my knees at the top of the second. I sat there in the sand panting and cursing, asking myself why I had come here at all - why had I left Shamsa for a fool's mission? I wondered if I would ever see her again. Suddenly I heard an unmistakable flutter of wings. I looked up and saw, standing smugly on top of Ata's broad head, a large black raven with piercing eyes and a shiny beak. She was almost identical to the one I had seen days ago perched on the head of the *khaluj* – the grieving she-camel - in the Wadi al-Ma.

Gap

I raised myself and made a motion towards the raven, who squawked, fluttered, flapped her wings, and flew off. She circled above us once, then glided to a dune some way off and

233

landed there. I suddenly remembered two things – first, that Rafig had described similar behaviour of a raven on *the Oversight*, who had led him to his son, Adnan. Second, that the raven was Adnan's spirit-bird. The oddest thing was that we had not encountered birds of any kind since entering *Old Man Sands* the previous day. I thought of the sobbing woman in the dark robe I had seen – or thought I had seen - moments earlier. I wondered if there were a connection between her and the raven – or if the raven was a hallucination, as the woman seemed to have been. I decided to see what would happen, and moved towards the bird, leading Ata after me.

The raven waited until I was within a few camel lengths, croaked twice, and flew off again, this time without circling. She glided away from my tracks, down a long avenue between the dunes. I knew I was taking a risk – it seemed absurd that a bird might be helping me intentionally. On the other hand, there was Rafig's story about finding his son, and I remembered him saying that crows and ravens were clever and were known to guide people in the desert. The raven landed on a dune, and began to hop up and down as if impatient.

I led Ata towards her and again, within a couple of camel lengths, she took off. This happened three more times and each time I told myself that following a bird was ridiculous, yet I did not give up. The third time she settled, I was leading Ata towards her, when a vaguely human call drifted across the desolation. The raven took off at once, and I saw her looping over us in a long ellipse. I battled frantically through soft sand in the direction I thought the call had come from. Suddenly I was out of the maze and on the edge of a dune slope sweeping down to the open sands. There were figures seemingly far below, us that could only be Rafig and his camel. I could no longer see the raven.

Almost wild with relief, I leapt down the slope with Ata skidding down behind me. Rafig saw us and waited for us to close the gap. He stood very still, his face impassive. I had meant to apologise, but could not find the words.

'I don't know what happened,' I told him at last.

'Azael's drum,' he said.

Dreaming

A little before sunset, we halted the camels in the lee of a crescent-shaped dune, hobbled them and gave them their nosebags. When it was full dark we made a fire - after what had happened that morning, in daylight, I was glad of the flames and the darkness. I was still shaken, and the circle of Grandfather Fire – extending to where the smoke could no longer be sensed - felt soothing and safe. We made bread in silence, and while the loaves were baking in the sand I told Rafig what had happened in the dunes. When I was finished I gazed at the old man's stern face in the firelight, knowing I had once again messed up, just when I had begun to believe I had things under control.

'Why did you do it?' he asked.

I swallowed guiltily. Azael's Drum had taken me by surprise, and I could not explain why I had felt the overwhelming urge to find the source - I now guessed it was not in any specific place. Neither could I explain why the drum-beat had sounded as if it were accompanied by human voices, nor where the pregnant woman with the swirling black hair had come from. The raven seemed an illusion too. On the other hand, the bird had brought me back in sight of Rafig, when the chances of my ever seeing him again seemed dubious. I had done the worst possible thing in the sand-sea – I had wandered off. Had I not made contact with Rafig again I would probably have gone round in circles till my water ran out, and both Ata and I died. I had the raven to thank for our survival.

'Why?' Rafig demanded again. 'Where did you think you were going?'

It was true that I had been lured by the voices, but there was also an element of rebellion in it, I could not deny that. I could have told Rafig at the time that I wanted to climb the dunes, but I had rejected the idea, and in fact, since I had probably known what he would say, I had defied him and his authority – the man, the friend, I had asked to guide me here.

'It was my *qarin*,' I said. 'My jinn. I thought I was doing well – since meeting Shamsa, I thought I had it under control. Obviously I was wrong.'

Rafig shook his head. 'Jinns are liars. They delight in hiding in the shadows till one thinks one is free. Just at the moment of triumph, the jinn strikes- he is always waiting, and he is always hungry. Yes, it was your jinn, and this time he almost got you. Did I not tell you that *Old Man Sands* was jinn country?'

'Yes, but I never understood how a jinn could be in two places at once.'

Rafig began to chuckle. '*Ma bt'arif lissi*? You haven't got it yet? There is only *one* place. There is only the Great Spirit and the Great Spirit's Dreaming.' Everything, you, me, the camels, Shamsa, the *Hurra*, Old Man Sands – even our dreams and the stories we tell, and the characters in those stories – are in the Dreaming. The jinn is in the Dreaming too, and so the jinn can be in the desert and in your heart, for desert and heart are both in the Dreaming.'

I scratched my head. 'But aren't the Great Spirit and the Great Spirit's Dreaming two *different* things?' I asked.

Rafig laughed. 'When you dreamed you saw a white leopard, were you not in the dream to see the leopard?'

'Yes.'

'So was the person you dreamed saw the white leopard part of you, or someone entirely different?'

'Part of me – the seer of the white leopard was a dream-version of me.'

'But not separate?'

'No. How could it be?'

'So the Great Spirit is not separate from the Great Spirit's Dreaming – they are one thing, not two. It is like Shadad the Hunter who dreamed the *Hurra* into existence, then awoke and found himself in the world he had dreamed. He was both the dreamer and the dreamed.'

I thought about it – it was hard, but I was beginning to get it. 'So we are both the Great Spirit *and* the Dreaming?'

'Ah – that's what I have been trying to tell you. We are like the ripples and the stream – remember?'

'Yes, the stream is the Great Spirit, and the ripples are the Great Spirit's Dreaming. The ripples represent finite life, the separate, individual life, and are a temporary activity of the stream – like the Dreaming. But there is nothing in the ripples that is not the stream – that is, the Great Spirit. The Great Spirit is the flowing stream - infinite and indestructible.'

'Now,' Rafig went on, nodding, 'imagine that the ripple in the flowing stream has a voice in its heart that keeps insisting that it is separate from the stream – that it is special and different and superior to all the other ripples, and that when the ripple dies there is nothing – no stream at all.'

'That would not make sense.'

'Of course – but that is what one's jinn does. It tries to persuade one that one is only a ripple and that the stream does not exist. In other words, jinns prevent one from seeing through the veil. They tell one that the world inside the veil is all there is, and within that world, you are special, or that you know better than others, or that you can mistreat others, or that you have been badly treated, that you are a victim. The jinn attacks those who desire power over others.'

'Not everyone has that desire.'

'Jinns are most active in those who are weak, who are afraid, who do not know who they are. One might say that those who are weak inside are the most inclined to make a show of strength. Those who are strong inside do not need to show it.'

'You're saying I don't know who I am?'

Rafig chuckled coldly. 'Did I make you to come here? Did I oblige you to live or travel with nomads in the desert? You are on this journey because you feel the need to find your true self. You left Shamsa, even though she needed your support at this time, because, for you, finding your true self was more important even than her.'

Now I felt angry. 'That's not true,' I stammered. 'I came to find the Lost Oasis.'

'What Lost Oasis? Where is the Lost Oasis? *The entire desert is the Lost Oasis*, you told me at the *Windmother*. You said you came to be healed - a voice told you in a dream of a white leopard, you said, so you know very well that the Lost Oasis is more than just an oasis ...'

'I still want to find it.'

He bellowed with laughter. 'Of course you do. And of course, your jinn wants to stop you. It wants to stop you so badly it's ready to kill you.'

'Why?'

'Because you will only truly be healed when you admit that your jinn is of no value, and you dump it in the desert where it belongs. This is the one thing it fears.'

'That is rubbish.'

Rafig cocked a hand behind an ear ostentatiously. 'I hear Brother Jinn's voice,' he said. 'He is furious when you suggest he is not real. Yet he is not. The real you is an unfolding of the Great Spirit - your soul, your true self – the part of you that is the stream, the part that never dies.'

I wanted to protest more, but what had happened that morning was against me. It was true – my jinn might easily have killed me in those dunes. I bit my lip, considered it for a moment. 'How long have you known all this?' I asked.

Roc

'The first step on the path is to be reborn,' Rafig said, 'but the end of the path is always the same – oneness with the eternal and infinite truth. Even as a child I knew this – perhaps we all know but it gets lost in us, depending on our surroundings. In any case, I wished to be a seer. Some of my friends made fun of me, others understood, and said I had the right qualities. I underwent many tests whose purpose was not for the sake of others, but for myself. My father – the Fish Eater – was himself a seer, and he sent me off alone in the desert to bring back water from a distant seep – a place where water gathers slowly.'

'Like when Khidir sent me to fill two water-skins?'

'Yes a little like that. My father said that, on the way, I might have a dream or a vision that would tell me whether or not I really wished to become a seer.'

'And did you – have a dream, I mean?'

'On the way to the seep, no. I lay down hungry on the cold sand every night – my father had forbidden me to carry food or a blanket. I had my camel, of course, but I carried only water, and fire-sticks to make a fire. I slept in snatches and though I dreamed, I could not recall my dreams – they did not make an impression on me.'

'I found the seep, but it was an *Umm Shash* - a place at the bottom of a narrow crevice, with only enough room to crawl down. One had to scrape away gravel to find the water, and it yielded only a bowl or two in a day, so the work was very slow.

'At night I rested near the seep, and, hungry as I was, I did not sleep well. I sometimes heard voices in the darkness, and thought I saw moving shadows. Then, one night I fell asleep and was woken by the sound of wings – the wings of a great bird descending. It was deafening, as loud as thunder, and a vast eagle-like bird – a roc - swooped down on me as I lay there. It grasped me in its talons and carried me off, and I was flying across the desert, and the world lay below me, then there was only the starry sky, and soon the stars lay below me too, and I was beyond the stars.

'Then I wondered where I was – how the Roc was carrying me. I no longer felt its talons and I realized with a shock that it was not carrying me at all, but that I *was* the Roc, not separate from the Roc, and that the whole world, the stars, the sky, and everything that existed was the Roc.

'I saw that the Roc was the Great Spirit, God, the Great Spirit's Dreaming, the Great Mystery, the One Absolute Eternal Infinite – those were just names for the one thing – that which could not be named - and the Great Roc was also just a name, a form in my dream, representing what could not be imagined, and had no form, and was not like anything, because it was the source of everything – not begetting and not begot.

'I was full of joy at this revelation – more joyful than I had ever been before – and suddenly I awoke and found myself in the desert, and it felt as if I had been reborn in this world, in this body, and the body itself was an illusion. All bodies, all forms, were what the Roc looked like from *inside* the veil, from inside the circle that I had believed was the separate *me*, and in my dream I had seen outside the veil. Then I had woken up again inside it.

'So I opened my eyes, and knew the truth - that the beings around me, the desert, the animals, birds, plants, wadis, and clouds, and everything – were *people*. They look different, but they grow from a common core, a common humanity, and humanity is not just *Bani Adam* - humanity *is*. Long before our Father Adam, humanity *is*. I knew that humanity was not just *Bani Adam*, but what the Roc is, what the Great Spirit is – the essence of being.'

'You mean, like humans in another guise?'

Rafig nodded. 'The bodies of animals, like our own bodies, are just appearances – they are what the Roc looks like from behind the veil, the place inhabited by the jinn that dies when the body dies. Those bodies are not permanent - they are taken off and put on like a garment.'

'Like the fox-woman in the story?'

'The quality that humans and other creatures have in common is their *humanity*, not their animality.'

'But what about your son – Adnan? Did you not say he had gone *beyond* the boundary?'

'Going *beyond* means that there is no boundary. The beyond is always there, but we do not experience it – it is not a wall but a veil. The danger with Adnan is that he will never find his way back into his own guise, and have to live on as a Ghost – trapped between guises.'

I suddenly remembered my own dream – the one that had brought me here. The White Leopard and the words, *the animals will heal you because you are animal and one of us*. When I reminded Rafig about this, he laughed.

'That was your interpretation of the dream at the time. Of course what the voice meant was *the animals will heal you because you are* human *and one of us,* but you could not have understood it that way then.. That is a measure of how far you have come.'

I nodded. 'Yes,' I said, 'I think I understand it now.'

Figure

Three days later we left Old Man Sands behind us, and were once again travelling on the *reg* – grey stony desert. It was better going for the camels than the soft sand, and they perked up slightly. That night we made camp by a brake of acacias, and the next morning, not long after setting off, we spotted what appeared to be a dark blemish on the skyline that Rafig said was *Saddle Unravels* – the last well on the Siren Road. The camels were thirsty and the water-skins flabby - we both knew that if there was no water at *Saddle Unravels*, or we were unable to draw it, we would have to turn back – and in this heat the chances of survival were small.

There was no wind that morning and the desert was still. We rode in silence, letting our camels pace in step until we came nearer to the blemish and it turned into a knoll above a line of thorn-trees. Almost at once we spotted a human figure there – the first human shape we had seen since Musa's wife, Khadija, on *the Oversight*. The figure suddenly stopped whatever it was doing and turned to watch us – perhaps in apprehension, I thought. We were deep in the *Hurra*, but though I was aware there was such a thing as camel-raiding - the *Amuck* - I also knew that hostility was not the nomad way. As we came closer, I saw that there was a host of four-legged creatures around the figure - goats and sheep. I glanced at Rafig and noticed his body had gone rigid and that his eyes were riveted on the standing figure. He suddenly urged *Hambarib* into a trot as if anxious to get closer, and I had to force Ata to keep up.

We trotted the camels closer and closer, and still the man – I could tell by now that it was a man – did not move. Rafig had not taken his eyes away, yet he had not pulled his rifle from where it was - slung from the saddle-horns. Evidently he saw nothing to fear. As we came nearer I noticed that the goats and sheep were scattered widely in stands of sword-grass along a shallow water course that fanned out in several lines from the knoll - a stony excrescence surrounded by tangled trees. There was no sign of the well, and I assumed it must be behind the knoll. A little closer and I saw that the figure was a young man - so lean he was almost emaciated. He was barefoot, dressed in rags, his hair a wildly tangled mass, his face as keen and alert as a wide-eared fox, his eyes almost chilling in their brightness, with a determined set of jaw. His face remained impassive as we approached. Then Rafig pulled up his camel abruptly, dropped out of the saddle, and rushed towards the youth. The next thing I knew they were hugging each other in a tight embrace. 'Peace be on you,' the young man said. 'I am glad to see you, father.'

Pulley

I couched my camel, dismounted, and went to greet him - I knew he could only be Rafig's son, Adnan. He gave me a firm handshake and we exchanged the customary greeting – his hand felt rough and calloused. Despite his wild appearance, though, there was nothing odd in his behaviour, and I found none of the hyena-like features I had been led to expect from Rafig's story. It crossed my mind that the old man might have been exaggerating.

'I will take you to the well,' Adnan said. 'The gear is hidden – you will not find it alone.' His voice was a low rasp, but there was nothing inhuman about it.

Leaving his flock to fend for themselves, he led us along a narrow path that snaked over a saddle between hills. Rafig walked close behind his son, his eyes riveted on him, talking to him whenever the tortuous track allowed it. I followed, leading our camels - the animals lifted their heads, pricked up their ears, and began to pace out, as if they smelled the water. Over the top, we descended into a sandy valley between rock walls – in the middle was a mound with a well-head – a raised stone plinth and a wooden pulley-frame. Adnan showed us a place to stop, and while we unloaded our camels he went off to retrieve the well-rope, bucket, and pulley from their hiding place.

'Is he alone here?' I asked Rafig.

'He is working as a herdsboy for a nomad family,' Rafig said. 'Their tents are pitched behind the ridge. He said they entrust him with the sheep and goats, and he has charge of the well.'

He gave me an equivocal glance and I remembered how Adnan had been stealing small-stock from nomads on *the Oversight*. Obviously he no longer felt the urge to do it, otherwise he would not be here. I almost asked Rafig if he believed Adnan was healed, but I thought better of it. Apart from anything else, I did not know exactly how to phrase the question – had he been ill, deranged, possessed by a jinn?

As if he had read my mind, Rafig said. 'Adnan is back.'

That said it all, I thought.

We laid out our equipment and raised the camels, and soon Adnan returned with a soft well bucket, a plaited leather rope, and a wooden pulley-wheel. We led our camels to the well-head, where the youth affixed the wheel to the spindle on the frame. He rigged up the bucket and rope, fitted the rope into the groove on the wheel, and gave the end to Rafig, who tied it to Hambarib's saddle.

'Now drop the bucket,' Adnan growled.

I picked up the bucket, let it drop into the well, and heard it hit the water far below. I waggled it around until I thought it was full, then gave the signal to Rafig, who drew the camel forward. The pulley groaned and the rope grew taut as the bucket came up. Adnan smiled, showing yellow teeth.

He and I carried the bucket over to a mud trough and poured the water in, then I led Ata to the trough to let him drink. He had not drunk since before *the Oversight* and he guzzled the liquid noisily, taking three or four deep slurps then raising his head, shaking his lips and blubbering, then lowering his head and slurping once more. It always amazed me how much a camel could drink in one go - I watched his abdomen slowly swelling, with pleasure and relief.

Rafig worked his camel back and forth, as bucket after bucket rose to the well head, to be carried to the trough by myself and Adnan. When Ata was satisfied, we hitched him to the rope so that Hambarib could drink. Once he had drunk enough, we filled all our water-skins, tied them, and laid them in the sand. Adnan detached the rope and coiled it, took off the bucket, and removed the pulley from the frame. He returned the gear to its hiding-place, and while he was gone, Rafig and I slung the water-skins and loaded the camels. Adnan arrived a moment later, and announced that he would go and fetch the sheep and goats. He directed us to his cabin further up the wadi, and said he would join us there.

Limits

The cabin turned out to be a makeshift hut of brushwood in a nest of large boulders, surrounded by thorn trees. There were a few pots and gourds there, and a three-stone fireplace with the remains of a fire. We unloaded the camels and dumped our gear in the shade of a large acacia, hobbled the camels and turned them out into the trees. We worked in silence. Rafig seemed preoccupied, and though he did not say so, my intuition told me that he was wondering why, if Adnan was healed of his madness, he was still living like a hermit, and why he had not returned home.

When the youth arrived with his flock, we helped him settle the sheep and goats in the trees. The three of us collected deadfall and brought it over to the grass hut, where Adnan twirled sticks and lit a fire. Beyond this grove of boulders and trees, at the base of the outcrop, open desert stretched on and on to the north. I knew that Siren Land and the *Great Green* lay in that direction, but they were months away. *Saddle Unravels* was the last well on the Siren Road, and the country between here and Siren was unknown, at least to us. Now we were at the limits of our known world, I began to understand just how vast was the territory beyond.

We had brought our cooking gear over and, once the flames were crackling, Adnan poured water and began to make tea. His actions were precise and focused, just as his work at the well had been – he had evidently not been permanently damaged by his experience as a *Ghost*. Still, he was slightly withdrawn, and I had not yet managed to build a rapport with him. I sensed that he and his father would have had a lot to discuss had I not been there, but I could hardly disappear into the desert, so, in order to break the ice, I asked him if he knew how *Saddle Unravels* had acquired its name.

Adnan smiled, as if he knew it was a ruse to get him talking, but he seemed to welcome this neutral subject.

'Once,' he said, 'a nomad was travelling in this area on a camel. He had crossed *Old Man Sands* and was looking for the Siren Road. It was night, and he was following the *Jadi* – the

North Star. Suddenly a terrific storm began – thunder boomed – 'agrabaan - lightning scorpions - stung the earth, wind howled, and rain slashed down. Terrified by the noise, the camel bolted. The nomad tried to stay on its back, but the leather bindings of his saddle had got wet in the rain. The saddle unravelled and came off, and the nomad fell off with it. The camel vanished in the storm.

'The nomad could not follow his camel that night. He covered himself with a cow-skin and by morning the rain had stopped. Since it had washed away his camel's tracks, though, the nomad had no idea in which direction he should go. Then a raven suddenly dropped out of the sky and landed nearby. The bird was hungry and the nomad found some grain in his saddlebag and fed him.

In return the bird told him that if he wished to find his camel he must walk to the distant hill. It took him a long while to get there carrying his saddle, but when he arrived, he found a deep lake stretching for three sleeps. The camel was there at the edge of the lake, his stomach swollen with water. The man called the place *Saddle Unravels* after what had happened, and though the lake soon disappeared, the well has been here ever since.'

'Ah,' Rafig commented, smiling. 'Trust Brother Raven to show the way.'

'I wonder if it was the same raven that saved me in *Old Man Sands,'* I chuckled. 'I didn't give it anything to eat.'

'A raven helped you in the *Sands*?' Adnan spoke with a trace of mockery. His eyes were bright, and there was a flicker on his lips as if he were laughing at me. 'The Great Spirit struck for you on that, indeed, for no raven lives there.'

I wondered if he did not believe me. If so, I understood – a raven had deliberately saved the nomad in the story, but that was just a story. I had seen it with my own eyes, but I myself found it hard to believe. Then I remembered that Adnan's spirit animal was a raven, and wondered if he was smiling at something else.

'So you heard *Azael's Drum*?' he asked.

'Yes. It was so loud, it nearly drove me mad.'

'The drum can rob you of your reason. It has led travellers to their deaths.'

I gave a low snort. 'I can well believe that. Does every traveller in the Sands hear it?'

'It is heard rarely. I have never heard it, for instance. Why do you say you became mad?'

'I said *nearly* mad. I saw a woman in the dunes – a pregnant woman dressed in black. She had long hair and was crying. I thought she was a hyena.'

He stared at me hard, and I realized what I had said. Rafig's story about his son as a hyena rushed back to me. The worst thing was that I did not know why I had said it – I had not intended to. Had I secretly wanted to provoke him? Was my jinn working in me? Whatever the case, it was too late. I had to tell him about the woman I had seen in a dream, the voice that had lured me into the desert that might have been a hyena, the hyena that we thought had followed us, the ravaged water-skin with hyena tracks, and the hyena I had shot at al-Gaa. Rafig joined in, nodding, affirming, adding to and clarifying what I said.

When we had told him all, Adnan took a deep breath, nodded and said. 'You are haunted by the spirit of a she-hyena – the she-hyena you killed at al-Gaa was carrying cubs.'

He is a Hyena

I noted his word *spirit*, and my first reaction was to say that the hyena that had torn open our water-skin on the way from al-Gaa must have been real enough. Then I realized he had mentioned a *pregnant* hyena, and I thought about my dream and my vision in the dunes.

'How do you know she was pregnant?' I asked Adnan.

The hint of malice in his look gave me a start. I glanced at him and realized that there was, indeed, more to him than there had at first appeared.

He added wood to the fire. I realized that it was getting dark – the shadows of the grass hut and the thorn trees were already starting to dissolve and merge with the earth and the sky had gone flint-grey, with a roil and flurry of raw red cloud hanging over the western horizon. There was silence as the world waited.

Adnan poured tea carefully into our glasses as if he had not done it for some time, then set the kettle back on the fire. I took the hot glass and sipped, and the others did the same. By the time I had finished the tea, the sun had gone and the desert was bathed in darkness.

'Should we bring in the camels?' I asked Rafig.

'It's safe enough here, and there is plenty,' Adnan answered for him.

'Let us leave them a while longer,' nodded Rafig.

The old man gazed expectantly at his son. Adnan set his glass down in the sand and cleared his throat. 'I have been away,' he said, and in the dusk his eyes were dark hollows with tiny pinpoints of red light in them. 'May God forgive me, father, but I have now returned.'

Rafig sniffed and nodded. For a moment I thought he might say something, but he did not. Adnan stared into the fire.

'When Zahara was married to Mughir,' he began, 'I no longer wanted to live in this world. I loved Zahara from the first day I saw her herding her family's goats and sheep – I thought her beautiful even then –she was beautiful both inside and out. I loved her and she loved me. We were closer than brother and sister. She was betrothed to Mughir, but she thought her father would listen when she said she wished to marry me, but he would not – or at least, he was overruled by his family.

'It was agony for me, not only because she was my life, but because I knew I was hers, too. If I had known she would be happy with Mughir, I would have accepted it for her sake, but I knew that the marriage meant for her only pain.   I would have killed Mughir, but that would have caused a blood-feud, and Zahara would have suffered even more.

'I could not stand to live with our clan any longer, so I ran away into the desert and lived on *the Oversight*, where there are water-springs and animals.   I lived among the wild beasts, catching snakes and lizards, eating small creatures – ground-squirrels, hares, and hopping mice – even coneys.'

'*Coneys*,' Rafig gasped. 'God forbid – to eat a coney is to eat a brother.'

Adnan shook his head guiltily. 'There was a clan of hyenas up there,' he said, 'but though I saw them, they did not harm me – they seemed to regard me as one of them. Sometimes I climbed on rocks and watched them hunting - I admired them and felt more and more drawn to them, almost as if I were of their clan. Then, one night, when Lady Moon was bright, and I was hungry, I met a she-hyena in the bush – the mother of her clan.   As I faced her she made a beckoning gesture with her left foot, and when I moved towards her she turned her back on me. I caught the scent of her hind quarters, and my spirit left me.

'When my spirit returned I was in a nomad camp where men and women were dancing by a flaming fire, and there was an old crone beating a drum and singing – she had red eyes, I noticed, and bristly hair on the back of her neck, and when she opened her mouth, I saw enormous teeth. She waved to me with her left hand, while singing in a voice that wavered between a cackling laugh and a whoop. As I danced among the men and women, I noticed that they, too, had bristly hair on the back of their necks, and ears the shape of leaves … the beat of the drum was mesmerizing and I could not see the faces clearly – I will never forget the words of the old woman's song.'

Adnan closed his eyes and began to rock backwards and forwards in the firelight. I glanced at Rafig, who was staring at his son with an expression I had never seen there before –fear, I thought. When the youth started chanting, his voice sounded so strange that I jumped.

'*The man who dances among us is a man.*

The people watch him with the eyes of men.

His body is the body of a man, but he is a hyena.

His eyes are the eyes of a hyena, but he is a man.

He is a hyena who is a man.

He is a man who is a hyena.

The people watch him with hyena's eyes.

He has the eyes of a man, but he is a hyena.

He has the ears of a hyena but he is a man.

He has the legs of a man, but he is a hyena.

He has the feet of a hyena, but he is a man.

He is a man and he is a hyena.

He is a hyena and he is a man.'

Adnan's chanting was so eerie, the words so strange, that deep down I felt an unfamiliar stirring. My scalp prickled. It was almost as if someone else was sitting here by the fire, not a nomad called Adnan - not a man at all. Suddenly, though, he stopped chanting, and opened his eyes. For a moment I thought I caught a hint of deeper redness in the dark sockets, the trace of the predator lurking. The song reminded me of the rock-pictures Rafig and I had seen at the *Horn Dance* – images from the Distant Time, of creatures who were half man, half animal, apparently taking part in a dance. The moment we had seen the pictures we had both thought of Adnan. It was as if that had been a premonition - as if Adnan was using words to describe that scene immortalized on the rock. Those images were from the Distant Time. Whatever had happened to Adnan, I thought, it was not something new.

Spirit Mother

'I saw that the other dancers were naked,' Adnan went on, 'men and women were dancing without clothes, quite unashamed, and the drum was beating. Then my *jibba* came off, and my *sirwal* came off, my slippers came off, and my dagger came off, and my wooden beads came off, and I was naked also. Then I began to shake and tremble and I felt pain and began to cry out. I realized that my ears had changed shape, and I had bristles on my neck, and my jaw felt wider and my teeth bigger, and my hands were the feet of a hyena.

'The dancers around me began to whoop like hyenas, and I began to whoop with them. I had taken on a hyena's spirit and it had awakened powerful feelings in my heart. I was slipping out of my skin-envelope and becoming something else. The old crone was still beating the drum but there was another figure standing with her, watching the dance – a lovely young woman, and a voice told me she was Spirit Mother – the mistress of animals. Finally, my awareness faded. I no longer knew anything, and after that I remember nothing until I awoke and it was morning. I was lying under a bush and there was no sign of the nomad camp or the fire or the dance – not even tracks.

'It had been a dream, yet not a dream because there was blood on my mouth and under my fingernails, and I could not recall how it had got there. After that, I felt changed. Many sleeps passed and there were long periods when I knew nothing and remembered nothing - I was alive, but I no longer *knew* I was alive. There were no voices in my head, no jinn, and during that time I was not able to think about Zahara, and the pain diminished. Those periods of being out of my skin-envelope became longer and longer, and in the end I felt myself switching back and forth between hyena and man, and though I was not a hyena, I knew I was not *not* a hyena either. Often I woke up with the bloody carcass of a sheep or goat with me and I knew I must have taken it from nomads, though I had no recollection of it.'

'The *Ghost*,' I murmured.

'Yes,' Adnan nodded. 'I heard that word from a nomad who crossed my path, though by then I could scarcely speak, and I sprang at him and caught hold of him and told him, "I still know, but the threads of light are fading, and I feel that I shall soon not know. You must leave while I still know." The nomad left quickly, and after that you came, father.'

'I followed the raven,' Rafig said. 'Your spirit bird.'

'I do not know if I sent the raven,' Adnan said, 'but when you came I recognized you. Your presence brought back memories of Zahara that were painful, because I had ceased to think of her except in moments. I felt I must slip out of my skin-envelope again – I did not know if I would find my way back then, so I left my knife in the tree to guide me. I have no idea how many sleeps I was away that time, but many I think. All I remember now is that I awoke from a dream and recalled that I had been visited by a woman whom I recognized as Spirit Mother, whom I had seen at that first dance. There were two other women with her, both equally lovely - one was Zahara, and the other a woman with two children. Spirit Mother spoke to me in a sweet voice, telling me that Zahara had crossed the Other Side, and was no longer with the living. The pregnant woman, she said, was also on the Other Side. She had been killed by one of my kind for no reason, and her cubs deprived of the chance of life. Spirit

Mother said that I should come and join them on the Other Side, where I would be the lover of all three – they were waiting for me there. I was Zahara's rightful lover, and as for the pregnant woman, she would take my spirit in compensation for that of the one who had killed her. I told her that I was sorry for Zahara and the pregnant woman, but I had no wish to go to the Other Side.

Then I woke up with my man-skin on and knew again, and remembered myself. I knew that my vigil for Zahara was over, and I could no longer stay. I found the place where I had left my knife in the tree, but you were no longer there, father. I did not wish to return to our clan, either. I found my camel, who I had let go *haamil*, still wandering on the mountain, headed into the *Hurra*, and met these good people who took me on as a herdsboy. Perhaps one day I shall return to our clan. This is all I need for now.'

The firewood popped and spat, and Rafig added more. For a moment we sat in silence. I was so stunned by the story I could hardly speak. I no longer asked myself if such tales were true. I knew it was true on some level, even if not on the level I had been brought up to regard as the exclusive domain of truth. I no longer believed in that, anyway. The part about the pregnant woman had come as a surprise, though, and once again I guessed there must be some truth in it.

'Was the pregnant woman the hyena I killed at al-Gaa?' I asked bluntly.

Adnan's gaze was hard. 'Yes, and I suspect also the woman you saw in your dream, and in the dunes. She will not let you go until she is satisfied. She wanted to take my soul instead, but I refused.'

'Can *I* refuse?'

'If you do not compensate her, she will haunt you always.'

'How can I compensate her?'

'You must meet Spirit Mother. She alone can tell you how.'

'How can I meet her?'

'She will come to you.'

Shortly, I got up to fetch the camels. Lady Moon was a silver sickle, and there were bright stars – I recognized the winged shape of *the Falcon* and the zig-zag line of *Coney Night Caller*. After I had brought the camels in and hobbled them by our sleeping place, I told Rafig and Adnan I was turning in. When I awoke some time later, father and son were still talking in low voices by the fire.

Poison

After *Saddle Unravels*, we were beyond the days, and I lost count of sleeps. The desert was a void without space and time, as if we had ridden across the border and entered the country of the real. That, too, was an illusion. The world was a web of stories told around a campfire in the evenings, weaving the landscape out of the darkness, and as Rafig said, the world was nothing like how we perceived it, for even the mountains and the wadis, and the stars and the sun, were the Great Spirit's Dreaming, seen from within the veil, and outside the veil it was beyond all imagining. Time itself could not be separated from distance, and though both time and distance were part of the Great Spirit's Dreaming, beyond the veil there was no distance and no time, only now. If time meant anything to us it was an excitation of awareness, like waves in the ocean of eternity, each wave a part of the flow's unfolding. There were sunrises and sunsets, there was the succession of heat and cool, wind, and calm, walking and riding, waking and sleep. I was absorbed into the land, and its texture and taste were my skin, its smells and sounds my body, its vistas layers of my senses that peeled off in horizon after horizon and bared my heart.

The camels never shied from the journey. Rafig never lost his steadiness. His eyes moved all day from skyline to surface and back again, and he made small adjustments to the position of his camel in accordance with the wind and the small shadows under stones. I began to feel that we were no longer humans and camels crossing the desert, for in the story we inhabited there were ripples and waves but no separate entities – everything was the flow.

The *Windmother* already seemed as far off as the Distant Time. The grooves of the Siren Road came and went, sometimes distinct, sometimes lost under layers of sand, only to reappear elsewhere. Occasionally there were way-markers – ancient cairns, conspicuous boulder-piles in high places, broken stone rings, even rock overhangs with engraved pictures of dancing men and cattle like those we had seen at the Horn Dance, though none so vivid. Twice we passed through gaps between cairns set on both sides of the grooves. Rafig called them *gates* and laughed out loud at these age-old jokes told by the makers – the absurdity of gates without walls, gates into eternity.

In one place we followed a series of cairns, each one in sight of the other, to a narrow gully beneath a cliff. Rafig said that there might be water there, and we hobbled the camels, and he climbed down into the gully with a wooden bowl. He was out of sight for a while and I sat fidgeting with the camels in the sun, until he re-appeared with a little water in the bottom of the bowl.

'One has to dig for it,' he told me. 'This is what nomads call *Umm Shash* – a slow seep.'

'How did you know it was there?'

'The language of the stones - five cairns in sequence like that, each just in sight of the others, means water.'

It took us the rest of the morning to top up a water-skin, taking it in turns to climb down into the hot, dark crevice with a skin and a bowl, scrape sand out of the seep, scoop up water, and fill the water-skin by feel. When the skin was full the one on top would hoist it up with a rope. It was exhausting work, and the seep was so slow that it yielded no more than half a skin, but as Rafig said, water was the gift of the Great Spirit, and to pass even a small amount by was to tempt fate.

We rode on and the days passed and we talked little, saving our strength for the travelling. There was no sign of an oasis. By day the heat baked us and the wind blew in our faces and against our backs and the dust became grit between our teeth. We took to riding after sunset, when the Lady Moon was up and the desert was a velvet blue cushion, while we turned the camels' heads to the *Jadi* with *Shadad the Hunter* rising to the southeast, and the rest of the stars so thick they vied for attention, and we spotted *'agrabaan* - scorpions of dry lightning - far off that lit up the black bones of hills for an instant before rendering them back into the body of the night. We rode until the moon went down and left us in ink-black darkness, as silent as the ocean deeps, with only the heaving of the wind like deep-water waves, then we stopped and toggled the camels close to our fire, and fed them grain in their nose-bags, and the circle of the fire was a magical circle in the great void and the endless night. We slept lightly and got up in the morning when the sun hoisted up the coal-dark curtain, and lodged salmon-pink and crimson on the world's edge, pulsating with all energy and all power.

There were no more seeps after the *Umm Shash*, and we were rationing our water, drinking one bowlful each a day, and our throats were parched. I was increasingly aware of the gamble we were taking, aiming for an unknown place neither of us had ever seen, on the assumption that we would find water there. As *Saddle Unravels* grew increasingly distant, so the chances of getting back there decreased. We had been lucky to find the seep, but Rafig commented that *Umm Shash* seeps were unreliable, and that it might not even yield water when we got back.

One morning, when the water in the skins had become so low that I knew it would not last another day, we sighted grey cliffs on the horizon, and beneath them upright totem-pole figures wrapped in cocoons of shadow. We stared, squinted, shaded our eyes, and I thought I could see trees. I remembered the time near Wadi Safra when I had mistaken a tree for a nomad, and the many illusions we had seen in *Old Man Sands*. 'Are those real or an illusion?' I asked Rafig.

He did not answer, and we rode on for agonizing ages before he said. 'Those are palm trees. This is an oasis. We have arrived.'

Closer up, the trees seemed to spread half way across the horizon, a tangled forest of palms, trunks, fronds, ribs, thorn-bush, and great clumps of green esparto grass like giant fans. The final moments before we closed with the treeline lasted an eternity, then we were inside the forest, inside blessed shade I had almost forgotten about after so many sleeps in the flaming wind and the glaring sun. We slipped out of the saddle and led the camels up a rippled dune and through the palm jungle, where shadows engulfed us, strange and unearthly after the searing light of the plains. We emerged on the other side and found ourselves looking down the dune-slope to a vast lake of blue-than-blue water, a dream out of a fairy-tale, out of all the lost oasis stories ever told. Water in the desert of deserts, in the hottest of hot seasons – this was the miracle we had been searching for. It was the oasis of the last story, and here was story's end. We hobbled the camels in the shade, and skidded down the dune to the lake edge. Rafig and I looked at each other – this water was the prize, and we had endured so much hardship, and risked our lives to reach it.

I bowed to Rafig. 'By the will of God,' I said. 'It is yours.'

He bowed back, then crouched and scooped up water in his palm. He lifted it to his lips with an expression of rapture, closed his eyes, and drank. When he opened his eyes they were wide with shock, and he spat the water out on to the sand, retching, coughing, wiping his mouth with the back of his hand. '*Poison*,' he spluttered. 'Not even a donkey could drink that.'

Mirror

A sulphurous stink wafted off the pool – neither of us had noticed it in our delight in finding the glittering sapphire water. Now I saw that the surface of the lake was also seething with flies – swarms upon swarms of them, hovering and circling, rising and settling, floating in living rafts. Their buzzing filled the air – another thing we had not noticed in our eagerness. I crouched down and lifted a handful of water up to my nose. It smelt like rotten eggs. I let it run through my fingers, and noticed that it left a white stain on my hand. I licked it – it was salt. The miraculous pool was more saline than seawater.

'The camels won't drink it,' Rafig opined, voicing my thoughts. 'They will drink brackish water up to a point, but not *that* brackish.'

It hit me that we were now in a terrible quandary. Our water-skins were almost empty, and there was no chance of us getting back to *Saddle Unravels* without water. It was *Ged* – the *Hot Hot* season – and travelling in heat like this we could last perhaps a day without drinking – two if we were sitting in the shade. The camels were tired and thirsty. They needed rest and water – a lot of water – and grazing if possible. We had put all our hopes on finding water at this oasis, and we had found it – a pool that seemed to match my wildest dreams – only to discover it had been another illusion. The water, as Rafig had said, was poison. I recalled that he had seen an unexpected problem in the *Sandlines*.

'*Leg Trip-Up*,' I said aloud.

Rafig nodded. '*Leg Trip-Up,* but perhaps not *Dragon's Tail.*'

We climbed back up the slope, tracing our tracks to the camels. We raised them and led them deep into the shade of the palm trees. At least, I thought, after many days under open skies, we were out of the sun and the baking wind. Unlike cultivated palms, the trees wore rough mantles of dark fibre - they looked like sombre sages wrapped in shawls. Rafig gazed up into the fronds and pointed out the large bunches of dates hanging there – the dates were enormous, and looked ripe.

'At least there's something to eat,' he commented.

He found a stone and hurled it up at the nearest bunch. 'I have not done this since I was a boy,' he laughed.

The stone fell short and dropped in the sand. Rafig picked it up and threw it again. Again it fell short. He threw it a third time, and it struck home - dates showered around us like hailstones. We collected them avidly. I put one in my mouth expecting to be overwhelmed by the delicious, honey-sweet stickiness of a fresh date. Instead, I bit into a hard nut-shell that cracked into fragments in my mouth, and dissolved into powder. I spat it out. I noticed that Rafig was having the same experience. He hawked bits of date into the sand and retched. '*No God but God*,' he said. 'These are the most horrible dates I have ever tasted.'

I was about to add something when a needle suddenly jabbed my neck. I jumped, howled, dropped the dates, and slapped at the place. A flying creature droned past my ear – then another and another.

'*Ba'uud*,' Rafig shouted, jiggling and whacking at his own face, '*Stingers.*'

At almost the same moment the camels went berserk, rising to their knees, straining at the hobbles, snorting, jerking, biting their own skin. Rafig and I rushed to grab the head-ropes, falling on our hands and knees to dodge thrashing heads and snapping jaws. The animals were in a frenzy, and I was worried that they would break their hobbles and rush off into the desert, never to be seen again – that would really be journey's end. Musa and Kabir had talked about an oasis being haunted by jinns, and now I wondered if the jinns were really *stingers*. Or perhaps these *stingers* were jinns.

'We have to move the camels to higher ground,' Rafig bawled. '*Stingers* like stillness and shade, they hate sun and wind.'

He pointed towards the sand-dunes overlooking the lake. There was no shade at all up there – not a single tree. That meant we would have to erect our flimsy shelter of acacia poles in the sun and the wind just as we did in open desert. I chuckled bitterly to myself, as I remembered Maya's story … *as soon as he was within the shade of the trees, he heard the tinkle of running water. It was like music to his ears... there were glittering streams, pools, springs and waterfalls and date-palms heavy with dates...*

The Lost Oasis was supposed to be a haven of cool shade and sweet water and ripe dates in the desert, but this was not even an imperfect copy of that oasis – it was a reverse mirror-image. All this way, I had dreamed that this place might be the Lost Oasis I sought - that I might find my true self here, and somehow be healed. Now the entire journey seemed a parody – as if the Great Spirit had turned out to be playing a cosmic trick - as if I had been lured here by a trickster jinn, who was now laughing in my face as cool shade became the haunt of flies vicious as hornets, as delicious dates became sawdust, as sweet, clear water became vermin-infested sludge.

We led the camels up the slope of the nearest dune. There were, at least, some clumps of brownish sword-grass up there that they could eat. We were searching for a place to put our shelter, when Rafig froze. He lifted his head, his nostrils flared as if he were scenting the air, and his eyes widened. He pointed south, the way we had come.

'See,' he said. '*The Poison Wind.*'

As if to emphasize his words, a gust of wind tickled my face like a warm feather. Looking south, I saw that the skyline was obscured by a moving wall of dust like a dark tidal wave, still distant, but excited and alive, a twisting, squirming creature of smoke and tendrils, creeping towards us.

'It comes slowly,' Rafig said, 'but it will be here by sunset. When it is upon one, one hears and sees nothing else. God is Generous, but if we have not found water by then, we will be in trouble.'

'Poison water, and now Poison Wind,' I said trying to sound optimistic. 'The Great Spirit really has *not* struck for us on this.'

In fact, this was the most depressing news so far. We had known the storm was due ever since the *Night Maidens* had fallen, but, although hot, the weather had remained steady. I had almost let myself believe we had been spared. Now, just when we needed it least, it was upon us.

We couched our camels on the dune-tops, unloaded them, and removed their saddles. We sent them off into the sword-grass in fore-leg hobbles. From our baggage, Rafig extracted our stained cotton *rakuba* and acacia poles. He knelt, drew his knife from its arm sheath, and began digging a hole in the sand. I drew my own knife – the one Brahim had given me – and joined him. I was determined that there would be no oval holes today.

Once the *rakuba* was up, we crawled in and sat in the shade. Leaning against our saddles, we shared a bowl of water. It was the dregs from the water-skins, gravy-colored and tasting of tar, but it was still better than the water in the pool.

'There *must* be sweet water,' I said. 'What about your father and the *Oasis of Last Chance—* didn't he find good water here?'

'We cannot be sure this is the same place,' Rafig said. 'It might be or it might not be. Sliman, Musa and Kabir talked about *the Outer* but none of them had been there, and none of them mentioned a pool of bitter water. As you said, no-one knows the names of the oases now, because the desert is changing.'

'A pool of bitter water?' I repeated. 'Haven't we heard that before?'

'I do not think so, and I am sure my father did not mention it, either.'

He paused, and seemed to be dredging in his memory. 'You say there must be sweet water here. It is true that there are usually seeps close to the surface in a place of palm-trees like this. We should search for signs of digging around the lake. We will split up – you go east, I will go west, and we will shout to each other if we find anything. We must work fast, though - we must find the seep, dig for the water, and fill our water-skins before the storm arrives.'

'Let's get moving, then,' I said.

We looped our head-cloths tightly around our heads, and crawled out of the tent into the sun. Rafig slung his rifle over his shoulder, and I picked up my camel stick. Both of us took wooden bowls from the baggage. The camels had already wandered some distance, and their heads were lowered and unseen among the fans of sword-grass. Beyond them, the wave of dust was creeping closer.

Rafig grinned at me. 'Don't get lost,' he said.

Free

Lost in the Lost Oasis. Despite our perilous situation, the idea made me smile as I tramped across dunes, trawled through tangled palm groves, and pushed through thorn-thickets, searching for signs of a seep. I had come looking for the Lost Oasis, because I had lost my true self, and because I believed deep down that I might find it in the remote reaches of this *Desert of Deserts.* The *Hurra* literally meant the *Free Desert* – the place one came to be free, where the nomads *were* free - but it also had connotations of *real, original, authentic* and even *pure.*

The oasis was enormous. I guessed it would take a day or even two to cross it from end to end. As I searched, I came across many tracks of wide-eared foxes, hopping mice, and gazelles, but since those animals mostly survived by acquiring water from other creatures, it was not a cause for celebration.

In an area of smooth sand at the bottom of a dune, I found the prints of a larger animal, and I squatted to examine them. It was the trail of a big hyena, no more than two days old. It was such a surprise that it felt like a slap in the face. I had not thought much about the hyena since talking to Adnan at *Saddle Unravels,* and after his astounding story I must have imagined at some level that I had eluded her. Now his words came back to me. *'She will not let you go until she is satisfied ...if you do not compensate her, she will haunt you always.'* Was this part of her haunting? The hyena might have lived here forever, of course, but if she had arrived recently from the direction we had come, then she had been travelling much faster than us, and had overtaken us on the way. The water, the wind, and now the hyena, I thought – all great problems came in threes.

At that moment I heard Rafig bellow my name, and, glad to leave the hyena tracks behind me, I hurried towards the sound of his voice.

Seeps

I found him in under some gigantic palm-trees, standing amid what appeared to be a miniature settlement of beehive huts – five or six of them. My mouth dropped open, but before I could speak, he pointed to the sand underfoot.

'Look at this,' he said.

The earth was churned up by the tracks of many animals, and covered in droppings. For a moment a sense of paranoia came over me, and I stared around as if strangers might spring out of the huts at any moment. Then I realized that the sign was old – made long before the *Night Maidens* fell. The huts themselves were partly derelict – the roofs of some had caved in. People had certainly been here, but not for a long while.

'Fish Eaters,' Rafig declared. 'This is their style. My guess is that they came for the date harvest, whenever that was. They must have stayed some time or they would not have built these huts. Have a look at those tracks. What do you see?'

I looked – there were camel-tracks, but also those of small stock. At first I thought they belonged to goats, but I was wrong.

'*Sheep*' Rafig announced. 'They brought sheep here. Sheep need to drink every day, and they won't drink brackish water. So there *is* a seep here, and it cannot be far, as the *Tu* would not have built huts a long way from water. By lighting smoky fires inside their shelters, they kept the *stingers* away.'

I nodded. '*Clever*. They must have hobbled their camels on the high ground like we did.'

Rafig nodded. He seemed to be enjoying the puzzle, but I reminded myself that finding the solution could mean the difference between life and death.

'If we follow these tracks,' he said. 'They may lead us to the seep.'

We trailed the prints through the palm groves, down to a dry-wash at the base of the dunes on whose tops we had left the camels. To the right, the palm forest stretched on into the interior of the oasis. The animal tracks petered out in the wadi - there must have been a flood here, I thought, and they had been washed away. There were camel and sheep droppings, though, and we followed them down the bed until we came to some mounds of spoil. Rafig crouched, examined the surface, glanced up at me. 'We dig here,' he said.

On our knees, we dug through the crust with our wooden bowls, piling up the sand nearby. Within an elbow's depth the sand was damp, and a little further down, water began to seep into the hole. Rafig tasted it and spat it out. 'No good,' he said.

I sniffed it and found that it stank of decomposing vegetation.

'It's the palm roots,' the old man explained. 'They taint the water. We will dig in another place.'

We dug some distance away, working more urgently this time. It was past noon, and the sky was smudged with ominous swirls of black and grey. There was already a tremor in the air, and the palm fronds high above us began to dance and whisper. Again we found a seep, and again the water was foul. We gave up, moving further down the wadi until we came across signs of diggings that looked recent. I was about to throw myself on my knees and start afresh, when I noticed the tracks of camels in the sand around them. They were not new, but neither were they as old as the Fish Eater tracks we had followed to the wadi.

Rafig scanned them carefully. 'Four riders,' he said. 'Nomads.'

We stared at each other, remembering the four riders Musa and his brother had spotted near the *Oversight*, and suspected of riding on the *Amuck*. Neither of us wanted to say the name *Arjan*, but I am sure it occurred to Rafig as much as it did to me. I recalled the tale of the Dove-Woman, and Shamsa's unexpected kiss.

'These are three days old,' Rafig said. 'The riders have probably moved on by now. Let us think about water.'

I nodded and we set to work, digging three seeps. The first two yielded water as bitter as the previous ones, but in the third, astonishingly, the water was fresh and clear.

We drank half a bowl each, but there was no time to rejoice. We hurried along the wadi bed and climbed up the dunes to fetch the camels. As we were fitting their head ropes, I glanced south. The dust cloud had grown larger now – a dark wave as high as a mountain. The air creaked and trembled. The smell of ash was in my nostrils and I tasted it on my tongue. We led the animals over to our flimsy shelter, packed up everything and loaded it. The high ground was not the place to sit out a sand-storm – we had to seek more sheltered ground. At the same time, the nomad tracks we had seen made me nervous.

Back at the seep we made a trough out of a shallow depression, covered it with a leather sheet, and watered the camels, taking turns to scrape up the water and pass the bowl to the other. Bowl after bowl came up and the camels slurped and gurgled as their bellies swelled – it seemed as though they would never be satisfied.

Finally, they sniffed at the water and backed off.

'*Camels Quench Their Thirst*,' I announced, remembering the *Sandlines* Rafig had thrown.

'Thank the Great Spirit,' said Rafig, 'Now the water-skins.'

The sky was a whirl of angry coils and spirals, and the palm-heads were dancing in the wind. There was grit on the breeze and snakes of sand swarmed and slithered just above the surface. We had barely started filling the water-skins, when the wadi bed suddenly snapped like a blown flag, shrouding us in dust. We wrapped our head-cloths round our mouths and clawed sand from our eyes. The palms trunks creaked, bending over as if bowing to the wind, and the fronds tossed and writhed.

Rafig and I scooped water from the seep in our bowls, and tipped it into the skins. It was backbreaking work in the simmering wind, but by sitting with our feet in the seep, we could fill the skins with one hand while holding their mouths open with the other. By the time they were full, we were both covered in dust and gasping for breath. We loaded the water-skins on the camels, got them up, and walked them down the wadi.

'Where are we going?' I bawled at Rafig.

'The huts,' he shouted back. 'They will give us a little shelter against the storm. By God, my father's people had the right idea.'

By now the sky was a vault of purple and grey and seemed to be bulging down to crush us. The wind roared and bellowed and the land underfoot trembled. The dust pulled at our heads and whipped at our eyes - we kept our faces down, and tramped on, aware only of the head-ropes coiled round our hands and the tug of the camels from behind. The storm was a *Windmother*'s fury, a raging dragon unleashed from the cave – a *flight* of dragons with great wings beating, coming down in successive waves, each wave more powerful than the one before. Every step was like pushing against a heavy door intent on closing. As we climbed out of the wadi the wind-creature grabbed at us, babbling and shrieking.

We dragged the camels up the slope till we came to the grass huts Rafig had found earlier, and unloaded in the palm grove opposite. We chose the largest and most intact of the huts and dived in with our blankets. Inside, the noise of the wind diminished and though the thin grass walls breathed in and out, they seemed to exclude the dust. There was a three-stone fireplace where the *Tu* had evidently lit smoky fires to keep the mosquitoes off, but we did not bother to light one. Instead we lapped ourselves in blankets and lay on our sheepskins, waiting for dark.

Crash

I woke in the night to find that the wind had dropped. There was a fire burning in the hearth, and Rafig was hunched over it in his blanket, with his back turned towards me. I saw that he was making marks in the sand with his fingertips – it was the *Sandlines*, I realized.

I watched him for some time until he sat back and sighed.

'What did you see?' I asked.

'It is not good,' he said softly.

'What? Tell me?'

'There are people here. Their intentions towards us are not favorable.'

A cold finger touched my heart and I sat up in my blanket. 'Who? Fish Eaters?'

'Perhaps. Perhaps others.'

'Maybe it's not true. You said your reading could be wrong didn't you?'

'God is All-Knowing, but don't you *feel* it?'

I thought of the hyena tracks and remembered that I had not mentioned them to Rafig.

'Yes, I do.'

'The camels have quenched their thirst, as the *Sandlines* told us at the start. Now we face *the Dragon's Tail* – the calamity. We must go.'

'Go where?'

'Go back. This is not the Lost Oasis. It is not a place of shady trees, ripe dates and singing streams – there are no beautiful maidens. It is a place of withered dates, vermin-infested shade, and bitter water.'

Bitter water. It was the second or third time Rafig had used that phrase, and suddenly I remembered where I had heard it before.

'*The Fish Eaters*,' I gasped. 'You remember - Atman and the others we met at the Beetle ….

" *… there is a place of palm-trees called* Bitter Pool *in our tongue. From there it is seven sleeps to Oyo, heading northwest, but the way is hard and waterless, across a plain called the* Plain of Straying, *and a treacherous maze of dunes we call the* Labyrinth of Sand. ...'"

Rafig sat up straight. 'By God' he said, 'I should not have forgotten that.'

'This must be the *Bitter Pool* they meant,' I said. 'It's clearly a known place to the Fish Eaters. They built these huts - you said they came here to harvest the dates. All right, this is not the Lost Oasis - but it's a stepping-stone on the way to somewhere else. What if *Oyo* is the Lost Oasis … ?'

'What if not? You may go on looking for the Lost Oasis till you reach the mountains of *al-Qaf,* and fall into *al-Kharaab*.'

I threw off my blanket. 'I'm not going back,' I said. 'I *am* going to find it.'

Rafig was quiet for a moment. 'Very well,' he said. 'I gave my word that I would go with you, but we must leave now.'

We emerged from the hut and found the camels still huddled under the trees. The wind had ceased altogether, and the palm-fronds had stopped whispering, though the night air was still heavy with dust. It was dark but there was a glow on the eastern horizon, and I realized that it would soon be sunrise.

'The wind will be back,' Rafig said. 'Soon after the sun comes up. That is the nature of the *Poison Wind.*'

We hung our water-skins, folded our blankets, laid them over the sheepskins on our saddles, and unhobbled the camels.

'*Listen,*' Rafig snapped.

I cocked my ears. At first, I heard nothing, then I picked up the faint murmur of voices drifting through the darkness. It might almost have been the low chuckling of hyenas, I thought.

'Is it Fish Eaters?' I asked Rafig.

'I cannot tell,' he said. 'I am not even sure those voices are human. Come on - let us …'

Pooommmppp. There was a startling bang, a burst of flame – something whizzed past my ear and hit a palm tree with a *thunk.*

'*Welcome home,*' I thought.

'*Mount up,*' Rafig hissed.

A moment later we were both in the saddle with the camels cantering through the soft sand down to the wadi where we had watered earlier. We rode along the dry-wash until it fed out into the open desert. Rafig took the lead, his head-rope in one hand and his rifle in the other. I felt Ata's feet slip, then gain purchase on stony ground. The camels began to run fast now, side by side, almost leaping forward, their great necks stretched out, their feet slapping lightly on the surface. I wondered how long they could keep it up.

There was another flat *pop* behind us, sounding closer this time. I ducked as a bullet sailed past me trailing fire like a shooting star. I smelled scorched gunpowder. Realizing that our assailants must be pursuing us, I glanced over my shoulder. Four men were coming after us, riding tall camels whose shapes stood out like strange spider-figures against the line of brilliance spreading across the distant skyline.

There was a gust of wind so powerful that it almost jerked me out of the saddle. I loosened Ata's head-rope and leaned forward, urging him on with my feet on his withers. The camels were running flank to flank, and Rafig's leg was touching mine. There was a third paper-bag bang, even closer than before, and I knew our pursuers were gaining on us. I tried to push Ata on faster. Another surge of wind blew grit into my eyes, and I blinked, cursing.

The sun was about to rise behind us, but the Poison Wind was creeping up from the south again in a seething wall of dust as high as a mountain. It would soon engulf us, I realized. At that moment Rafig leaned across my pommel and yelled in my ear. 'The camels are slowing down. Soon our pursuers will catch us.'

'*What?*' I shouted back, not understanding.

'Turn your camel so that the wind is behind you. It will carry you northwest, towards Oyo - the way you wish to go. Do not change direction. God willing, I will catch up.'

The camels' feet were still pounding and it took me a moment to fully grasp what he was saying.

'Wait,' I yelled. 'There are four of them. Let me ...'

Rafig put out his left hand and touched my arm.

'You must go on,' he roared. 'This is your time. Find your true self. Go in the safe-keeping of the Great Spirit and remember always that you are the Great Spirit's Dreaming. I will follow you if God strikes for me on this, or we will meet again on the Other Side.'

'*What?*'

Rafig slowed his camel, and before I knew what he was doing, he had wheeled into the light. It happened too quickly for me to change pace, and by the time I looked he was far behind. I saw four dark camel riders bearing down on him out of the sunrise, saw Rafig urge Hambarib straight towards them. I saw him raise his weapon, saw the puff of smoke, heard the pop. I turned to steer Ata to the north and heard more flat thumps from behind. I glanced back again just in time to see Hambarib stumble and crash.

Then the Poison Wind engulfed me.

Shelter

Visibility was no more than a camel's length. The wind roared, bellowed and droned like hollow organ pipes. It came in waves, lashing at me so strongly that I had to drop out of the saddle and continue on foot. I wound my head-cloth about my face, and tied Ata's head-rope to my wrist so that I would not lose him in the storm. I was not afraid of being pursued as I knew the dark camel-riders could not find me, but all I could think of was Rafig and that last image of Hambarib as he fell. Pressing ahead with my journey was out of the question. Rafig had told me to go on without him, saying that if I kept the Poison Wind at my back it would push me in the right direction. He had suggested that he might catch up. I did not care about that, though - we had eaten bread and salt, and I would not continue without finding out what had happened to him.

I stamped on, head down, forcing one foot in front of the other, hauling Ata, desperately searching for shelter. The wind became hotter, gusting behind me in blasts like a flow of volcanic fire, roasting me alive. The heat was painful, exhausting – my heart was beating in my ears, and my brains boiled. The ground underfoot was stony, and, after what seemed many hours, I happened upon an outcrop that looked as though it might afford some refuge from the wind. I found the side away from the storm, couched Ata, hobbled him close, unloaded and unsaddled. I slung my water-skins from the saddle-horns and covered them with a spare blanket, so that the hot wind would not leach away the moisture. Then I went to ground under my blanket, shrouded like a corpse from head to foot.

I did not sleep, but kept myself covered, knowing I had to trap as much moisture as possible under my blanket, to prevent my body from dissolving into vapor. As I lay there, face down, I went over Rafig's last words. His *'we will meet again on the Other Side'* sounded ominously as if he were accepting death, and intended to sacrifice himself deliberately for my sake. I kicked myself mentally for not having wheeled my camel to challenge our pursuers when he did. We were companions and we should have faced the attackers side by side. It was true that I had no weapons but a camel-stick and a knife, and could not have done much, but it would have been two against four instead of one against four.

I wondered again who the dark camel-men were. I knew now that Fish Eaters used *Bitter Pool*. The huts we had slept in were disused, but the oasis was huge and Fish Eaters might easily have been lurking in another part of it. On the other hand, there were the four sets of camel-tracks we had found in the wadi. Rafig had been sure they belonged to a party of nomads from the south, and we had already heard the news about four nomads suspected of going on the *Amuck*. Having seen the conditions, and how few herds and flocks were around, though, embarking on a raiding expedition in this season did not seem a very sound option I knew that raiders did not target travelers, but grazing herds or caravans. What about the idea that Arjan and his cronies might have set out to make sure I never returned to Shamsa? They would have had to take on my bread-and-salt companion, Rafig, too. Yet, as I had learned, the journey to *Bitter Pool*, involved considerable hardship – even if Arjan had known where we were heading, it hardly seemed worth the effort. I was a stranger from nowhere, with no ties other than companion status, and if they wanted to get me out of the picture, it would have been easier if I was alone. Any harm done to Rafig was likely to start a blood feud with a neighboring clan - a serious consideration for Arjan. The more I thought about it, the more unlikely it seemed.

I wondered, too, about jinns – the jinns that were said to inhabit lonely places like the *Bitter Pool* oasis. On hearing the voices of our attackers, Rafig had said that he was not sure they were human. Then there were the recent tracks of a hyena, like the tracks we had been finding at intervals since I had shot the she-hyena at al-Gaa. I might once have dismissed such ideas as superstitions, but after all I had experienced since leaving civilization, I was aware that there was a whole numinous dimension to the world that had been hidden from me in my previous life.

Other Side

At noon, the wind dropped. I dragged myself up, talking to Ata as I loaded him. He nodded at me sagely as if he saw everything. I mounted and turned his head back the way I thought we had come, but our tracks had been swallowed by the wind and there was nothing to follow. Now unshrouded, the sun's fire blazed along the crests of sand hills in the distance, shaking out heat devils that smoldered all around. I recognized no landmarks - the landscape had been shrouded by the storm that morning, and with the sun directly above, it was hard to gauge the direction accurately. The one known place I was hoping to see was the oasis. The encounter had occurred a little way outside it, and though the camels had been running, we could not have been very far from the palms when Rafig had turned.

Strain as I might, though, I could see no oasis. On our approach from the south, I remembered – only a day earlier – the trees had appeared to stretch across the entire horizon. Now it seemed that the storm had covered the place – either that or the desert had swallowed it whole. There was no sign of it. I remembered the youth in Maya's story - he had dropped date-stones in the desert to retrace his steps to the Lost Oasis, but had never found it again. I rode on and on towards the place I thought it should be, but still I saw nothing. The sun descended slowly from its zenith, and the shadows under the stones began to lengthen. There was not a breath of wind now, and it was hard to imagine that this had been the site of a raging sandstorm earlier.

I stopped suddenly, realizing that I had been heading southeast, *away* from the oasis. I tried to reorient myself southwest, but there was nothing on the horizon but a shimmering lake – a glittering, quicksilver mirage. I rode towards it until it suddenly vanished without trace. I halted again.

'*I'm lost,*' I told Ata. '*I'm lost in the* Hurra. *I'll never find Rafig. What if he's lying wounded somewhere?*'

To my surprise, Ata raised his muzzle and snorted emphatically, exactly as if he thought I was talking nonsense. I was just telling myself that I had read too much into it, when he moved, wheeling round in a half circle and orienting himself northwest – the opposite direction from the one I was heading in.

'*Not that way*,' I said, straining on the head-rope and trying to pull him round. He snorted once more, and strained against me in a way I had only seen camels do when prevented from going to grazing or water. He turned northwest again and planted his front feet widely apart.

'*Come on*,' I said. I pulled on the head-rope for the third time, but again he would not budge. This was the direction I was supposed to go in, I thought, remembering Atman's words '... *seven sleeps to Oyo, heading northwest ... the way is hard, across a stony plain called the* Plain of Straying, *and a maze of dunes we call the* Labyrinth of Sand ...'

It was as if Ata knew that, and was telling me to stay on course. It seemed sensible. The way I was going, I would never find Rafig, even if he was still in the place where we had encountered the dark camel-riders. Moreover, he had seemed to foresee that, telling me, *You must go on. Find your true self. Go in the safe-keeping of the Great Spirit.* He had said that he would catch me up, and he would only be able to do that if I stuck to the direction I had planned – the northwest bearing. It was a heavy decision, though. I had seen Hambarib crash, and though it was possible that he had stumbled rather than been hit by an enemy shot, I could not be certain. If Hambarib was dead or badly hurt, Rafig would have no means of catching up, even if he was himself unscathed. Of course there was also the possibility that he had been captured by the dark riders.

In the end, I felt I had no choice but to follow Ata's urgings: I did not even know where I was, and I knew nothing in the desert was more fatal than travelling in circles. In the end I loosened the rope and let the camel have his head. Whatever Rafig had said, though, I felt a heavy stone in my heart, as if I had broken our bread-and-salt pact.

A little before sunset I descended into a wadi that ran through interlocking granite ridges. There were trees on the wadi bank, and I came across a grove of *arak* bushes that was exactly what I had been looking for – Rafig had always said that a stand of *arak* made a better shelter than a tent. I unloaded Ata, removed the saddle, and slung the water-skins. I hobbled him, fed him grain in a nosebag, and filled a bowl with water from a water-skin. It was the first water had drunk since noon, and it had a faint taste of palm roots. I remembered how Rafig and I had only yesterday dug out the seep in an oasis that seemed to have disappeared off the face of the Earth. It was a story from the Distant Time - it had happened in a different world, long ago.

It was then that my grief at Rafig's disappearance hit me. I had kept it low all day, pushed it to the back of my mind, but now I could no longer resist it. I had come to rely on Rafig's knowledge, kindness and generosity – his *muhanni*, and his mastery of the *Sandlines*. He might be all right, but the odds were that he was not. *I will catch up with you*, he had said, *or we will meet again on the Other Side.*

I laid out my sheepskin, wrapped myself in my blanket, and slept.

Pool

There was a wide pool of dark water in a great chasm, at the base of sheer cliffs that rose directly out of it on both sides, and touched the sky. There was a forest of trees in the chasm – all of the same family as the Sky Tree on *the Oversight* – and Rafig had told me she was the last of her kind.

I sat by the pool and watched a wild ram saunter down to the water's edge. The wild ram had enormous spiral horns – four hand spans, I judged. It was like the wild ram from the story of Kabaysh – the one that the shepherd had rescued from the *gelti*.

The wild ram called out with a man's voice for *Snake-Woman*, and shortly a beautiful, slim woman, with long black hair that covered her body, appeared from the water. She carried a plant with her, and she stepped out of the water and embraced the wild ram, and rubbed the plant in his eyes. The plant was a mushroom.

The wild ram was a man. He was a wild ram with the spiral horns of a wild ram but he was a man. He was a man with the hands of a man, but he was a wild ram. He was a ram with the feet of a ram, but he was a man. The woman was a woman, with the hair of a woman, but she was a snake. She was a snake with the head of a snake, but she was a woman. She glided in and out of her snake-skin. She was a woman but also a snake. The two embraced with entwined bodies, and plunged into the water and disappeared beneath the surface, making waves and ripples in the pool. After a while the wild ram emerged from the water laughing and ran off.

I watched all this with envy. After the wild ram had gone, I called the Snake Woman, and a snake appeared from the water. The snake coiled itself around my legs and body, and it grew huge, as long as a tree is tall, and then it became smaller until it was my size, and it was a woman, gliding out of her snake-skin, a woman with long hair, looping her body around me, and our bodies entwined. The woman carried a plant in her hand - a mushroom. '*This is Orotalt*,' she said, and she rubbed it into my eyes. Then we entwined again, and after a while, we plunged into the pool together.

Under the surface of the pool there was another country, where there were the tents of people who were hyenas. They had the heads of people, but they were hyenas. They had the feet of hyenas, but they were people. They had the hair of people but they were hyenas. They spoke the language of men, but they were hyenas. Grandmother Hyena and Grandfather Hyena were cooking food on a fire outside their tent – they were cooking the meat of a hare on the fire - for some children who were sitting on a mat nearby. They offered some of the meat to me. I saw that the meat was rotten and had maggots in it, and I would not eat it.

Then Snake Woman said to me, 'I am al-Lat, Earth Mother, Mother of Spirits, and this is our country, *Tihamat*. Grandmother Hyena and Grandfather Hyena have lost a daughter, who was carrying twin children, and these children here have lost a mother and siblings, thanks to you, who mortally wounded her with your weapon and left her to die.'

'They're animals,' I said.

'No,' she said, 'they are humans. They may appear to you as animals, as you appear to them, but in their own country, as you see, they are humans. They live in tents, with their kin, they cook food on the fire, herd camels, marry, have children and follow *muhanni*. For them you are an animal who has strayed from your humanity. By killing Hyena Woman you broke the law.'

'I know. I am sorry,' I said. 'How can I make up for it?'

'You must leave your skin-envelope,' she said, 'and you must come here to *Tihamat* and become human, and be my lover and give your soul to me, and stay forever with me in this *Land of Shadows*. She smiled at me, the smile both of love and desire, and the smile of a snake, with a snake's eyes.

I recoiled. 'I cannot do it,' I said. 'I have to find the *Oasis of the Last Story*, to find out what happens in the end.'

'You will never find out what happens in the end. Not until you sacrifice what you hold most dear.'

Out of the corner of my eye, I saw that Grandfather Hyena had a mushroom in his hand and he rubbed it in his eyes, and he was a hyena with gnashing teeth, and his wife was a she-hyena with gleaming eyes, and the children were young hyenas with bristling neck-hair, and the Snake Woman was a snake with a flicking forked tongue, and all of them were coming after me. I ran away and swam up to the surface of the pool and splashed out of the water, and rushed off into the forest, and there I came face to face with a wild ram, who was laughing.

Then I woke up and the dawn was a pink slash across the desert, and I was lying under an arak bush and Ata was staring at me with tired but inquisitive large eyes.

Sign

I took out a pot, and set to work making dough to bake the bread that would last me the day. As I twirled fire-sticks, I saw the sun climbing up in a brilliant aura of light to the east, with no trace of yesterday's dust. The sticks produced smoke, and the grass exploded in a gush that became something much louder, the wings of a Great Roc approaching from behind.

It was not the Great Roc, it was a flock of grey cranes – a great swarm of flying people, darkening the desert sky for as far as I could see. I remembered my vision of grey cranes on the night-ride to al-Gaa - so long ago now – and I recalled the words of Hassan, our host in the Wadi al-Ma. *'The Children of Adam do not control the growing of the grass, nor the blooming of the trees, nor the flight of grey cranes across the desert.'*

I was transfixed by the sheer power of the flow, and I knew now that this power was the Great Spirit's Dreaming - the wind in another guise. The flock changed direction then, wheeling in a perfect spiral movement like the flap of a cloak. For a moment I slipped out of my skin-envelope and my spirit was with the flying people - feeling the wind breathe, moving to a rhythm, drawn by an intent. There was only one creature in all creation, and I was it, and all of it was my true self.

The flying people passed and the sense of flight disappeared, and I was standing by Ata in the desert, by a fire, watching a flurry of dots hanging over the skyline. My gaze fell on my shadow, an elongated shape to my left, and I realized what had just happened. The grey cranes had been flying due north, but had altered course before my eyes, turning northwest. They had given me a sign, showed me the way, just as the raven had done in Old Man Sands. I stood up straight and watched the last specks disappear over the horizon, and saw, in that direction a double-peaked hill, like two fangs, standing where the cranes had passed.

'God is generous,' I told Ata. 'We have found our known place.'

Straying

Beyond *Twin Fangs*, the desert became an endless plain of grey dust, without dunes, and only the occasional wadi and stunted white-thorn, with bare crags far away, providing the sole landmarks. I realized this must be the *Plain of Straying* - that Atman had talked about. Like *Old Man Sands*, there was little here one could use to judge distance and scale, nothing to attract the eye but whirling dust-demons, and shimmering heat-haze, and the silver-flickering mirrors of the devil.

The days were hot, and the surface heat burned through the soles of my slippers, and my breath came in gasps. Each morning, as noon approached, Ata would begin to shake his head ruefully and roll his enormous eyes, picking his way gingerly across the baking surface. I no longer rode, as I could see that Ata's strength was fast ebbing away. Sometimes his legs trembled. His breath was labored, and he winced from a sore that had appeared on the inside of one thigh, where it rubbed against his chest-pad. I knew from my time with Brahim's herd that this was called *zabata:* it was caused by fatigue.

There was nothing for Ata to eat on the *Plain of Straying*. When I led him, he no longer strained on the head-rope– instead, he would nuzzle against my back, or nibble at my ear, hopeful, I thought, for the grain I could only give him in tiny amounts. When we halted for the night, there was no tussock-grass for him to graze on, and no thorn-bush to browse, and as soon as I removed the saddle, he would roll over on his side with his head on the surface and remain like this till sunrise. He would gaze at me sadly with those big, dark pools of eyes – I could almost hear his reproachful voice in my heart.

Since Rafig had been carrying most of the remaining food, leaving me with only flour and a few dates, I had to ration both food and water. I would spend the first hour every morning baking enough *Umm Duffan* to last the day, but the loaves were getting smaller, and though I carried some firewood with me, it, too, became scarce. I found some *tombac* leaves in the bottom of a saddlebag and sucked them to assuage the craving for food. Stuck between the gum and the lower lip, one leaf would last the entire morning. It took the edge off the hunger, but did nothing for thirst.

After seeing the grey cranes, I had felt confident that I could find the way to Oyo. I kept the wind in my right nostril, and watched the shadows of the stones, as Rafig had taught me, but after a time the mournful monotony of the landscape began to wear me down. Often I saw the flash of sunlight on water in the distance, only to find that it was another mirage. When the wind dropped, I would catch my breath, and start thinking that I had lost my way, especially at noon when the shadows under the stones were reduced to nothing. I knew that once the sense of disorientation took control, panic set in, and panic in the desert meant almost certain death. I had to stop, breathe deeply, pick out one of the ridges in the distance that seemed to be in the right direction, and fix my eyes on it. It took all the willpower I had to stay on course.

The worst thing was that, while the landscape was utterly desolate, with no sign of life at all, we were not alone. On the second morning in the *Plain of Straying* I awoke to find hyena tracks all around my camp. The tracks did not come near my sleeping place, but formed a complete circle around it, at about the same distance as what Rafig called *the circle of Grandfather Fire* – the magical border between the camp and the wild. I discovered that the tracks came from the south, and followed them a little way, to where they seemed to disappear, swallowed up by the sand. Returning to Ata, I told him. 'That hyena came from nowhere.'

Ata nodded his head, licked his lips, and stared around nervously.

When we set off that morning, though, I had the distinct feeling that we were being followed, and now and again it became so strong that I had to look behind. Occasionally Ata pulled on the head-rope and when I turned round I realized that he too was scanning the desert to the rear. I saw nothing but our own tracks and the endless desolation, yet as the day passed the nagging feeling continued. Whatever my senses were telling me, my intuition said that something was not right. That night, just before I rolled into my blanket, I heard the whoop and low chuckle of a hyena from what seemed to be some distance away. Though I lay awake half the night, listening, it did not come again, and in the morning I found no tracks at all near the camp.

Woman

On what must have been the fourth day after the grey cranes the wind dropped and I began to feel certain I was going in the wrong direction. I scanned the far distance for the peak I had been focusing on, but it seemed to have gone. I was suddenly so confused that I made Ata wheel round, and began to follow our own tracks. Mine and Ata's prints were clearly etched into the surface, but after a few moments I came across a third set, dogging and crossing over ours. Chilled, I stopped to examine them. They were close enough for us to have seen what was following us, and whatever it was had vanished without trace. I had expected to see the tracks of a hyena, but I was wrong - these were the footprints of an unshod human being. And I was experienced enough to know that they had been made by a woman.

'*A woman is following us,*' I told Ata. The camel's eyes bulged at me as if he could not believe what he had heard.

I had to make a concerted effort to control myself. The tracks were there, but that was impossible, I thought. Nobody, neither man nor woman, could travel in the *Plain of Straying* without a camel or at least a donkey to carry water, and there was clearly no camel or donkey. Not unless the animal was hidden somewhere, and in this desolation there was nowhere to hide. If the woman had been following us, where was she now? Her footprints simply vanished like those of the hyena I had seen earlier. I could not help thinking of the *Snake Woman* I had dreamed of – *al-Lat, Mother of Spirits* – who had told me that to do penance for killing the hyena I would have to sacrifice what I held most dear. What I held most dear at that moment was my life and Ata's – I wondered confusedly if I was expected to sacrifice one of them, or both.

In the end, I simply turned my back on the strange tracks and headed in the direction I had been going, forcing myself to focus, finding my high point on the horizon, and homing in on it again. There was a mist in my head, but no matter how it swirled I kept my eyes on that point, and the head-rope firmly coiled around my fingers. Sunset came and our shadows fluttered ominously across the surface like great dark moths. As darkness fell, I thought I heard footfalls behind me. I stopped and looked around, but saw only the gathering gloom. *Did you hear that?* I whispered to Ata.

He shook his head from side to side.

We pressed on a little further, and now I fancied I could hear voices drifting out of the desert. It sounded like girls singing, and I remembered my experience in *Old Man Sands* and shuddered. This time I would not go and investigate. The voices came again, mocking, yet strangely seductive. I tried to close my ears to them but they penetrated deep into my heart. I thought longingly of Shamsa, then of the Hyena Woman I had seen in a dream, of the Snake Woman, and Adnan's dead love, Zahara.

I dragged Ata on, and the eerie voices came with us. Ata seemed nervous. He kept gazing around him, and his legs trembled as he walked, and he sometimes gasped with pain from the *zabata* sore. I wondered how much longer he could keep going. His eyes started out of his head and he seemed terrified.

I made camp and settled down. As I lay in my blanket I heard footfalls approaching and voices taunting me at close quarters – this time I could not tell if they were men, women or animals – it sounded like a mix of all. I sat up and scanned the night. Suddenly I glimpsed twin pinpoints of white light - eyes glaring at me from the blackness. Then there was another pair, and another and another, watching me, winking at me. The cackling and chuckling and murmuring continued and suddenly it was everywhere around me, echoing backwards and forwards, now close to me, now far away, like Rafig's voice in the *Sandlines* trance. I stared around frantically, left, right, behind, and in front, but saw nothing. Ata lifted his head and pricked up his ears. I was in the most desolate place in the world, quite alone but for a camel, and yet I was surrounded by this chorus of strange, unseen creatures. A deep wave of horror tugged at me like a current, and I had to hold on to the horns of my saddle to stop myself from jumping up and rushing into the night. I shivered, cowering under my blanket, wondering what would happen next.

Then the voices stopped and the eyes were gone. There was stark silence, no movement, no scampering or twitching - nothing but the yawning stillness of the desert night.

I lay awake until first light, sitting up every time Ata shifted. I rose at sunrise and circled the camp looking for tracks, convinced that I would find many. I found none at all – none but the ones we ourselves had made.

As the sun rose further, I smelled ash and sourness, and saw that the southern horizons were blurred with dust. The Poison Wind was on its way again, and I guessed it would be here by mid-morning. I felt drained and lethargic and had to force myself to get going. Once on the move |I could not jettison the feeling that there was someone else with me - a sinister presence trailing behind. I could feel the stirring of the storm on the air, adding to the sense of disquiet. As the day grew hotter and air movement increased, thirst and hunger began to claw at me. The grey plain stretched around me, equally featureless in all directions except for the edges, that, as the storm crept up, unravelled into smoke. Ata snorted, groaned and rumbled, and his legs shook. Twice he sat down and the second time he refused to budge. He erupted in a paroxysm of powerful sneezes, spluttering and twisting on the head rope, until, after a particularly strong sneeze, a segmented white maggot as long as my finger dropped out of his nostril and wormed away. For a moment the camel stared at it, horrified at the thing that had been growing inside him. I had seen this happen before with Brahim's herd, and knew the maggot was the larva of the botfly - a creature that laid its eggs in a camel's nose. The fact that it had emerged now, though, seemed a warning - a sign that its host was on its last legs. I shuddered, and for a moment I lost my sense of self completely, lost my moorings, my eyes turning first one way then another. I felt a new terror welling up inside and I froze, not knowing whether to go on, turn left or right, or go back. I could not go on, but I could not stay here either. My mind became a scream of pure dread. I had to yank and cajole Ata till he rose shakily to his feet, and I saw that the light had gone out of his eyes. I had to force my legs to move, to pull him along, and every step was agony. It was as if my limbs and head were being wrenched from my body, tearing me to shreds. I thought of the Wind Scorpion who had once been a man, and whose body had been dismembered by giants – that was how I felt. I thought about the Wind Scorpion's journey to the *Oasis of the Last Story* – I had desperately wanted to get there, to find out how the story ends.

There was a snarl of wind and the air became thick with dust. I saw silver snakes of fine particles slithering across the surface. I was on the verge of total panic, yet I held on, gripped the head-rope, forced myself forward, and, just a moment later, I glimpsed in the distance a wall of sand dunes looming out of a dry-wash that seemed from here to be clothed in trees and bushes. An intuition told me that I had crossed the *Plain of Straying*, and had reached the limit.

Only the other lay beyond.

Farewell

The dunes lay above us like jelly-mold castles, heaving, seething and quivering in the storm. Though visibility had already diminished, I could see that the wadi was a *sayl* that I thought must carry water off the dunes when it rained – its sandy bed, lined with green-leafed acacias, caper-trees, evergreen arak, and yellow esparto-grass, twisted its way round the edge of the dunes for as far as I could see.

As soon as we arrived among the trees, Ata plonked himself down. He lowered his neck and rested his head in the sand, a sure indication that he was beyond exhaustion. I unloaded him, piled the equipment under a tree, and removed the saddle. I did not try to hobble him. He blinked at me as if in gratitude, but did not lift his head. A low groan came from somewhere deep down in his throat.

I patted his neck and stroked him, knowing what I had to do. He seemed to pick up my thoughts, and I felt that he could see through the veil into my mind.

'Thank you, friend,' I said. 'You were Ata for a time, and you helped me, and did my bidding, but you never belonged to me. Now I release you. There is food for you here, enough that you will not need to drink, at least for a time. Now you can be free.'

I stood up and, slapping him lightly on the neck, and heaving on his legs, I managed to get him to his feet. He stood there uncertainly, as the wind sifted dust around us, and his legs quaked. I put both arms round his neck, untied the head-rope and slipped it off. It was the first time I had ever seen him without head-rope or hobble, I thought. He raised his head and stared into my eyes, and I saw sadness there. He blinked again. *'You will not survive without me*, a voice said. *The way has been hard, but I feel for you.'*

'The Great Spirit only is All-Knowing,' I said out loud. 'Earth Mother told me I must sacrifice what I hold most dear, and I have held you dear. After this, all I have to sacrifice is myself.'

I chucked him under the lip and he mustered the energy to snap at my fingers.

'Go, find the *Night Camels*,' I said. 'Rest with them. Go in peace and the freedom of Earth Mother, and if the Great Spirit wills, we will meet again, if not on this plain, then on the Other Side.'

Ata snorted once, then turned and began to shuffle painfully down the wadi towards the densest stands of trees, pausing every few steps. I watched him go until the Poison Wind gushed through the tree branches and lifted blankets of dust off the wadi bed, hiding him in its shrouds.

Leg Trip-Up

From the gear I took only my camel-stick, my knife, a water-skin that was almost empty, and my *sufun* bag containing my diary in a rubber sack, pencils, fire-sticks, a packing needle and thread, and my now useless torch. The windward faces of the dunes towered above me – much steeper than those in Old Man Sands – and though I missed Ata, I knew he would not have managed to climb them anyway.

I laboured up the first slope, and as the sand-sheets rasped, the grains grinding against each other, chattering, and rumbling with fiendish voices. Blown sand screeched down on me in waves and rose in trembling veils so that I could see no more than a few arm-lengths above. The dunes were like the legendary giants of the Mushroom Rock that I had visited with Brahim's herd, I thought - giants awoken after untold ages, still furious that the wide-eared fox had stolen fire from them, their outstretched hands strangling me, trying to suck me in, to absorb me, grasping at my body, snatching at my head. My legs plunged deep into the sand and extracting them was agony. I pulled my head-cloth over my mouth and gawped around in confusion at a world that had lost its familiar dimensions. This was a theatre of ghosts, where every line and surface I thought was solid dissolved as the wind blew, and the light changed, and the shadows wavered, and the sand danced and pirouetted around me.

I crawled over the dune-crest, sashayed down the leeward slope into sand that rumbled like Azael's Drum. I crept over sand-crevasses, tottered along razor-sharp ridges, as the tides of sand flowed, rippled, reformed around me. There was no thread to follow out of this warren, and there was no turning back, I realized. '*The wind is behind me,*' a voice said. '*I can neither outrun it nor resist it. I am the wind, and I am the eye of the wind, and I am that which the wind blows, that blows the wind.*'

So I no longer cared which way I was going – my head whirled, and I gave myself up to the sands. I stumped on, bent double against the dust, calf-muscles screaming, pacing on half blind through sand up to the knees, advancing through the sand swells and the flying grit, as the wind and the heat and the sadness gradually pulled me to pieces. I dropped down from the dunes on to level sand, but still the dust demons chased me, hacking at my head, rasping in my ears. I stumbled into soft sand and stumbled out, slipped over sharp rocks. Swell after swell of dust slapped at me, each successive surge whipping away my breath. I fell to my knees, got up again, tottered a few more paces, and tripped over something lying in the sand.

Leg Trip-Up, I thought.

It was a dead camel, lying with its legs drawn up and its neck stretched out in a sweeping curve. At first, I thought it must be Ata, and that I had come round in a circle. I quickly realized it could not be, though, because this camel was mummified like the carcass we had come across near Shamsa's camp in the Wadi Safra. It was half buried in sand, and the hide was pulled tight over the bones, split open here and there so that bleached white bone showed through. The eyes and organs were gone. And there was another difference, I saw – the camel had only three legs. Its left rear leg was missing – the bone had been cut through and the flesh sheared off at the stump.

I pushed myself to my feet wondering what had happened to the leg, and who might have been here before me. There was no way of telling how long the carcass had lain in the sand – no sign that it had been gnawed at by scavengers. The thought entered my mind that it might have belonged to another seeker like myself, another contender for the secret of the Lost Oasis. Perhaps many had tried, and none had succeeded. Maybe they were those like the boy in the story who had spent themselves trying to find the place for the second time.

I clenched my fists and trudged on and on, with no idea of passing time. I was in a no-man's land, a limbo where time had stopped, I thought - I had always been there and always would be. My heart thumped like a kettledrum in my ears, and my breath came in painful stabs. The wind wailed and howled, and the sand trembled. The dust ripped at my head and gouged at my eyes and my legs were so painful that every step was agony. I knew I could not continue much longer, and only sheer special-forces willpower kept me planting one foot in front of the other.

My foot hit something else in the sand and I fell on my hands and knees. I thrust myself up on my haunches, gasping for breath, and squinted at the object I had stumbled over. It was a grotesque angular appendage with strips of skin clinging to lengths of polished bone, ending in what looked like a two-fingered claw. It was the remains of a camel's leg – the leg of the mummified camel I had found earlier, I guessed. I could not tell how far I had come since finding the three-legged carcass, but it seemed some distance. When I examined the thick thighbone at one end, I saw that it had been hacked off, not with a knife as I had first thought, but with an axe. It struck me that whoever had been with the dead camel had severed one of its legs and carried it with him for food, but, finding it too heavy, had dropped it in the desert.

Once again, I wondered who this person was who had come here before me, who was ahead of me by who knew how long. I forced myself to my feet, feeling that some hidden force was drawing me on. I pushed myself forward, sobbing, flailing through the clouds of dust. Abruptly, I felt the surface descending, and almost at the same time the wind dropped slightly, allowing me to see that I was passing between ranks of rotting stone ramparts, beneath hills like enormous clamshells. In the distance, I glimpsed the ghostly outline of a vast rock wall with peaks and pinnacles that seemed to stretch on forever, like the mountains of al-Qaf, at the end of the world. By the time I reached the valley floor though, the dust had veiled it again, and as I inched my way forward, I saw what appeared to be a bundle of rags lying on the surface. A chill passed through me as I sensed what it was. I began to tremble. The storm was angry, dark, thick with demon faces, and the rocks glimpsed dimly around me were gaunt fingers whose forms filled me with dread. A voice rasped in my ear in a deafening whisper, *'There is a dead man here.'*

Corpse

The corpse was lying on its side, its hands in front, feet sticking out from under the hem of a ragged *jibba*. It was stiff, frozen in position, as if it had been there forever. It occurred to me that the wind had dropped. I scraped dust out of my eyes, but somehow I dared not look closely at the features. I saw that the skin of the face was as thin as parchment, pulled tight over the skull, and looked away.

I noticed that the corpse was clutching something smooth in its hand. It looked familiar, I thought. I examined it gingerly through the stiff dead fingers, afraid of what I might find, but deep down I knew what it was. It was a stone axe, the work of the Anakim – identical to the one I had picked up near the Horn Dance with Rafig. It fitted into my hand perfectly, just as that one had.

I felt frantically in my pocket, realizing that it was some time since I remembered the weight of the stone axe there. I delved my hands into both pockets, squeezed the material as if the stone might be lurking in the folds. It was gone, and so was the arrowhead I had found at the same time. I stared at the axe in the corpse's hand - it was mine, I was certain of it. I thought of the three legged camel carcass and how its fourth leg had been cut off. This was surely the axe that had done the job. Like me, the dead man had been seeking the Lost Oasis, but, exhausted by the *Plain of Straying* as Ata had been, his camel had foundered. He had cut off the leg so that he would have food on the rest of his journey, but after staggering on for a while he had been overcome by exhaustion and dropped it. He had forced himself further but had not got very far before he himself expired – from thirst, hunger, extreme fatigue – who knew?

I avoided asking myself how, if this man had come here before me, he could possibly be holding a stone-age tool I had been carrying in my own pocket. Instead, I began to prize it from his fingers, exerting all my strength, bending them back until the knuckles cracked. When the axe finally fell into my hand, though, it felt red hot, as if all the heat it had absorbed lying in the desert over the ages was pouring out of it at once. I yelped and dropped the stone into the sand. At once, it turned into a botfly maggot and wormed away. I shouted out again, but instead of watching the maggot, I forced myself to look at the dead man's face for the first time.

It was like looking in a mirror. If not my identical twin, the dead man was me.

I staggered backwards. Hot pains shot through my chest and my heart felt like a weight. I tried to force myself away, but found that half my body was paralysed. The pain was a stab in the heart so agonizing that I screamed and fell on my hands and knees. I screamed again.

The desert looped and swung drunkenly around me, but I dug my fingers into the sand and crawled forward shrieking, struggling down a long dark tunnel with no end.

Way

All I remember after that is that I found myself alone in the desert in what seemed quite a different place from where I had found the corpse. I had been walking a while, when the Poison Wind started up again, stronger than ever. I could not see the way ahead, and the blast became so intense that I had to cover my face and force myself forward bent almost double. After a while I came to a rock wall and, following its line, I eventually discovered a small cave where I found respite from the storm.

I fell asleep, but something woke me in the night, and I realized that the wind had dropped. Lady Moon was clear and her light filled the cave and I saw to my surprise that the walls were moving. The rock was alive and it was undulating like a piece of cloth in the wind, and there was a voice that rose and fell with the undulation of the rock, sounding now like the wind roaring, now like a gentle breeze in palm-fronds, now like the song of a stream after the rains, now like the voice of a young woman.

'*These walls are not walls, but a veil and what lies beyond is the other that is not other, but is usually hidden from your sight.*'

'Who are you?' I asked the voice.

'*La ana walla inta*' the soft, woman's voice answered, 'neither I nor you, but Self – not *my*self or *your*self but *the* Self.'

I realized then that the rock walls were as thin as muslin and I simply pushed my way through to the other side, and found myself in another place, another desert, and standing on a dune in front of me was a woman, and the woman was lean and graceful and long-legged had long fair hair that was luminous in the moonlight, and was itself the colour of moonlight. She beckoned me to her and I saw that her eyes were white and had no pupils, and that instead of feet she had the feet of a large cat. The woman was a white leopard, I thought.

She stared at me and her eyes sparkled, and I remembered the glittering eyes I had seen the previous night on the *Plain of Straying*. This time I was not afraid, though, and when I looked closely at the woman, I knew that she was not a leopard as I had first thought, but a cheetah, and her shimmering white coat was entirely without markings. She was the white leopard I had seen in my dream in civilization – or what I had thought was a white leopard.

She was the cheetah whose tracks we had picked up near the Horn Dance – tracks with the claws showing, not retracted like a leopard's. She had been a cheetah all along.

As I stood there, the soft girl's voice spoke in my head, '*the Lost Oasis was always what is most human in you. When you killed my spirit at al-Gaa you killed yourself. Hyena Woman was human too, for in their own country hyenas are people like you.*'

I felt light as the wind and without fear. Fear was my jinn speaking, the *qarin* – the evil twin I had left dead in the desert. I was empty now, a void, and the ultimate part of myself, nameless and divine, could finally expand. There was no barrier between me and the world – my existence and that of the animals, plants and everything else, was continuous, for everything that existed was the Face of God and everything was of the Great Spirit.

As I looked at the Cheetah-Woman, I saw that she was none other than the Snake Woman and the Hyena-Woman I had seen in other dreams and visions, that she was herself Earth Mother, and the Mother of Spirits, and that all animals and plants and all creatures were part of her dreaming, just as her dreaming was the Dreaming of the Great Spirit.

'Now you have reached the limit,' Cheetah Woman said. 'You have made penance for your acts. You are no longer pursued. You have left your body in the desert, and now you may join me as my spouse, for I am deeply in love with you, as with all your kind, and I welcome you to live with me on the Other Side.'

I knew what the woman said was true, and it was the most tempting offer I had ever heard – she was lovely beyond loveliness and nothing could have been more satisfying than to join her on the Other Side. But something held me back – somehow I did not wish my body to end as a corpse in the desert. Somehow my journey was not over and I had not found out how the story ends.

'No,' I said. 'Thank you, but I am not yet ready.'

The woman nodded gravely, and I watched her as she slunk away towards a gaping dark portal in the rock wall that had appeared behind her. The white cheetah stopped at the shadowy threshold and turned her head towards me. The moonlight-white eyes flashed once. '*Come then,*' she said. '*I will show you the way.*'

Who?

When I opened my eyes, a young woman was crouching over me dabbing my lips with a damp rag. I sat up slowly, and she moved back a little, watching me.

'Don't try to get up,' she said. 'You need rest before you go to the cave.'

'What cave?' I asked, thinking I had not heard correctly. My voice came out as a croak.

'The Dreamer's Cave.'

I stared at her, wondering if I had understood. She was dressed in a blue wrap, and braided black tresses fell across her bare shoulders. She was slender and wore loop earrings and bracelets. She reminded me strongly of Maya – the woman who had first told me the tale of the Lost Oasis. I had never thought to ask the storyteller where she came from, but for a moment I was almost certain this was her.

She handed me the rag and nodded to a bowl of water at arm's length. 'Dip the rag in and suck the water from it,' she told me. 'You were parched when we found you - your lips were cracked and we had to keep them wet. At first we thought God had taken you unto God, but then we saw you were breathing.'

'When *who* found me?'

'My sisters and I found you, just outside *the Labyrinth*. We brought you here on a donkey.'

'Labyrinth?'

'The dunes – we call it the *Labyrinth of Sand*.'

I nodded, remembering that Atman, the Fish Eater, had mentioned this place when describing the way to Oyo. I also recalled the body I had found in the sand. 'What about the other one?' I asked.

She shook her head, making a face. 'There was no other. It was a strange thing, because my sister, who was the first to see you, swore that you were not breathing when she found you, and that you started breathing afterwards, but I thought she must be mistaken.'

She laughed merrily. 'Your spirit left you for a while, that is all.'

I suddenly remembered Ata and the three-legged camel. 'Did you find a dead camel also?' I asked. 'One with three legs?'

She laughed and shook her head.

I dipped the cloth in the water, held it to my lips with a trembling hand. I felt the moisture soothing the cracked skin, unclogging my mouth. My body ached from my ordeal in the

Plain of Straying and *the Labyrinth*. I looked around and found that I was sitting on a mat in the shade of a tree with a gnarled trunk half as wide as a camel. I squinted at it and realized suddenly that it was kin to the Sky Tree at the top of the pass on the *Oversight* – the kind Rafig had said once grew everywhere.

The young woman's eyes followed mine. '*Tarout*,' she said. 'These *tarouts* are all that remain of the sacred forest that flourished here in the Distant Time. The stories say the *tarouts* were tall even then.'

'*Tarout*,' I tried the word out, and remembered where I had heard it – it was the tree in the tale of the wide-eared fox who had stolen fire.

I noticed that this *tarout* was one of a series of equally enormous and ancient-looking trees running through a wadi that wound down into a ravine between sheer sided sandstone cliffs. I felt that I knew the place, that I had been here before, then I remembered my dream of the Snake-Woman, the wild ram, and the pool. I had seen this place in my dream.

Around us, the wadi opened out and the sandstone buttes stood far apart – rough scree-sides whittled by wind and rain into slabs, terraces, cliffs, blocks and pinnacles. The *tarout* trees formed a sort of forest within the gorge, and among the trees there were a dozen circular lodges with brushwood walls and grass roofs - larger versions of the Fish Eater huts I had seen at the *Bitter Pool* oasis. Women and children moved around the lodges, and there were goats and sheep flocks under the trees. I did not see any men.

'Where is this?' I asked.

'This is Oyo, where our people live.'

'Your people? You are Fish Eaters … I mean *Tu*?'

She smiled. 'Yes, we are *Tu*, and we have been here since the time of the Anakim, our ancestors. They left this region when their cattle could not live here - when the Great Waters became dunes and the rivers turned to sand.'

I was startled. He words remind me of the visions I had had when I picked up the hand-axe near the Horn Dance – the one I had prized out of the hand of a corpse that looked exactly like me. It had burned my hand and I had last seen it squirming away in the guise of a botfly maggot. I felt in my pockets. Both the hand-axe and the arrowhead were gone. I noticed, though, that my *sufun* bag, knife, and camel-stick were still there. I vaguely recalled that I had had a water-skin, but like the stone axe, it was gone too.

I was still pondering this when the woman withdrew a little way, calling out names. Two young girls emerged from a brushwood lodge nearby, one carrying a skin bag, the other a tray bearing utensils. They laid the things front of the woman.

'Your daughters?' I asked.

'My sisters,' the woman said. 'I am Sabba, these are Lila and Asha.'

The girls came up and greeted me – they were twins, with mischievous brown eyes and braided locks, dressed in drapes of thin cloth. They shook hands and peered at me.

'Who *are* you?' one of them asked.

The question bothered me. I thought of the self I had been before the desert – the soldier, the teacher, the *civilized* man. That was a false identity built on memories and experience, and it was that self, I knew suddenly, that I had left lying in the sand. It was the self-important self, the jinn-self, the *qarin*-twin, the shadow side of that identity, who resented any affront to his own feeling of entitlement – the self who had killed a friend through negligence, fought in a war, wilfully separated from Rafig in *Old Man Sands*.

I saw with sudden clarity that I was no longer that self, or at least, while that self was still with me, I was aware of it, and it could no longer harm me unless I allowed it to. I had seen through it and knew it was not my true self.

'I don't know,' I told the girls.

They laughed as if they had expected this answer and danced away hand in hand.

Sabba fetched firestones and collected kindling. She twirled sticks to make a fire, then set a clay pot of water on the flames. She roasted coffee beans on a flat iron spatula, mashed the beans in a mortar, and added them to boiling water in the pot. When the coffee was ready, she poured it into a spouted bulb of red clay of a type I had never seen among nomads. She brought it over to me with a tiny cup. She crouched down elegantly and poured coffee into the cup, then set the bulb in a nest she scooped in the sand. 'Drink,' she said. 'Coffee. The *Tu* way.'

She sat with me while I sipped the coffee. The aroma alone was enough to revive my senses, and after three cups of the bitter but rich and powerful liquid, I felt renewed.

'Is this the Lost Oasis?' I asked.

'Oyo is a mountain,' Sabba said. 'To journey from one side to the other takes perhaps ten sleeps. There are pools here, palm trees, gorges, caves, camps, and villages. Some people call it Nyssa.'

'Ah,' I said, nodding. 'I came in search of the Lost Oasis, and I have travelled a long way through hunger, thirst, heat, storm, and weariness. My guide and I were attacked by … *enemies* … and I lost him. My camel was dying so I released him and let him go *haamil*. Is this the end of my quest?'

Sabba smiled. 'That is for you to decide.'

From the way she spoke it sounded almost as if she had been expecting me.

'Do you know me?' I asked.

She looked at me with dark eyes like fathomless pools. 'I know you,' she said. 'You are of Adam's Children.'

She left me alone for a while and I sat gathering my strength, thinking about Rafig, about Ata, and about Shamsa. I wondered if I would see any of them again. Then I wondered if I were still dreaming.

I gazed around, noticing that the vast trees were in bloom with white flowers, and that the air was full of their scent. The forest was alive with birdsong, and I noticed the coming and going of bee catchers, fly catchers, rollers, weavers, and other birds whose names I did not know. The sand around me was scattered with gazelle prints, and the meandering tracks of skinks and lizards, and I glimpsed a small pink snake coiling hastily into its burrow.

My gaze fell on a black beetle laboring up a mound of sand, rolling a ball of camel dung with her back legs, leaving a trail as intricate as a filigree mesh. The sand was soft, and the creature was having a hard time of it, slipping down, and starting again with dogged determination. Once she lost her balance completely and rolled over on her back, letting the ball roll down to the bottom of the mound. She wiggled her legs until she righted herself, then went to collect the ball. She never seemed to consider the idea of giving up on this route and trying a gentler approach. I watched her struggle, following every move, willing her to succeed, becoming absorbed in her toil.

And then I knew.

She was the sun goddess rolling her eye across the edge of the world, returning from the shades of night with the gift of light, reborn and engendering all life in that ball of fire. She was the sun, and the sun was the spirit in my body, and her light touched all creation, and all creation flourished, and the sun and the beetle were the same with the same being running through them – the same breath, the same wind, the same spirit, that was myself, and the *tarout*s and the valley. I remembered how the camel Agha had carried the sun after we had left Shamsa's camp, how Shamsa's face had been radiant in the naked light, and how we had experienced each other without estrangement or separation.

Now it was the beetle's turn to carry the sun, to be the sun, and I was the beetle, seeing what the creature saw, feeling what she felt, knowing what she knew. There was no veil between us – I *saw*. I was drawn into her being and into her world with a sudden intense awareness of beauty that changed everything and turned it inside out. I was no longer a stranger, sitting under a tree, in an island of life in a sea of emptiness, I was a feature of the landscape. I was not at a spot in remote desert, but a place connected by a web of spirit, wind, breath, to every other place that existed, or had existed, or would exist – and all those places moved through this place, though me, and my body was a place and all worlds moved through it. The spirit that ran through me ran through all creatures, through the moon, the clouds, the rain, the wind, the sky, through the movement of seeds, and birds, and animals, through the movements of the stars. With a surge of elation, I remembered that there was no *here* at all, either -there *was* no present, and no me, either – those were just ephemeral appearances, transient forms, momentary attributes of an underlying and overlying consciousness - and in that consciousness everything else existed. I did not live in the universe: the universe itself was the creation of the Great Roc - the universal mind.

I was brought out of the vision abruptly by the sound of stone scraping on stone and I looked around to see Sabba grinding grain on a hand mill, almost identical to the ones I had seen nomad women using in the Wadi al-Ma. That took me back to Shamsa, and I realized that Sabba must be preparing polenta for me. Abruptly I began to feel awkward. Although her younger sisters were still around, the absence of men started to bother me. Sabba had rescued me, probably saved my life, treated me with great charity, listened to me attentively, and had not questioned me as to why I was there. Yet there was something about the situation that did not feel right, and I could not help wondering what the men would say if they returned and found me there.

It was a while before the polenta was ready, and as I waited, I felt increasingly uncomfortable. When she finally brought the food over in a wooden bowl, I was tempted to eat a few mouthfuls and run away. She had been so hospitable, though, that I could not bring myself to do it. I had just started eating the polenta when she said, 'The men are back.'

I glanced round and saw a party of four men striding towards us, leading their camels. The men wore desert-stained *jibbas* and, with their shocks of bushy hair, they looked wild and ferocious. A shiver ran down my spine.

Then I noticed they were smiling.

They came straight up to me and as I stood up the one who looked the eldest among them said, 'Welcome, welcome. We trust our sister has treated you well. Your coming is blest.'

I shook hands with them, realizing that I had been misled by my own prejudice. These men did not fear or distrust me because I was a stranger. To them, I realized, I was not a stranger but a fellow human, and of humans they expected the same decency and respect for others they would themselves have shown.

Daud

The nomad who had greeted me first was called Daud - Sabba's elder brother, he said. A small goliath of a man, he had a beardless, humorous face and hair as bushy as a thorn tree, with a carved wooden hairpin stuck in it. He wore no shoes and had large hands and feet.

He gave the head-rope of his camel to one of his companions who led the animal off towards the trees with the other men and their animals.

He sat down on the mat opposite and searched my face.

'We followed your tracks from northwest of *Bitter Pool*,' he said. He held up a thumb and four broad fingers. 'Five sleeps.'

I flushed, realizing that Daud and his Fish Eater companions had tracked me here. That suggested that they were the Fish Eaters who had come after us at the oasis, and who had shot Rafig.

I cast around wondering what to do. I felt cornered. Sabba had retired to her lodge, and the others vanished into the trees. There was nowhere to run, I thought. 'Why did you shoot Rafig?' I demanded.

Daud shook his head. 'We did not shoot him,' he said calmly. 'We picked up your tracks one sleep northwest of the oasis, in a valley where there were arak bushes.'

That must have been where I saw the grey cranes, I thought.

'We tracked you to *Twin Fangs* and then across the *Plain of Straying*, but we were too far behind to catch up, and then we lost you in the *Labyrinth*. We must have overtaken you there, because we arrived at Oyo yesterday. We were in another camp when we heard that our sisters had found a traveller on the edge of the dunes. We guessed it might be the same man we had been tracking and came to find out.'

Daud had remained sitting. His attitude was well-meaning, and I felt disarmed. I

I did not relax my guard, though. I noted that he had not asked who Rafig was, suggesting he knew already that I had had a companion. The idea that Sabba and her sisters had found me by chance in the sand-dunes was hard to believe. More than this, though, my intuition told me that Daud was holding something back – I sensed he had not told me everything, and that could mean that he and his companions had really shot Rafig and were trying to cover it up. With what advantage, though, I asked myself? Since I had been at death's door when Sabba and the girls had found me, they could easily have just left me there.

I restrained my fears and deliberately invited Daud to share the rest of my polenta. He hesitated for a moment, then sat down and tucked in. Though I ate little, I was aware that we had just made a bread-and-salt pact as strong as the one I had shared with Rafig. I knew Daud knew it too.

Afterwards we drank water from a water-skin and washed our hands, and Sabba reappeared with more coffee. She gave us both a cup, then sat down at a short distance and watched us drink.

'Today you must rest,' she said, addressing me. 'In the morning, if you feel stronger, I will take you to the cave.'

I lowered my glass. Sabba had not asked me whether I wanted to go to *the cave* – whatever it was. I recalled her remark about visiting the cave just after I had come to my senses. It was as if my visit to the cave was somehow preordained.

'The Great Spirit bless you for saving my life,' I said, 'and for your hospitality. I am not aware what this … *Cave of Dreamers* … is, though, and I don't know why I should want to go there.'

Daud and Sabba laughed. '*Sahih*?' Daud enquired. 'Is this the truth? But it is why you have come.'

'How do you know why I have come?'

The Fish Eaters laughed again. 'It is foretold,' Daud said. 'In the *Sandlines*.'

I sat up. 'You are a seer?' I asked him.

'No, no,' he chuckled. 'Not me. My sister here – the *Kahina* Sabba – is the seer. Young as she is, she is a very good one. There are many *seers* among the *Tu*, but more women than men. Women are more sensitive, perhaps. They carry a gift that goes back to the Distant Time – to our ancestors, the Anakim.'

'How do you know that?' I demanded, remembering that Rafig had acquired the *Sandlines* from his father, a Fish Eater, and that Atman – the *Tu* who had told us the tale of the *Night Camels* – had also been gifted.

'You will understand,' Sabba said. 'When we go to the cave.'

I was tempted to resist, to demand why I had not been asked if I would like to go to this cave – as surely befitted a guest. It felt as though they assumed they knew why I had come here. Once again, I considered if it might be an elaborate trap of some kind, but then that seemed pointless, I thought. I had nothing, not even a camel, and if they wanted to get rid of me they had no need to lure me to a cave.

I scanned Daud's face, and he smiled back at me warmly – too warmly.

There is something he is not telling me, I thought again.

'What will I find in this cave?' I asked.

'What you do not expect,' Daud laughed.

Orotalt

That night I slept under a *tarout* in a woven covering Sabba brought me. I was shattered after my journey and glad of the rest. I still felt the effects of thirst, as if my guts, lungs, and brain had been scoured with sand, leaving me weak and light-headed. There had also been the trauma, first of losing Rafig, then setting Ata free, then finding a dead camel and my own corpse in the desert. I realized that what had happened in the dunes was a series of hallucinations, but I must have been at death's door to have been in such a state, I thought. I slept fitfully. In the morning Sabba woke me when the day was a rosy daub across the ragged outline of the hills. She told me to get ready for the journey to the cave. Once again,

I felt like resisting, but I restrained myself and said nothing. We set off shortly after first light, with a large white donkey that Sabba drove in front of her, following the wadi down into the gorge. Here the *tarout* forest gave way to a series of elongated pools lying at the bottom of cliffs so sheer and high they took the breath away. It was like walking about in the bottom of a well. The rock walls were yellow sandstone, scoured and striated as if successive chunks had been sliced off with a giant knife over the ages, as water had seeped into the gorge – one had to tilt one's head far back to see the tops. As we rounded the nearest bend, I caught my breath for the second time. Hundreds upon hundreds of camels were watering at the pools – scooping up water with their heads lowered, hooting, snorting and shuffling, kicking up clouds of dust. They were attended by Fish Eater herdsmen who wore their hair in uncut plumes with ornate wooden hairpins, and were dressed in tattered *jibbas* of the same yellow as the sandstone, with waistcoats, thick skin belts, and curved daggers. Unlike the nomads, many of them worked bare-chested, wearing only *sirwal*. They were either barefoot or wore sandals rather than slippers. I noticed, though, that the *Tu* camels were generally thinner than those I had seen in the Wadi al-Ma – many were black-and-white pied, a race I had not seen in nomad herds.

We left the camels behind and came to part of the gorge where the bed was narrower and the pools smaller, with a little vegetation. Once, I heard a scrape of sand and was astounded to see the glitter of scales as a sleek dark shape launched itself into the water, sending ripples across the pool. I glanced at Sabba in amazement, wondering if I had seen right.

'Was that …?'

'Brother Crocodile,' she laughed. 'He is small, and he eats only fish.'

'There are fish in these pools, then?'

'Of course. Mostly catfish.'

'And do you really eat them?'

'Mostly we leave them for the crocodiles.'

'I never expected to see a crocodile in the *Hurra*.'

'They have been here since the Distant Time, but in those days it is said they were much bigger, and they could eat a fully-grown man. There was once a man called Shadad …'

'You mean the hunter?' I cut in. 'The one who came dancing through the desert in a dream and named all the places?'

She beamed. The donkey slowed to nibble at some plants, and she made a chucking noise to encourage him.

'Yes,' she said. 'The one who is up in the stars. The story goes that Shadad never had any luck hunting gazelle or spiral-horn white antelope. All the other men of his clan would bring back game, but not Shadad, even though he was the strongest man of all.

'Then one day, while he was out hunting in *Tu,* he came to a dried-out pool in a gorge, where he found a fat crocodile who could not move. "Is there water near here?" the crocodile asked him. "Yes," Shadad replied, "there is another pool nearby that, as far as I know, never goes dry." The crocodile asked Shadad to carry him to that pool. "I cannot move by myself," he said.

'Shadad was wary of the crocodile's teeth and agreed to do it only if he could bind the animal's jaw. The crocodile accepted, and Shadad bound his jaw with his head-cloth, and carried him to the other pool on his back.

'When they arrived, he untied the binding cautiously and stepped away. The crocodile dived down into the water once, twice, three times. After the third dive, he surfaced. "Since you have been so kind," he said, "I will tell you how you may have more luck in the hunt. Go into the *tarout* forest and you will meet a gazelle doe. Do not shoot her with your arrow, for she will have many children. Further on you will meet a *jadi* – a young gazelle. Do not shoot him for he will be the father of many children. Further on still, you will meet an old buck gazelle, who has lived a long and fruitful life and fathered many children. He will give himself to you."

Shadad left the crocodile and entered the forest, and it happened just as the animal had said. He did not shoot the doe nor the *jadi,* but only the old buck. He brought the gazelle back to his camp and told the clan what had happened, and from then on the people knew the lore of hunting, and after that, Shadad always had the best of luck.'

I listened to the story fascinated, remembering what had happened at al-Gaa. The *Tu,* I realized, had specific taboos about which animals could be hunted, as embodied in this story. I was sure the nomads did too.

Sabba led me out of the gorge and into a corridor-like canyon, with a bed of soft sand. We followed it until we came to a place surrounded by rock overhangs. She let the donkey browse, and led me over to the walls.

'Look at this,' she said.

The rock was covered in engravings of men and animals. They were slightly different in style from the ones I had seen at the Horn Dance – the human figures were more detailed, and there were large bull-like animals with wide horns engraved so that the heads pointed upwards. There were zig-zag patterns, with grids, spirals, and whorls, and what appeared to be giant mushrooms. I gaped at them, remembering my dream of the Snake-Woman, and how she had rubbed a mushroom into my eyes. In fact, with every step I took I was having a sense that I had been here, seen all this before – was Sabba really the Snake-Woman, I wondered?

The most curious engraving was that of what appeared to be a bee-faced man with a human body, clutching what were obviously handfuls of mushrooms.

Sabba pointed first at the bee-faced image, then at one of the giant mushrooms engraved separately. '*Orotalt*,' she said.

Kibela

'What is Orotalt?' I asked, remembering suddenly that I had heard the name in my *Snake-Woman* dream.

'In the Distant Time,' she said, 'when men talked with plants and animals, Orotalt walked in Nyssa. Orotalt could appear in any skin-envelope he chose. It might be a man or a woman, old or young, or an animal – a hare, a raven, a wide-eared fox, a night-calling coney – even a mantis or a bee. Orotalt could be heard everywhere - in the voices of animals and birds, in the buzzing of bees, in the wind, in the trees, in the grass, in the water, in the heat of the sun, the light of the stars, the patterns of the clouds.

'Then the wind changed and Orotalt vanished from the mountain, and his voice could no longer be heard. A woman of the *Tu* called Kibela went looking for him. She searched for him everywhere. She looked in every cave, in every gorge, and on every cliff-top, but could not find him.

'All she found was a wide-eared fox whose leg had been caught in a hoop snare. Kibela released the wide-eared fox from the hoop snare and sent him on his way. Before he went, the fox said. "You are seeking Orotalt, and for your kindness you shall find him." He told the woman that in the nearby valley she would find a grove of *tarout* trees, where some cows had been resting. He told her to sleep there.

'Kibela thanked the wide-eared fox and set off into the valley. She found the *tarout* trees and saw the place where the cows had been resting, where they had left their manure. She went a little farther and fell asleep under a *tarout* tree. In the night there was a great storm, with Thunder Beings, and Lightning Scorpions that stung the earth in the place where the cows had left their manure. In the morning she found that a ring of mushrooms had grown in that place. The mushrooms spoke to her saying. "We are Orotalt. If you wish to speak with the Twice Born, eat us."

'Kibela ate the mushrooms and heard a buzzing like that of a great bee. She buzzed off to a cave, where she met Orotalt. When she returned, she took the rest of the mushrooms back to her clan. Thereafter the secret of the mushrooms was passed on through the *kahins* and *fakis* – the mushrooms were the portal one must go through to be with Orotalt.'

Sabba pointed out the zigzag lines on the rock wall. 'This is the lightning,' she said. 'Orotalt grows only when the lightning strikes a place where cows have left manure on the earth. There are no cows here now, and the *tarout* forests are but a semblance of what they once were. Even storms are few. Orotalt no longer grows except in one place, and even there it is barely living.'

'Is Orotalt a mushroom or a man?' I asked.

'Orotalt can appear in any guise,' she repeated. 'He can be a tree, a flower, or a mushroom – even a storm or a flood. Orotalt is both man and woman, and neither. He is the *Twice-Born*, the *One That Comes*. He comes with messages from the Great Spirit, of whom there is none beneath and none beside, and he is of the Great Spirit's Dreaming.'

I suddenly remembered that the Hermit of al-Gaa had talked about a god called the *Twice-Born*, and about a shrine built to him in the desert by the Anakim – and a town – the *Town of the Twice Born* - that might be the origin of the Lost Oasis legend.

I was excited. Connections seemed to be coming together here, like the intertwining strands of the great spider web Rafig had talked about. I wanted to ask more about Orotalt, but I checked myself. I knew Sabba was preparing me for something, and I guessed I would soon to find out what it was.

We continued along the corridor for some time until it opened into a wider gorge with *tarout* trees and steep, sloping walls covered in stony scree. I realized that we had come round in a circle and were now further up the main gorge from where we had started. I took my *sufun* bag. Sabba hobbled the donkey in the bushes, tied a sash round her waist to raise the hem of her wrap, and slung a leather bag over her shoulder. She handed me a small water-skin. 'Come,' she said. 'It is time to climb up to the gate.'

Eden

The entrance to the cave was invisible from below, and to get there we had to scramble along a winding path up a steep slope through the stony scree. Still weak from my travels, I struggled to keep pace with Sabba, who climbed ahead of me, barefoot, moving with effortless grace.

She stopped to give me a moment's rest, sweeping aside her dark hair, and offering me a slender hand. I sat down on a rock, trying to catch my breath, and feeling a little abashed that this slim young *kahina* should be so much fitter than me. At once I felt a cool breeze on my face, and realized that, while I had scarcely noticed it on the way up, this scree-side was exposed to a northerly wind that felt quite different from the wind that had carried me here – the hot wind from the south.

'The wind is so cool,' I remarked.

Sabba laughed. 'Oyo is the place where all winds meet.'

She pointed out the gorge below with its series of pools standing out in the sun, crystal blue, and still surrounded by hundreds of tiny camels. It occurred to me that this deep gorge had been scored, carved, and weathered over aeons by the action of wind and rain.

In the other direction, I saw that the *tarout* trees stretched far outside the entrance of the wadi so that, in the distance, the desert appeared to be a boundless forest of green. Beyond its canopy, dark peaks and pinnacles loomed on the horizon. The scale of the plateau was awe inspiring, I thought. It made *Bitter Pool* look like a pale imitation. The Lost Oasis story Maya had told me that day, spoke of *deep caves, tangled forests of giant trees, and lovely young women*. This place seemed in keeping with that.

We continued upwards, and the going became increasingly difficult. My breathing grew heavier, and I found I could not keep up with Sabba, who seemed to become lighter and more quick-footed as she climbed. Often, she had to wait for me. Suddenly, though, she was smiling at the cave entrance – it yawned behind her, low and wide like a giant mouth, shielded by loose boulders. The wind was strong here, and so cold that I was reminded of my experience at Elai - how I had dropped the well bucket from freezing fingers. That was when I had met Rafig, who had helped me find my way here. I was glad to step into the shelter of the overhang.

Once we were through the opening, I was stunned to see how vast the cave was. The ceiling soared so far above us that I had to crane my neck to see it. Sabba drew me further inside to where the rock walls were covered in paintings. I gasped. These were not matchstick-men engravings like those I had seen down in the rock corridor earlier, but real paintings in chalk white and ochre – not scrawlings, but dynamic, living art, painted by loving hands, scores upon scores of pictures, some faded, others superimposed on previous ones, so they appeared to present layer upon layer of images, done over countless ages. Here were all the animals I had seen in my visions of the green desert, and more – elephant, giraffe, buffalo, oryx, spiral-horn white antelope, wild ram, ostrich – even hippopotami and rhinoceros. Other pictures showed domesticated animals — the longhorn cows with swollen udders I had seen in the Horn Dance pictures, fierce-looking bulls, and long processions of fat sheep whose insides seemed to be illuminated in white. Sometimes animals were shown in interaction with long-limbed stalk-headed men, running with what looked like lassos, spears, or bows and arrows. In other pictures men and women were gathered in groups, probably dancing – their hands were open, palms uppermost, fingers spread, in the same way that the nomads presented their hands to invoke the Great Spirit's blessing. Instead of the animal-heads on human bodies I had seen previously, though, the human figures had mushrooms where the heads should have been. I examined some of them carefully – the mushroom shapes could not have been hats or wigs, because they grew directly from the stalk-like necks. Curiously, many had what appeared to be shoots or mycelia in place of feet.

I peered at these figures closely, seeing the beauty in them, wondering at the way the artists had managed to express life through the suggestion of movement. There was something radiant and unearthly about the pictures, and I wondered why many of the human figures had mushroom heads and mycelia

I recalled the giant mushrooms carved on the rocks in the corridor-canyon, and how Sabba had remarked that these plants were rare.

'Look at this,' Sabba said, indicating a painting I had not noticed. It showed three horses with riders, arranged horizontally, painted in red ochre. The animals were clearly horses, yet they were like no horses I had ever seen in real life – their legs were stretched out almost vertical in a way that suggested flying. The riders, painted in cameo, were braced backwards, indicating speed. These humans, I noted, were stalk-heads rather than mushroom-heads, and they were shown with fringes of hair flying backwards in the wind.

'*Dream horses,*' Sabba commented.

She showed me a small figure beneath the horses – a red-ochre stalk-headed human lying prone. She drew my attention to two objects lying near the figure. I scrutinized them. It was hard to make out – they might have been almost anything - but what I saw was a bag like the one Sabba was carrying, and the segment of a mushroom that seemed quite out of proportion. Sabba indicated the prone figure. '*Kahina,*' she said. Then she pointed to the mushroom segment '*Orotalt,*' She drew a line to the flying horses with a finger, and repeated. '*Dream horses.*'

I wondered why she was talking like this. Then I realized she was trying to express something quite complicated in simple terms and wanted me to use my imagination to grasp it.

I considered the strange flying horses and the prone figure. *The figure is a kahina*, I thought. *She is in a trance and is experiencing the flying horses as part of her dream. That is why Sabba calls them dream horses.*

Sabba nodded as if privy to my thoughts, keeping up semi-dumb show.

When I opened my mouth to speak, she laid a finger across her own lips. She drew me a little further on and pointed to a painting of a cow with a fat udder, drew a line to a dancing mushroom-head. *A connection between cattle and mushrooms*, I thought. *The Anakim – Ancestors – were cattle nomads. The land was green and well-watered in those days.* Then I remembered Sabba's comment in the canyon earlier. The mushrooms once grew in places where the cattle had fertilized the earth, when those places were struck by lightning. *These mushrooms grow in cattle manure – there is the connection,* I thought.

Sabba showed me a place to sit in the sand, near to the rock wall, and sat opposite me, cross-legged. She dipped into her bag and brought out some kindling, a pair of fire-sticks, and a handful of dry grass. I watched silently as she twirled the sticks, produced smoke and heat that ignited the dry grass, carefully placing the kindling on the growing flame, starting with tiny pieces of wood, and building up with larger and larger pieces. I stared at the flame entranced, feeling as so many times before, the transformative power of Grandfather Fire. When it was burning well, Sabba took the water-skin from me and laid it next to her. Then she slipped a small rawhide bag from the larger one and set it between herself and the fire. She fixed me with a grave look. For a moment I saw a shadow in her face, and was reminded again of Maya, the storyteller.

'I know why you are here,' she said. 'You are here because you felt there was something devouring you, something you felt was missing, and you could not say what it was. You came here to be healed.'

The animals will reveal the lost oasis. They will heal you, because you are animal, and one of us.

'You asked me if this was the Lost Oasis,' she went on. 'Yes and no. No, Oyo is not lost. Yes, what you see is a faded version of what it once was. Is this the Lost Oasis? Perhaps, but you have glimpsed the Lost Oasis many times on your journey, I think.'

I thought of the sandburs we had harvested and the watermelon patch that had saved us when it fruited, then vanished into the earth, leaving its seeds, which might blossom again when the rain fell. I thought of the *Lush* pastures that I had not seen but only heard of, where rich grass and flowers bloomed right across the desert, feeding the nomad herds for a while, fading away to dust. The pastures would appear after a season or several season, but never in quite the same place again. I recalled the relics of the Anakim people that spoke of a time when the entire desert had been green.

'I have seen it,' I said.

'Here at Oyo, called Nyssa in the Distant Time, the Ancestors lived in a green world that flowed with milk and honey – trees grew in deep forests around lakes and rivers, and there were animals of every kind.'

'*The Garden of Eden,*' I said.

'The Ancestors had a means of seeing through the veil that hides the Great Spirit, painted on these walls, and that is why this is called the *Dreamer's Cave.*'

'The mushroom,' I said.

She opened the small skin bag and tipped out some brown kidney-shaped flakes into the palm of her hand. I leaned forward and saw dried toadstools.

'*Orotalt,*' Sabba said holding them up. 'Orotalt is the mediator of Lost Oases, both flourishing and dying at the same time. Orotalt is male and female, young and old, wise, and insane, all of these and none of them. *He-she* is the trees, and the flowers and the grasses. *He-she* is all the animals – the four-leggeds, the crawlers, the flying ones, and the swimmers, but has a special kinship with cheetahs, leopards, lions, and hyenas. *His-her* closest followers are women, who can tear men apart. *He-she* is called the *One of Many Names*, the *Twice Born*, the *One Who Comes* but also the *Masked One* and the *One of Many Forms*.

'Orotalt is the messenger of indestructible life, for death is not the end – we are all part of the Great Spirit - and the Great Spirit endures forever.'

She offered the dried fungi to me and I took them in both palms and examined them.

'In the Distant Time, it is said, men and women would come to Nyssa from all directions to take the sacrament and participate in the Great Mystery. I am offering this sacrament to you. You are free to choose, but the offer is made only once.'

'If I take it, will the secret be revealed?' I asked.

Sabba watched me with a half-smile. 'Only the truth will be revealed.'

I shifted my gaze to the dried flakes of mushroom and back to Sabba's face. I was risking my life, I realized. Mushrooms could be highly poisonous. I asked myself if I trusted this young woman whom I had met only a day earlier. I knew that I had intuitive faith in her, just as I had trusted Rafig from the start.

I put the dried mushrooms in my mouth and swallowed them.

It was quiet in the cave. Sabba unlaced the water-skin and gave me a drink, then drank some water herself. She retied the skin and took a small drum from her bag, held it between her knees and began to play a rhythmic beat. The drumming seemed to reverberate from the rock walls, echoing back and back so that I was suddenly caught up in a wave of sound and was drawn into it as I had been drawn into the flight of grey cranes that had swept over me in the desert. It was the same slow rhythm I had heard in their wings. Sabba began to chant, a sweet, haunting song, and her voice came from within me and blended with the drumming so that I was floating on a flux of feeling. The sound possessed me and was all of me, and suddenly the sound was a horse I was riding bareback among other horses that were cantering and rearing and neighing, and galloping faster and faster and faster, so that I had to lean forward against the wind, and I felt the wind rushing in my hair, felt the wind on my face, and the horse rushed on still faster until it was no longer running but flying on the wind, streaking towards the horizon on the high stream of eternity.

Dance

I was sitting by a campfire in the desert. It was night and the stars were vivid and as numerous as celestial termites, but this lushness of night pastures was familiar, and I knew them well. Zahara was a fiery mouth dropping to the dark horizon, and above me I saw constellations scattered like dewdrops across the night's velvet cover – the Night Maidens, the Grey Crane, the Wide Eared Fox, the Raven, Coney Night Caller, and the Falcon.

There was a hooded figure opposite me, Now, as I looked, I saw that, in fact, the figure was not hooded, but had a mask where its head should have been. I felt the utter, paralyzing terror of the Great Mystery – the brief flicker of finite life and the unspeakable power of the life that went on forever, the breathing force of life, and the dreadful manifestation of death lurking in its midst. This life was consciousness, the entity that gave birth to suns, held up stars, moved planets, lay in the tides and the wind and the rain. It was the force that had burst out when I had met Shamsa. It was dreadful, awful, overwhelming.

I knew I was in the presence of Orotalt - I had been drawn into the primordial mystery, the Great Mystery, the *Misterion*. Only a short while ago, there had been a moment in the desert when I might have chosen death. It would come again, but now I knew.

'You knew?' a voice asked.

'There was no Lost Oasis,' I answered, and it was as if a stranger was speaking. 'The Lost Oasis was always with me. I carried it here.'

'You followed the path.'

' '*I*' had to follow the path until I could abandon my false self - I could never have unveiled my true self without it. It had to die before I found the Lost Oasis but separating was so hard my body was almost thrown away, too.'

'The path leads nowhere,' the voice said. 'It has no end.'

'I see that now. It was the journey itself that taught me everything, and what I learned was simply what I already knew, but did not know that I knew. The self I thought was '*I*', was not the true self. The true self is not a person. The true self lies beyond the veil. I am the wind, and I am the *I* of the wind, and I am the rain and the stars and all that is. I am the Great Spirit, no more and no less than everything, for the whole universe is the Great Spirit's Dreaming, and every form that is, is the Great Spirit in another guise, and the way the Great Spirit appears from behind the veil. Now I know that my task was not to find something missing, but to uncover something already there.'

'You dreamed the animals would heal you.'

'Yes, but now I know that animals are human, and that what they share with humans is their humanity, and to rediscover the truly human, to end the illusion of separation, is healing.'

'Very well,' the voice said. 'There remains the secret. Do you know what the secret is?'

'Love,' I said without hesitation. 'The Great Spirit is consciousness and consciousness is love. Love is pure and joyful and harmonious and knows nothing of evil. Evil is only the absence of love. Evil is what happens when we get trapped behind the veil, and believe the veil is the whole world. We are manifestations of pure love – that is the nature of consciousness. When there is cruelty or hate that is an aberration. The universe appears to be a multiplicity of forms, but only from behind the veil, for it is of one substance, and that is love. Love is reality and what is real is love. There is nothing more.'

'Then let us be silent.'

The wind blared suddenly, welling up from the bowels of the desert, and the wings of great birds were beating, bulls were bellowing, there came the thump of thunder, lightning seared the night sky.

I was alone, yet I was sitting on the other side of the fire, and now I was taking off a mask, and seeing the world beyond the mask, and the fire and the wind and the stars were inside me, and I was both old and young, both man and woman, both wise and insane, both flourishing and dying at the same time.

The flames sputtered and became flares of firelight on the walls of a cave. There were figures dancing around me. I could hear pipes and strings, hear the rhythm of drums, feel the dancers swaying. Out in the great river valleys and on lush prairies beyond the cave, men hunted giraffes with lassos or tracked antelopes with bows and arrows. They herded cattle in endless procession down the rivers to the great lakes. The dancers danced around me, and the seasons passed, and the moon rose and set, and the rain clouds raced across the sky, and the rains came and went, and the grass grew and died, and the rivers ran and dried up, and the lakes rippled and dried out, and the wind lashed the sand of the lake-beds into labyrinths of dunes, and the sun sucked up the water until it became thick with salt, and then there was no water but only shining salt pans called the Devil's Mirror. The prairies became sand sheets and desolate plains and the cattle nomads wandered down the dry riverbeds until they came to the banks of the Nile in the east, or to the green mountains of Siren in the north, and there they settled and created civilizations. Only a few hunters and goat herders remained in the desert, and the paintings dancing on the rocks, and the legend of the Garden of Eden, the lost paradise that existed in the green desert before civilization was born. I witnessed this majestic story as the pipes piped and strings reverberated and drums beat and the music spun me round like a leaf and whirled me faster and faster on a cosmic spiral, round, and round, upwards and outwards on a melody exquisitely sad, exquisitely beautiful, until my being exploded with ecstatic joy.

The vision vanished and the dancers vanished, and I was alone in the cave, with the wind roaring outside, so deep, so terrible, it seemed to shake the Earth. I heard the wind rustling in the massed fronds of invisible palm trees and found myself sitting by a dying fire.

Returned

The long shadows told me it was late afternoon. Sabba was no longer present, but there was a dark hooded figure sitting on the other side of the fire. When I sat up, the figure lifted its head.

'The Great Spirit be blest' said a voice. 'You have returned.'

I knew the voice, and hearing it filled me with joy.

'*Rafig*,' I said.

The figure opened his hood and Rafig was there, looking no different from when I had last seen him near *Bitter Pool*.

Is this a dream also? After the worlds Orotalt has taken me to?

'Rafig, is this really you?' I asked.

We embraced each other in the nomad way, and I felt flesh under the desert-stained shirt. Then we sat down together by the remains of the fire. Rafig picked up some stubs of wood and began to rekindle the flame. I found the discarded water-skin. It was still half full. I handed it to Rafig who shook his head. '*You* drink,' he said softly.

After I had drunk and the fire was burning, I asked. 'Where is Sabba?'

'The *kahina* left you in my safe-keeping.'

I searched the old man's wizened face. 'I saw you fall from your camel,' I said. 'I heard the shot. I thought the bandits had killed you.'

'They were not bandits,' Rafig laughed. 'They were Fish Eaters – *Tu*. You have met them – or one of them. Daud, Sabba's brother.'

I was still light headed after the trance and I felt confused.

'I don't understand.'

'It was a mistake,' Rafig said. 'They had been herding camels at *Bitter Pool* for a while, and some of their animals had been taken by a party of nomads on the *Amuck*.'

'The party of four we first heard about from Musa on the *Oversight*?'

'Yes – we found their tracks in the wadi, remember?'

'We thought that might be Arjan and his friends.'

'I do not believe it was Arjan. Daud and his folk found our tracks in the oasis and, realizing that we, too, were nomads, thought we were with the raiding party. That is how I read their intentions in the *Sandlines*. They did not mean to kill us, only to frighten us off – that is why their shots were wide. They could have hit us had they really wanted to.'

'You fired at them, though … I saw Hambarib crash.'

'I fired over their heads – that is nomad custom. That they hit Hambarib was unfortunate. They had not meant to shoot him. He was wounded, but still able to walk, though not to travel. They helped me take him back to *Bitter Pool* where I released him *haamil*. If God wills, he will find the *Night Camels*.'

'I had to release Ata too.'

Rafig nodded. 'I explained everything to Daud, and said that you were heading for Oyo, hoping it was the Lost Oasis that you were searching for.'

Rafig glanced round at the rock paintings. 'He told me about this cave – the *Cave of Dreamers* - and how his people had preserved the old ritual of Orotalt handed down over the generations from the Distant Time. I told him I believed that this was what you sought.'

'That is why they assumed I would come to the cave,' I said.

Rafig nodded. 'It is also why they did not tell you I was here. I did not wish to meddle.'

'Is that why you turned back at *Bitter Pool*?' I asked. 'The Poison Wind was almost on us, and we could both have escaped under its cover. You had no need to hold them off.'

For the first time ever, I saw slight awkwardness in Rafig's smile. 'I realized that they were not bandits and I turned to reason with them,' he said. 'That is what I told myself at the time. Yet deep down I knew that you must find your own way on this last part of your journey – just as my father sent me off alone to have a vision when I was a boy. I could only take you so far. It is true that I had sworn not to abandon you and that we had eaten bread and salt, so it was a hard decision, but I had intended to follow you. Daud gave me a camel from their small herd, and as they were heading for Oyo, where I had never been, I travelled with them. We found your tracks on the way, in the wadi of the *arak* bushes, where you slept. We lost your tracks in the *Labyrinth of Sand* and arrived here ahead of you here two days ago in the morning. I think you know the rest.'

I nodded.

'It remains only for you to tell me what you learned.'

'I learned that there was no Lost Oasis,' I said. 'It was never lost. It was always there, only I could not see it – it was hidden from my sight. The Lost Oasis is the life that flourishes for a moment and then dissolves in the wind, only to bloom again later. The flower blossoms for a moment then fades, but indestructible life goes on. It is the same for all of us, the animals, the plants, and the Children of Adam too. In civilization they teach us that life ends with our death, but that is not so – the self we think we are – the jinn that is born with us, and that tells us we are different and separate - does not even exist, or at most is a momentary shadow. The true self lives forever.'

'Then all your trials in the desert were in vain?'

'No. I could not hear the Earth while the jinn's voice was chattering, neither could I truly feel myself of the Great Spirit. I had to clear myself of everything that could be desired - to go beyond fatigue, beyond hunger and thirst, beyond dreams and hopes, beyond happy and beyond sad. My false self had to die, at least momentarily, so that my true self could live, and when that part awoke, I knew that *I* had existed long before I was born, and would go on living after my death. I might have discovered that elsewhere, but I did it in the desert.'

Rafig smiled, as if he had known this already. 'And the secret?'

'Love,' I said.

'What about joy?'

'If one knows love, one feels joy. It is the same.'

Rafig smiled. 'Then I read the *Sandlines* right after all.'

No Separation

We spent the night in Rafig's camp in the gorge, where we laid out sheepskins and blankets under *tarout* trees. He showed me the pair of camels the *Tu* had given us.

'*Given* us?' I asked in surprise.

'God is generous. We are strangers in need. Would we not have done the same for them?'

I nodded, remembering the way Rafig had insisted that we lend our camels to help Shamsa's family move to Hassan's camp. It was *muhanni*, I reminded myself, the true law of the desert. Daud and others had also given Rafig provisions – grain, flour, dates, liquid butter, tea, and sugar – enough to take us back to the Wadi al-Ma. There was also a saddle and equipment for me, to replace the gear I had left in the wadi before the *Labyrinth of Sand*.

In the morning we saddled and loaded the camels - trim piebald animals with the *Tu* fish-brand on their flanks - and moved down the gorge to Sabba's lodge, where we met Sabba and Daud and other members of their clan. I had to restrain myself from thanking them, not only for taking me to the Dreamer's Cave, but also for their generosity and hospitality. Knowing thanks would not be welcome, though, I resolved again to help any strangers in need I might meet, especially Tu.

Later, we watered the camels in one of the pools beneath the towering sandstone walls, where, as the previous day scores of other camels pushed their way to the water's edge, snorting and hustling amid layers of dust. I could not help noticing, though, that many of the animals were thin, with the ribs pressing through the skin of their flanks.

'The rains have been poor in *Tu* this season,' Rafig reminded me. 'The grazing is sparse. That is why many Tu are moving into nomad land.'

I thought once again of the Lost Oasis story – how the sun, wind and rain and the plants were like performers in a cosmic ballet, forever rotating around each other, ebbing, flowing, advancing, receding, forming, breaking, yet never abandoning the eternal dance. That was Orotalt, I realized.

In the evening we gathered at Daud's lodge, where two goats had been slaughtered in our honor and many of the clan came to eat with us. Afterwards we sat under the stars and drank coffee, and Daud asked us how we would get back to the Wadi al-Ma.

Rafig replied that instead of retracing our steps to *Bitter Pool,* we would cross the *Plain of Forgetting* – the route that lay to the south, mentioned by Atman – the Fish Eater who had first told us about Oyo. 'My father once mentioned it,' he said. 'Although strangely, he always called this area *Tu* – never Oyo or Nyssa.'

'*Plain of Forgetting*?' I said. 'It's as if we had stolen fire, like the Wide-Eared Fox.'

Rafig and the others laughed. 'Perhaps this is the Fire Mountain,' Daud said, chuckling. 'Perhaps we are the Giants guarding the secret.' He paused. 'Yet crossing the *Plain of Forgetting* is a hard way. It is the *Ged*, and there is only one watering place on that route – *Waterskin Rupture*. It will be much shorter for you, though - nine sleeps to the mountain your people call the *Oversight*.'

Later, Sabba came to talk to us. 'I do not ask about your experience,' she told me, 'because I know one cannot describe it in words.'

'That is true,' I replied. 'I had glimpses through the veil before on my journey, but this was as if the whole veil was lifted, and I saw things as they really were – that there were no barriers between us and … well I saw the Great Spirit, but that name says nothing about what it was like. One could never tell that story.'

'Did you see Orotalt?'

'Yes. I talked to him. Apart from dancing in a cave, and music and a vision of the desert when it was green, that is almost all I can describe.'

For a moment, Sabba looked sad. 'You are not obliged to leave,' she said. 'You are welcome to stay. There may be other secrets you have not learned.'

I glanced at her quickly, wondering if I had heard a compliment or an invitation. I had been acutely aware of Sabba as a beautiful young woman – that was why I had felt so awkward to be alone with her at first. I did not think she was married, yet I had never imagined that there could be anything between us. Her eyes were on me and for a fleeting moment I saw in her face once more the image of the Spirit Mother – *al-Lat* - the woman I had met in various guises in stories, dreams, and visions over the past days. The last time we had met she had tried to entice me to the *Other Side* to be her spouse, and I had turned her down.

I thought of Maya the storyteller – the living image of Sabba. In her story, the youth who had found the Lost Oasis had decided to return to the outside world – had he refused the same offer, I wondered? He had gone back to his village only to find that his sweetheart had married someone else. That made me think of Shamsa. If Arjan had not left the Wadi al-Ma before we did, he must have been there all the time. I felt suddenly anxious about Shamsa, and the emotion surfaced as a desperate craving.

'There is someone waiting for me,' I said, blushing.

Sabba giggled. 'You are blest,' she said. 'Remember, though, that you are always welcome here.'

'If you can find us again,' Daud laughed. 'Oyo is a big place, but it is never easy to find.'

'We will leave date-stones in the desert,' I joked.

Sabba stood up and we shook hands. 'Go in the safekeeping of the Great Spirit,' she said, 'and though we may not meet again, in our hearts there is no separation.'

Rupture

Once the sandstone peaks of Oyo had melted into the desert behind us, it was as if a gate had slammed shut and we had cast off into a stream of oblivion. The things I had experienced came back to me in dreamy, dislocated images, and though, if I chose, I could still hear the voice of Sabba, saying *in our hearts there is no separation,* sometimes I could no longer recall her features, nor the details of my stay with her and the Fish Eater clan.

On the *Plain of Forgetting* there was no surface movement but that of our own shadows, and the play of wild colors on the world's rim at sunrise and sunset. I had crossed great featureless spaces on the way to Oyo, but this was a place chilling in its barrenness, where each day became a mirror of the previous one, where the lava surface was so hard that the camels left no trace, passing across it like dust devils, like ghosts who had not been there at all. Rafig navigated solely on the wind that blew almost always in our faces, coming in successive blasts of fire that made me gasp, as if stabbed with red-hot blades.

On another level the pain and discomfort did not bother me, and neither did my thoughts wander as they once had. I did not replay the past, nor fantasize about the distant future - my only purpose now was Shamsa. The craving I had felt when I had remembered her in Oyo, though, had vanished. I had realized that it was jealousy I was feeling – the thoughts had come up only when I had thought about her marrying someone else. That was unworthy – the old *qarin* talking. I would not worry about her nor make up any narratives in my head. I would trust her and see how things were when I arrived.

Though there had been times on my journey to Oyo when I had felt at one with the landscape, the feeling now never wavered. I realized that this sense of connection came from joy in being – a sense that was present despite the harsh conditions. The wind was not our enemy, the wind that scorched us gave us life.

The voice that I had thought of as my self was mostly quiet, and the voice that remained talking did not exalt my uniqueness, my self-importance, my difference, neither did it, inversely, make me feel morally superior. I felt confident but not haughty, and I knew that this had always been the way of Rafig and the other nomads I had met. They had the skills and the knowledge to adapt to a world that outsiders saw as harsh, but never had the arrogance to believe they could control it. If the challenge exceeded the best they could offer, then fate would go as she must.

The *Plain of Forgetting* was lifeless except for two coal black crows who seemed to acquire an interest in us and followed us from the second day. As we rode, the birds would fly ahead, rising, circling, and dropping, perching on the desert surface to await our coming. When we neared them, they would flutter off again, wheeling on the wind, then landing ahead exactly as if they had appointed themselves guides. When we made camp at sunset, the birds would alight close to us, hopping, cawing, and posturing, fixing us with beady eyes, until I fed them a few scraps of dried polenta, or a handful of grain. 'Crows are wise birds,' Rafig reminded me. 'One finds them always in pairs – Brother Crow and Sister Crow. They warn us of dangers.'

The crows would vanish during the night, but return in the morning, hovering over us as we loaded the camels, sometimes perching impudently on the camels' heads. After we had struck camp, the flying people would land and investigate the place where we had slept, teasing out any edible morsels that might have been overlooked. During the day they would often disappear for long periods but would return sooner or later.

'Crows fly to the ends of the earth to bring back news,' Rafig explained. 'It is bad luck if they do not reappear.'

On the seventh day, though, the crows did not come back, and that was the day we ran out of water. From the early morning my mouth felt like sandpaper, and by mid-day our lips had cracked, and our tongues had become so bloated and covered in mucus that we could no longer swallow. Just before sunset, though, we came to a deep gully that could not be seen from afar, and we dismounted and led the camels down into a dark defile between narrow basalt walls. Rafig declared that this must be *Waterskin Rupture* – the only watering place between Oyo and *the Oversight*.

'Why does it have that name?' I asked.

'In the Distant Time, a traveler dropped a water-skin here when stung by a scorpion. The skin split open and filled the stone basin that is still here.'

We found the basin in a wide arena that opened out of the defile and discovered that it held a little water. We couched the camels there and let them drink, while Rafig filled a bowl, scraping it along the stone bed. He offered it to me, but I refused and, as custom demanded, insisted that the old man drink first.

After we had slaked our thirst, we lay back against protruding boulders in the long shadows, as the evening cool began to seep into the gully. Rafig's eyes closed, and I felt my own eyelids flicker – my body was heavy, and suddenly I was very tired. A soothing voice crooned in my ears and I thought it was the voice of Sabba, as she had sung in the Dreamer's Cave, coming from far off. In my thoughts I was poised on the bank of a river whose current ran calm, deep and silent. I was about to tumble lazily in, when a more strident voice crowed *'ahoy'* so loudly that I jumped and sat up.

I saw at once that the camels were gone, and that the two crows were back perching right in front of me, peering at me with accusing black eyes. I had no doubt that the sound had come from them. It was full dark, and I did not know how long I had been asleep. I rose to my feet and the birds took to the air, cawing. Rafig woke and grasped the situation at once.

'No God but God,' he declared. 'I should have recalled the story.'

'What?'

'That at *Waterskin Rupture* the water has a quality that makes one sleep. My father told me about it, but I suppose I never believed it. I fell asleep like a donkey, without unloading or hobbling the camels, and now they are gone.'

We hurried along the defile and climbed the slope at the far end. At the top we stood and stared north into the deepest darkness. There was no moon. The night sky was a veil of dust, and the stars peered through it like bleary eyes. Rafig cast around for tracks, but we both knew we would not find any on this hard surface.

We were quiet for a moment, then Rafig said. 'They will head back to Oyo. I believe I could find my way even with no moon, but we will not catch up with them. If there was any grazing on the way, they would stop there, and we might stand a chance, but there is none. Like this they will keep going till they arrive home.'

'They let us down,' I said, remembering how Ata had run away on the third day of my journey, how he had become a trusted friend, and how I had released him before the *Labyrinth of Sand*. I wondered where he was now: I hoped he was safe with the *Night Camels*.'

Rafig shrugged. 'Those were Fish Eater camels. They did not wish to leave their homeland.'

'God is generous,' I said. 'Obviously they were just on loan.'

'In any case this is my fault,' Rafig said. 'I should have made certain we hobbled them. The story of the *Father of Hobbles* was one of the first lessons I learned – about the nomad who fell asleep without hobbling his camels, lost them all, and ended up hobbling himself to wait for death.'

'Do you think it's true about the water?' I asked. 'Or were we simply too tired to bother.' Rafig shrugged, and we both fell silent, pondering the immensity of the desert and the sheer depth of the darkness. Oyo was seven sleeps away, and that meant the Wadi al-Ma – and Shamsa – was comfortingly close.

'The Sky Tree is only two sleeps from here,' said Rafig, as if reading my thoughts. 'I know the way. We do not need the camels. Let us go in God's safekeeping. We start now.'

'We have no water-skins,' I reminded him.

'I know. Before the sun comes up, we must travel far.'

Rise

We were still tired from the long ride and drowsy - perhaps from the tainted water of the stone basin, or perhaps not. We pressed on fast, aware that we must make the best of the darkness, and with the exertion our heads cleared. Rafig followed the wind, and the stars when they glinted more strongly through the skein of dust and towards morning he halted in his tracks and pointed at a tight cluster of stars that had appeared just above the horizon.

'No God but God,' he exclaimed. 'It is not possible that we have been away so long.'

'What is it?' I demanded.

'*The Night Maidens,*' he whispered, as if unable to believe it. 'The *Ged* is over. The *Night Maidens* rise.'

Then I remembered. I had last seen the star-cluster the evening Shamsa and I had said goodbye.

When daylight came, though, we were still on the *Plain of Forgetting* and there was no sign of *the Oversight*. As the edge of the world turned crimson, we stopped to rest for a few moments, and the crows came back, dropping out of the sky and shuffling around us, leaving tracks like stars. I noticed the tracks and ran my fingers across the surface. It was sandy – already the landscape was changing. The sunrise came in vibrations of light and color like drumbeats in my ears, as gush of liquid fire flooded the horizon, its rhythm falling away to the low cadenza of the desert. The sun appeared like an upturned golden boat, and as it cast off from the land hot winds were unleashed from its mantle. We struggled on across the plain, and wind and sun baked us. By mid-morning, our tongues had become so big with thirst that we could not swallow or talk, and soon we were bent over with the kind of kidney pains I remembered from the salt caravan. My eyes started to dry out and it felt as if they were sinking slowly into my skull. My insides had been scraped with a rough stone, my head began to gyrate, and my legs faltered as if the flat surface had tilted sideways, trying to tip me off. Rafig caught me with a lean arm.

'We are close,' he said. 'The Great Spirit give us strength.'

He slipped his hand under my shoulder and helped me along, and I was filled with gratitude to this old man who had guided me and stayed with me, and come back to me after my ordeal, and risked his life so that I might attain my purpose, and I knew I had never felt such love for a person as I felt for Rafig, and it was as if the two of us were the same being.

We staggered along with our arms locked around each other, our breaths coming in ragged accord, our slippers tapping on the hard ground, trying desperately to stay upright, and from time to time the two black crows landed before us, posturing, and fluttering their wings, lifting their black beaks as if goading us on and pointing the way. Not long before sunset, though, we saw the birds flitting in front of us, and almost fell over the edge of the world.

The *Plain of Forgetting* dropped away beneath us and shattered into fragments and boulders. The wind sobbed, catching its breath, and the sky was suddenly full of clouds that had not been there a moment before, dashing across the horizon and fracturing into frayed clusters. The valley below was a carousel of light and shade, spawning coils of silver dust, with the hint of a mountain lurking in the distance. I saw a scorpion-sting flash, and a moment later the hot sky rumbled with thunder. We slid and stumbled down the slope, falling, catching each other, slipping, staggering on again. Before we reached the bottom, though, a high, cool wind touched us, and rain rushed across the landscape, hitting us with the force of a tidal wave, soaking us instantly. We reached a wadi at the base of the slope and sat in its bed panting. In moments we were waist-deep in a raging torrent.

The sun had already gone down, and we had no choice but to stay where we were, as the water flowed under us and through us, and seeped into our being. Twigs and bits of camel-dung bobbed against our bodies. The rain came in waves, rising and falling, slopping down our necks, slashing at the land around us. The ground trembled. Thunder spoke with a voice like splintering wood, and the night was split with brilliant spider-legs of lightning. There was no point in trying to move – there was no hiding place, I thought. I had never felt so vulnerable, so abjectly at Earth Mother's mercy. Yet there was a thrill in knowing with all my senses, her raw transforming power.

'*Let it come down*,' Rafig shouted over the noise of the rain. 'The nomads have been waiting a long time. If it is like this in the north, the *Lush* will be a carpet of yellow flowers.'

'We finish with joy,' I yelled.

We sat in the rain all night, and in the morning, when the eye of the sun opened hazily, we rose out of the waters, shivering, our limbs numb and our teeth chattering. We walked a little way barefoot, carrying our slippers which had become shapeless hollows of leather. I felt reborn – the thirst had gone and I felt I had been cleansed, the self I had been was washed away.

We sat down on a damp sand hill, and hung our shoes on a thorn-bush, waiting for the sun to dry them. I laid out the contents of my bag – luckily, the rubber bag my diary had been sealed in had preserved it intact. Rafig opened the breech of his rifle, removed the cartridge and the firing mechanism and set the various parts on stones.

The desert plain had become a mandala of colors – blood-red, orange, gold and brown streams flowed everywhere. To see the desert transmuted by water like this, I thought, was to understand the Lost Oasis tale in all its glory.

I tried to think about Oyo –Sabba, Daud, the *tarout* trees, the crocodiles, the piebald camels, the rock pictures, the Cave of Dreamers - and found that the memory had faded. I could recall the story, but the details had become vague. The narrative in my head was like the rock paintings I had seen – a few strokes captured movement vividly, but the full richness of the experience had gone. It was like a dream that fades on awakening – certain images remain but the sequence of what actually happened one cannot recall.

'Do you think you could find your way back to Oyo?' I asked Rafig.

The old man scratched his head. 'I thought I could,' he told me, 'but now it has become … unclear. So strange my father never mentioned Oyo or Nyssa. Now it feels as if we were never there.'

Reflections

As we sat, regaining our strength, I was astonished to see a furry animal scamper out of the bushes and run along the wadi-bank with an odd half-hopping gait. The creature was the size of a large hedgehog or a rabbit, with short legs and tiny feet, a pointed snout, black eyes, and what looked like a friendly expression. I noticed that it had no tail.

'What is that?' I asked Rafig.

'That is a coney,' he said, smiling. 'They name her *Coney Night-Caller*, because she calls to others – to lost ones, perhaps - at night. Her voice carries a long way.'

I suddenly remembered the coney whose rasping voice Shamsa and I had heard in a tree high above us the last time we had spoken – the time she had kissed me. She had said that the coney was calling to her lost lover in the desert. I realized with a start that though I had heard talk about the coney – and there was a star constellation with that name - this was the first time I had ever seen one.

'The coney is sacred,' Rafig said. 'Of all animals it is most like the Children of Adam.'

'Do you think she is showing us the way?' I asked.

Rafig nodded. 'Yes. She tells us that nomads are near.'

The coney had already vanished, but her tracks led south along the wadi, and Rafig said this would lead us to *the Oversight*

We decided to continue upstream along the bank. We collected our few belongings, put on our slippers and soon found ourselves walking through a new-born world. The stream grew narrower, and soon the outline of the mountain became clear through the haze. We were weary and heavy-footed and each step took an effort, but the sight of the mountain spurred us on. After what seemed like an age, we passed through some thorn-scrub and climbed a steep sandy slope until we saw clear water lying in a depression below us. The pool was silent and still – dragonflies of vivid blue and red swooped across it, leaving tiny ripples where they touched the surface. We were already thirsty, so we shuffled down to the pool, drank our fill, then sat at the edge, contemplating our reflections in the water.

'This pool has been dry for many seasons,' Rafig told me. 'I know it well. I came here first when I was a small boy. I had never seen still water like this before. I was amazed at my reflection. They told me that it was me, and for a very long time afterwards I lived with the memory of that reflection, thinking the image was myself.

'Next time I came here I was a youth – not quite a man – and I was shocked at the changes I saw in my reflection. I had been carrying that first picture around in my heart ever since, believing it was me. The reflection showed someone quite different, yet why, I asked myself, did I feel that there was another Self, who had not changed at all despite the changes I saw in the water? Why did I feel that there was a Self that had been *I* even before I had first seen my reflection here?

'I returned the next season but it was not the same. There was a drought on the land, and when I climbed down to the pool I found it was completely dry. That hit me hard because my water-skin was almost empty and I had been relying on the pool to save my life. It was then, as I sat here staring at the bare sand where I had previously seen my own reflection, that I understood. My reflection was gone, yet I was still here, the same *I* that I had always been. My reflection in the water had never been my True Self, but only an appearance, *me* seen from another point of view.

'I was still just a youth, it is true, but it was then that I knew, for the first time, that I need not be afraid of death. I knew that what would vanish when I died was only a reflection, not my True Self. That Self had been there before I was born, had continued unchanged throughout my boyhood and youth, and would remain after God took me unto God, just as I was still here, sitting in the same place, although the water and my reflection in it had gone.

'I managed to get back to my tents that time, thanks to God and the kindness of the nomads I met on the way, but I never forgot the lesson. Now, I am here with you, and the water has returned, and I see my reflection in it once more. I see in it signs that I am a *shayb*– an old man. The most important thing I have learned in my life that I am not my reflection. The reflection is not my Self, nor is your reflection your Self. Just as Lady Moon told Brother Hare in the tale, nothing that lives ever really dies. When our part in the Great Spirit's Dreaming is over, the image we may have believed was our self, dissolves. We simply merge back into the Great Spirit – the Lost Oasis – where we have always been.'

He paused and we both stared at our reflections in the water.

'That is my story,' he said. 'I am glad I have told you.'

'Yes,' I nodded. 'That is the best story of all.'

We dragged ourselves up and got going again, and soon found the mouth of the wadi that fed the pool, following the narrow goat-path that ran along its bank as the water-course spiralled up into the hills. Before long the path led us into a gorge thickly forested with acacia trees whose leaves sparkled with raindrops. Here last night's rainwater had already run away, and the wadi was starting to dry out. We left the bank and walked along the sandy bed, weaving around blue stones and boulders that had been fashioned by water into a mosaic of shapes and sizes.

We were startled by a piercing whistle that rang across the wadi. Rounding a twist in the wadi bed I saw a nomad herdsboy, with scores of camels of many shades, browsing in the thorn trees. I was just raising my hand to wave to the boy, when Rafig touched me on the arm. I turned my head and gaped. Along the entire dappled length of the creek as it climbed away from us, on both sides, amongst the thorn thickets, a whole clan of nomads – men, women, and children – were on the process of erecting tents. In every patch of hard ground between the trees lay piles of saddlery, the frames of litters, folded rugs and blankets, leather, and straw vessels. Women in wraps of bright colours swarmed excitedly around the tents while men and boys herded camels that stomped around in the bushes. We wandered towards the nearest tents, bemused by the noise, chatter, and bustle, after days of being alone.

'*Peace be upon you,*' a voice called. '*Thank God. You have arrived.*'

Arrival

A youth was grinning at us from the bushes, and an instant later I recognized Zubayr, the Fish-Eater youth who had travelled with us on the salt caravan from Saadig's camp. Rafig seemed pleased to see him, and I felt overjoyed. The youth jumped down from the wadi bank and rushed to embrace us both, shaking hands, releasing, then shaking again. 'You have been away so long. Thank God you have come back safe. Praise to God for your safe arrival.'

In a moment, others had joined him - they took our arms and led us back up the slope, to where someone laid out a mat in the shade of some old thorn trees. Before we could sit, we were surrounded by men and women wanting to shake our hands, as if in our absence we had somehow become holy. Children stared at me and the tiny ones poked at my legs with stubby fingers. I was dazed by the sudden attention and my head began to swim.

Zubayr arranged leather saddle cushions for us to lean against. We sat down and the crowd gathered around us as if awaiting our benediction. Women brought a bowl of water and a bowl of camel's milk. While we were taking turns to drink the milk, Rai turned up with Hassan, and it took me a moment to remember that they were Shamsa's father and uncle.

'Thank the Great Spirit for your safe arrival,' Hassan boomed.

'It has been so long' Rai said. 'We thought God had taken you unto God.'

'We must have lost track of sleeps,' Rafig said. 'Last night we saw the *Night Maidens* rise.'

'Where are your camels?' Rai asked. 'You did not come out of the *Hurra* in the *Ged* on foot?'

'We had Fish-Eater camels …' I began, but words failed me. Like everything else that had happened at Oyo and on the *Plain of Forgetting*, the particulars had become hazy and blurred.

'Did you find the Lost Oasis?' Hassan demanded.

Rafig and I looked at each other.

'It's a long story,' I said.

'Tell us,' someone demanded. Others murmured and nodded in assent.

I tried to recall what had happened at Oyo, but where was Oyo? I was no longer sure. Glancing at Rafig, I could see he felt the same.

I strained my memory, but it was like trying to bring back a dream that has gone. I felt in my *sufun* bag – apart from Brahim's knife and my clothes and slippers, it was the only thing I had that had survived the journey. I found my diary, tipped it out of its rubber case, and

310

scrabbled through it. The pages that should have contained my entries for Oyo were blank. I could not remember having made any, either.

I stowed the book back hastily in its rubber packet.

My head began to throb, and I clenched my fists, felt my heart thump. As if from far away I heard a woman's voice crying 'Leave him alone. Can't you see his spirit is suffering?'

Then Shamsa was there.

Kissed

When at last we were alone, Shamsa said. 'Thank the Great Spirit for your safe arrival. The lover was far away for so long, but *Coney Night-Caller* called for him every night.'

'We saw her further down the wadi,' I said. 'She brought us here.'

'Tell me, did you find the missing part of yourself?'

'There was no missing part. How could there be? I was wrong to think there was. It was my true self, and it was with me all the time, but I was not aware of it. I only had to draw back the veil. You knew, didn't you?'

'I knew, but I could not tell you. You had to discover for yourself.'

I paused and looked at her carefully. Her eyes were the same eyes, and her braided hair foamed over her bare brown shoulders. She was not wearing a nose-ring, I noticed, or any of the emblems of marriage.

'Where is Arjan?' I asked in a quiet voice.

'He married,' she said, her eyes sparkling. 'To my cousin, Dhara – a very pretty girl.'

I smiled and took her hand – it was small and warm. 'The moment we met, I recognized you,' I said. 'I knew you. I have always known you. You have always been part of me, and always will be.'

I wanted to tell her how I had denied that feeling in myself, because I had felt unsure, felt that I was not yet whole, not yet a complete person. She was myself already and we were each other - the joy she felt would be my joy, and the pain she felt would be my pain, just as our pain and our joy could not be separated from our love for the land, our love for the Earth, our love for all people, for the whole of existence, because the Earth, Existence, Being, God, the Great Spirit, the Universe, were only names for our awareness of it, and that was love itself. Like everyone else, I had always known that, but I had been blind to it. My journey in the desert, my search for the Lost Oasis, had revealed to me what I had always been aware of at some level – the Lost Oasis was love. I did not say this, because Shamsa already knew, and when she kissed me for the second time ever, the world vanished for an eternal moment, and then there was nothing more to say.

Joy

Rafig and I slept under the trees in Zubayr's camp that night, and he told us that he had decided not to return to Saadig's family. 'Saadig is a good man,' he said, 'may God's blessing be upon him. While you were away, though, I met a girl in the old camp in Wadi al-Ma called Idraya – another cousin of your Shamsa. If you marry Shamsa, and I marry Idraya, our children will be related.'

Zubayr was already helping Idraya's father as a herdsboy, he said, but had looked after the six camels from the salt-caravan that Rafig's kin had not come for. Rafig said that he would take the two riding camels for himself and me, and that Zubayr could have the remaining four towards his bride-price. The youth looked pleased.

'If the scouts' report from the *Lush* is good, you will need the camels,' he said, 'because tomorrow the clan will begin the migration to the north.'

Rafig shook his head. 'Tomorrow I will return to my own clan,' he said. For a moment his eyes became misty and I knew he was thinking of his son.

'What will you do about Adnan?' I asked.

'God is All Knowing. After I have rested, I will go back to *Saddle Unravels*, and see if he is ready to come home.'

When I woke at sunrise next morning, Rafig was gone.

The first thing Zubayr told me was that the scouts had returned from the *Lush*. 'God is generous,' he said. 'The rain has been good, the water pools are full, and the grass is blooming. Now, after all this time of drought and waiting, you will see the real Lost Oasis.'

'So Rafig left?' I asked.

'He got up with the Morning Star,' Zubayr said. 'I gave him some saddle gear and he chose one of the camels and set off. He told me to tell you to go in the safekeeping of the Great Spirit, and though the days may be lost, the lesson is not lost, and to stay on the path even though it has no end. He said you would understand.'

I nodded. 'Without a handshake or anything,' I said.

Zubayr laughed. 'You know nomads do not like farewells. That is not their way. For though we may not see each other again, in our hearts there is no real parting.'

I nodded. 'That is true,' I said, remembering Sabba's words.

The women were already dismantling the tents, folding them carefully, packing things into pots, sacks, saddlebags, and boxes. The men went off to bring in the flocks of goats and sheep, and the camel herd. They separated the house camels from the milch camels. They couched them by the women, who harnessed and saddled them, and set up their litters for the nursing mothers and small children.

I worked with Shamsa and the others, helping to roll tents and fasten loads. As I hefted sacks and slung water-skins, I reflected as I had when we had helped her family move, on how little the nomads owned. Their entire world had to be carried on camel's back, so anything that was not a necessity was a burden. When the nomads moved, they left almost no trace - every sign that they had been here would soon be hidden, every vestige of their sojourn would revert to the Earth.

What struck me most, though, was the way they worked so harmoniously together, with a tangible sense of joy. Their custom of *muhanni* – kindness, mutual aid, generosity, and mutual well-being – was, in the end, just another word for love. They were in tune with nature, with the rhythm of the Earth, and they loved and cared for each other, and for Earth Mother. Having found this lost world, I knew I could not go back to civilization. I would stay here in the desert, would walk my path with this woman and these people for as long as the Great Spirit allowed.

Finally, the men mounted their camels and drove the herds and flocks before them through the acacia forest. Shamsa and I helped the women climb into their litters and passed up the small children. Then I mounted the camel Zubayr had chosen for me, with Shamsa behind. The camels rose to their feet, tossed their heads, and snorted. A palpable sense of excitement ran through the clan. They were moving at last. The rain had fallen, and the grass was growing. It was the season of migration to the north, and all was right with the world.

Not Lost

Many sleeps later, on our way to the Lush, we halted to rest in the Wadi Safra, not far from the place where Rai's tent had been pitched when Shamsa and I had first met. While the others were adjusting their saddles and litters, Shamsa and I wandered off a short distance and sat down in the sand. The wadi – a dead land when we had last seen it - was now a vein of green trees and rich grasses, brimming with brilliant yellow flowers, alive with the sound of bees and birdsong.

I looked west. Far beyond the horizon lay a mountain called Oyo or Nyssa, an oasis, where cattle nomads from the Distant Time had left signposts to a magic portal – an opening into the story of all that had ever been or ever would be.

I turned to look east. *Long, long ago, a young man and a beautiful young woman met in a desert place where there had once flowed a great river.* Long, long ago, the river had poured into the Great Water at the same spot where a young man had once stood on the edge of the great desert, seen a camel-herd, and dreamed of finding the Lost Oasis.

The Lost Oasis was never lost. The nomads are not lost, neither is the young man lost, nor is she lost, the young woman who walked with him for a time. They are the Earth's story. Listen to Earth Mother. She is telling that story still.

The (re is no) end

A Nomad Cosmology

The Lost Oasis	1)*Al-Wahat al-Ghayba* (lit. the Unseen Oasis) In myth, a lush green place of cool water and shady trees in the Sahara – sometimes inhabited by beautiful maidens. Travellers may happen across it, but can never find it twice. 2) Ephemeral fertile place that vanishes and appears again - a symbol of finite life (*bios*) and indestructible life (*zoe*).
Distant Time	The remote past – the time of the Ancestors, when humans could become animals, animals could become humans, and both spoke the same language.
Pharoah's Road	Ancient caravan route running northeast across the Sahara then parallel with the Nile to Egypt. The route was known in ancient Egyptian times, before camels came to Africa.
Hare's Ladder	Mountain west of Elai crater, in myth used by trickster Hare on his errands for Lady Moon.
Qoz (or Goz)	Relict sand-dune country of scrub savannah on the southern edge of the Sahara.
Devil's Mirror	Mirage, especially on desert salt-pans, the remains of great lakes that existed in the Sahara in the Distant Time.
Al-Qaf	In myth, the mountains at the end of the world.
Al-Kharab	In myth, the Great Abyss at the end of the world.
Old Man Sands	*al-'Urug ash-Shayb.* Sand Sea north of the Horn Dance ridge. In myth created by the serpent-man Azael, whose drumming can still be heard there, and may lead travellers to their death.
Sky Mountain	In myth, the mountain used by Wind Scorpion to climb up to the sky and steal the basket of stories from Sky Father.
Fire Mountain	In myth, the desert mountain inhabited by the Fire Giants, the only beings who knew fire before it was stolen for the Children of Adam, by the wide-eared fox.
Saddle Unravels	Last known well on the Siren Road, north of Old Man Sands

Siren Road	Ancient desert route thought to lead to Siren, in Libya (possibly Cyrene) Said in myth to have been made by the Anakim giants on their exodus from the Sahara as it turned to desert in the Distant Time.
Great Roc	In myth, an enormous bird capable of carrying a camel in each foot. A symbol of the One Absolute Eternal Infinite, or the Great Spirit (consciousness).
Poison Wind	The *simoom* – fierce, hot sand-storm arising at the beginning of the *Ged* – the Hot-Hot season - blowing from the south.
Amuck	Camel raiding among nomads. Not considered stealing, as all camels are thought ultimately to belong to God, it is carried out according to rules. Any deaths or injuries incurred are subject to blood-compensation.
Umm Sagar	Watering place on the Pharoah's Road
Elai	Crater with deep and shallow wells on the Pharaoh's Road
Mushroom Stone	Wind abraded stone (yardang) on the Pharoah's Road. A *hattia* or sacred site where no animal can be killed or tree cut down.
Hurra	Deep desert, the Desert of Deserts, lit, the *Free Desert*. The deep Sahara, stretching from near the Nile Valley to Cyrenaica in the north, and the Maghreb in the west.
Al-Gaa	Lit. *the Bottom*. Rock salt oasis west of Elai, relic of a great lake found there in the Distant Time.
Lush	Deep desert pastures often flourishing in the season of rains, the destination of seasonal migrations for all nomad groups.
Wadi Safra	*Yellow Wadi* - the relic of a great river (the Yellow Nile) that once flowed east across what is now desert, from Oyo to the Nile.
Wadi al-Ma	A forested wadi, once part of the river system that included Wadi Safra. Site of nomad summer camps.
Nyssa	Ancient name for Oyo. Legendary mountain, said in Greek mythology to be the birthplace of the god Dionysos.

Oyo	'Fish Eater mountain' – a vast sandstone plateau in in the deep desert, containing camps, villages, caves, water pools, palm groves and *tarout* forests. Once a site of religious mysteries.
The Oversight	Volcanic mountain between the Wadi al-Ma and the Hurra
The Outer	The last oasis on the route to Libya. Called Bitter Pool by the Fish Eaters (Tu).
Tarout	Saharan cedar. Abundant in the Distant Time, the relics of cedar forests still exist in Oyo, and there is a single very ancient specimen on the Oversight – known as the Sky Tree
Sky Tree	The last *tarout* left in nomad territory, at the top of a pass on the Oversight.
Orotalt	Sacred mushroom, probably pscilocybin, that once grew in the cedar forests in Oyo and elsewhere. Associated with cattle manure, the fungus may have flourished when Oyo was frequented by cattle nomads in the Distant Time. Rock pictures of mushrooms and mushroom-headed humans are found at Oyo and other Saharan sites.
Orotalt (2)	Archaic Arabic name for the god known in Greek Mythology as Dionysos – the god of transcendental experience, also called the *God who Comes* – a messiah figure thought to have originated in north Africa, who may have been the archetypal fore-runner of Osiris, Christ, and others. One common aspect of these three deities is that they died and were resurrected. Dionysos is also known as the *Twice Born*.
Kibela	In ancient Greek myth, Cybele, mother of Dionysos. In Tu myth, the woman who discovered Orotalt, the sacred mushroom,.
Tu	Literally 'kin' – the people of Oyo and that region lying west of nomad country. 'Fish Eaters' to the Arabic-speaking nomads. The element *tu* is found in the names of several indigenous Saharan nomad groups including *Tubu* and *Tuareg*
Plain of Straying	*at-Tiih*. A desolate, almost featureless pumice plain northeast of Bitter Pool.

Plain of Forgetting	A lava plain south of Oyo. Also the desert featured in the story 'How the Wide-Eared Fox Stole Fire' that causes travellers to lose their memory and die.
Labyrinth of Sand	Maze of dunes lying on the edge of Oyo mountain to the southeast.
Horn Dance	Long ridge running north-south, north of the Oversight. Site of Anakim camps in the Distant Time, with many artifacts, rock pictures and stone rings.
Windmother	Weathered outcrop at the northern end of the Horn Dance. In myth a woman who keeps the wind tethered in her cave in al-Qaf mountains, who can appear as a crone or a beautiful maiden.
Sanya	Pl *sawani*. Deep well, measured in *men* – that is, the height of a man with one arm extended above his head (roughly 2 metres).
Haamil	A camel released to forage for itself in the desert.
Khuluj	A she-camel who has lost her calf
Aghbash	fem. *Ghabsha*. Off white or dirty white – colour only applied to camels.
Majnun	Lit. possessed by a jinn – insane. Also- Imbued with divine ecstasy.
Bowga'a	Lit. treachery. Breaking the bread-and-salt pact of travelling companions – a serious breach of honour resulting in ostracism.
Qarin	also *garin*. Jinn born with a person and dying with them - a twin self that might be identified with the false self or ego, tempting people into selfishness, arrogance and greed.
Well of the Catfish	Shallow well in the Wadi Safra, in myth inhabited by Labuna, a giant catfish whose origin goes back to the green Sahara of the Distant Time.
Night Maidens	The Seven Sisters or Pleaides, a constellation whose fall marks the beginning of the Ged – the Hot Hot season.
Lightning Scorpions	*Agrabaan*. Flashes of lightning esp. dry lightning.

Snake Woman	An incarnation of *al-Lat* or Earth Mother. In nomad myth snakes are associated with life (indestructible life – *zoe*), probably because of their ability to shed skins.
Yellow Nile	In myth, a river said to have flowed from Oyo mountain west across the Sahara into the Nile in the |Distant Time.
Sunset Land	*Maghreb* – the desert to the west of Fish-Eater land.
Siren Land	Land lying north of the Hurra, in Libya – probably Cyrenaica
Shadad	The Hunter – a constellation identified with Orion. Mythical character from the Distant Time, said to have dreamed into existence the Known Places of the Hurra. Shadad is the subject of many stories and is also said to have introduced the idea of *muhanni* to the nomads.
'Urf ar-Ruhhal	Nomad oral tradition and customary law
Dobbayt	Nomad poetry, said to have the rhythm of a camel's pace.
Spirit Mother	An incarnation of Earth Mother, responsible for animals and plants.
Al-Lat	Lit. the Goddess – Earth Mother
Sakanab	The news. Exchanged when nomads meet in the desert, includes details of environmental conditions – rain, growth, winds, clouds et al.
Tihamat	In myth, the *land under the ground,* Land of Shadows or Underworld.
Al-Falak	In myth, the Dragon - dweller in the Underworld. The dragon has a knowledge of the stars, clouds, winds and waters.
Sandlines	*Khatt ar-Raml,* also called Earth Magic or Striking Sand. Nomad system of divination through marks in sand.
Ged	The *Hot-Hot* season in the desert (as opposed to *as-sayf* – summer – and coming in the middle of it.)
Ghost	Nomad who has become a *wild man*, and lives with the animals in the desert as one of them.
Jadi	1)North Star – Polaris. 2) A young gazelle
Waswasa	Demon whispers. The internal dialogue of the *qarin* or ego.
Veil	*Khashfa*. In Sufism, the 'barrier of dissociation' that prevents individuals from perceiving that they are part of a greater transcendent

whole – the One Absolute Infinite Eternal, Great Spirit, or consciousness. Seers and prophets are those able to see through the veil – the 'doors of perception' that are flung open during a transcendent experience, including one induced by Shamanic trance, meditation, or entheogenic substances.

Father of Hobbles	Cautionary tale told to nomad children about a nomad who forgets to hobble his camels in the desert, awakes to find them gone, and hobbles himself to wait for death.
Slant	Pass on the north side of the *Oversight* mountain, leading down into the Hurra.
Umm Shash	A seep or water-source, usually in a rock crevice, where water accrues slowly
Muhanni	Nomad values – kindness, generosity, mutual aid, mutual well-being.
Misterion	Ancient Greek. The *Great Mystery* or the first mystery, connected with the *Eleusinian Mysteries* – the core of ancient Greek religion. The *misterion* refers to *zoe* – indestructible life, or life after death.
Dove Woman	Tale of a bird-woman whose feather coat is stolen by a man who forces her to marry him, with dire consequences.
Hyena People	In myth, a community of skin-walkers - humans able to become hyenas and hyenas able to become humans.
Wadek	Animal fat often used for medicinal purposes
Dom	*Medemia argun*. Type of palm tree bearing edible fruit
Gontar	Nomad measurement of weight – lit, a camel-load – very approx. 300 kilograms.
Umm Kabut	Spider – web weaver
Kahin	Fem. *Kahina*. Seer, diviner
Haskanit	Also *aniti*. Sandbur grass. Wild goat-grass with highly nutritious but prickly seeds used by nomads to make bread, probably since the Distant Time.
Ram's Trail	The Milky Way

Sangura	Hard desert surface – best going to camels.
Faki	Holy man, Sufi, shaman – used as a title.
Salt Bush	
Grasping	Deep well north of the Wadi Safra: an '*ayn* or 'eye' replenished by a spring
Rakuba	Makeshift shelter of cotton cloth on wooden poles used by camel travellers against the mid-day heat.
Awda the Blind	Legendary blind caravan guide, said to be of the Hyena People.
Hajin	Fast riding-camel. Racing camel.
Elbil	Also *al-ibil*. Nomad camel herds as opposed to house camels.
Inderab	Light, flexible wood used for modifying saddles to carry heavy salt-packs
Firestones	Nomad fireplace of three stones arranged in a triangle – the fire is lit between them and the cooking pot placed on top.
Fox Woman	Story a wide-eared fox in human form who marries a nomad, with sad consequences.
Wadi al-Ma	Lit. 'the valley of water'. Long, forested wadi in nomad country south of the Hurra. Site of summer camps for many nomad clans.
Tani	fem. *Tanya*. Lit. *two-tooth* – immature camel whose age is denoted by two prominent front teeth on the lower jaw.
Whitethorn	*Acacia tortilis* - white-thorn acacia.
Heraz	*Acacia nilotica*
Caper	*Capparis decidua*. *Tundub*. Caper tree
Kabsh	Ram. Cognate with *Kabaysh*, legendary shepherd, discoverer of the Lush pastures, who also first bred desert sheep.
Zabata	Sore on camel's inner thigh where the forelegs rub against the breast pad caused by hunger and fatigue.
Baa'ud	Mosquitoes
Sayl	Small water-course, usually flowing into a wadi.

'Ushub	Vegetation, grasses.
Shugga	Rectangle of woven goat's and camel's hair, stitched together with others to form a nomad tent.
Day's Heart	Evening Star
Zahara	Morning Star
Raven	Bird believed by the nomads to be close to humans, with the ability to show them the way in the desert. Ravens are sacred and are never killed by nomads.
Crow	Seen by the nomads as another kind of raven, with the same qualities.
Coney	*Wabir*. Hyrax. Mammal the size of a large hedgehog living in trees and among rocks. Believed to be sacred by the nomads, who consider it a close human relative.
Spiral Horn	
White Antelope	Addax. *Bagr al-Wahesh*. Now rare but once abundant in the desert. Considered by the nomads the most beautiful of all antelopes.
Waterskin Rupture	The only watering place in the Plain of Forgetting – the water is said to have soporific qualities.
Kayfana	In nomad dialect 'like us'.

Printed in Great Britain
by Amazon

20596432R00183